A STEADFAST SURRENDER

"This may well be Nancy Moser's best novel yet. A wonderfully entertaining story that will have book discussion groups all over the country buzzing."

DEBORAH RANEY, AWARD-WINNING AUTHOR OF
A SCARLET CORD AND *BENEATH A SOUTHERN SKY*

"If you felt that God was asking you to sell everything you own and follow Him blindly, would you do it? *A Steadfast Surrender* is a wonderfully compelling tale of someone who does just that. Yet Nancy digs deep beyond the single act of obedience and gets to the heart of our desire and struggle to hear God's voice. This gripping drama will challenge your own spiritual journey—what I love best in a novel!"

CLAY JACOBSEN, AUTHOR OF *INTERVIEW WITH THE DEVIL*

"Nancy Moser writes compelling fiction that teaches. As I read *A Steadfast Surrender,* I couldn't help but reevaluate my own obedience to the one I call Lord. You won't want this story to end."

LOIS RICHER, AUTHOR OF THE CAMP HOPE SERIES

"*A Steadfast Surrender*—an out-of-the-ordinary reading experience that's probing and daring. *Try it!*"

LYN COTE, AUTHOR OF *AUTUMN'S SHADOW*

"*A Steadfast Surrender* is a challenge to every reader to listen a little more closely to that still, small voice of God; to boldly take the path few others have chosen; to seek God's will in every situation. Nancy Moser's witty style will keep the reader enveloped in the lives of the citizens of Steadfast, Kansas, through the final revelation of God's plan for them."

HANNAH ALEXANDER, AUTHOR OF THE HEALING TOUCH SERIES

"Once again, Nancy Moser manages to weave drama, a bit of suspense, and spiritual challenge into an entertaining whole, complete with a surprise ending."

JANELLE BURNHAM SCHNEIDER, AUTHOR OF *RIVER OF PEACE*

A
[Steadfast]
Surrender

A Novel

NANCY MOSER

Multnomah Publishers *Sisters, Oregon*

A STEADFAST SURRENDER
published by Multnomah Publishers, Inc.
© 2003 by Nancy Moser

International Standard Book Number: 1-59052-143-9

Cover image by Alan Thomas/Photonica

Multnomah is a trademark of Multnomah Publishers, Inc., and
is registered in the U.S. Patent and Trademark Office.
The colophon is a trademark of Multnomah Publishers, Inc.

Poem used in chapter 12 on p. 167 is by an unknown author.

All of the Shakespearean dialogue spoken by the character
Harold Shinness is taken from actual plays by William Shakespeare.

Unless otherwise indicated, Scripture quotations are from:

The Holy Bible, New International Version © 1973, 1978, 1984
by International Bible Society. Used by permission
of Zondervan Publishing House

Other Scripture quotations:

The Holy Bible, King James Version

Printed in the United States of America

For information:
MULTNOMAH PUBLISHERS, INC.
POST OFFICE BOX 1720, SISTERS, OREGON 97759

Library of Congress Cataloging-in-Publication Data:

Moser, Nancy.
A steadfast surrender / by Nancy Moser.
    p. cm.
ISBN 1-59052-143-9 (Paperback)
  1. Women--Kansas--Fiction. 2. Rich people--Fiction. 3. Kansas--Fiction. I. Title.
PS3563.O88417S74 2003
813'.54--dc21

2003004863

03 04 05 06 07 08 09—10 9 8 7 6 5 4 3 2 1 0

I dedicate this book
to the steadfast life and love of my parents,

Lyle and Marge Young.

Thank you, Dad and Mom, for everything.

NOVELS BY NANCY MOSER

A Steadfast Surrender

The Seat Beside Me

The Sister Circle

Time Lottery

THE MUSTARD SEED SERIES:

The Invitation

The Quest

The Temptation

*You will keep in perfect peace
him whose mind is steadfast,
because he trusts in you.*

Isaiah 26:3

Prologue

His eyes are on the ways of men; he sees their every step.
There is no dark place, no deep shadow, where evildoers can hide.

JOB 34:21–22

THE GIRL WRAPPED THE PILLOW around her ears, muffling the argument in the kitchen above her. She hated when grown-ups fought. Before her parents were killed, *they* had fought. A lot. Never caring if she heard. Wanting her to hear?

She couldn't blame words for her pain. Words didn't kill. In fact, death made most words as worthless as a puff of air in the wind. *"Don't worry, Sim, everything will be all right."*

She expelled her own puff of air and let the pillow fall free, allowing her aunt and uncle's shouts to reach her. Their words were meaningless. Powerless. They couldn't hurt her. She wouldn't let them.

The basement darkness was so thick it throbbed like a smothering blanket. Her uncle had given her a night-light to help her find her way to the toilet in the unfinished storeroom nearby, but the girl chose the dark. It matched the color of her life. She didn't need—didn't want—a room with a moon to light it, or yellow curtains with ruffled edges, or a wicker rocker inhabited by an unused teddy bear. Special places like that were reserved for babies who wouldn't come. Not for an orphan too old to count for anything.

The air conditioner chugged to life, muffling the angry voices. Sim turned onto her side and closed her eyes, then opened them again, finding no difference in her sight; it was as if she were blind. It was appropriate. Darkness had been her companion since the car accident.

But soon…soon there would be light. There *had* to be. She

would fight for it. Soon she would be free and on her own, running in the light. Soon she would be away and everything would be all right.

It was a promise she had made to herself. One she dared not break.

One

The rich man will fade away even while he goes about his business.

JAMES 1:11

THE INTERCOM BUZZED. "Claire, your husband, line one."

Ex-husband. Claire Adams's money-grubbing, selfish, two-timing ex-husband. "Tell him I'll call him back."

"I already tried that. He says it's an emergency. He says he'll hold."

He can hold till the Second Coming, for all I care.

"Claire?"

"All right, all right, I'll take it." She settled in behind the desk at her mosaic studio, closed her eyes, and tried to find the calm before the storm that was… "Ron. My two-timing ex. What can I do you for?"

"Plenty. Obviously. But besides that, I have a proposition for you."

"Haven't you done enough propositioning?"

"Very funny."

"Do you hear me laughing?"

"Are you going to dredge up the past or can I talk about our future?"

"We don't have a future, Ron."

"Don't be difficult."

She opened her mouth to respond, then closed it. Talking with Ron made her emotions dry and brittle, like a slice of bread left on the counter overnight. She mentally tapped into a verse that had been her mantra during the divorce: *"O God, you are my God, earnestly I seek you; my soul thirsts for you, my body longs for you, in a dry and weary land where there is no water."* Ron had offered no water. No refreshment. No relief. Only the refreshment of God had seen her through his womanizing and her eventual surrender of their marriage.

"CeeCee?"

She took a cleansing breath. "Can we wrap this up, please?"

"Don't be so quick to cut me off. This benefits you too."

She snickered.

"You like boating, don't you?"

It took a second for the word to register the word. "Boating?"

"I want to buy a boat. I want you to pay for half."

Her laugh was full now. "And why would I do that?"

"Because I'd let you use it. Like I said, you like boating."

"I *liked* boating. Past tense. Those days are over, Ron. And since you dumped me for a younger model, I think it's inappropriate for me to pay for half of a boat *she* will use."

"But CeeCee, you know I've always wanted one." Ron could make instant gratification an Olympic event.

"Then buy one. But leave me out of it."

"You know I don't have that kind of money. You've always made more than me."

Ron's ego hadn't liked that fact when they were married, and he had taken advantage of it since the divorce. Claire had been generous in the settlement, willing to give up some cash and possessions for the whole thing to be done with as soon as possible. Maybe that was a mistake. "Do unto others" was hard to maintain when *others* got greedy. She sucked in a breath and steeled herself. "My answer is no."

"No?"

"Why doesn't your beloved Tiffany pay for it?" There was silence, and Claire began to laugh. "She's left you, hasn't she?"

"I kicked her out, not that it's any of your business. She was an absolute leech."

"I know the feeling."

"You should see the bills she ran up."

"A disgusting opportunist."

He sighed. "So I'm alone now. All alone."

"Oh, I'm sure you'll find another young babe to keep you warm."

"Tiffany was hardly young. She was thirty."

"And you are?"

"You know very well how old I am, and my love life is none of your business. Not anymore."

But it had been her business once. Ron left Claire because a pretty girl stole his heart and promised him a life of passion and adoration. Lola lasted thirteen months before Ron realized her portrayal of a high-living Lolita was a front for an empty bank account that she wanted Ron to fill. Besides, Lola the Lolita liked to roam more than her Lothario.

In spite of Ron's infidelities, Claire had wanted to work things out. Not because she loved him so much, but because she knew it was the right thing to do. Saying "till death do us part" in a church had meant something to Claire. Yet just as it took two to argue, it took two to make up. And Ron hadn't wanted to work at their marriage. Not after he discovered other women who made him feel young again in a way Claire couldn't. Or wouldn't.

She didn't blame him entirely. Just mostly. Claire knew she worked too much and had tunnel vision toward her art. But in her own defense, she'd never forgotten a birthday or anniversary; she'd hung up Ron's towels without complaining; and she'd made him his favorite cheesecake, which was unsurpassed by any la-di-da restaurant charging six bucks a slice, even though it kept her in the kitchen way past her preferred time limit.

Claire realized Ron was still talking. "—suppose I'll have to cancel the order, though I already had a weekend planned."

"Poor baby."

"Don't be mean. I thought you could be a little generous, what with your recent success. I saw the article in *Newsweek* about your work. But I guess I—"

"Generous? Don't you dare talk generous with me. Who got the good cars? Who got the house?"

"You said you didn't want them."

She *hadn't* wanted them, preferring to start fresh, but that wasn't the point. "I have to go, Ron."

"What if we go 60-40?"

"Bye."

"Uh-uh, don't you dare hang up on—"

She dropped the phone in the cradle and immediately longed for a nap. What she had once celebrated as Ron's spunk, she now saw as plain old petulance. After twenty years of marriage, he'd changed.

And you didn't?

She frowned. Had she? What traits had Ron found initially charming in the twenty-five-year-old Claire Adams, up-and-coming mosaic artist extraordinaire? Had her ambition and creativity turned into something less desirable at age forty-five? Had fame and money irreparably changed her?

Actually, it didn't matter whose fault it was. Their marriage was over. It still hurt like a gaping wound, and every call, every contact with Ron added a handful of salt.

She shoved all thoughts of him aside and was actually pleased when her stomach growled. Needing and wanting to eat were good signs. For months the necessity of food had been a burden, and she'd ended up losing fifteen pounds.

The divorce diet. If only she could package it.

Lunch and a meeting at the gallery beckoned. She stood to leave just as the line buzzed again. "Call on line three, Claire. It's your pastor."

Claire could hardly skip that one—and she didn't want to. The previous Sunday they had dedicated the mosaic altar she'd created and donated. He was probably calling to share some compliments with her. She picked up the phone. "Pastor Joe. All's well with the altar, I hope?"

"An altar fit for a King. We're extremely grateful for it."

"You're welcome."

"But I have a favor to ask of you."

"Uh-oh. I feel a request for a matching baptismal font coming on."

"Actually, I need your culinary expertise."

For a moment she was speechless. "Surely you jest."

"Oh, you'll do fine. We have the administrator of a Denver shelter visiting. She's been talking at the circle meetings and will give a speech at the congregational dinner tomorrow night. She's staying at the Martins'. But tomorrow—Saturday—the Martins have some softball function for the kids, and Molly and I have a bowling tournament—"

"How's your game?"

"I've hit three digits."

"Ooh. Strike three, you're out."

"Wrong kind of strike, Claire. Anyway, we wondered if you would entertain the administrator tomorrow noon. Have her over for lunch."

During the divorce Claire had taken solace in the church she previously ignored and discovered the benefits of becoming a joiner. She was now on Pastor Joe's ready-willing-and-able list of volunteers and didn't really mind. Giving back eased the pain of what she'd given up.

"You'd like her, Claire."

She sighed. "Does she have a name?"

"Michelle Jofsky."

"Wouldn't you rather have a couple do this?"

"I think she's been coupled out. An afternoon woman-to-woman would probably be a relief. She's a baseball fan, just like you. Sometimes eating pizza and watching baseball is a thousand times more satisfying than a four-course meal."

That made it easier. "Pizza I can handle. Baseball, huh? A Royals fan, I hope?"

"Cubs. You'll have to duke it out."

"I'll kick in my Christian tolerance. For one afternoon. As a favor to you."

"And God."

"Who we both wish were a more avid Royals fan."

"I'll call Michelle and tell her to be over at noon. And Claire? This is a good thing you're doing, and I'm proud of you. But…"

"But what?"

"Be good. Okay?"

"Hey, you started it. But never fear. I'll give it my best shot."

❧　❧　❧

Michelle Jofsky tried to block out the noise of the Martin boys arguing over a video game in the next room. She tried to concentrate on the Bible in her lap. It wasn't easy.

She enjoyed traveling and talking to churches about the Salvation Shelter where she worked. And she really didn't mind staying in people's homes. Most of the time. It wasn't that she was used to silence. She wasn't. Her apartment was above the shelter and there was always noise. People noise. Since being at the Martins' she'd realized it was mechanical noise that grated on her nerves: TV, computer, stereo. How could these people ever hope to hear God if they never allowed silence into their lives? She'd said something to the youngest boy, but he merely turned the volume down from deafening to annoying.

She'd escaped to her room, starting her so-called quiet time with a prayer for tolerance and a dose of God-sent concentration. She opened her Bible at random, willing God to lead her time with Him. It opened to Colossians. She read: "Devote yourselves to prayer, being watchful and thankful. And pray for us, too, that God may open a door for our message, so that we may proclaim the mystery of Christ, for which I am in chains. Pray that I may proclaim it clearly, as I should. Be wise in the way you act toward outsiders; make the most of every opportunity. Let your conversation be always full of grace, seasoned with salt, so that you may know how to answer everyone."

She looked up. Interesting. Especially considering all the speaking she'd done in the last two days. And tomorrow night was the big congregational dinner. Good words. Appropriate—

A tap on the door. "Michelle? Phone."

She left the guest room to take the phone in the kitchen. It was Pastor Joe.

"How you faring, Michelle?"

She glanced at the alien battle being played out on the computer screen across the room and remembered the verse's admonition to have her conversation be "full of grace." "I'm doing fine, Joe. What's up?"

"How'd you like to watch baseball and eat pizza with Claire Adams, one of our single parishioners?"

Baseball, pizza, single… "That sounds heavenly."

He chuckled. "I thought you'd say that. And I think you'll find Claire a fascinating woman. She's a mosaic artist on the verge of famous. She's had shows in London, Venice, Cincinnati…"

"Cincinnati?"

"I guess art appreciation knows no bounds. Noon tomorrow, okay? Claire's looking forward to the opportunity to meet with you one-on-one."

The verse offered a reprise: *Make the most of every opportunity.* Michelle's insides pulled, and she caught her breath. She knew what that feeling meant. This was not going to be an ordinary pizza lunch. "I look forward to it."

She loved when God got her guessing.

By the time Claire got off the phone with Pastor Joe, she was on the verge of late. In order to get to her meeting at the gallery on time, she took a shortcut and got lost. Now, though she'd figured out where she was, she had no choice but to grab some fast food. Fast.

She stopped at a traffic light and scoped out the neighborhood. Garbage hugged the curb, there were bars on the windows of a beauty shop, and an abandoned car was permanently installed on a side street with a cat lounging on its hood. It was not the best part of town, but it would have to do.

Claire spotted a McDonald's one block ahead and turned into the parking lot, heading toward the drive-through. It was blocked with orange traffic cones and a sign: *Please excuse the inconvenience. Come inside to order.*

Come inside? Who had time to go inside?

Her stomach rumbled its vote. She'd have to make time.

Claire parked her silver Lexus close to the front door, where she could keep tabs on it. She went inside and was relieved to see that the line was short. She ordered a #1, supersized, with a Coke. She handed the teenager a fifty. The boy studied it as if it were foreign currency.

"Got anything smaller? We're not supposed to take bigger than a twenty."

Claire opened her billfold and fanned through the bills. She'd just cashed the check she'd received for the sale of her latest commission—a mosaic coffee table—and had specifically asked for hundreds, not wanting her billfold to be too thick. "Sorry, that's the smallest I have."

She suddenly noticed she had an audience. Seven sets of eyes bounced from her billfold to her face, then back again. Her cheeks grew hot. Her heart skipped a beat. She folded the billfold shut.

A manager walked near the boy. "Go ahead, Marlon. Give the lady her change."

Marlon handed Claire her change and her order.

Claire hurried to her car, got in, and locked the doors. She put the sack on the seat so she could tuck the change away. But when she opened her billfold, she lingered, seeing with fresh eyes what the people in the restaurant had seen.

The stack of twenty-five hundreds stared back at her. The crispness of the bills contrasted with the wrinkled, much-used bills she'd gotten for change. Two thousand five hundred dollars. Claire's average weekly amount. Cash for spending money.

Most people would have accepted that amount as a decent *month's* wages.

She'd just paid for a fast-food lunch with a fifty-dollar bill. *"Sorry, that's the smallest I have."* She hadn't meant to sound uppity, but the very fact that she thought nothing of paying with fifties and hundreds was as symptomatic as it was ridiculous. Was she so immune to wealth that she could flaunt it with abandon? Did she care nothing about the reactions of those around her, who by seeing her riches might feel their own lack more deeply? To say nothing of the temptation.

She looked at the inside of her car. It still had the new car smell and the "In Transit" sticker on the back window. CD player, cell phone, cassette. Air-conditioning, antilock brakes, cruise control, dual air bags. A laptop computer sat on the floor of the passenger side, safely tucked away in a leather case.

Even her clothes…no funky Bohemian attire for this artist. For some reason people expected her to wear Indian-print skirts, sandals, and have long hair that had more *poof* than style. Claire would never tolerate being a stereotype. When she was in her studio—dirty with tile dust, metal shavings, and grout—she opted for comfort rather than style. But in public she leaned toward Armani, or her suit of the day, which happened to sport a Donna Karan label. To obtain the impeccable look of success, she only bought the best. Her shoes and matching purse had been purchased from a pricey catalog, and a Rolex adorned her wrist. It was one of two she owned: one gold, one silver. To match her accessories of the day.

Her stomach clenched. She fumbled with the keys. When the engine revved to life, an old man near the entrance of the restaurant looked up, then away, as he shuffled to a trash can, pushed open the swinging lid, and grabbed a crushed sack.

What's he doing?

Claire sat transfixed. The man opened the sack and peered inside. His hand disappeared and came out with two French fries, which he stuffed into his mouth. Another dig brought out the last few bites of a hamburger. He shoved it in his mouth, licking his fingers.

Claire smelled her own lunch, sitting unopened on the seat beside her. Supersized. The sheer quantity of the meal repulsed her.

Before the thought moved from synapse to synapse, Claire grabbed the sack and the drink, opened the car door, and walked to the man. "Sir?"

He looked up. There was a crumb poised on his whiskers.

She held the food in his direction. "I've already eaten. Would you like this meal? It's a Big Mac. Large fries?" She tried a smile.

The man looked at the sack, practically drooling. Then he squinted at Claire and smiled back. "That depends. What's the drink?"

"Coke."

The man nodded. "Nifty. You got a deal."

Claire returned the nod and headed back to her car, feeling virtuous. She noticed her billfold on the seat. An idea overwhelmed her.

No, you're thinking crazy…a meal is one thing, but—

She turned back to the man. He was walking away. "Sir?"

He turned.

Claire looked down at her shoes. How could she do this without hurting his pride? "You...do you have a wife?"

"Not anymore."

Oh, dear. "You have kids?"

"Two or three."

Whew. Claire reached into the car and grabbed the billfold. She withdrew the bills, not even looking at them, afraid she would chicken out. "Here. Buy them a Christmas present."

The man stared at the wad of hundreds. He squinted at the summer sun. "But it's June."

"Birthday then. Buy them something special." She backed toward the car.

The man stared at the money, then at her. "Why you doing this?"

Claire bumped into the car door. She reached backward for the handle, then shrugged and managed a shaky laugh. "I have no idea."

The man scratched his head. "Whatever the reason...God bless you, ma'am."

Claire's heart beat through her blouse. She felt something swell inside her, like a dam ready to burst. She got in the car and put it in reverse, nearly backing into a passing vehicle. As she pulled around the building, she noticed two cars using the drive-through.

There were no orange cones in sight.

Claire found a day-old donut on the studio table that served as lay-out space, lunch table, and chair if she felt the need to gaze at her work from a new angle. She poured a cup of coffee and sat on the table to eat. Her heels skimmed the concrete floor.

From across the warehouse-sized space, her head metalworker, Darla, turned off her blowtorch, flipped up her mask, and came toward her. "Those are from yesterday, you know."

She shrugged.

Darla tilted her head. "You look...odd. Didn't it go well at the gallery?"

"I never got to the gallery."

"Why not?"

Claire thought about telling Darla about giving all her money to the old man, but stopped. Not only would her friend think she was insane, she had the feeling if she shared her good deed with anyone, it would be spoiled. But oh, how she would like to brag. She took another bite of donut. "Long story for another day, another time. How are things going here?"

Darla studied her a moment longer before pointing to where she'd been working. "The base for the Oswald dining room table should be ready this afternoon, and Sandy is putting away the shipment of smalti that came in this morning. Everything should be ready to go. All you need to do is finish up the mosaic."

Claire snickered. "Inspiration on demand, huh?"

"You always manage to come through."

She swung her legs back and forth. "I don't feel very creative right now."

Darla changed her weight to the other foot. "What's wrong? You seem restless."

What's wrong? What's right? What's real? What's unreal?

When Claire didn't answer, Darla continued. "They're expecting it the end of this week. Do you want Lana to call and tell them it will be late?"

Claire took a deep breath, then removed her jacket and headed to where her work clothes were kept. "No. I'll get to it. Right now."

Darla followed her. "Claire...what aren't you telling me?"

She forced a smile as she hung up her jacket. "It's nothing for you to worry about. Honestly. It's nothing for anyone to worry about. It's a good thing. I think."

"A good thing. Even more reason to share."

Claire pinched her lower lip. "But not now. Not yet." She took a cleansing breath. "Now go on. There's work to do."

And thinking.

Two

"Ask and it will be given to you; seek and you will find; knock and the door will be opened to you."

MATTHEW 7:7

SATURDAY NOON, THE DOORBELL RANG. Claire answered it to find a fiftyish woman holding a pizza box while the pizza-delivery car drove away. It took Claire a moment to sort through the scene. "Michelle?"

The woman raised the box and inhaled. "I smell pepperoni."

"Good nose." Claire took the pizza and stood aside so her guest could enter. Claire dug into her jeans pocket for the money she'd put there for the pizza man. "Here, you beat me to it."

Michelle waved the money away. "I'll supply the pizza if you supply an unlimited supply of iced tea."

Claire smiled. She liked Michelle. "One cold one coming up."

They moved into the kitchen area. Claire got out plates and napkins. The smell of pepperoni and cheese filled the air. She noted Michelle was a good six inches shorter than she was and fifty pounds heavier. But what Michelle lacked in height, she made up for in pluck. Claire liked how she made herself right at home, opening the cupboards, getting out two glasses, and filling them with ice.

"Nice place."

"Thanks." Since Claire gave Ron the house, she'd moved into this three-bedroom townhouse. Although it was a step down in size, it was comparable in quality and luxury. Not that she *needed* marble countertops or crown moldings, but she was used to them. "The game doesn't start for half an hour."

Michelle pulled out a stool at the breakfast bar. "Then let's sit here."

22

"Sure." As Claire sat and they started eating, she suddenly realized she needed to come up with conversation. She'd been counting on the game negating any need for her to be wise and witty.

Michelle beat her to it. "Pastor Joe says you're rich and famous."

Claire choked. Michelle patted her on the back.

"You okay?"

Claire took a sip of tea and wiped her mouth with a paper napkin. "You just surprised me, that's all. And Pastor Joe told *me* to be good?"

Michelle shrugged. The glint in her eye hinted there was more to come. "I work in a facts-based business. I prefer to slog through bushes rather than beat around them."

"What bush are we talking about?"

"Money."

Claire's stomach sank. Pastor Joe was going to pay for making her spend the afternoon with a fund-raiser. If he'd wanted a donation, he should have asked. She might as well get it over with, give the lady a check, and hope the baseball game would start early.

She stood to get her checkbook. "I can give you something for your shelter."

Michelle shook her head. She nipped a string of cheese with her fingers, then licked them noisily. "I don't want your money."

"But you said—"

"I said I wanted to *talk* about money, I didn't ask for any."

Claire returned to the stool. "You don't want my money?"

"Not your guilt money."

"Excuse me?"

Michelle shook her head while patting a napkin to her mouth as she finished chewing. "Maybe I'd better start over."

Claire took a sip of tea and set her glass down hard. "Maybe you'd better."

"I run a shelter for indigents in Denver."

"I know that."

"I live in a room on the second floor. I eat with the homeless. I have few possessions I call my own." She swiveled in her seat and extended an arm, taking in the hearth room, the breakfast area, and the kitchen. "You have so much."

This sounded like a trap. "But you don't want my money."

She held up a finger. "Your guilt money."

The appeal of Michelle Jofsky's make-herself-at-home nature dimmed. "If this is how you fund-raise, you'd better think of a new approach."

Michelle faced her, stool to stool. "That's just it. I don't think I'm here to get money from you."

"You don't *think*...?"

She took a breath. "I'm sorry. I'm being way too blunt. I get that way when I'm excited."

"And what are you excited about?"

"Opportunities."

"Such as?"

Michelle turned back to her pizza. "Are you open to Him, to *things?*"

Him. God. "What kinds of things?"

Michelle looked at Claire straight on. "Feelings. Hunches."

"Women's intuition? That sort of thing?"

"Beyond that." She wiped her palms on her thighs. "Oh dear, there's no subtle way to breach this thought I have, this notion, this nudge."

"Then just say it. I can take it. I promise."

Michelle studied her a moment. "I think you're the reason I came to Kansas City."

Claire finished chewing. She didn't like the sound of this. *The Twilight Zone* had been cancelled years ago. She did not need to experience one of the lost episodes. She got up from her stool. "Want some more tea?"

"No thanks."

Claire didn't either, but she poured some anyway. She also took another slice of pizza, though the thought of eating more was unsettling.

"You want to know why I think you're the reason I came here?"

"I'm not sure. But tell me anyway." Claire mentally braced herself.

"The answer is: I don't know."

Claire's shoulders drooped. "Should I be relieved or disappointed?"

"I wish I could be more specific. Sometimes it is and sometimes it isn't. Specific, I mean."

"It?"

"My hunches. Feelings."

"This happens often?"

"Often enough."

"But you said you were a facts-based person. Hunches are not based on facts."

"Sure they are. It's a fact that I got a feeling about you. I can choose to ignore it or accept it. Go with it. This time I went with it. I came here this afternoon, didn't I?"

"To tell me…?"

"I don't know."

Claire shook her head and glanced at the TV. *Come on game. Start!* "Are your hunches always so vague?"

"Not vague, just nonspecific."

"I don't see the distinction."

"The urgings I have, the nudgings, are very real and more than mental. They're so strong they almost give me a physical push. I *know* I'm supposed to do something; I just don't know the details."

"Give me an example."

Michelle ran a finger across the condensation on her glass. Then she nodded. "Ten years ago, before I started to work at the shelter, I was walking in an industrial part of town when I had an urge to turn right and go down a specific street. I had no reason to turn, and to tell you the truth, I was running late and really needed to keep going. Since then I've learned it's best to follow through with these promptings. It's become an obligation."

"Says who?"

Michelle smiled. "We'll get to that. Anyway, I turned right. I hadn't been down that street before, but I knew it led to the railroad tracks. Yet there was a kind of purpose in my walking, as if there was something I was supposed to see. So I kept my eye out for a reason I was being brought there, searching for the last piece to the puzzle.

When I got to the tracks I saw a bunch of lean-tos, the kind the homeless make out of boxes and boards. More than anything, I wanted to turn around and get out of there. That kind of poverty and desperation made me uncomfortable, you know?"

"I can imagine."

"But then I saw an old man lying right next to the tracks, so close that his back was against a rail. Passed out. As soon as I saw him I felt a rumbling in my feet. The lights of a train came closer. It blared its whistle. It was like a scene in a movie. At first all I could do was shake my head no. This was *not* happening. Then I snapped out of it, ran to the man, and rolled him away from the tracks. Just in time. I saved him. My following the nudge saved him."

"Very admirable. So you're here to save me, even if I'm *not* passed out in the path of an oncoming train?"

"But maybe you are."

Claire stood and paced near the counters. "Look around. I'm perfectly safe. No trains in sight."

"But you may be on the wrong track."

Claire had had enough. "Excuse me, Ms. Jofsky. You don't know me well enough to know what track I'm on, much less if it's wrong, and I resent—"

Michelle pushed her plate away and rested her arms on the counter. She looked down at her clasped hands.

Michelle's calm was infuriating. "Don't just sit there. Defend yourself!" Michelle shook her head. The noncombative action took the steam out of Claire's engine. "You've got to admit it's mighty strange, your coming into my home, telling me you don't want my guilt money, telling me you were sent here, telling me I'm on the wrong track and in the path of an oncoming train."

When Michelle looked up, Claire started at the tenderness in the woman's eyes. "Let me back up to something I know for certain," Michelle said.

"Good idea."

"I believe we've each been created with a unique purpose. We've been placed in this unique time, in this unique position and place, in this unique set of circumstances to *do* something unique. We just have to find out what it is. *You* need to find out what it is."

"And that's why you're here."

"Maybe." Michelle took a deep breath and glanced at the front door. "When I drove up to this house I had a feeling…and when I came in and saw how you live and felt the wealth—"

"This place is hardly ostentatious. My ex is the showy one. This place is minimal compared to—"

Michelle raised a hand. "I'm not condemning you. Not at all. Earning a lot of money is not a sin. In the Bible, there were lots of rich people. King David and King Solomon were very rich, and God didn't hold their wealth against them." Her eyes lit up. She put a hand to her mouth. "Do you have a Bible?"

"Of course I have a Bible."

"Get it."

Claire retrieved it off her bedside table and held it out to Michelle, but Michelle pushed it back toward Claire. "No. It's for you to read. You to find."

"Find?"

"The verses that will help you understand."

"What verses are they?"

Michelle headed toward the door, her face drawn with a puzzled look. She stopped to answer. "Maybe the book of Mark…no. I won't say more. Read *the* Book, Claire. See where *He* takes you." She opened the door.

"But the baseball—"

Michelle shook her head. "Some other time. Prayers to you, Claire. I think you may need them."

Claire took the Bible to her favorite chair. She sat down and held the book in her lap but did not open it. The entire encounter had been too weird, too left field. Michelle blustered in like a storm, stirred things up, then left, leaving Claire blown away, stunned. Maybe she should just turn on the television and let the baseball game consume her, forget she'd ever met Michelle Jofsky—the strange woman whose purpose was obviously to confuse everyone she met.

But Claire couldn't. Not today. Not after she'd been spurred to give a week's wages to a stranger. Not since a conversation with her ex-husband reminded her how shallow their life together had been. Not since Michelle Jofsky dropped into her life.

What if Michelle was right? What if she'd been brought to Kansas City just to meet with Claire? Claire knew God worked in such ways—more than people knew. She had to open the Bible. She had to at least be willing to *see*. Maybe the verses she'd read would be nothing, and she could grab the now-cold pizza, her now-warm tea, and watch the game until she slipped into the blessed bliss of a Saturday afternoon nap.

She closed her eyes and took a deep breath. "Okay, God, show me what you want me to see." She opened the Bible, feeling it fall toward the New Testament. She looked down at the page. Mark 10 was laid out before her.

She shivered. Michelle had mentioned the book of Mark. The stakes were raised. This was not a coincidence.

She began to read: "As Jesus started on his way, a man ran up to him and fell on his knees before him. 'Good teacher,' he asked, 'what must I do to inherit eternal life?' "

As soon as she read the first line she knew—she knew—what verses these were: the Rich Man verses. She knew the story. But there was more to her shock than recognizing a familiar biblical event. These verses, this story—this charge—had been dogging her for the past few months. And here they were again.

It had first come up at her Bible study. No big deal. An interesting lesson. But then she heard it on the radio, read it in a magazine, and heard a veiled reference to it on a sitcom.

And now this…

This could not be a coincidence.

She took a cleansing breath and returned to the Bible to finish the passage.

"Why do you call me good?" Jesus answered. "No one is good—except God alone. You know the commandments: 'Do not murder, do not commit adultery, do not steal, do not give false testimony, do not defraud, honor your father and mother.'"

"Teacher," he declared, "all these I have kept since I was a boy."

Jesus looked at him and loved him. "One thing you lack," he said. "Go, sell everything you have and give to the poor, and you will have treasure in heaven. Then come, follow me."

At this the man's face fell. He went away sad, because he had great wealth. Jesus looked around and said to his disciples, "How hard it is for the rich to enter the kingdom of God!"

Claire's heart pounded. She put a hand on the page, covering the words. *No, no… This isn't what You want me to do. Not this.*

Claire closed the Bible with a snap. She tossed it on the table, found the remote, and clicked it, bringing the baseball game to life. It was the top of the first inning. The Royals were up. The bases were loaded. There was a pitch. Ball met bat. The crack echoed. In one moment the ordinary path of a good hit grew wings. Would it be a grand slam?

The camera panned, following the flight of the ball. Claire held her breath. The moment was magic as the epitome of baseball perfection hung in the air: a possibility, a hope, a chance.

At the wall, the ball was caught.

The runner was out. The possibility dead. The hope dashed. The chance missed.

Go, sell everything…then come, follow me.

A possibility? A hope? A chance?

Claire flipped the channel.

Three

*"I will not sacrifice to the LORD my God burnt offerings
that cost me nothing."*

2 SAMUEL 24:24

CLAIRE BLINKED. The sound of the television entered her world.

She looked at her hand and found it grasping the remote control. A glance at the screen showed Cary Grant and Grace Kelly driving on a winding road along the French Riviera. She knew the movie. Some Hitchcock flick. It was near the end, and she didn't remember seeing any of it. Her mind was sleeping yet still consumed with a jumbled missive of five words. Variations on a theme: *Sell everything and follow me.*

Every time she repeated the words, her thoughts raced around a track, returning to the place they'd started. Sometimes the crowd yelled "Go! Go!" spurring her on. But more often, the crowd sat in a shocked silence that she would even consider such an idiotic thing. Round and round she ran, never finishing. Never being done with the race.

Sell everything and follow me.

The idea was preposterous. There was too much at stake. Claire had started creating mosaics full-time ten years ago. Before that she created on the side, trying to fit inspiration into the other to-dos of her day. Success had not come easily. It took three years for a gallery to show interest in her work, and then only a piece or two. Finally, after one exclusive showing—and a wonderful article in *Time* magazine about a mural she'd done in the entryway to a renowned museum— she'd become a hot name. She'd opened the Claire Adams Gallery.

She'd done commissions for movie stars and CEOs of Fortune

500 companies. Her art provided enough income for her and Ron to build a house in the best part of Kansas City—a house that sported a four-car garage (including the corresponding vehicles), three fireplaces, a wood-paneled study, a walk-in pantry, a media room complete with theater seating, and closets large enough to house their extensive wardrobes.

Through the years they tried to have a child. There appeared to be no physical reason they couldn't have kids—and because the finger of fault wasn't pointing directly at either of them, Ron refused to adopt, insisting that someday the miracle would happen. But when they neared their forties, Ron closed up shop on that dream and declared that children simply wouldn't fit into his lifestyle anymore. He was right about that one. Dealing with children while being unfaithful would have been tricky—though not impossible—for the ever-resourceful Ron Adams.

Childlessness was Claire's oozing wound. She always assumed she'd be the mother of two or three. She dreamed of kids she could cuddle, help with their homework, sing with in the car, and read to before bedtime. She prayed fervently for a child, argued with God, made deals, cried, and even feigned apathy, hoping God would slip a baby into their lives while she wasn't looking. But with each passing year that was a testament to God saying no, Claire felt the wound of barrenness break open, making her weaker—if not physically, at least emotionally—exposing dry places in her soul.

Perhaps that had contributed to the demise of their marriage. Ron must have felt Claire's capacity to love being eaten away. So he turned elsewhere. Could she really blame him? She would go to her grave wondering why God had withheld this one blessing.

What *was* a blessing from God was Claire's artistic success. She had come to realize that if God was behind her childlessness, He was also behind her financial prosperity and status. Which was why she was generous with her giving. There was a verse: "From everyone who has been given much, much will be demanded; and from the one who has been entrusted with much, much more will be asked."

She accepted that. Embraced it as her responsibility. But certainly God didn't want her to give it *all* away? Without children, without

Ron, all she had left was her work and the fruits of her labor.

Follow me.

Wasn't she already doing that? Ever since the divorce she'd gone to church, read the Bible, and talked to God on a regular basis. He was her Father, her Counselor, her Savior. She gave to the food bank, the mission projects, and had even donated the mosaic altar to the church—a piece of art that was worth tens of thousands of dollars. If they needed a new roof, they only had to call her for a check. The church was a big part of her life. Wasn't that enough?

Everything.

Claire zapped the TV to silence. She threw the remote on the floor. This turmoil was Michelle's fault. What right did a stranger have to come into Claire's home and tell her tall tales about being sent for some purpose?

A new thought jumped front and center: *Michelle wants me to give all my money to her shelter!*

Suddenly one plus one equaled two. Michelle Jofsky wasn't some holy woman with a special God-sent mission. She was a fund-raiser in need of money. A slick shyster looking for a chump with deep pockets. Her rejection of Claire's guilt money was a clever ploy.

Well, she'd gone after the wrong dupe this time. This sucker was closing up shop. Out to lunch. Don't call again.

Claire glanced at the time. Seven-fifteen. She'd wasted the entire afternoon agonizing over some pitchman's spiel. And to think Michelle was going to address the congregational dinner tonight— might *already* be addressing tables and tables of potential patsies, who were waiting to have their pockets picked while their minds became burdened with guilt trips.

Claire pushed herself out of her chair. "Oh no you don't, Michelle Jofsky. Not with my church, you don't."

Claire was late. The dinner had started at six-thirty, so by the time she got to church, Michelle was already at the podium, her victims full and complacent, their minds numbed by tuna casserole and apple crisp.

Claire slipped into the room and found an empty chair at a back table next to the Snyders and the Andersons. They nodded their greetings, then turned their attention back to Michelle.

She's probably told them the same bunkum she told me. Messing with their minds, just like—

"So you see, the gospel message can be told even to those who have had no experience reading the Bible. That's what we try to do at the Salvation Shelter. We meet each individual wherever they're at in their spiritual journey. We don't overwhelm them with too much too soon. But remember, none of us has to have all the answers. But we are asked to give the *reason* for our faith. 'Always be prepared to give an answer to everyone who asks you to give the reason for the hope that you have.' We need to share what God has done in our lives."

Aha…this is where she'll tell people to sell everything.

"For most of the men and women who visit us at the shelter, a good meal and a kind word are the starting point. We can't overwhelm them with talk of God's love and eternal life when they're experiencing bitterness and an aching stomach. Patience is the key." She smiled. "You don't beat people over the head with God's love; you pat them on the back. And we need to keep in mind that it's not up to us to close the deal of Jesus' offer of salvation, but just to plant the seed. Show them someone cares. Hopefully, they'll begin to wonder about the peace they see within *us*. Hopefully, they'll want some of that for themselves and they'll ask. And when they do, we'll tell them the source of our peace."

And if you really want to help these people you will sell everything and—

"God cares for the homeless as much as He cares for you and me. Jesus died for all. We can't ever forget that. Thank you."

Applause. Claire looked around the room, frowning. People were smiling, nodding their heads. They didn't look as though they'd been asked to sacrifice their entire livelihood.

Ken Anderson put a hand on the back of Claire's chair. "Sorry you missed the bulk of her speech. She's good."

"What did she talk about?"

"The usual stuff. How we need to reach people by example."

Vivian Anderson chimed in. "She gave us some case studies of people whose lives have turned around because of help from the shelter. She was homeless too, you know."

"Michelle was homeless?"

"By choice."

Claire didn't understand. Vivian moved her chair closer, eager to share the story. "She grew up in a wealthy family. She earned a degree, even worked in the family business for a while. But then she gave it all up. Went out on the streets to live."

Claire's stomach knotted. "Why?"

Ken hemmed Claire in on the other side. "After saving a man from being crushed by an oncoming train she had a vision. Kind of like Paul, in the Bible, on the road to Damascus. She thought she saw Jesus and heard Him talking. The vision told her to give up everything and follow Him."

"There was some verse…" Vivian reached for a piece of paper she'd used to take notes. "Here it is: Mark 10—"

"Seventeen through twenty-three." As Claire said the words, the breath went out of her.

"That's it! You know those verses too?"

Claire could only nod.

"Anyway, it was a fascinating story. Ms. Jofsky wasn't suggesting we all do what she did. After all, there are different definitions of *everything*, of the one thing that keeps us from truly following Him, but I admire her for—"

"Here she comes now."

Ken and Vivian stood, and Claire turned her head in time to see Michelle reach their table. Hands were shaken all around, but Claire couldn't find the strength to join them. She noticed Michelle's concerned look.

After more small talk, the Andersons moved on and Claire felt a hand on her shoulder. "How you doing, Claire?"

She shook her head at Michelle's question.

"I was hoping you'd come. I wanted you to know you're not alone."

Claire looked up. "Alone?"

Michelle looked around the room, giving a just-a-minute wave to some people who were waiting to chat with her. She spoke low, for Claire's ears alone. "Not everyone gets asked to do what we've been asked to do—not in this exact way. We should feel honored."

Claire found air enough to snicker. "That's *not* how I feel."

"I know it's hard, but—" Michelle looked up when her name was called, nodded, then looked back to Claire. "Give me ten minutes to do the post-talk shuffle and then we can go somewhere to talk."

Michelle moved into the crowd.

Claire escaped into the church library, taking a seat facing the door so she could watch the narthex yet stay out of sight. She did not feel up to dealing with chitchat. One comment about the weather or the Royals and she would lose it. Her mind was focused on the problem at hand and had to stay that way. Her future depended on it.

A stream of people began to leave. No one noticed her. Finally she heard Michelle's voice rise above some laughter. Claire stood. Her movement drew Michelle's eyes as she walked past the library door. Michelle turned toward a couple. "I really appreciate your kind words. I'll be in church tomorrow morning before heading home."

The couple kept walking but Michelle turned into the library. "You ready?"

Claire felt as if she were going to burst. "Definitely."

"Then let's go. I'll drive."

It was a deal.

They pulled out of the parking lot. "You want coffee?"

"I want answers."

"You're upset."

Claire laughed. "Oh no, this kind of thing happens to me every day."

"This *thing* is wonderful."

"This *thing* threatens to ruin my life."

"Or save it."

Claire angled toward Michelle. "You knew what I'd find in the Bible, didn't you?"

Michelle shrugged. "I suspected. I did not *know*. That was between you and God. That's why I backed off. I didn't want to overstep my bounds. You had to seek His guidance by yourself—or not."

"At your talk tonight, did you ask anyone else to give up everything?"

Michelle looked shocked. "Did you expect me to?"

"Actually, yes. After I pulled myself out of the daze you left me in, I remembered the dinner and hurried there to stop you. I figured you to be a con artist."

"For telling you to read the Bible?"

"For coming to my house and telling me I was the reason you came to Kansas City. That's mystic voodoo stuff."

"What you call 'mystic voodoo stuff' is standard operating procedure for God."

Claire couldn't believe this woman. "So you do this all the time?"

"Not this specifically. But other things."

"Like what?"

Michelle stopped at an intersection. She looked at Claire. "God is at work everywhere. He can implement and initiate anything He wants. Most people are too close-minded to be aware of His promptings. So when He can't use one person, He uses someone else. His purposes *will* be accomplished, one way or the other."

"So you're one of the open-minded ones?"

"I am now."

Claire raised an eyebrow, hoping Michelle saw her skepticism. "Since your vision? That was a new addition to the bum-on-the-tracks story you failed to mention before."

Michelle shrugged. "It happened afterward and was definitely a turning point. I'd felt God's nudgings before, but I usually turned them off."

"Turned them off. You make them sound like a light bulb."

"Perhaps *shut them out* is a better way to say it. Closed the door. I'd feel spurred to do a certain thing, feel deep in my gut that it was the right thing to do, but then I'd start rationalizing it, letting the world's outlook intrude. Often I'd mentally shut the door in order to get it out of my sight." She sighed deeply and pulled into the intersection. "I was pretty stubborn. The railroad incident and the vision were God's way of getting my attention."

"I didn't have a vision."

"Maybe you didn't need one. God operates on a case-by-case basis. What works for one person doesn't always work for someone else. Our God is very good at dealing with people one-on-one."

"You make Him sound like an omnipotent caseworker."

"In a way He is. Caseworker, Father, Savior, Protector, Friend, Lord… He goes by many names. He fills many roles. Every role. You know this, Claire. I know you do. He wouldn't be offering you this opportunity if you weren't a woman of deep faith."

Claire shook her head. "Though my faith *has* gotten stronger in the past year, it's far from deep."

"Faith is a progressive thing, Claire. One act of faith leads to the next—as we can handle it."

"But what He's asking me to do…"

"It's not for everyone."

"No kidding. You said I'm supposed to feel honored about this?"

"He doesn't give us any task we can't do—with His help."

"Oh, I'm sure I *can* do it. It's more a question of do I *want* to do it."

"Do you?"

"Not really."

Michelle laughed. "An honest woman."

"Did *you* want to do it?"

Michelle hesitated. "Not at all. I'd grown up with money. I liked having money. Whatever I wanted, I could have. It wasn't easy giving that up."

"But you did it."

"It was the best thing I *ever* did."

Claire didn't want to believe her. "What did it get you?"

"Freedom."

"Huh?"

Michelle laughed. "Your eloquence is overwhelming."

"Then explain."

"The freedom to let God provide. The world tells us to excel, to *get*, to *have*…" Michelle paused a moment. She flicked her thumbnail against her teeth. "Let me ask you a few questions. How many cars do you have?"

"I have two and my ex has two."

"How many can you drive at once?"

Claire saw where this was going. She didn't like it.

Michelle didn't wait for an answer. "How many televisions do you have? Telephones? Empty bedrooms? Pairs of shoes?"

"So we're all supposed to live in a one-room house with one television, one phone, wearing our one pair of shoes."

"The point is, how many of these things do we need?"

"I'll say one, but—"

"So you *need* a television and a telephone?"

"I don't *need* much of anything. Give me a floor to sleep on, some bread and water, and I'll survive. But that's not living."

"So possessions make a life?"

Claire sighed. "Of course not. You're twisting things. We can't take it with us, but while we're here, it's sure nice to have. Possessions merely make a life better."

"So you're a better person for owning many things?"

"They make *life* better, not *me* better."

"What makes *you* better?"

Claire looked out the car window, trying to think of the right answer. "Being a good person makes me better. Doing good things for others." She thought of something Michelle was probably waiting to hear. "Believing in God makes me a better person."

Michelle raised a finger. "So are you a better person *because* you believe in God, or do you believe in God because you are a better person?"

"Which came first, the chicken or the egg?"

"Something like that."

"You're scrambling my brain, Michelle."

"I'm trying to simplify things."

"Then try harder."

Michelle stopped at a traffic light and tapped her thumbs against the steering wheel. She was silent until the light changed, her words seeming to find movement with the movement of the car. "Having money frees us to help others. When we're just starting out, we don't have a lot of extra to give. We're in the prison called *survival*. But once we get past supplying the basics for ourselves and our families, money frees us to look beyond food and shelter. We can use it on bigger and better toys, or it can give us the opportunity to invest in God's purposes instead of our own. 'Every good and perfect gift is from above…'"

"I know that. I know God's given me what I have. And I think I'm pretty generous with the giving back."

"Ah…the how-much-is-enough dilemma."

Claire shook her head. "You're putting me in a no-win situation. If I set a limit on what I feel I owe God, then I'm an ungrateful fool. But if I say He can have it all, then maybe I'm a reckless one."

"A fool for Christ."

"Ha, ha."

"I can't make your decision for you, Claire. All I know is that I was led to share the opportunity with you. I've never regretted *my* decision. Whatever I've given away has come back to me tenfold in peace, satisfaction, and a deeper knowledge of Him." She shrugged. "Those elements are priceless."

"But intangible."

Michelle considered this a moment. "Not really. Though they affect the heart and soul more than the physical body, they are very real. The body dies. The soul lives forever. Isn't that worth the investment?"

"But *everything*. Sell everything?"

Michelle sighed. "I was hesitant to tell you any of this, because I believe the command to sell everything is referring to more than possessions. To some people possessions aren't the issue. They might be challenged to sell their pride, or their busyness, or their need for attention. Whatever keeps us from full surrender to God needs to be sold, done away with."

"But you think with me, possessions and fame are the issue."

She shrugged. "Aren't they?"

Claire didn't answer.

"I'm not suggesting it will be easy. Money and status represent your accomplishment. Your hard work. The world judges people based on what they have and what title they hold. But God doesn't. Sometimes achievement and money keep us from putting Him first. You can give God a dollar and He appreciates it, but if it doesn't hurt a little—if it doesn't cost you anything—what kind of offering is that?"

"Give till it hurts."

"Remember the story of the widow's mite, Claire?"

"Kind of." *Not really.*

"The bigwig Pharisees with their fancy clothes and high-and-mighty attitudes made a big production about giving their offerings at the temple. *Look at me. I'm so good.* But then a poor widow slipped in and gave one penny—all she had. Jesus said she was better than the rich men because she gave *everything,* quietly, unobtrusively. The Pharisees merely gave a small portion of their wealth and did it for all to see."

"So it's all or nothing? That doesn't sound right."

"Giving something is better than nothing, but giving it *all* is a privilege. It's total surrender."

Claire rolled her eyes. "Oh, right. I forgot. It's an honor."

"That's up to you. You can look at it as an honor or a burden. God is not going to force you into it."

"He's not going to take everything away if I say no?" Claire felt ridiculous for saying it out loud, but it *had* crossed her mind, and she'd already lost so much. No children. No marriage.

"He could, but He probably won't. God's big on free will. And He doesn't want you to obey Him grudgingly. 'Each man should give what he has decided in his heart to give, not reluctantly or under compulsion, for God loves a cheerful giver.' "

Claire laughed. "What did you do? Store up these verses just for me?"

Michelle's voice was serious. "Just for *me.* I need reminding. Too often."

"So you still struggle?"

"Of course. Easy, it's not. And there are days when I'd like to call my seventy-year-old parents and have them send me a one-way ticket home. I'd dive into the cushy bed in their guest room, have the maid make me a steak, a baked potato slathered with a pint of sour cream, and strawberry cheesecake."

"I make a great cheesecake."

Michelle smiled. "And I thought all you made was pizza."

Claire noticed they'd entered a questionable part of town. "Where are you going?"

"Don't ask me. I'm just driving. I don't live here, you know. Direct me."

Claire saw a McDonald's up ahead. Within a second she realized it was *her* McDonald's. "Pull in there! That's where this all started." Claire told Michelle about the old man and giving up a week's salary. Michelle pulled into the parking lot, and Claire was out the door before she'd shut off the engine. "I have to see it again. I have to."

Michelle scrambled after her.

With one foot inside the restaurant she stopped and sucked in a breath. She raised a finger. She pointed at an old man—*the* old man—seated by the window. Her voice was a whisper. "That's *him!*"

Michelle put a hand to her mouth. "Oh, oh no…"

"What?"

"That's *my* man too. The man I pulled off the railroad tracks."

Claire and Michelle moved to his table. He wasn't dressed as shabbily as he'd been the day before, but wore a nice pair of khakis and a plaid, long-sleeved shirt.

"Sir?" Claire said.

The man looked up, then smiled as if it were the most natural thing in the world to have two crazed-looking women standing before him. "Well, I'll be. It's you. Nice to see you." He looked to Michelle and his face changed from unconcerned interest, to curiosity, to recognition. "Oh, my. Denver, right?"

Michelle fell into one chair with Claire falling into the one beside her.

The man took a bite of his Big Mac. "My, my. The Lord continues to amaze."

Claire ignored him a moment and turned to Michelle, who was staring at him, shaking her head. "Are you *sure* this is the man you saved from the train?"

Michelle nodded.

"Oh, yes, indeedy," the man said. "That was quite a thing you did. I'm mighty glad you heard His call and followed it. That was one time where I was a bit wary of His instructions."

His…? Claire wasn't sure she heard right. "What are you talking about?"

He dabbed his chin with a napkin. "The Lord instructs and I follow. Most of the time, anyway. But going down to the tracks and lying against the edge like that…" He shook his head and nodded toward Michelle. "That was a risky one. I prayed a lot, lying there, waiting for you to come." He shrugged. "But hey, John 10:3, I always say."

"I don't know that one."

Claire glanced at Michelle. A verse she actually didn't know?

He cleared his throat. "'He calls his own sheep by name and leads them out.' He called. I answered. You answered."

This was ridiculous. Claire leaned on the table. "You answered…by lying on a railroad track?"

"That, and coming to this place for you."

Claire's heart threatened to beat through her chest. "God told you to come to this McDonald's so I could give you all my money?"

The man shook his head and put his sandwich down. "Let me explain. Twelve years ago I was at a crisis point in my life." He pulled the cuffs of his shirt down, the action drawing Claire's eyes. There was a smattering of scars on his inner wrists.

He noticed her notice, pulled up his sleeves, and displayed them for both to see. "You've seen my stripes. Yet my wounds are nothing compared to His. 'By his wounds we are healed.' " He took a deep breath and put his hands in his lap. "The details of my crisis are inconsequential. What's important is that God drew me close and got me through it. I was so thankful that I dedicated the rest of my life to Him. And lo and behold, He took me up on it. Soon after, I found Him spurring me to go places at certain times. At first I resisted, thinking there was no way God could or would be telling me to go shoot hoops at a certain park, or dress in a suit and eat lunch at some corporate cafeteria. And yet, when I followed—when I continue to follow those nudges—things happen."

"Like what?"

"When I open my eyes and heart to the moment, I usually cross paths with a soul in need of His assistance, in need of getting in touch with a part of His plan."

"I'll repeat my previous question," Claire said. "God told you to come to McDonald's so I'd give you all my money?"

"Nah. I go *where* He sends me, *when* He sends me. I don't know the *what* and certainly am not privy to the *why*. In fact, I've come to see that it's important not to interfere and make things happen." He shook his head. "I gotta admit, that took some practice. A body starts seeing what *could* happen and wants to push things. It's hard to hang back and let Him have His way." He smoothed the edge of the Big Mac wrapper on the table. "Answer this: Did I do anything to get you to give me your money?"

She thought back to the sight of him scrounging in the garbage. He hadn't been begging, nor had he even asked if she could spare a dollar. Until she'd offered her lunch, they had not made eye contact. Nope. The idea had come from her. From God. She shook her head.

He smiled. "That's what makes it so exciting, what makes me keep on keeping on: the element of free will that has the opportunity to play itself out. Or not."

"So this is what you do? Travel around following God's nudges?"

He grinned over his burger. "As I recall, it can pay quite well."

"I'm not sure I like providing someone with a windfall," Claire said.

"Sure you do." He winked. "It made you feel great, didn't it?"

He had her there. "Does something like this happen every time you feel called to go somewhere?"

"Nope. Sometimes I go to a place and hang around for hours and nothing comes down. At least nothing I know of."

Michelle leaned on the table. "That means your nudge was false."

He shook his head. "Though there's no perfection in what I do, I don't think that's the case. I'm supposed to be there, but the applicant doesn't show."

"Applicant?"

"That's what I call 'em. They're given the opportunity to apply their faith and say yes to God, but for some reason they say no, and miss the blessings that could have been theirs."

Suddenly Claire's lungs felt as if they were being squeezed. "I wonder how many times I've missed the blessings. I'm pretty stubborn."

He moved to touch her hand but stopped short. "Don't beat yourself up over it. We all miss out. Just take heart in knowing this time you said yes."

"Where's your next trip?"

He ate a fry. "Don't know yet."

Claire rubbed her face, trying to press some logic into her pores. "I can't believe this is what you do for a living."

"It's what I do to truly live. And He provides the living. Between God-gigs, I find a job and settle in for a spell. But I don't settle too deep. Got to be ready to go when He calls."

"And how exactly does He call you?" Claire asked.

"Same way He calls any of us. A feeling, a nudge, a stirred-up need to move forward. The more a person listens and follows through, the more He calls. The trick is to prove yourself dependable."

"Obedient," Michelle said.

The man nodded. "The wonder of the *O*-word." He held the box of fries toward each of them. They declined his offer. "I must say, meeting you two a second time, that's special. He doesn't often let me witness the aftermath of my gigs, so I'm thankful He brought you here today. It's nice having a chance to talk shop with two of the applicants."

"Applicants for *what,* is the big question," Claire said.

He shrugged. "What's He asked you to do?" His question was simply stated, as though there was nothing more natural. "He *has* asked you to do something, hasn't He?"

Claire nodded. "I'm supposed to give up everything and follow Him."

He chuckled over his burger. "Giving me twenty-five hundred dollars was a good start."

"Oh, she's got lots more than that."

Claire flashed Michelle a look.

The man didn't seem the least bit impressed. "Are you going to do it?"

"I don't know."

"That's understandable. Maybe the broader question is are you ready to go where He's leading?"

Again, his question was the essence of simplicity—and understatement. It was like a doctor asking a patient in the midst of a heart attack, "You feeling a bit under the weather?"

He was waiting for an answer. Claire sighed. "The trouble is, I'm not sure where He's leading or what comes after."

"*I* haven't a clue. But it'll be good, you can bet your life on that." He laughed. "Bet your life...that's a good one."

"So my life depends on my saying yes to this?"

His face turned serious. "Every life depends on saying yes to God. Although you *can* say no, the yeses are much more fulfilling." The man pointed a fry at them. "Have you ever wondered if before Moses, God asked other men to lead the Israelites out of slavery in Egypt, but they all said no? Four hundred years of men saying, 'No thanks, I'll pass.' Maybe Moses was the first to say yes. Did a good job too. Oh, he messed up a few times, but all in all—"

"How do you know this?"

"Don't *know*, just speculating. The thing is, usually something happens in our hearts when God makes us wait—He's waiting on us a lot more than we're waiting on Him. Yet the Hebrew slaves waited four hundred years to be set free, and the Bible doesn't say a thing about any change happening in their hearts. So maybe the wait was for another reason."

Claire looked to the front of the restaurant, where people were ordering hamburgers and chicken nuggets with no clue about the conversation that was going on just a few feet away from them. The overhead speakers sang, "Raindrops Keep Falling on My Head."

"When does God have to know my answer?"

"Now would be good."

"Now?"

He grinned. "Now earns brownie points."

"God gives brownie points?"

The man dragged a fry through a dollop of ketchup. "Again, that's my spin on things, not His. But He does like an eager worker.

Proves your faith, you know. And you wouldn't want to miss those blessings, would you?"

Claire looked to Michelle. For once, the woman was silent, yet by the way she pursed her lips, it was evident that doing so was a struggle.

"So what happens if I do what He's asked? Will an angel chorus sing hallelujah or something?"

The man smiled. "You've seen too many movies."

"Then what does happen?"

"You do it. You follow through. Talk is cheap."

"But giving up everything is going to be very expensive."

"Compared to what?" he asked.

The question of the century. "So I give up everything. Then what? I mean, will I receive further instructions?"

"Like I said, too many movies. This isn't *Mission Impossible,* nor am I an angel from that TV show."

The man *could* pass for Della Reese's brother.

"You will not find an envelope with a to-do list, if that's what you're asking."

Claire felt a hand on her arm. Michelle's voice was low and smooth. "God will let you know what to do. It'll all fall into place. It did for me. As long as you keep yourself open to it."

"Whatever *it* is."

The old man's face changed, losing some of its lines. *"It* is the will of God. And *it* is very, very good." He pushed himself back from the table, gathering his garbage. "If you'll excuse me, ladies. *I* have places to go, people to see."

"So now what?"

Michelle took a deep breath and looked around the restaurant. "Want a burger? You'll need to keep up your strength. Giving up fame and fortune is hard work."

"I never said I was going to do it."

Michelle laughed. "Oh, you'll do it. If I had another fortune to give up, *I'd* do it all over again." She looked to the door where the old man had left. "We never asked his name. We should have asked his name."

They sat in silence a moment. "I've got to get out of here." Claire headed for the exit.

Michelle ran after her. "Where to?"

"My studio."

"But it's Saturday night."

Claire waited to answer until she got in Michelle's car. She shut the door, then looked straight at Michelle and pointed to the ignition. "My studio, Ms. Jofsky. And don't get in my way. Not when I'm trying to earn brownie points and not miss the blessing."

Michelle's face lit up. "You're saying yes?"

Claire closed her eyes and sighed a sigh she would remember for the rest of her life. "I'm saying yes. God help me."

Michelle laughed. "Oh, He will. He will."

Four

Another said, "I will follow you, Lord;
but first let me go back and say good-bye to my family."
Jesus replied, "No one who puts his hand to the plow and
looks back is fit for service in the kingdom of God."

LUKE 9:61–62

CLAIRE WATCHED MICHELLE SLEEP, slumped in the chair next to the workspace. It was three in the morning, and though Claire had tried to get her to go home, Michelle resisted, wanting to stay while Claire worked things through.

Worked things through. Easier said than done.

Claire resorted to her tried-and-true method when confronted with a dilemma: She worked on her mosaics. She thought more clearly when her hands were busy. Plus, there was the added necessity of completing the commission for the Oswald family. If she was giving up everything to leave life as she knew it, she had an obligation to follow through with her commitments.

She nipped the edges of a piece of gray tile and fit it into place, finishing off a storm cloud. The details of giving up everything had turned out to be more complicated than she thought. Giving up the house, the possessions, the money was doable. But the fame. The recognition. Claire knew her fame would live on—at least for a while—riding on the crest of her existing work. But when that work was sold? When the world realized there would be no more Claire Adams mosaics? Then what? Would the very scarcity of her work make her even more famous? Or would the lack of having her art in the public eye make her fade into obscurity?

The unknowns made her stomach clench and her mind reel.

Yet even they were acceptable. What was hard to let go of was the art itself. The act of creating. Her talent was a gift from God. How—and why—would He want her to give it up? It didn't seem logical. But then again, logic was man's quest, not God's; it was a desire to explain what often could not be explained.

Michelle stirred and slid her body from a slumped to sitting position. She moaned. Her muscles had to be sore from sleeping in such an awkward position.

"I must have dozed off."

"Can't imagine why. It's only three in the morning."

Michelle stretched until her muscles shuddered. "I haven't pulled an all-nighter since college. They were stupid then, and they're stupid now."

"Exactly. Go back to the Martins'. You have a plane to catch tomorrow."

Michelle ran her hands over her face. "I can sleep on the plane. But what about you? Aren't you tired?"

Claire laughed. "Don't stop me now, Michelle. I'm on a roll for the Lord, thinking up a storm while my hands are creating a storm cloud."

"Do you always leap into things so vigorously?"

Claire thought for a moment. "I'm good at making quick decisions. Ron says I'm *instinctively instinctive.*" She sighed. "It takes him a week to decide what color socks to wear."

"But at least they match, right?"

"Wanna bet?" Claire leaned toward her work, snipping a tile to shape. "I guess with this current opportunity it's jump in or jump ship. I'm afraid if I let myself think about it too long I'll chicken out and let rational thought take over."

"God doesn't want you to be irrational."

"I'm not. But the excitement of the faith-challenge gets me going until the reality of the follow-through makes me pull up short. I want to do the right thing, I'm honored He's trusting me to do this, yet a part of me is still hesitant and I'm afraid that hesitancy will never completely fade."

"You're probably right."

Somehow, hearing that made everything better. If it was all right to proceed in spite of the hesitancy, then maybe it could be done.

"Before I fell asleep you were talking about a financial package to offer your employees."

Claire pushed her doubts into a corner. "Just because I'm crazy, doesn't mean they should suffer. And the gallery can continue selling my pieces." She looked up. "I'm going to have the proceeds sent directly to you."

"Me?"

"For the Salvation Shelter."

Michelle put a hand to her chest. "I never meant for you to do that."

"I know you didn't. That's why I'm doing it." Claire grinned. "The truth is, when I saw how pitiful you looked all slumped in that chair—snoring like a foghorn, I might add—I had no choice. It was between your charity or giving all my wealth to the Society for the Preservation of the Carpet Beetle. You won."

"I'm honored."

"Rightly so. It was a close call." Claire pushed another tile in place, turning it ever so slightly with her finger. "I wish you could get it in one lump sum, but—"

"I'm not picky. Too many zeroes and I get giddy." Michelle bit her lip, her eyes darting. "But to satisfy my curiosity, how many zeroes are we talking about? Eventually?"

Claire laughed. "Greed becomes you."

Michelle blushed. "It's not greed; it's just that I'd like to know so I can plan—"

Claire stopped the woman's defense with a hand. "You don't have to justify anything to me. You have a right to know, and though I don't have a final number, and though the sales of my existing pieces will extend over a span of months—if not years—we're talking six figures."

Michelle's eyes threatened to drop onto her lap. "Hundreds of thousands?"

"Give or take."

"I had no idea." Michelle kept shaking her head. "That's truly a fortune. I didn't have to give up nearly that much."

Claire's throat was suddenly dry. *Is it too much? Is God asking too much?*

Michelle leaned toward her. "Uh-uh. Get that doubtful look off your face. I shouldn't have said that. You don't need me making you question your decision. It's obviously right. You've been running on full throttle ever since we left McDonald's."

Claire arched her aching back and held the position until the ache melded into a modicum of comfort. "But maybe I'm going over-board. Maybe I've gotten caught up in the swell of the idea without thinking about the ramifications—"

Michelle walked to the mosaic, grabbed Claire's hand, and gave it a sharp slap. "No! Stop second-guessing yourself."

Claire rubbed the back of her hand. "You're asking the impossible."

Michelle hesitated only a moment. "We need to pray." Without any more preamble she knelt on the floor at Claire's feet, took her hand, and bowed her head. "Lord, we think we understand what You want Claire to do. And she's ready to do it. But she's feeling some doubt—I'm afraid I caused it by comparing what she has to give up with my own situation. Forgive me for that, Lord."

Claire opened her eyes. She didn't want Michelle feeling badly. But Michelle did not return her look. Her face was drawn, her fore-head furrowed in deep concentration as she continued to pray. Claire closed her eyes as she listened.

"If it's Your will that Claire give up her wealth and fame for You, then give her a sense of peace that can only come from You. If she's on the wrong track, and this is not Your will, then let the unease con-tinue, and lead her toward stopping the process."

Claire felt Michelle's grip ease and opened her eyes again. Michelle was looking at her. "Do you want to add anything?"

Claire wasn't used to praying out loud—at least not with an audi-ence. But she did have something to say. And now was the time. She closed her eyes and began. "Dear Lord, I can't say as I'm pleased with the situation You've put me in. I guess I should call it an opportunity, though You'll forgive my lack of total enthusiasm. But I'll do it. I *will* do it, if it's what You want. Yet I have so many questions… I give up my art, sell my townhouse, sell my vehicles… I'll be free of any encumbrance—which I'll have to admit, is kind of appealing—but then what?"

As a deep sigh escaped her, Claire found herself relaxing. It was a relief to let her doubts and questions into the open for God to handle. "Like Michelle said, if this doubt is from You, then let it continue and I'll stop this thing, chalk up one sleepless night as small payment for keeping my lifestyle. But if this doubt is *not* from you…then make it go away." She opened her eyes and looked to Michelle. "Amen?"

Michelle smiled. "In Jesus' name, amen." She stood, rubbing her knees. "I think that's about it. How do you feel?"

Claire sat back, trying to assess her state. She took a deep breath. Blinked a few times. "Better. I think."

"Peaceful?"

Claire did another scan of her emotions and was disappointed. "Not quite. But better."

"Give it time. Though we'd like instant answers to our prayers, we don't always get them."

"Bummer."

Michelle laughed. "I still believe God wants you to do this."

Claire nodded. "Time will tell."

Michelle drove Claire to her car in the church parking lot. Claire had just enough time to go home to shower and change before the early service at church.

She fished her keys from her purse. "Are you going to get into trouble with your host family? The Martins will think you're a bad girl for being out all night."

"I called them and said I was with you. I said we were working on a project."

"That's the truth. Will I get to talk to you before you head back to Denver?"

"Probably not. They've got me set to speak at the eleven o'clock service, and then I'll be off to catch my plane at two-thirty."

Claire took one last look at this woman who had been instrumental in changing her life so completely. She was nothing special to look at. Not particularly pretty—especially with the dark circles under her eyes. Yet she had been an instrument of God. "I feel like I've known you for years, and it's been less than twenty-four hours."

"An eventful twenty-four hours."

Claire would not argue with that one. With a sigh she extended her hand across the middle console. "I won't forget you, Michelle Jofsky."

Michelle shook it. "Nor I you. Call if you need me. And keep me informed where God sends you."

Tears threatened. Claire got out of the car and bent down to say one last thing. "Be watching for the checks. Do good things with my money."

"I'll do better than that. I'll do *God* things."

Claire nodded. After all, that *was* the point.

Claire headed home to get ready for church, yet she was wary about spending time alone. Would her resolve dampen when she was alone with me, myself, and I?

It didn't. As she stood in the shower of the townhouse she would soon be selling, she found herself singing quite loudly and quite off-key, "He's got the whole world in His hands." She laughed at her own elation.

Maybe this would be easier than she thought.

But then again, maybe not.

Claire *had* to tell someone about her plans. It was like the fuse had been lit on a wonderful secret, and she would blow up if she didn't share it.

She walked into the church and scanned the narthex, looking for someone to brag to. Too bad it was in bad taste to wear a placard that said *I'm giving it all up for God—are you?*

She spotted Mandy Everett, smiled, and waved.

Mandy came toward her. "All right. What's going on? If I turned off the lights, you'd glow."

So glad you asked. Claire pulled Mandy to the side. "I'm glowing because my life is about to change."

Mandy gasped and squeezed her arm. "You're getting married."

Claire laughed. "Don't you think I'd need a man in my life in order to get married?"

"A technicality."

"Nope, I'm a free agent—as far as men go, at least."

Mandy gave her a puzzled look. "My brain does not decipher cryptic messages on weekends so you'll have to be more—"

"I've got a secret." Claire felt like a teenager.

Mandy leaned close. "Which you *are* going to tell me right this minute."

"If you insist." Claire waved at some other people she knew coming in the front doors, but she didn't make an attempt to draw them over. Not yet. One at a time. Claire took a deep breath. "I'm going to give everything away."

"Everything of what?"

"Everything. Every thing. All I own."

"Why?"

This was the hard part. "Because God wants me to."

Mandy lowered her chin and raised her eyebrows in a look Claire had seen before. "And how exactly did He instruct you to do this? A divine e-mail? Heavenly airmail? Or maybe a singing telegram with an angel chorus?"

"You can't be skeptical when I haven't even explained."

"I'm getting a head start."

Claire's thoughts bounced between telling Mandy about Michelle or bringing up the Bible verses in Mark.

"I'm waiting."

Claire gave her the condensed version of what had happened with Michelle. Mandy's reaction was as dull as the *uh-huh*s of a bored psychiatrist. Claire's enthusiasm died. "So, uh…that's it. Tomorrow I tell my employees I'm closing up shop."

Mandy blinked. Then she sighed. Then she changed her weight to the other foot. "You're crazy."

Those two words stabbed Claire's bubble like a needle. "But it's the right thing to do. God's chosen me to do this. He wouldn't ask unless He thought I could—"

"Well, la-di-da, aren't you special?"

Claire took a step back.

Mandy brows lifted another fraction. "Why has He chosen *you?* Why not someone else? Why not…me?"

Oops. "I don't know, Mandy, and maybe *chosen* is too strong a word. God's given me the opportunity. It's up to me to do the choosing—to choose to do it or not."

"But why *would* you? God's the one who let you get rich and successful in the first place. 'Every good and perfect gift is from above,' and all that. Why would He want you to give it all up? It doesn't make sense."

It did this morning, with Michelle.

Claire looked at the exit. Maybe she should skip church today, stop at the bakery and buy a dozen cream-filled long johns and a monster hazelnut cappuccino. Go home and wallow in her confusion until the sugar and caffeine overdose zapped her brain back to reality or made her slip into catatonia.

"I don't want to put a damper on your enthusiasm, Claire, but you're talking like an alien being. What happened to Claire Adams, the woman who fought her way toward owning her own gallery and having showings around the world? Claire Adams who can outshop Imelda Marcos, who buys a new vehicle every two years whether she needs it or not?"

"I…I have too much. I don't need it."

Mandy slipped her hand through Claire's arm. "None of us *need* it, darlin'."

The statement both confirmed and horrified Claire. "Some people *need*, Mandy. We've just climbed the ladder too high to see them. But they're there. On the ground. Maybe they're even holding the ladder for us."

"That doesn't mean you're supposed to jump off and join them.

Give your 10 percent to the church. Hey, give *30* percent, I don't care. But don't give up everything you've worked for on a whim."

"But what happened to me…those things are not whims. They're real."

"Real strange."

Claire was conscious of her heart beating. Maybe she and Mandy didn't understand each other as well as she'd thought. "What about the peace I'm starting to feel about the decision? That's usually a sign that a person's made a good choice."

"A person can talk herself into anything, Claire, you know that. I can feel peaceful about buying a three-hundred-dollar pair of shoes if I try hard enough. I doubt God's behind that."

Mandy was mixing her up, stirring a pot that didn't want to be stirred. Mandy's husband waved his wife over. The service would start in a few minutes.

Mandy turned to leave, then put a hand on Claire's arm. "I'm sorry if I put a damper on your plan, darlin'. But I simply can't believe God would tell you to do such a misguided thing. I'm concerned. I want you to be careful. Think things through. You're known for your ability to make snap decisions, but sometimes it's best to let things stew. Give them time to settle."

Claire didn't want to stew. She didn't want things to settle. And she certainly didn't want to doubt.

She wanted to act. And so she did. She straightened her back and looked her friend in the eye. "You wondered why God didn't choose you to do this, Mandy? Because you would have said no."

She walked toward the sanctuary, leaving Mandy's chin resting on the floor.

Claire slipped into a pew for the nine-thirty service, face hot, heart pumping. She knew she had multiple chips on her shoulder. How *dare* Mandy deride her decision? She needed support and encouragement. After all, she was going to do something few people had guts enough to do. God had chosen *her*. She had been *called*.

As the prelude began, she looked at the people in the congregation. God hadn't called them to make this sacrifice; He had called *her*. He trusted *her*. She needed to trust Him to give her confirmation that her decision was right.

She remembered Michelle's directions to be open to His will. She closed her eyes for a quick prayer. *Make things plain.*

With a sudden thought she opened the bulletin to see if the Scripture reading for the day happened to be Mark 10:17–23. She was disappointed that it wasn't. *You missed a good opportunity to drive home the point, Lord.*

The congregation stood to sing the opening hymn. Claire cleared her throat and shuffled her shoulders, trying to get the chips to fall away. If she was going to get anything out of the service, she needed to purge the anger and the I-should-have-saids from her mind. She had to make room for God.

Claire loved to sing the alto part during the hymns. It brought back memories of high school chorus, standing on wobbly risers, wearing a new dress for a concert. She was only an adequate singer. But when all the voices rose together to praise God, her voice gained strength and talent took second place to enthusiasm.

Yet today, as she sang the words to the unfamiliar hymn…

> *Go, labor on: spend, and be spent,*
> *Thy joy to do the Father's will,*
> *It is the way the Master went;*
> *Should not the servant tread it still?*

The notes caught in her throat. It was as if the words were meant for her.

She felt the eyes of Dan Hutchins, sitting to her right. She met them. He raised an eyebrow, as though to ask, *Are you all right?* She managed a smile, then noticed she didn't just have Dan's attention. In the row in front of her, she spotted Mandy whispering behind her hymnal to another acquaintance. Their eyes flitted back to Claire. Mandy's husband also glanced in her direction and shook his head ever so slightly. Obviously, he'd already been told her big news—and judged her.

News was spreading…and from the looks on people's faces, the reaction wasn't positive.

I'm being deemed a crazy.

The hymn continued:

> Go, labor on: 'tis not for naught;
> Thine earthly loss is heav'nly gain;
> Men heed thee, love thee, praise thee not;
> The Master praises—what are men?

Claire's legs were weak. *Go, labor on…the Father's will…earthly loss is heav'nly gain…men praise thee not…the Master praises…*

As the gossip spun around her, she realized she was living out the words of the hymn. People did *not* understand. Would not. Could not?

She felt a hand on her forearm. It was Dan. "You okay?"

Without consciously making the decision to do so, she edged her way toward the side aisle. She ignored the puzzled looks of the ushers in the narthex and hurried out of the church.

As Claire sped home she had to laugh. She'd asked God to "make it plain." She'd expected an answer to her prayer that was uplifting, encouraging. Something that would make her *feel* the blessing of her sacrifice. Instead, He showed her the reality of it. Gossip. Ostracism. Misunderstanding. It was almost as if God had offered her a further challenge: *Knowing what you know now, do you still want to do it?*

Did she?

As she pulled into her driveway, she noticed something taped to her door. It was a piece of white paper, folded in half. She opened it and scanned to the end of the message. It was from Michelle.

Dear Claire:

   I read a verse this morning and found it an affirmation of my own choice. Perhaps it will help you too.

   "Then I heard the voice of the Lord saying, 'Whom

shall I send? And who will go for us?' And I said, 'Here am I. Send me!'" (Isaiah 6:8).

Don't get bogged down in the details—financial, emotional, mental, and spiritual. God has asked you a question. Answer. Then trust Him to handle the rest. He knows what He's doing. Focus on Him.

I am here for you. Any time. Any place.

Michelle

Claire sank onto the front step and read the note again.

Focus on Him.

That was the key. When she thought about *her* sacrifice, *her* assignment, all sorts of unruly thoughts popped up like weeds in a beautiful garden. The only way to get rid of the weeds, and to prevent more from growing, was to keep her mind, eyes, and soul focused on the Gardener Himself. He would tell her what to do. He would even take care of the weeds.

He'd asked a question and she'd said yes.

That question—and that answer—was the essence of everything.

Five

*I consider everything a loss compared to the surpassing greatness
of knowing Christ Jesus my Lord,
for whose sake I have lost all things.*

PHILIPPIANS 3:8

IT TOOK TEN DAYS for Claire's lawyers to work out the details of her life. Or, actually, seven days to handle the details after three days of trying to talk her out of it. Today she implemented that plan, hoping that it would give her a satisfying feeling of accomplishment or closure. Instead, it left her numb.

She sat behind her desk at the studio and let it sink in. She'd just had a meeting with her studio workers after spending the morning at the gallery trying to calm Regina, the director. *None* of them understood what she was doing. *All* of them thought she was out of her mind.

Was she?

Her life as an artist was over. Her employees had generous compensation packages, and the proceeds of her art was set to go to Michelle's Salvation Shelter, so Claire was now out of the entire process. She was a nonessential, a minor detail, as her existing art went on without her and any future art died before it was born.

"Claire?"

She looked up. Darla stood in the doorway.

"I wanted to wish you well."

Darla had the most to lose. She'd been with Claire since the beginning. "Thanks. I'm so sorry—"

She took a step into the room. "Don't be sorry. At least this explains your odd mood the other day. And though I can't say I completely understand, I've always respected your faith. I even started going to church because of you."

Claire snapped out of her daze. "You did?"

"Sure. When you were going through your divorce it was completely different from how my divorce played out. You seemed to find an inner calm—even when your world was going crazy. I wanted that."

Claire touched Darla's hand. "I just wish it hadn't taken a divorce to get me there. I wasted so much time being a casual Christian."

Darla laughed. "That's an interesting term."

"Interesting, but apt. For years—decades, actually—I believed the basics but took them for granted, not giving any more effort than necessary. Basically I figured I could handle things on my own, and when I couldn't, I'd send up a quick prayer, expecting a quick answer. It was a very one-sided relationship: God gave and I took." She snickered. "Pretty dumb, huh? Rude even."

"Pretty normal, I'm afraid."

"Funny how the blessing of my divorce has been a stronger faith."

"For both of us."

Claire shook her head. How could she have been so blind? The most important person in the studio had built her faith right before her eyes, and she hadn't noticed? Her work was demanding, but had she let the logistics of the business overshadow the people *in* it? Perhaps it was good she was getting out.

On impulse Claire asked, "Darla, would you be my contact here at home? I'd like to have someone I could call—if I need to."

"Sure, but…" Darla shifted her weight to the other foot.

"But what?"

"Don't you want your contact to be someone…maybe your best friend?"

The fact she didn't have a best friend was pitiful. "You're my friend, aren't you?"

"Of course."

"We've known each other for years, haven't we?"

"Years."

"Then be my contact. You're the only one who knows about my

personal life *and* my art." She drummed a pencil on the desk. "It's quite a privilege, you know. You'll be privy to all sorts of inside information."

Darla grinned. "Isn't that illegal?"

"Only on Tuesdays."

Darla nodded. "I'd be honored, Claire. And I wish you the best. You're one brave lady."

Or a stupid one.

Claire needed to clear her head, which meant a visit to an art gallery. Strolling through other artists' creations was a comfort, proof she was not alone in her work.

Work she was leaving behind.

The Nelson-Atkins Art Gallery always had something to grab her interest. But today, she didn't feel like seeing the works of Pollock, Calder, Titian, or even Rubens. As soon as she entered the columned portico, she was drawn to a temporary exhibit, "Midwest Masters: Paintings by and About the Midwest." She strolled before paintings of all styles and mediums, finding comfort in the familiar scenes of open fields, sprawling lakes, and soldierlike rows of trees framing family farmsteads. But the exhibit didn't just capture the pastoral beauty of the area. There were paintings of bigger cities too: St. Louis, Kansas City, Lincoln. And still others of the small towns that dotted state after state.

Then a small-town scene captured her attention, though she couldn't pinpoint why. It wasn't extraordinary. The picture depicted a town square, featuring a courthouse in the center and an old-fashioned library across the street. Both buildings were made of tan stone. A flag flapped in the wind, while benches dotted the common area in front of the courthouse. A dozen people strolled through the scene. Smalltown, USA. It was a setting that could be replicated a hundred times across the area. Maybe that's what drew her to it. The stability, the promise of calm. The never-changing steadfastness.

She glanced at the title plaque: *Steadfast, Kansas.*

Steadfast.

She held her breath, her eyes darting across the paint strokes one more time, searching, claiming the scene as her own as if she had a stake in its colors, lines, and forms.

Claire backed up until the back of her calves found a bench. She sank onto it, her gaze glued to the painting. *Her* painting. Her opportunity.

Her future?

A shiver confirmed the idea that had taken root.

She was going to Steadfast, Kansas.

As soon as Claire got back to the studio she went to her computer and searched the Internet for information on Steadfast. There wasn't much. The town didn't have a website, so the only information she could gather was generic. Founded in 1886 with a current population of 3,386.

Could she actually go to a town based on so little information? For one thing, she was not a small-town type of woman. She'd lived in Kansas City her entire life and enjoyed the constant activity of the big city. What would she do in a town that wasn't much bigger than her neighborhood?

And yet the memory of the painting haunted her. There was no denying she had been drawn to it, mesmerized by the feeling it invoked. By the peace it represented.

Peace. Was that what she was searching for? Not exclusively.

Since she was giving up everything, she assumed God would have a big assignment for her. A heaven-inspired project only she could accomplish. Something worthy of her sacrifice. And that meant work. Not peace. And not sitting around in a town where she'd be pegged a stranger with her first stroll up Main Street. They'd ask questions she couldn't easily answer. Wouldn't it be better to fade into the anonymity of a city where whos, whats, and whys were ignored?

She logged off the Internet, more confused than ever. Maybe she was rushing into this. The business end was set, and she'd put her townhouse on the market. But maybe she needed to slow down. The only sense of direction she'd received had been in regard to Steadfast,

Kansas, and that didn't seem to fit. So maybe she should just hold off a bit and—

The intercom rang. Lana's voice said: "Your realtor on line one, Claire."

Good timing. Though she and her agent, Angie, had talked about lowering the price on the townhouse, Claire could now tell her that she was going to remain firm on the price. Best not to be rash.

"Hey, Claire. Want to hear something amazing?"

"Sure."

"I had a couple come into the office looking for a townhouse. They were very specific about their wants, even which direction the house would face—west. Plus, they wanted oak woodwork in the hearthroom and kitchen area, and you know that most of the newer homes have the enamel-white trim and—"

Claire felt a now-familiar stitch in her stomach. "And my townhouse would be perfect for them."

Angie hesitated, but only for a second. "They'll pay full price."

Claire's breath left her.

"Plus, they want immediate possession."

"No, no, no."

"What do you mean *no?*"

No, no, no collided with *yes, yes, yes.* There was no turning back. It was a do—

"It's a done deal if you say yes," Angie said.

Claire laughed. "Been there, done that."

"What?"

"Yes, Angie. I say yes."

So much for holding off. *Steadfast, here I come.*

The buyers of Claire's townhouse liked more than the west entrance and the oak moldings. They liked Claire's furniture, *and* the pictures on the walls, *and* the gewgaws on the mantle…

Sold!

It was disconcerting how fast—and effortlessly—the trappings of her life were jettisoned. Two weeks from first look to closing. She felt like Jonah's shipmates in the storm, throwing everything overboard to lighten the load that was her life. She only hoped *she* wouldn't be thrown over too. Or, if she was, that God would provide a nice big fish to swallow her up. And spit her out?

The proceeds from the sale of her home, vehicles, and possessions were being divided between twelve charities. Her lawyer suggested narrowing it down to six, but Claire decided to give some to many, rather than a lot to a few.

She stood in the entry and looked back at her home. Although the buyers had wanted most of Claire's possessions, she'd singled out a few items of sentimental value and passed them out to family members. A niece received her grandmother's silver tea set; a nephew was given her father's fishing trophies; and Claire deemed her sister the caretaker of the family photographs and Grandma Morris's wedding china, including the soup tureen with the chip on the handle.

Once she started going through her possessions, she was amazed at how little was truly important. She'd filled an entire house with pretty things that pleased the eye but did nothing for the heart or soul.

And her wardrobe...Claire loved clothes. In her youth she bought in quantity, but in the past few years she'd found that buying fewer, classic pieces was the wiser choice. She had beautiful suits, most with matching shoes. The question was, what should she give away and what should she take with her? She vowed to whittle her belongings down to one small suitcase and an oversized bag that she could carry on a bus easily. But what kinds of clothes would she need in Steadfast, Kansas?

What was she going to *do* in Steadfast, Kansas?

Claire was an organizer. She lived out of her day planner. She was used to having her time scheduled and certain. To go to a small town in southeastern Kansas without knowing who, what, when, or how she was going to live was...unsettling. Would she need suits? Jeans? Sackcloth?

Logic suggested because God was having her give up everything, He was probably directing her to a simplified life. Therefore, no need for designer clothes. Wistfully bidding her beautiful things good-bye before bringing them to the Women's Career Center, she settled on a khaki skirt and pants, a few pairs of jeans, a denim dress, and an assortment of tops and blouses. One black blazer. At the last minute, she threw in a pair of black dress slacks. Her fifty-seven pairs of shoes had been pared to four: tennis shoes, black flats, sandals, and one pair of tan pumps. Two pairs of earrings: one gold and one silver. She sold her Rolexes and gave the money to the church's mission project. It was pitiful how two watches could provide Bibles for 2,438 people. She bought herself an inexpensive Timex.

The one thing she'd kept was Grandma Morris's necklace. It had sat in her jewelry box for years, appreciated but unworn. While cleaning out drawers, Claire put it on and discovered she liked the feel of the cross on her chest—and the way it was always handy to run a finger across if the need arose.

Claire touched that cross now as she stood in the doorway, ready to say good-bye. She felt small and vulnerable without the things that had shaped her identity. She was left with just herself—

And You, Lord. Stay close. I need You.

And so, with one last wistful look, Claire Adams closed the door on her old life.

Claire hadn't ridden on a bus since a church ski trip in high school. That bus had been loud and crowded. This one was quiet and sparse.

People chose their seats carefully, keeping their distance. Claire understood. They may have been fellow travelers heading in the same direction, but by their symbolic choice to be separate, they indicated that was all they had in common. *Leave me alone, and tell me when we get there.*

Not that anyone was hostile or unfriendly. This was the Midwest. You looked at people when you walked down the aisle. You smiled. You said hello. But then you dissolved into your own little habitat, turning your head to the window to watch the rest of the world flash by.

An hour out of Kansas City, Claire checked the money in her billfold. That had been another hard decision: how much money to bring with her. Her lawyer suggested she keep a savings account—perhaps holding ten thousand dollars—in case of emergencies. But

Claire rejected the suggestion. If she had a contingency plan—if she had a way out—she might take it. *Everything* meant *EVERYTHING.*

At first she'd felt guilty keeping *any* money, but then she realized she would need money to get to Steadfast, and some for motel and food until she got a job or—

Or what?

Had she left one profession only to be sent to Steadfast to fall into another? Just like that? Although she had no proof, Claire didn't think this was the way it would work. God had plenty of people to work in normal jobs, and He wouldn't have asked her to give up everything to work in a Burger King somewhere.

At least…she hoped not.

Surely her job would be more unconventional and would involve working with people on a one-on-one basis. Something…*inspiring.* Meaningful. Profound.

But she'd need a place to sleep and she'd need to eat. Hence, she needed money. The amount she'd settled on came about oddly; but in retrospect, seemed appropriate.

Claire had a habit of leaving money in odd places: purses, jars, dishes on the counter. Loose change. A few bills. Throwaway money. Yet when she began to gather it together…when she took it to the bank and cashed it in—earning the oddest look from the teller—she had $397.32.

Not a small sum to have lying around. Yet a miniscule sum with which to start a new life. She'd already had to spend $32 to get the bus ticket. But God would provide. Wouldn't He?

So her total net worth was now $375.32. By the world's standards she was a failure. But by God's standards? Good thing His view of a person's worth was different.

She looked at her watch. Within an hour she would arrive at her new home. *But I don't have a home.* Her new town. *Where I know no one.* To start over. *Doing what?*

She sucked in a breath. Her chest tightened.

What have I done?

❧   ❧   ❧

Steadfast.

The city sign was ordinary. Even in the moonlight Claire could see the holes from kids taking target practice with their BB guns. And the final *t* was slightly obliterated by a glob of bird doo. But as the bus passed by, with the Kansas wind making the sign vibrate on its post, she knew—she *knew*—this was the place her new life would begin.

There was no bus station in Steadfast, only a bus stop in front of the courthouse. The scene was surreal, the painting come to life. But the town square was dark. Steadfast was a passing-through point, and as such had a late arrival time. It was after 1 A.M.

The driver helped her with her suitcase, looking around the empty streets. "You got someone coming to meet you?"

She picked up her suitcase. "I'll be fine." She was tempted to add a line about a friend picking her up but didn't want to start her new life with a lie.

The driver didn't look convinced, but he went back to the driver's seat. The doors closed. The bus drove off, leaving her.

Alone.

She made herself breathe. In. Out. In. Out. *It'll be all right. Please, God, make it be all right.*

She looked around. She'd been dropped in the middle of a set for the *Andy Griffith Show.* Did the people fit the profile that ticker-taped through her head? Two-parent families with a dog that lived in its own house out back; a high school football team that rose above all odds to take state; bake sales and car washes to earn money for a new roof on the fire station; and the requisite town drunk, town gossip, and town floozy.

Steadfast, meet Claire Adams.

I'm here, Lord. Now what?

She yawned. Although she'd slept on the bus, a crying baby had prevented total rest, so the first order of business was finding a place to sleep. Although she wasn't picky, she didn't want to draw attention to herself. Park benches were too public, and the filth of back alleys was beyond the scope of her tolerance. She may have given up everything she owned, but she had standards. She did a three-sixty. A hardware store, café, antique store, bar, grocery.

No motel, hotel, bed-and-breakfast, or Room for Rent sign. Most little towns had a motel on the edge of town, but which edge? Claire didn't feel like wandering the streets at one in the morning, no matter *how* safe they might be.

The courthouse loomed large, the tan stone of the region making it appear strong and impenetrable. A flag flapped to her right. She looked at it. There was the other building shown in the painting. The library.

Claire walked toward it. She had always liked books—or the idea of books. Yet as a mosaic artist, she hadn't had much need for Chaucer or Dickens. When was the last time she'd read for pleasure? Her excuse had been lack of time. Ha. She had time now. Plenty of it.

She scanned the building. The sheer size of it brought back wonderful memories. As a child, she and her cousin used to go to the neighborhood library every Saturday morning. They'd loved the musty smell of old wood and books and had claimed a favorite corner to read in, giggle in, and, as they grew older, watch boys from.

She paced the library's perimeter, sizing it up like a cowboy eyeing a horse he wanted to buy. It was one story tall, but set up high, with worn stone steps leading to a newer, glass front door. There was a small, attic-type window on the front and a—

Claire stopped. She backtracked a step. Was that a light shining in the attic? At one in the morning? She stared at it, then smiled and whispered into the darkness, "The Lord turns my darkness into light."

The light drew her in, a beacon in the night. She did another three-sixty. Yup. It was the *only* light in the buildings edging the square. This meant something. Either she trusted God to take care of her needs, or she didn't. And her most immediate need was a place to sleep. What safer place than a library?

"Okay, Lord. Here goes."

She walked to the door. It was predictably locked and for a moment her hope shut down. Then she thought: *What about the back?* She realized the chances were slim, but…

The back door opened when she turned the knob. Claire shoved it open a few inches, waiting for some alarm to sound. The only sound was the drone of the cicadas in the huge maple trees overhead.

She nudged the door farther open. It hit something. She peeked inside and found a stack of boxes partially blocking its swing. The moonlight revealed a storeroom with an overhead projector, shelves holding office supplies and books, and a few broken chairs.

She slipped inside. Although she would have loved to turn on a light, she didn't dare. As harmless as she was, she *was* an intruder. She closed the door behind her and felt a button on the door knob. The door had a lock. Lucky for her the door wasn't used often enough for someone to check whether it was locked or not.

Claire gave her eyes a moment to adjust to the dark. She moved to a wide, swinging door straight ahead. She edged it open and peered at what had to be the main library. Although she was tempted to take a tour through the books she'd neglected, she had not been drawn to this library in the wee hours to read. She'd been drawn by a light. A light in the attic.

She turned back to the storeroom and found what she was looking for. To her right was a narrow stairway with a rickety railing. At the top landing was a door.

The door was ajar. But there was no light.

Her heart pounded. The absence of light when there *had* been light was disconcerting. *Maybe someone's up there.* If so, they wouldn't appreciate being disturbed in the middle of the night.

Yet it had been the only light in a dark night. And she was tired. God had led her this far. She had to trust Him. Besides, what were her options?

"Hello?"

The sound of her voice was like a slap in the silence.

No answer. She started up the stairs, jerking when she broke through an invisible cobweb. Obviously no one had been up here in a while.

Then who turned off the light?

Claire hesitated. She found it hard to swallow. *Trust Him. It's just a light. Go on. Quit acting like a child afraid of the boogeyman.* She climbed the rest of the stairs with a new—if somewhat feigned—determination. At the landing, she hesitated, then peeked inside the room. Moonlight streamed through the window, coming to rest on the glass of a picture sitting on the floor, leaning against a crate. Could that have reflected like a light?

"Hello?"

No sounds.

She pushed the door open and walked in. Although there were more shadows than light, Claire could see that the walls of the attic were partially finished, as if someone had gotten a deal on a few sheets of wood paneling. Its bare beams were bound together by cobwebs. The dark corners revealed three dormers, each with a small window. The center dormer to her right had a makeshift window seat built within the grasp of its three walls. A faded rag rug marked the center of the room. Perhaps some librarian once used this place as a getaway?

Dusty crates, old card catalogs, a trunk, a few tables and chairs. What? No freshly made bed waiting for her? She smiled.

Claire dropped her suitcase on the rug, opened it, removed some of the clothes, and rolled them into a pillow. She unbuttoned her denim dress and used it as a blanket. Her shoulder and hip objected to the solidity of the floor. Her mind flitted to her king-size four-poster with the padded pillow-top mattress. Maybe if she thought soft thoughts?

After a short time, her body forgot the fact that it was uncomfortable and eased itself to sleep.

Welcome to Steadfast.

Six

*"But as for you, be strong and do not give up,
for your work will be rewarded."*

2 CHRONICLES 15:7

CLAIRE WOKE WITH A SORE BACK. *It feels like I've been sleeping on the—*

She opened her eyes and remembered. She *was* sleeping on a floor. She sat up, and her denim-dress blanket fell off her shoulder. The library attic was friendlier by day, with sunlight streaming in the three windows. With a groan, she pushed herself to her feet, looked around, and felt her eyes widen and her heart lift.

In one of the dormers was a single bed, complete with metal headboard. It reminded her of a hospital bed. She dragged it out and placed it perpendicular to the window closest to the stairs. She bounced on the mattress. It was only three inches thick, and the metal webbing beneath it squeaked and squealed at her movement, but it was better than the floor. A real bed. Civilization. To think she'd been this close to a cushioned sleep.

She looked inside the crates, one by one. Most contained books and papers, though she did find a few candles and a book of matches. As there was no electricity, candles would have to suffice.

In the trunk she found a stash of old blankets, two small pillows, and a couple of ratty terry towels. She put them to her face and inhaled. Musty, but they seemed clean—and better than nothing.

She rearranged a few crates, creating a bedside table. She blew the dust off a bookshelf and unpacked her clothes. There. All moved in. All ready.

But for what?

Claire still had no clue as to why she'd been brought here. Yet once she allowed herself to be still, she realized something new had been added while she slept: an antsy feeling, as if an important event was on the verge. Her insides pulled with anticipation.

What's going on, Lord?

He gave her no immediate answer.

She stretched, her muscles complaining about the hard night. Never again. Now she had a bed. And who was she to complain? Free lodging was free lodging.

The first order of business was a bathroom. She looked at her watch. Six o'clock. The library wouldn't open until nine or ten. It was safe to venture downstairs.

She grabbed a towel from the trunk, her toiletry bag and a change of clothes, and found the restrooms through the swinging door, to the right, off the main room. It felt wonderful to wash her face and brush her teeth. After making quick work of minimal makeup, she assessed her appearance. She adjusted Grandma Morris's necklace, letting her fingers linger on the cross. Her eyes strayed to her hair. Perhaps there was good reason she'd gotten it cut short and permed a few weeks ago. Traveling hair. Attic hair. But how she would love a shower.

She shrugged to her reflection. "Deal with it." At least her reflection didn't argue.

She ventured into the main library. In the half-light of dawn she saw it was a large rectangle. A librarian's desk and checkout area were between her and the front door. To the left, computers stood at attention, guarding the book stacks. Much remained in shadow.

Claire's stomach rumbled. Sleep, bathroom, food. The necessities of life were raising their hands, vying for attention. Actually, they'd been very patient. Yet Claire didn't want to leave the sanctuary of the library until she had a plan. And in order to get a plan, she had to ask the *Planner.*

She noticed a Mr. Coffee. A half-full pot of yesterday's brew beckoned. She didn't want to risk filling the library with the luscious smell of fresh-brewed, so a cup of cold would be better than nothing. Caffeine was caffeine.

She poured herself a cup, gulped half of it, and took a seat at the librarian's desk. Then she bowed her head, supporting it with her clasped hands. "Lord, I'm here. Thank you for the place to sleep last night and the coffee this morning. But tomorrow, if you can conjure up a donut, I'd be grateful. As for today... "She peeked over her hands, her mind swimming. "What am I supposed to do? Why have you brought me—"

A car door slammed. Her heart attempted to climb back from her toes. Claire moved to the window behind the desk, being careful to stay hidden. A young woman wearing floral gardening gloves removed flats of flowers from the back of a minivan, placing them near the flowerbeds at the foot of the flagpole.

Help her.

The impulse was so clear it was nearly an order.

Claire looked heavenward and saluted. "Yes, Sir."

Merry Cavanaugh got the last of the flower flats from her van and stood over them, leaning on a spade. She mentally planned their placement in the two symmetrical beds edging the corners where the street sidewalk met the sidewalk leading up to the front door. The existing plantings were pitiful. Four gangly rosebushes that would never produce a rose, and two yews that had never met a garden shear. The yews could be trimmed, but the roses would have to go. In their place Merry would plant red begonias, white impatiens, and blue lobelia. If a library couldn't be patriotic, what could?

Jered Manson, a teenage friend of hers, had offered to help, but if he showed up it would be a miracle worthy of fireworks. Jered was big on good intentions and short on follow-through, and yet she continued to give him chances to help, recognizing his need to be needed. The boy's problem with tardiness (if he showed up at all) was directly related to his drinking with two no-goods every evening. She was trying to pull him under her wing. If she didn't...he'd be swept away. Lost.

She knew what that was like.

A woman strolled up the sidewalk at her left. Merry didn't recognize her, but due to the early hour she pegged her as an exercise walker. Merry nodded a greeting, then placed the spade in the dirt beside a rose bush. She stepped down hard and was relieved the ground did not resist.

"Need help?"

The woman had stopped nearby. "No, I'm fine." Merry moved the spade a few inches to the right and made another cut into the earth. Then another.

"What did that rose bush ever do to you?"

Merry looked up. "What?"

The woman pointed to the bush. "You seem intent on doing it in."

Merry felt ridiculously defensive. "It did itself in. All branch and no bud. It doesn't deserve to live."

"My, my. Does this indicate a general hatred of roses, or this one specifically?"

Merry checked her attitude. She should be penalized ten yards for unnecessary brusqueness. It had become a bad habit. She leaned the spade on the sidewalk. "I haven't seen you around before."

"I'm new in town." The woman held out her hand. "Claire Adams."

Merry removed a gardening glove and shook her hand. "Merry Cavanaugh. I'm fairly new here too. Four months, next week."

"An old-timer compared to me. I just got in last night."

"Quick! You still have a chance to get out."

"You don't like it here in Steadfast?"

Merry chastised herself. Bitterness was not becoming. "Let's just say it's a little small for my taste."

"Then why are you here?"

Because I couldn't stay there. At home. My empty home that used to be full of life. My dead home. She offered her standard answer: "A friend of my mother's lives here. She told me of a job opening. I moved."

"That's nice."

Merry shrugged and nodded toward the library. "The friend practically lives in the library, and when the old librarian retired…" *Blanche felt sorry for me and conspired with my mother to force me toward a new start in a new town.*

Claire's swallow seemed deliberate. "You work there?"

"The sole staff is me, myself, and I. They obviously didn't mind that I had no experience whatsoever."

"I'm sure they were thrilled to have—"

"I think Blanche called in some favors. Made people feel sorry for—" She stopped. She hadn't meant to bring it up. Why did she always bring it up?

"Why would they feel sorry for you?"

Merry looked away, put the glove on, and shoved the spade into the dirt. She leaned it back until the roots tore, then nodded to the flat of impatiens. "I'll get these out if you'll put the new ones in." She glanced at Claire's hands. Manicured. Sculptured nails. "Sorry, I don't have another pair of gloves."

"No problem. How do you want them placed?"

Merry explained the red, white, and blue layout and went back to extracting the rose. Claire tapped the edge of a six-pack against the ground, loosening the plants.

Merry was relieved Claire hadn't pursued her question of the town's pity, but still wanted to get the conversation safely headed in a new direction. "What are you doing out so early?"

"Helping you."

Merry stopped digging and squinted. Apparently Claire was as good at being evasive as she was. "That has got to be the simplest answer I've heard in a long time."

"Thank you. I think."

"Oh, let me assure you, it's a compliment. Nothing seems simple anymore. Not people. Not circumstances. Not life." *There I am, doing it again.* "Don't mind me. I talk too much—or at least say too much."

"So there's something you don't want to say?"

Merry dropped the spade and yanked at the rose bush. The remaining roots tried to hold on, but she ripped them in two with a strong tug. She tossed the gangly mass on the grass. Claire was looking at her, waiting. "I don't even know you."

"Hey, as of a few months ago, you didn't know anyone here. Or don't they know the details either?"

"Oh they know." Merry grimaced. "Blanche made sure of that. It's no secret. Everyone in the world knows."

Claire's right eyebrow raised. "Now you *do* have me intrigued. What was your name again?"

And away we go… "Merry Cavanaugh."

Claire cocked her head. "It doesn't ring any bells. Should I know you?"

Merry sighed. If Claire was going to stick around it was going to come up anyway, so she might as well get it out in the open. "Remember the Sun Fun plane that crashed into a lake seventeen months ago during an ice storm? The helicopter rescue? The—"

"The hero who kept handing off the line to the others? Yes! I remember watching it on TV." Claire put a hand to her chest, holding some emotion in. "What that man did…it was so moving. It made me wonder if I would have done such a thing. It—" Her expression changed, and Merry could practically see a new train of thought derail her words. "Were *you* on that plane?"

"I was one of the five survivors."

"The hero saved you?"

"Henry Smith was his name. Yes, he saved me."

Claire got to her feet. "Oh my, what you must have been through. To be saved like that."

"My husband and son died."

Claire took a step back. "Oh." Then her eyes showed recognition. "The young mother…you're *her?*"

"That's me. One young mother, off on a pleasure trip to Phoenix to live it up with a college chum. One selfish, dissatisfied, unappreciative wife and mother who didn't know what she had until she lost them."

"I'm so, so sorry."

Merry moved to the next rose to sacrifice. "They died, I lived. End of story. Or end of their story. Mine goes on, or attempts to. I'm only thirty. I never considered myself widow material. One of God's little jokes."

"I don't know what to say."

"You married, Claire?"

"Divorced."

"A different kind of widow. A different kind of grieving, but you grieve just the same. Right?"

"I suppose I do."

Merry swiped the back of her hand over her forehead, feeling speckles of dirt attach to her skin that only got worse the more she rubbed. "Don't mind me. I'm perpetually weary. I moved to Steadfast to start fresh, but I'm not doing a very good job of it."

"At least you're trying."

Merry shrugged. How could she feel so old? She was only thirty, but she felt at least a hundred.

"Did you move here permanently?"

Merry glanced at Claire. "Right or wrong, I dropped down roots immediately. Bought an old Victorian over on Maple. Peeling paint, warped doors, and ceilings decorated with brownish rings that look like illustrations of amoebas. It needs fixing up and I need to keep busy. It seemed a good match." She snickered. "Like I say, I'm weary."

Claire went back to the flowers and Merry dug up the other roses. Silence separated them, but in an odd way, seemed acceptable. Claire didn't make her feel odd or bad about who she was or why she'd escaped to Steadfast.

It was a relief.

Jered Manson was late. But it wasn't his fault. If only Moog and Darrell would quit buying the beer, he'd quit drinking it, and quit being hung over. He'd really wanted to help Merry plant the flowers this morning. He'd intended to be there. He'd even run through yards to try to make it there, not daring to drive and risk waking his dad. But when he turned into the square he saw Merry with another woman, putting the empty flower containers in the back of her van.

It was too late. He was too late. Again.

At that moment, Merry looked up. "Jered!"

He ran a hand through his hair and walked toward her, wishing he weren't so sweaty from the run.

Merry held her ground, tapping her watch. "You're too late."

He felt his face redden. "Sorry."

Her shrug was a dagger. "I had other help." She turned to the woman standing next to her. "Claire, this is Jered Manson; Jered, this is Claire Adams. She's new in town and a very good helper."

Implying I'm not?

"Nice to meet you, Jered." Claire shook his hand.

"Yeah. Nice to meet you."

Merry continued. "Jered's interested in a career in music, being a performer, composing."

He immediately forgave all insults to his work ethic.

"What kind of music do you like?" Claire asked.

"Rock. Sting, Billy Joel, and Elton John."

"Good choices."

Merry smiled. "We've been researching music companies on the Internet at the library, trying to piece together how Jered should go about pursuing his dream."

"You have a big dream."

An impossible dream. "Yeah, well…"

"He can do it." Merry's smiled warmed him. "*If* he ever learns to be on time."

He accepted her scolding.

She looked back at the flowers. "But since we're done here, you can go home, Jered."

When Merry and Claire started chatting without him, he had no choice but to leave. He walked toward the park in the square, taking a seat on a bench. Then, making sure no one would see him, he removed the picture from his pocket. It was half the size of a snapshot—torn in half by his own hand. It was a picture of Merry in a baseball cap, smiling at the camera. Her arm was around the shoulder of a boy, but his face had been torn away as unnecessary. Jered stared at the picture and imagined Merry's arm around his shoulder. Proud of him. Happy to spend time with him.

At the sound of a horn he looked up. His father drove up, his elbow resting on the opened window. "What are you doing out this early, Jered? I wake up and find you gone, but your truck's still at home. Since when do you go anywhere without your truck?"

Jered rushed to the side of the car, not wanting Merry to witness him getting in trouble. "There some law against getting up early?"

His father snickered. "Law, no. But face it, getting up before noon is not your usual modus operandi."

"Huh?"

His father sighed and nodded across the square at the diner. "Since you're up, let's eat. I have a favor to ask of you."

So that's it. An ulterior motive. Jered was used to those.

Claire swept the last of the dirt off the sidewalk. She arched her back. The effect of the physical labor on her floor-stiff muscles was a mixed bag. Some muscles felt better, some worse. "All done."

Merry took the broom and tossed it in the back of her minivan. "Thanks for the help." She dug in her pocket for her car keys. "I've got to run home and get cleaned up before work. Can I drop you back at the motel?"

Claire was a little taken aback. She'd never said she was staying at a motel—obviously *the* motel—but didn't mind that Merry assumed she was. "No, I'm fine. It was nice to meet you, Merry."

"You too, Claire."

And that was that. Obviously, Merry assumed a lot of things. She'd never even asked Claire why she was in Steadfast. As a stranger, Claire had expected a lot of questions from the small-town residents. Maybe Merry hadn't been overly curious because she was a big-city transplant herself.

But beyond expecting some what-are-you-doing-here questions, Claire had expected helping Merry Cavanaugh would make the eager ache in her gut go away. But her good deed seemed to be only that. A good deed. The gnawing feeling that something important was going to happen held fast. If only she knew whether the upcoming event would be good or bad. She assumed good—since she believed the feeling came from God—but one could never be entirely sure about such things. Unfortunately, Claire had found during her short tenure with God that being in tune to His guidance was an inexact science and too often tainted by her own will, a pesky mood, or whether or not she'd had enough sleep. All she could do was keep her eyes and ears open and try to do the right thing.

Claire looked to the diner across the street. The lights were on. Her stomach cast a vote.

The bell on the door to the café announced her arrival. It was obvious the Plentiful was the A.M. hub of Steadfast. There were only two empty tables. The waitress looked in her direction, and Claire held up a single finger. The waitress nodded toward the table by the window.

A glass of water appeared, as did a menu. Claire handed it back. She knew exactly what she wanted. "Do you have biscuits and gravy?"

"Wouldn't be allowed in town without it."

"Then that's what I want."

"Coffee? With…?"

"Cream."

The waitress laughed. "I like a woman who knows her mind—and knows good food. I get tired of fruit cup ladies."

"Fruit cup ladies?"

"Dieters." The waitress whispered it as if it were a dirty word.

Perhaps here, it was. Claire noticed a dry-erase board heralding the daily specials. She guessed that the *Flapjack Fiasco* at $3.99 and the *Breakfast Bonanza* at $5.99 tasted like heaven but contained double the calories most dieters ate in an entire day.

"Back with your coffee in a jiff."

Claire turned her attention to the other diners. In a corner was a table of men with farm caps. A discussion of seed corn prices rose and fell. At the counter looked to be a few truckers dining alone, with the rest of the tables made up of people dressed for work.

A man with a stunning shock of slicked-back dark hair was seated in the other window table across from that kid, Jered Manson. Jered's back was to her, so she didn't greet him. He probably wasn't too keen on seeing her again, considering he'd just been chastised for being too late.

The difference in the two males' attire was striking. The man was dressed a step above the rest of the diners, like some kind of visitor from Hollywood—a dandy in a cream-colored linen suit. The boy wore ragged jeans and a baggy T-shirt. His hair was close-cropped, like it was growing back from being shaved. He had two earrings—in the same ear. The two of them could be featured in a poster showcasing the generation gap.

Help him.

Claire blinked at the inner order. She was supposed to help *another* person this morning? But how?

She tried to zero in on the conversation the man was having with the teenager.

"I don't care what your plans are this morning, Jered, nor do I want to listen to your whining about having a hangover. I need you to wait tables for the lunch crowd. End of story."

"I hate waiting tables for you. I'd rather wait tables where real people eat."

The man leaned forward across the table, but Claire could still hear his words. "You want to work in a junk diner, fine, get a job here. But I've spent years giving Steadfast a fine restaurant, and I'm not going to let you defame Bon Vivant."

The boy slumped in his chair, his arms crossed. "Let me go home and sleep."

"I will not. Something got you up this morning—even though you won't tell me what it is—and you're not going back to bed. It's good you're up when normal people get up, no matter what shenanigans you indulged in the night before. That's all a part of consequences, Jered. You'll have to forgive me if I thought it would be nice for the two of us to come here for breakfast. I can't help if you're feeling—"

"I thought it was a junk diner."

The man hesitated. "It is. But they happen to make the best cinnamon rolls in existence. You like them too."

"Don't pretend you're doing this for me, Dad. And don't pretend you came looking for me because you were worried. You just hunted me down to butter me up so I'd come to work."

"That's not—"

The waitress stopped at their table. "More coffee, Bailey?"

"No thanks." He checked his watch. "In fact, can we have the rolls to go?" His face lit up. "Hey, Annie, I'm in a bind today. Want to come wait tables for me? All you need is a pair of black pants and a white shirt. I'll supply the rest. I'd need you from eleven to—"

"Work a shift here and then work a shift for you?" She snickered. "Dream on."

Bailey's shoulders slumped. "Actually, it's a double shift. One waiter is sick, and I fired the other. I need someone through dinner too."

She pointed the coffeepot at the boy. "Have Jered do it."

Jered shook his head. "I'm not feeling too good."

Annie raised an eyebrow. "Sorry, Bailey. Can't help you. But if I run into anyone who wants to run their feet into the ground for ten hours, I'll let you know."

Help him.

Claire shook her head. She was tired. She didn't want to be a waitress. She'd never been a waitress.

In a minute Annie came back with two Styrofoam containers, and the man and boy moved to leave. Claire avoided his eyes as he walked past. *Ah, come on, Lord, can't we hold off until tomorrow? Can't we ease into this?*

Annie poured Claire's coffee and pulled some cream tubs out of her pocket. "Food'll be up in a jiff."

A question formed. "Who was that man?"

Annie looked toward the door. "That's Bailey Manson. He owns the fancy restaurant on the edge of town. Bon Vivant."

"He needs waitresses?"

Annie eyed her. "You a waitress?"

Claire sighed. *I am now.*

Bailey Manson said all she needed were a pair of black pants and a white shirt. Claire had both. Odd how the black dress slacks had been an afterthought.

But how to get inside the library to retrieve them and change? Sneaking in the back door at one in the morning was one thing, but attempting it during the day was another.

Are you sure I have to do this, Lord?

In response, her stomach swelled with a new dose of anticipation—or was it indigestion from the double helping of biscuits and gravy? Maybe she was misinterpreting its urgency. Nothing had happened so far—except she helped Merry Cavanaugh and was now thinking about helping Bailey Manson.

So why this feeling that time was short?

Claire saw Merry's car in the parking lot but no others. She strolled between the bank on the corner and the library, pretending to take note of the plantings along the edge. Then she slipped behind the building and made a beeline for the back door. She hesitated only a moment. She tried the knob.

It was still unlocked.

She cracked it open and listened. All sounds of activity were muffled, as if they came from the main library.

She peeked inside. The storeroom was empty.

Pooh. "Okay, Lord. Okay." The whisper followed her as she slipped upstairs to change into a waitress.

As soon as she entered the waiting area, Claire knew Bon Vivant was not the usual small-town restaurant. Meat loaf and mashed potatoes were *not* on the menu. There would be no free refills of Coke or place mats for children to color while they waited for grilled cheese or chicken nuggets. Each water glass would contain a slice of lemon. She saw damask tablecloths, fresh flowers, and subdued lighting, and she recognized the music of Fauré.

This was an anniversary and birthday restaurant.

Then she saw it: one of her mosaics adorning the wall of the waiting room. She moved close and touched the tiles. She remembered making it. If memory served, it had been purchased from the gallery a year—

"I'm sorry, but we're not open until eleven." Claire turned to find Bailey Manson sticking his head in from the main dining room.

She stepped away from the mosaic, not wanting to risk a connection. "I'm…I'm not here to eat, I'm here to work."

Bailey's body followed his head into the foyer. He gave Claire the once-over. "Black pants, white shirt…a bit confident, are we?"

Claire shrugged. "I believe my confidence fits nicely with your desperation."

He blushed. "It just so happens I need a waitress. How did you know?"

"I heard you talking to Annie at the diner."

He nodded. "Right. I did say something to her, didn't I? When I first saw you, all dressed and ready to go, I thought you'd been sent by Santa Claus."

Would you believe God?

Bailey glanced at his watch. "No matter. Time's a'tocking." He opened a closet and removed a bin of red cummerbunds and bow ties. "You'll need these." A waiter appeared in the doorway to the dining room. "Stanley, this is… I didn't even ask your name."

"Claire Adams."

"Claire. My name is Bailey Manson, and this is Stanley. Stanley, Claire will have section B. Teach her the ropes." He put a hand on her shoulder as she walked past. "You do know how to wait tables, don't you?"

She would soon enough.

Bailey singled out the key to Bon Vivant as he held the door open, letting out the waiters. "Night, Stanley. William, Roberta."

Claire was the last one out. "A moment of your time, Ms. Adams?"

She stood outside the front door while Bailey locked up. Her legs throbbed. Her feet were leaden. The cicadas chanted a droning night rhythm that matched the pulse of her headache. She had five minutes of sanity left before she would explode.

"You did well." Bailey walked toward his car, trading one key for another. "You've obviously waited tables before."

"No." The one-word answer was all she could manage.

Bailey stopped walking. "Then you are the fastest learner I've ever seen. How many evenings a week can you work?"

"None."

"You don't want to work—?"

"No. Sorry." *I'd never survive.* Claire looked at the moths diving at the streetlight in a suicidal frenzy. She considered joining them.

"If you didn't want to work for me, why did you come to the restaurant and apply?"

"I didn't apply. I came to help."

"You showed up wearing the right uniform. Certainly a white shirt and black pants are not your usual summer attire."

"No."

"So you showed up in my restaurant's waiting room, just as I needed someone to work—for a one-night stand?"

"Unfortunately, that's all I have to give."

Bailey expelled an exasperated sigh. "It's too late for games, Ms. Adams. Let's bypass the reason you showed up and saved my skin. The fact is, you did it. And now I want you to do it again, on a regular basis. Good help is as hard to find as a cool breeze in August."

Claire shook her head. She didn't want to argue with him. She didn't want to explain. She just wanted to get back to the library and die. She wasn't sure why she'd been spurred to work for Bailey, because the feeling of anticipation had not lessened. If anything, it had gotten more insistent. But she was fairly certain being a permanent waitress at Bon Vivant was *not* her present fate. Or doom.

Thank God.

Bailey unlocked his car and got in. "You're an exasperating woman, Claire, but I suppose I should thank you and count my blessings. At least I had your services one day. Will you grace me with your presence again?"

"Perhaps."

Bailey rolled his eyes and started his car. "Keep me in mind if you ever feel like helping out."

Not in this lifetime.

Claire was glad the library was empty because she couldn't have tiptoed if she tried. Her head and torso wanted to be in the attic, but her legs and feet were content to stay at the bottom of the stairs. She pulled herself up each step, leaning on the creaky railing.

She'd always prided herself in being a hard worker, but she was used to the work of the mind and hand more than a full-body workout. She hadn't signed on for this.

She looked across the attic where her marginal bed waited.

Home sweet home? If she weren't so tired it would be laughable.

She collapsed on the mattress and fell into a sleep born of hard work.

Claire opened her eyes. It was still dark. She glanced at her watch. It was a little after midnight. She was still wearing her waitressing clothes.

It didn't matter. Sleep. Sleep mattered.

She turned onto her side, snuggled her cheek against the flat pillow, and closed her eyes.

Wake up!

She sat up in bed. Her eyes darted, trying to capture the cause of her unrest. The anticipation that had plagued her for days gnawed with fresh teeth.

Claire crawled out of bed and moved to the window seat, looking across the town square. The moon cut a swath through the trees. The flowers she'd planted with Merry cast irregular shadows. It had been a long day. Yet somehow, it wasn't over.

The ache grabbed. Her heart began to pound. And she suddenly knew.

Tonight. Tonight was the night.

Someone was coming.

Seven

Trust in the LORD with all your heart and
lean not on your own understanding;
in all your ways acknowledge him,
and he will make your paths straight.

PROVERBS 3:5–6

SIM LOOKED OUT THE WINDOW of the bus. They had just returned from a bathroom break and everyone was awake and talking, even though it was nearly midnight. She wished they would be quiet. Their conversations frayed her nerves. How could they talk about sports or weather or work as though those things were important? They belonged to the *before* world. They didn't belong to *now*. Or even *later*.

At least they weren't talking to her. The wall Sim had erected between herself and the world was doing its job. On her side was grief. On their side was the rest. The rest meant nothing to her. Not anymore.

If only fear would stop threatening the wall. She could see it peeking over the top, ready to pounce when she wasn't looking. Who knew which meddler would get suspicious of a kid traveling alone and confide in a cop, who would then call her aunt and uncle? At every stop, Sim expected to feel a hand on her shoulder: "Where you going, girl?" or "Why are you traveling alone?"

I'm traveling alone because I am *alone. And I'm going…away.*

They'd want to know her parents' names. She'd laugh and say, "That's a good one," and they'd get testy and pull her aside and find out where she came from and why she left. But they wouldn't understand. They'd look at her chopped-off, red-streaked hair, her heavy eye makeup and nose ring, and think she was a druggie. She wasn't but didn't mind that people thought she was. It made them stay away. She didn't want their pity or their sickening, helpful words.

Cops were different. They were drawn to her eccentric looks. And if *they* noticed her… *Trouble at three o'clock. Watch her.* Then they'd arrest her and put her in a jail where she would always—and yet never—be alone. In jail, fear would be her bunkmate.

There was too much at risk to look people in the eye. Best to fold into a seat and disappear.

A bump in the road knocked Sim's head against the window, jolting her awake. It took her a moment to remember where she was. The darkness didn't help. The reading lights of a few sleepless passengers reflected off the glass. She stretched, then rubbed the crick in her neck. She looked out the window. Shadowed farm fields flew by, an unending blur lit only by the moon and the headlights.

The bus slowed and there was the grind of a downshift. Sim sat up straighter, hoping to spot a marker that would tell her where they were. A sign came into view, announcing a town.

Steadfast.

The word grabbed her. She spun around, as if the back of the sign would tell her more. She tensed as they slowed, passing a darkened restaurant, some houses, a farm implement dealership, a gas station.

She grabbed her backpack from the overhead rack and hurried to the front of the bus.

"Hey, girl, get back to your—"

"I want off!"

The driver pointed out the window. "This isn't anybody's stop. This is Stead—"

"Steadfast." Sim moved to the top of the exit steps. "This is where I'm supposed to get off."

"Can't be. We're just passing through. Let me see your ticket."

"I want off!"

Drowsy eyes peered over the tops of seats.

The driver pulled over. "What's the rush, girl? This ain't your stop. I know it."

"It *is* my stop. I have to get off." Even as she heard herself saying the words, they made no sense. Why the urgency? Why this place?

"You got somebody picking you up? It's late. Nothing's open."

"I'll be fine." She waved a hand toward the door.

Shaking his head, the driver opened it. "You be careful."

Sim raced down the steps and away from the bus before someone could stop her. It pulled away, marking its exit with a fog of diesel exhaust. As its sound receded, she was struck by the silence of the town square. She was used to a big city where there was always something open. Yet here, every storefront was dark. No cars. No people. Crickets chirped. A streetlight hummed.

Why did I get off here?

The last five minutes played back like a dream she was watching from a distance. It made no sense.

Sense or no sense, she was here. And here was as good a place as anywhere. Sim looked for a place to go, a place she wouldn't be found.

A courthouse crowned the square, looming large and ominous, its stone reflecting the moon.

Can't go there. Come morning, it'll be full of people asking questions. I want somewhere quiet—

The flapping of a flag drew her attention across the street. Below the flag, red, white, and blue flowers gave the old building a friendly touch. The flag went limp against its pole. A sign above the front door read STEADFAST LIBRARY.

Steadfast. Sim crossed the street.

Claire saw her. A girl getting off a bus in the square. Bodywise, she looked to be thirteen, maybe fourteen, but she dressed older. Tougher. After the bus pulled away, the girl hesitated. There was no one there to meet her.

Except me.

Claire took a step away from the window. She put a hand to her midsection, gauging the bite of the anticipation. It was gone. It had been replaced with certainty. This was it. This was what she'd been waiting for.

But a *girl?* What was she supposed to do with a girl? She wasn't good with kids, had never had much experience with them. If she were in her house, it might be doable, but she was living in the attic of a library. What could she do to help a strange girl while she was hiding out in an attic?

A moment later, Claire heard the back door of the library hit against the stack of boxes. Why wouldn't her heart stop pounding? It was loud enough the girl could probably hear it.

Claire cracked open the attic door and saw the girl slip inside, scoping out the storeroom, picking up books, setting them down. Her face was fair and sculptured, perhaps marking an ancestor of Nordic descent. Her features possessed the inkling of beautiful, like a promise that could be kept or broken. But her hair was awful, chopped off at the chin in uneven chunks of fake red. And was that a nose ring?

Yet even in the shadowed room, Claire could see by the way the girl's eyes took in her new surroundings that she had smarts. And courage. There was no fear in her eyes, just curiosity.

The girl tripped over air, making Claire smile. Adolescence was such an awkward time. Feet as big as pontoons with no cooperating muscles to steer them.

Potential. That's what she had. Maybe that's what they both had. Potential to be used by God. To find their unique pur—

The girl turned her head toward the attic door, and Claire's stomach grabbed.

It was time.

Was that a door?

Sim adjusted her backpack and paused at the bottom of a narrow staircase. At the top of the steps, a door stood ajar. She wanted to call out, ask if anyone was up there, but didn't dare. *She* was the intruder.

She climbed the stairs, testing her weight on each one. No sounds gave her away. Her fear of the darkness was tempered by her need to find a safe place to stay.

She stood at the door and pressed her cheek against the jamb, trying to see through the crack. The moonlight fell over a window seat and a shelf with clothes. She pulled back. *Someone lives here.* She turned to retreat down the stairs when a woman's voice came from within the room.

"Come in."

Sim's heart zipped through her body. She swallowed.

"It's okay. Come on in."

Sim held her breath and jabbed the door so it opened on its own. She let herself breathe when she saw the woman standing on the other side of the room. She looked harmless enough: slim, fortysomething, short hair. She looked like Mrs. Barrett, the principal of her middle school. She wore black pants and a white shirt. "Who are you?"

"Claire Adams."

The woman lit a candle on a small table. Sim wished the flickering light would reach into the far corners of the attic, where the monsters lived. She shoved away such childish fears and looked around. Boxes and cobwebs. Pretty bleak. "You live here?"

"For the moment. Come—"

"You homeless or something?"

"Not exactly. But for the moment this is my home."

She snorted. "Some home."

"And where's *your* home?"

Sim felt herself redden. She shouldn't have made fun of the woman's quarters. At least she *had* a place to stay. Such as it was. She straightened her back. "I'm traveling right now."

Claire raised an eyebrow.

"I *am* traveling."

"Where to?"

"Places." Claire didn't ask more, and Sim let herself breathe. "I can't believe they actually charge you for this place."

"Actually, they don't."

It took her a moment. "You're hiding out?"

The woman shoved her hands in her pockets and shrugged. "Let's just say I'm biding my time."

"No one knows you live here?"

"You know."

"Besides me?"

"No one."

She pointed to the light. "Hasn't someone noticed the light through the window? Seen you come and go?"

"Not yet."

"You sure?"

"I don't think I'd still be up here if I'd been seen." The woman sat on the window seat, dangling her legs. "What's your name?"

Her mouth told the truth before her brain could think of a lie. "Sim."

"That's an odd name."

"It's short for Simone." She shrugged as she yawned. Her body demanded sleep.

"You're tired. We can talk tomorrow. You're welcome to stay, Sim."

Her body warred with her mind. The world didn't work this way. Strangers didn't offer strangers lodging for free. And strange ladies didn't offer to share their rooms with kids—unless they had something weird on their minds. Sim knew about such things. She'd seen it on television. Her eyes strayed to the bed. "You're not some pervert, are you? Or some escaped convict hiding out from the feds?" She immediately regretted the words. If Claire *was* some wacko, now she'd get mad and do something really bad.

"I'm harmless."

"But you want me to stay. That's kinda…weird."

"The Bible says we're supposed to share with people in need."

Sim took a step back. "Oh. You're one of *them.*"

"Them?"

"Religious fanatics. Spouting Bible verses and yelling at people to 'repent or be damned!'" She'd seen their kind on TV too.

Claire shook her head. "Right message, wrong method."

"You're not like that?"

"No."

"But I bet you can quote Bible verses."

"Occasionally. How about you?"

"Uh-uh. Not my style." She pointed at Claire's necklace. "You wear a cross. I bet it's not a fashion statement either."

Claire touched it. "It was my grandmother's."

"Peachy keen." *That was rude.*

Claire dropped her hand. "You can have the bed. I'll put some blankets on the floor over—"

"Uh-uh." Sim took another step toward the door. "I'll find a place downstairs. There's no one else here, is there?"

"Just us."

"Then I'll stay. One night. I need a place to—"

"Hide?"

Sim escaped downstairs.

And so it began.

Claire peeked through the door separating storeroom from library and watched the girl sleep. Sim had moved three armless vinyl chairs together and was stretched across them, her head on her backpack, a sweatshirt covering her shoulders. There was no way it could be comfortable. She slept, her mouth open, snoring softly. Claire understood why she hadn't wanted to sleep in the attic with her. Being streetwise was probably an attribute—and a necessity—amid the evil of the world. But it was sad. Where was the trust anymore? Why did suspicion have to reign?

And what was Sim's story? What had brought her to Steadfast on a bus in the middle of the night? She seemed so independent, stubborn, headstrong. And wary. If Claire told her how she'd anticipated her arrival, Sim would be out of there.

Claire went back to the attic and lay down. She closed her eyes, but her thoughts spun.

Okay, Lord. She's here. Now what?

❧   ❧   ❧

"Get up."

Sim moaned.

Claire nudged her. "Up, kiddo."

Sim peeked out from beneath her arm. "What time is it?"

"Six-thirty."

She groaned. "No way."

"Up."

Sim squinted at the light coming through the windows. "Why?"

"We have things to do."

"I'm doing what I want to be doing."

"We don't always get what we want."

She groaned. "You think that one up all by yourself?"

Cocky kid. Claire took Sim's hand and pulled. Sim rolled off the chairs onto the floor with an *oomph*. Claire moved to help, but Sim pulled back, and her words came out in what could have passed for a snarl. "Don't touch me and don't tell me what to do."

Claire retreated, hands raised. *What brought that on?* "You have to get up. People will be coming." She nodded toward the restrooms. "The facilities are over there."

Sim got to her feet, gathering her backpack. After using the rest room, she joined Claire in the main library and began wandering around in the shadows. "So this is it, huh?"

Claire took a deep breath, loving the smell of paper and ink. "One of these days I'd love to see this place with the lights on."

Sim cruised the nearest shelf, putting her eyes close to the bindings, trying to read them in the dim morning light. "Ah! Here's my favorite: *Atlas Shrugged.*" She handed it to Claire.

"You've read *Atlas Shrugged?*" Claire asked.

"Haven't you?"

Claire had the book on her shelf at home but had never tackled it. It was huge. It weighed every ounce of its thousand pages. Though she knew that *not* choosing a book simply because of its length was juvenile, it had been a factor.

Sim turned to the stack on the other side of her aisle. She pointed.

"And Tolkien. I've read The Lord of the Rings series three times. Don't you just love it when Frodo realizes that only by leaving the shire—that place he loved the most—would he be able to save it?"

Claire felt like a pupil being given a quiz when she hadn't read the material.

Sim's eyes widened a fraction. "You *have* read Tolkien, haven't you?"

"Actually, I haven't had much time to read in the past few years. I've been—"

"People can make time. They just don't." Sim looked right at her. "Am I right?"

Claire wanted to argue but feared it would come out whiny and defensive. "Right."

Sim's fingers skittered over the bindings. She pulled out a book and held it out to Claire. "Here's one even you should have read. *Huckleberry Finn*."

Claire felt an absurd surge. "I *have* read that one. It's about a kid. A runaway." She paused, zeroing in on the implications. "How appropriate."

Sim shoved the book back in its place. "Who said I was a runaway?"

"Aren't you?"

"If I'm Huckleberry, then you must be Jim." She leveled Claire with a look. "You a runaway slave?"

This girl wouldn't let her mind rest a minute. It was too early to be astute and witty. Claire needed coffee. "Let's get out of here."

"It's early. The library doesn't open for hours. We have tons of time."

The ignorance of youth. "Nobody has tons of time, Sim."

"Oooh, deep thoughts. *Now* I'm impressed."

Claire ran a hand through her hair. "I'm hungry. I'm going to change clothes and grab something to eat. We can either go to the café or pick something up at the grocery—"

"You go ahead. I'm fine."

"Suit yourself." Claire moved toward the attic, wondering why God had sent her an adolescent. Punishment, no doubt.

❧   ❧   ❧

Sim rummaged through the library storeroom. Book junk. Pretty boring.

Then she saw it. A door. It was blocked by an old photocopy machine. There was something exciting about a blocked door. It made her think they were trying to hide something. Maybe there was something important in there. Something valuable. Treasure.

She knew her imagination was working overtime, but treasure or no treasure, she still needed to see what was in there. She shoved the machine aside and opened it. She switched on a light. "Hey, lady!"

The woman appeared at the top of the stairs, buttoning a blue shirt. "The name is Claire."

Sim closed the door and stood in front of it. "Come see what I found."

Claire descended the stairs. When she was close, Sim opened the door with a flourish. "It's a shower!"

Claire poked her head inside, taking it all in. She flipped the water on. "It's old but it works. Oh, I've been wanting a shower."

"What have you done up until now?"

She was running back up the stairs. "I've only been here two nights and…" Her voice faded as she disappeared into the attic. It picked up again when she reached the landing to come down. "…it's a real luxury."

"You've only been here two days? I thought…you acted like you'd been here a long time."

"Nope. Newly arrived, just like you."

"Why did you come here?"

Claire paused at the door to the bathroom, a towel and bottle of shampoo in her hand. "I came here for you."

"What?"

She went inside and closed the door. "Give me ten minutes and we'll talk."

You'd better believe it.

❦   ❦   ❦

Claire was true to her word. Ten minutes later she came out rubbing her hair. "That felt wonderful. A bit cramped, but wonderful."

Sim crossed her arms. "Glad you liked it. Now spill it. What did you mean when you said you came here for me?"

Claire strapped on her watch and checked the time. "Let's get out of here before people show up. We need groceries and a cooler. You like chocolate donuts?"

"Not really." But she walked toward the door. Sim loved chocolate donuts.

Claire noticed Merry enter the front door of the grocery store. She pulled Sim toward the line at the checkout lane even though they weren't through shopping.

"What the—?"

Claire leaned close. "It's the library lady. She's here."

"So?"

"She might see us."

"So?"

Claire had to think a moment. Maybe it was all right. No one knew about them staying in the attic. She rubbed her eyes. "I'm turning paranoid."

Sim leafed through a *People* magazine. "Get over it."

"Claire Adams." Merry Cavanaugh walked toward them. "The bedding plants are still alive twenty-four hours and counting."

"Glad to hear it."

Merry glanced at Sim, then away, then back again. "Who's this?" She didn't look like she really wanted to know. Claire couldn't blame her. Sim's appearance screamed, *Leave me alone!*

Claire panicked. "This is…my niece, Sim." Her heart flipped at the lie. Why did she say that?

Sim's mouth dropped open. Claire put a finger under her chin and shut it. "It's not polite to gawk, kiddo."

Merry raised an eyebrow, then held out her hand. "Nice to meet you, Sim. I'm Merry Cavanaugh. Your aunt was quite a help to me yesterday."

"Yeah, she's quite the helper, my *aunt.*" She shoved the magazine back in its stand and flashed Claire a look. "Good old Auntie Claire."

Claire felt herself redden. What *had* she been thinking, telling Merry that Sim was her niece? She hated liars—and lying. Plus, it wasn't a comment that could be easily undone.

Sim's face lit up. "Hey, Ms. Cavanaugh. Do you need someone to help at the library? I need a job."

Merry blinked twice, the crease between her eyebrows telling its story. "Well, I don't—"

"I may not look like your usual nerdy bookworm, but I've read tons. The classics. Ask Claire." Sim nudged her. "Tell her about *Atlas Shrugged,* and Tolkien, and Twain."

It was their turn to check out. Claire put a loaf of bread on the conveyor belt. "It's true she's read those books, but I don't think—"

"I really want the job. I'll work hard. Promise."

Claire knew there was no legal way Merry could deny Sim a job.

"You *do* need help, don't you?"

Merry cleared her throat at Sim's pointed question. "Actually, it's just me, and summer *is* our busiest time. And the board *did* approve a part-time helper, but the boy I hired didn't work out."

"So the position's open?"

"Yes, I guess it is."

"Good. I'll take it."

Merry's smile was uncertain, her sigh deep. "Well, then. Who knew I'd come in for a can of coffee and end up with a new employee? What an interesting surprise. Why don't you come in this morning at nine and I'll give you a tour."

A tour wouldn't be necessary.

As soon as Merry left, Sim pounced. "What right do you have to call me your niece?"

Claire countered, lowering her voice. "What right do you have to get yourself a job?"

Sim glanced at the checkout lady, who looked in their direction, then away. Sim turned her back to her, speaking to Claire alone.

"Hey, it's *my* life, lady. No matter what you tell people, we are *not* in this together. I need some spending money so I got myself a job, which proves I can take care of myself." She sidled past the cart. "So 'bye, *Auntie* Claire. See you later."

Claire wanted to run after her, but she was stuck. She had food to pay for. She offered the clerk a weak smile. "Kids."

The woman nodded.

Niece? She called me her niece!

Sim stormed across the street and past the town hall. She plopped on a bench. Claire was weird, and Sim wanted nothing to do with her attic hideaway and her—

"Donut?"

A chocolate donut appeared in front of her face from a hand extending over her head. Sim took it and tore into it.

Claire moved into view. "Hey, I'm sorry. Merry caught me off guard. I didn't know what to say. But I shouldn't have lied. I shouldn't have."

"How about saying I'm your friend, an acquaintance? But your niece?"

Claire took a seat at the far end of the bench, putting a Styrofoam cooler full of groceries between them. "I panicked." She took a bite of her own donut. "And what about you? A job? Where'd that come from?"

Sim angled to face her. "No one can ever accuse me of being a free-loader. I take care of myself. I pay my way." She glanced at the cooler and reached into her pocket. "What do I owe you for the donut?"

"My treat."

Sim slapped a crumpled ten-dollar bill on top of the cooler. "I don't take handouts."

"I don't want your money."

The bill skittled in the breeze and blew to the ground. "You'd better take it, 'cause I'm not moving."

The ten dollars did a flip across the sidewalk and jumped onto the grass. Sim shoved the rest of the donut in her mouth and licked her fingers noisily, pretending to be oblivious. It was a battle of wills. She needed that ten dollars. She only had forty-six more.

But as the bill continued its journey across the lawn, Claire gave in first. She went after it, capturing it with her foot. She shook the money at Sim. "You are an exasperating child."

"Gee, Auntie. Be careful or you'll injure my self-esteem."

Claire stuffed the bill in her pocket and returned to her seat. "It appears you have plenty of that—and then some."

"Got any more of those donuts? I deserve ten dollars' worth."

Claire sighed but took the lid off the cooler. "Help yourself."

"Don't mind if I do."

"As soon as we're done eating, I need to get this cooler back to the attic. Care to be lookout?"

Sim slanted her a look. "Maybe."

"What's that supposed to mean?"

"You've managed to put off explaining your comment about being brought here for me. I'm not moving until you do." Sim flicked a donut crumb off her leg. A bird hopped over to peck at it.

Claire glanced at her, then away. "You have to keep an open mind, Sim. This isn't your normal explanation."

"My real aunt and uncle sent you, didn't they?"

"Who?"

Oops. "Nobody. Go on."

"You ran away from an aunt and uncle?"

Sim shoved her spine against the back of the bench. "We're not here for my story; we're here for yours."

"How about my story first, your story second?"

"I'm not promising a thing." She tossed the bird another crumb. "You going to tell me, or not?"

The way Claire's face relaxed gave Sim the feeling she was going to get the truth—no matter what it was.

"God sent me here."

Sim blinked. "That wasn't in my top ten of expected answers."

Claire shrugged. "It's the truth."

Sim stood and gestured toward the library. "You lied."

"No, I didn't. God sent—"

She faced her. "You lied. You said you weren't one of those religious fanatics."

"I'm not." Claire sighed deeply and her face battled. "Perhaps I should start from the beginning." She looked at Sim, her eyes desperate. "Will you listen? Really listen? With an open mind?"

She sat. "Give me your best shot."

"I gotta hand it to you, Claire. That's a good story. Bizarre, but good."

Claire sighed deeply. "Thank you."

"But I also think it's stupid, giving all your money away. I've got tons of money and I don't plan to give it away."

Claire's eyes grew wide. "You…have tons of money?"

Sim slammed the palm of her hand to her forehead. "Why do I keep doing that? Letting things slip?"

"You're only thirteen."

"Fourteen."

"You're just a kid. Perhaps an honest kid who isn't used to lying?"

Not hardly. "You don't know anything about me."

"Then tell me. It's your turn. Tell me your story. Tell me how you came to be here."

She sat up. "I'm a mass murderer on the run."

"Sim…"

"Fine. I'm a child star going undercover for a part."

Claire took a deep breath. "We made a deal. I told you my story, now what's yours? I'll keep your secret if you'll keep mine."

Sim did a double take. "Nobody here knows what you just told me?"

"Nobody."

"So you're going to keep hiding in the attic?"

"I don't have a lot of funds. Until I get further direction, this is where I have to stay."

Sim laughed. "Direction from God?"

"He's the boss."

"You're a stitch, Claire. If you get any extra messages from heaven, let me know, okay?"

Claire shuffled her shoulders. She tossed a big chunk of donut on the ground and the birds converged. "Now, out with it."

Sim looked her in the eye. "You promise you won't tell?"

Claire raised a hand. "Cross my heart."

I'd like to believe you. Sim looked down at her hands. The blue nail polish was chipped and worn. Just like she felt. She glanced at Claire's hands. Fake nails, but one was broken off. Somehow that one imperfection…

Maybe Claire was telling the truth. Maybe she *had* given it all up. And if she had, maybe she'd understand why Sim had given up *her* old life. In a way, they were the same. Runaways. Outcasts. Besides, Sim was beginning to like her. The woman listened as if what Sim said mattered. An adult who listened. A new experience. And Claire didn't talk down to her like some adults did.

Sim turned her fingernails under and made a decision. "You guessed right. I'm a runaway. I'm an only child. A *real* only child. My parents are gone. Dead." She spit out the last word.

Claire blinked twice. "Oh my. I'm so sorry. You must be terribly sad."

It was too small a word for what Sim felt. She shrugged, then stood again, unable to sit with an audience so close. "They died in a car crash." She used her hands to illustrate her words. "One semi hits one BMW and the semi wins. *Splat. Bang. Boom.* They're gone and I'm alone."

"But not alone."

She shoved her hands in the pockets of her jeans. "Alone."

"But you mentioned an aunt and uncle. They took you in?"

Her chest tightened. She paced one step right, then back, over and over. *Leave. Run. Don't look back.*

"Sim…" Claire stood.

She raised her hands like a shield and took a step back. "Don't." Claire sat.

"I won't go back."

"You don't have to."

"I don't—?"

"You don't. But I would like to understand why you ran away."

Sim looked at Claire, gauging her motives. Her eyes seemed sincere. The way she sat, the way she moved and talked…she seemed at peace with herself and the world. Peace. Peace was not allowed on Sim's side of the wall. If only it were.

She was suddenly tired. Everything was mixed up. She sank to the bench, leaned her forearms on her knees, and stared at the ground. "My parents died on December 22. They were coming back from a corporate Christmas party. No one was supposed to tell me Dad was drunk, but he was. He caused the accident. They both died. Cook was the one who woke me up, said they were dead." She looked over at Claire. "Funny how fresh that moment stays. I'll never forget the pink roses on Cook's bathrobe that night. They're in my head so clear I could draw them. She sat on the side of my bed and talked with that Polish accent of hers, going on and on. I don't remember the words, other than *dead* and *accident*. But I remember the roses on her robe." She shivered. "My aunt and uncle wanted to put roses on the coffins, but I wouldn't let them. No roses. No pink roses."

Sim was glad Claire didn't say anything. She'd had enough words from people feeling sorry. She was surprised Claire didn't look embarrassed. That's how most people looked when she brought up that night. Like they'd rather get a tooth pulled than listen. Because if they listened, then they had to react. And nobody knew how to react to death. Death was a wicked relation everyone preferred to ignore and certainly didn't want to invite into their lives.

"I was given to my dad's brother and wife. But they didn't want me. Aunt Susan is obsessed with having a baby."

"But you're a child, their—"

"Their nothing." She spun toward Claire. "Didn't you hear me? They want a *baby*. Not a teenager. They don't care about me. They only took me in because there wasn't anyone else and they wanted my trust fund. As long as I live with them, they get to use *my* money to try all their fertility stuff. But when I turn eighteen, it's all mine." Sim tapped a hand on the top of the cooler. "And they're having a grand time of it too. Buying themselves a new car and a big-screen TV. Pretending to be sad when all the time they were scheming to get rid of me so they could get *all* my money; maybe buy themselves a baby through the black market or something."

"Sim…"

"It's true." She crossed her heart, then saw Claire's look. *I should have known you wouldn't believe me.* "Believe me or not, I don't care. They didn't care if I was around. My parents always said it was good my aunt and uncle didn't have kids because they're too set in their ways, though if you ask me, my parents had no right to talk. I was a mistake."

"Never."

"It's true. My parents didn't want me. My birth was an accident, just like their deaths were an accident. Two blips on a screen that only messed things up." She flicked away a tear and sniffed. Stupid tears didn't help anything.

"I'm sorry, Sim. Really sorry."

Sim saw the compassion in Claire's face, but she couldn't give in to it. She'd die if she gave in. She stood, moving away. "I don't need your pity. I'm doing what I want to be doing. It's over. Done. It's no big deal. I—"

"You belong here. And so do I. God brought us together."

As nice as it sounded, it was way too weird. "God didn't do anything. *I* did. I got myself here with my own planning, my own smarts. And I don't need you, Him, or anyone, to tell me some plan. I'll make my own plans, thank you very much."

"But—"

She grabbed another donut and adjusted her backpack on her shoulder. "But nothing. You want help getting that cooler to the attic or not? I've got to get ready for work."

With Sim at work in the library, the silence in the attic fell like a heavy curtain. Sim had a job among the people of Steadfast. But what about Claire? Should she go out and do odd jobs? She sat on the window seat but felt no push to do such a thing.

She sighed and pulled the Bible into her lap. *Show me what to do, Lord.* She let the Bible fall open to the middle and began reading in

Psalms. There was such emotion there, such help no matter how a person was feeling.

Then one verse stood out among the rest: "Be still before the LORD and wait patiently for him."

Claire laughed softly. How appropriate for God to ask her to do the two things she was *not* good at doing: being still and waiting. She was a take-charge person. She made things happen. The fact she was sitting in an attic in Steadfast was proof of that. With amazing quickness and fervent activity she'd done all God had asked her to do. And now Sim was here. Certainly there were things to be done. Places and people to see.

Claire looked at the verse again. *Be still before the Lord.*

Yeah, right.

Wait patiently for Him.

Pooh. Not what she wanted to hear. She flipped to the back of the Bible, to the concordance. The verse she wanted to find was one that would tell her, "Charge ahead!" or "Go for it!"

She found one "charge" reference in Jeremiah: "Charge, O horses! Drive furiously, O charioteers!"

Forget that.

As for "go for it"? She was not surprised to find the Bible devoid of the twentieth-century phrase. A lot of *go here* and *go there,* but nothing that fit what she wanted to find.

Unfortunately, there *were* a lot of references to waiting: "'Therefore wait for me,' declares the LORD," and "Wait for the LORD; be strong and take heart and wait for the LORD."

Then she found one with a new twist: "Blessed are all who wait for him!"

Blessed?

Well, then.

Maybe she'd give it a try.

Eight

Flee the evil desires of youth,
and pursue righteousness, faith, love and peace,
along with those who call on the Lord out of a pure heart.

2 TIMOTHY 2:22

MERRY PUSHED THE BOOK CART through the fiction stacks, heading toward the far corner. She heard Harold's humming before she saw him. "Morning, Harold."

Harold Shinness glanced up, then immediately looked to the floor like a wallflower at a junior-high dance. "Good morrow, cousin." He curled his sixty-year-old body on the vinyl chair, protecting his opened book.

"What are you reading today?" He positioned the book so she could read its cover. "*Mutiny on the Bounty.* That's a good one."

He raised his face, his voice deepening to the mellow tones of an actor. "Good friends, sweet friends, let me not stir you up to such a sudden flood of mutiny."

Merry shook her head, amazed. Harold had been a brilliant teacher at the high school, but ever since his wife had died, he'd withdrawn into this odd man who only spoke Shakespearean quotes, as if he'd etched the pages in his mind to displace the grief.

Hey, whatever worked.

"Who said that?" Merry smiled. "Caesar?"

"Antony." He pulled a stick of black licorice from his pocket, pinched a lint-ball off the end, and held it out to her.

Merry took it, understanding it was his way of saying thanks for the chair in the corner—Harold's undesignated yet sacred chair that no one else disturbed.

In spite of his odd habits, Merry liked Harold, just as she liked the two other regulars who had rooted themselves in the old library. Even in her short tenure here, the regulars had evolved into a gathering of kindred spirits. Merry was now the trunk, and they were the branches, each individual and unique, yet bound together, sap and sinew. Merry recognized their literary tastes and took pleasure in showing them new books. In turn, they seemed to recognize the intensity of her pain and—knowing there was little mere mortals could do—provided her with the simple constancy of their presence.

Merry stooped to retrieve a few pieces of colored tile. The fallen tiles from the dilapidated wall mural near the front door tended to migrate across the library floor like sorrowful parts of a broken family in search of a home. She'd been told that the mural was originally a pastoral of the Kansas countryside, but now it resembled a tattered crazy quilt with small areas of color broken by blotches of dismal gray cement.

She brought the tiles to number two of the library's regulars. The elderly man sat on a stool by the mural, placing tiles on the wall. Merry stood behind him a moment, trying to figure out what he was creating. She couldn't imagine anything bright red being in a field of blue. But who was she to question art? When Ivan had volunteered to repair the mural she jumped at his offer. Of course, she *assumed* he knew what he was doing.

"Morning, Ivan."

He glanced up, then went back to his work.

"What's that you're working on? A red…?"

He sat back and looked at the mural. "I'm not sure yet. I'm thinking it might be a nice place to put a barn."

Okay… "But why the blue? If you surround it with blue won't it look like it's floating in water—or the sky?"

He swiveled to face her, a hand on his hip. "Who's the artist here, Merry? Me? Or you?"

"You, definitely you. But I'd still like to see a drawing of what you have in mind."

He tapped his head. "Don't need it on paper. I've lived in this town all of my seventy-four years. I remember what the mural looked like—one of the few people in town who does." His chin lowered and he looked at her through gray lashes. "And since I *am* doing the work for free…"

"Lay off?"

"Wise choice."

She changed the subject. "Where's Blanche this morning?"

Ivan nodded toward the other end of the library. "She's at those computers again. I think she's having an affair with some Casanova in Idaho." He readied another red tile for the field of blue. "She certainly won't look at me anymore."

"I'm sure that's not true. Want me to eavesdrop for you?"

"Not for me. Not my business who she daddles with."

"Then I'll do it for me. We don't want her getting caught up in something she shouldn't, do we?"

"Whatever."

Merry knew what damage living in the land of What If could cause. Not being content with what you had could be an evil thing and should be nipped in the bud, burned at the stake, decapitated in the guillotine. After all, hadn't an absurd What If caused the death of her husband and son? If only she'd been content with being a wife and mother, she would never have gotten on that plane heading to Phoenix to have fun with her old roommate. And if she hadn't made her discontent known, Lou would never have felt compelled to come after her, dragging Justin onto the plane as a surprise.

The plane that crashed.

The crash that killed them.

All because of her.

Merry closed her eyes and pulled in a slow breath, a habit when memories and guilt hovered too close. *Enough. I'm starting over.*

She exhaled the memories and moved to the computers. She stood behind Blanche but couldn't read what was on the screen other than to know that some sort of on-line conversation was in progress. Blanche's fingers typed as fast as she normally talked. Merry cleared her throat.

In one movement, Blanche stopped typing and wrapped her

arms around the monitor, blocking the screen. When she saw it was Merry, she let go.

"Don't scare me like that! I thought you were Ivan. That old artichoke thinks he can run my life."

"That old artichoke is concerned about you, Blanche. We've all heard horror stories of people getting involved on the Internet."

Blanche juggled her shoulders. "Last time I checked, I was fifty-three years *over* the age of consent. I've lived through two husbands, four wars, six ornery children, and a passel of grandkids who've never heard the word no. If I can handle that, I can handle a Romeo from Toledo."

"You're talking to a man from Toledo?"

She raised her fist. "Toledo today, tomorrow the world!" She leaned toward Merry. "He thinks I'm thirty-five."

"You're tiptoeing through dangerous territory, Blanche."

She waved the concern away. "Tiptoeing, my big toe. I'm stomping through." She lowered her voice. "It's not like I'm ever going to meet one of these Don Juans."

"Did it occur to you that they may be in their seventies too?"

Blanche put a hand to her mouth. "They'd lie to me? They wouldn't dare—"

"You dared."

She made a face and turned back to the computer, moving the mouse to sign off. "Go tell that old rutabaga he's victorious. I'll be over to properly annoy him in a moment."

As Merry turned away, she caught a glimpse of Ivan's eyes before he turned back to the mural. She wondered why the two friends didn't get married and be done with it. Blanche had confided that they'd been tormenting each other for nine years—faithfully and exclusively—until Blanche had discovered the Internet.

She noticed Harold leaving, hiding *Mutiny on the Bounty* beneath his jacket. "Bye, Harold. See you later."

He nodded and hurried out. She returned to the front desk and jotted down *Mutiny on the Bounty*. He'd bring it back tomorrow. Harold wasn't good at checking in and out, but he was great at reading and bringing back.

Sim had only been on the job an hour when she saw it. The weirdo—that Harold guy—stole a book. And none too smoothly either.

Not that she cared much about stealing in general. She'd done a bit of shoplifting herself. But taking a book. Books were sacred. Special.

Sim glanced at Merry to see if she'd noticed. But Merry was oblivious, working at her desk. It was ridiculous. If the librarian didn't protect the books, then who—?

Sim left her book cart, burst through the front door, and bounded down the steps. "Hey, you! Harold!"

The old man stopped at the curb across the street, one foot up and one foot down. He held the book beneath his jacket, its edge peeking out. His face was a mixture of curiosity and fear. A car drove between them, and Sim touched its back bumper as she crossed the street toward him.

She walked past him, to the sidewalk, hoping he would follow her. It made her nervous the way he straddled the street and safety. Relief eased through her when his lower foot joined its mate on the sidewalk.

He looked at her.

Now what? "I…I saw—"

Merry burst through the library doors. "Sim!"

She rushed down the steps toward them, and Sim saw fear on her face. *Does she think I'll hurt the guy?*

Merry reached them and put a hand on Harold's shoulder. "You all right, Harold?"

He opened his mouth to speak, but Sim interrupted him. "He stole a book." She pulled it from his jacket. "See?"

Merry took the book and handed it back to Harold. "I know what books he has. We have an understanding, don't we, Harold?"

"I rather tell thee what is to be fear'd than what I fear; for always I am Caesar."

Sim stared at him. *What does that mean?* Harold pulled a piece of licorice and offered it to her. "Uh…no thanks. I already ate."

Harold cocked his head. "Youth, thou bear'st thy father's face;

frank nature, rather curious than in haste, hath well composed thee."

Merry put a hand on both their shoulders. "Well, then. *All's Well That Ends Well,* right?"

Harold bowed. Then he nodded at Sim and scuffed off across the square.

Merry looked after him. "He's such a sweet man. A gentle man."

An odd man. But apparently one who hadn't stolen any book. "I'm sorry, Merry. I didn't know."

"How could you?" They headed back to the library. "I should have warned you. You were only trying to protect the library."

"Protect the books."

"You really appreciate literature, don't you?"

"It's better than real life."

Merry paused on the front steps. "My, my. You're way too bitter for your years."

"Is there an age limit?"

Merry apparently changed her mind about going up the steps. She pulled Sim to the side. "Care to tell me about it? Why are you here with your aunt? Where are you parents? Why Steadfast?"

Sim shoved her hands in her pockets and looked over the square. "I don't want to get into it."

Merry looked at her a moment, then touched her arm. "I see pain in your eyes, Sim. I know that look. I've been there. I *am* there. Whenever you want to talk, I'll listen, okay?"

Sim nodded and went inside. Why did everyone think she needed help? She could handle things.

She could.

Really.

Be still and wait.

Pooh.

Claire folded a newspaper into accordion pleats and held them at the end. She fanned herself, but it didn't do much good. There was no air conditioning in the attic. And no bathroom. And more critical than both of these, there was nothing to do.

But be still and wait.

Claire looked out over the square. She'd just witnessed a scene with Sim, Merry, and an old man. A book had exchanged hands. A small drama in which she had no part. And that had her grinding her teeth.

She'd come all this way, sacrificed so much, to sit in a hot, dusty attic? Alone? It didn't make sense. When Sim had appeared in the middle of the night, she'd been sure the girl was the reason she'd been led to Steadfast. But Sim wasn't cooperating and didn't want Claire's help. She didn't even particularly want Claire's company. And now Sim had a job and was making friends, while Claire had nothing.

She looked around the attic—her own little apartment. She'd been so proud of finding it, like it was meant to be. She'd found a place to stay. She'd befriended Merry. But now Sim had taken over Merry. Nothing seemed to fit. Maybe this whole thing was a mistake.

She continued to fan herself, thinking back over all the steps that had led her here. Had she interpreted something wrong? Taken off in a direction that was a dead end? Perhaps her fascination with the Steadfast painting was a fluke. Perhaps she'd read too much into it. Perhaps she should still be living in her town house, working at the studio, sitting at her drawing board, creating her next great piece of art.

She pulled back as a bird flitted close to the window, its wings brushing the glass. It flew away, soaring toward the trees in the square. Free.

This was ridiculous. If a bird could be free, so could she. It was time to leave her prison.

She found her shoes.

Claire walked into the library. It was odd, coming in from the front with the lights on. As soon as she entered her eyes were drawn to the right. A ceramic tile mosaic adorned the wall. It was a six-by-twelve-foot mural—or had been, at one time. Most of the quarter-inch tiles were missing, leaving gaping holes in a pastoral scene. A stool sat empty in front of it, ready for some artisan to fill it. To fix it. To complete the work.

She ran a hand over the existing tiles, snaking past the bare patches. Her mind immediately began to fill in the blanks. *Oh, Lord. I am supposed to be here, aren't I?*

"Hey, Claire," Merry said from the front desk. "Come to check up on Sim so soon?"

Sim appeared from between the stacks and gave Claire a dirty look.

"Actually, no. I was just passing by." She turned toward the mosaic. "It's quite a mess, isn't it?"

Merry patted her pocket, then pulled out some small tiles. "More fall off every day."

Claire's insides did double flips. A mural that needed an artist. Surely this was not a coincidence. Maybe this was the reason she'd been brought to Steadfast. They needed her expertise.

Her eyes grazed over the needy mural, her mind scrambling to create a total picture, a maze of mental colors swirling and rearranging themselves as each vied for its proper position in her newest creation. Who would have thought that a small town such as Steadfast could not have just one, but two Claire Adams creations?

Her mind let go of the artistic process and inserted thoughts of a big unveiling. The mayor standing at her side in front of the sheathed mural, ready to unveil. Claire would pull the drape away. Oohs and aahs. Applause. The key to the city. Shaking hands. Attempts to be humble amid her own pride and sense of accomplishment.

Pride. Accolades. Applause.

Forbidden fruits.

Claire was aware that Merry was telling her about the history of the mural, but she couldn't listen. Not when she was fighting a war. She'd given up her art, and with it the pride and the applause. God had asked her to give up everything. And everything meant everything.

This is a test.

The realization slammed hard. A mural in need of an artist was not a ticket for her to go back to her art, but a test for her to pass by, to surrender her art. God was asking her, *Were you sincere in giving it up for Me? Or will you renege the first chance you get, grabbing back that which is no longer yours?*

Merry was still talking. "...and here's our resident artist." She angled to include an old man who was coming back from the direction of the rest rooms. "Ivan, this is Claire Adams. Claire, this is Ivan, our artist."

Claire had to force herself to remember the niceties of shaking his hand. "You're...you're doing this?"

"You bet."

"You're an artist?"

"Nah. I'm just a retired old coot Merry conned into doing the work for free." He squinted at the mural. "I may not get it back exactly the way it was, but I'll give it a good shot. Haven't got anything else to do."

Anything else to do? The way Ivan approached the art was like a knife's jab to Claire's sensibilities. Art was important. Creating enriched people, brought joy and even insight into their lives. It was *not* something you did because you didn't have anything better to do.

Merry moved to the mural, to an area directly in front of a stool. "We appreciate your efforts, Ivan, though I'm still trying to figure out how this blue and red patch fit in."

Claire's eyes also sought an explanation. Where the rest of the mural was done in subtle variations of colors blending together like the shading of a painting, Ivan had placed the brightest red tiles next to the brightest blue. Fine, if he was creating a modern abstract, but not at all in keeping with the landscape composition—

Ivan returned to his stool and flipped a hand. "Don't bother me, Merry. I'm creating."

Merry's nervousness showed in her smile, but she stepped away, attempting to draw Claire with her. But Claire didn't want to go. The mural needed her. It was screaming for her expertise. Ivan was ruining it. She felt like a surgeon being asked to watch a rookie resident attempt a complicated operation. To stand back and not intervene would be an act of neglect, malpractice—

Or obedience.

Claire grimaced. What had the old man at McDonald's said? *"The wonder of the O-word."* Ha. Some wonder. She fingered her necklace.

Merry called to her from the counter. "Claire?"

She was forced to turn her back on the mural and was surprised to find it was one of the hardest things she'd ever done. She walked toward Merry, but the magnet of the mural attached itself to her, trying to wrench her back. If only Merry would extend a hand and pull her to safety.

But Merry was straightening a pile of bookmarks, oblivious to her struggle. "How can I help you this morning? You in need of a good summer read?"

Confronted with the question, Claire didn't know how to answer. Why was she here? Because she was lonely, confused, in search of some reason—

A loud thud drew their attention. Their eyes were drawn to Sim as she shoved a book into its space with extra force. The girl's glare could have drawn blood.

"She doesn't seem too happy to see you."

Claire looked at Merry and shrugged. "I...I think my presence offends her independent nature."

"I've noticed she likes to be in control."

Claire was snapped into the moment. "Has she done something wrong?"

"No, no. She's caught on remarkably fast, but..."

"But what?"

"I have the feeling she thinks she can run this place better than I can."

Claire shook her head. "It's good to know I'm not the only one who feels intimidated by that particular teenager. Though in my case it's not 'that particular' anything. Teenagers intimidate me. Period. They're different today. More worldly. Less innocent."

"They need us more than ever but want us less and less."

Claire pondered that. Did God feel the same way about people in general?

Merry sat at her desk. "So. Once again the question: How can I help you this morning, Claire?"

With one last look at Sim, Claire realized if she was going to figure out why she'd been led to Steadfast, she needed to be close to Sim and Merry and the others whom God had brought before her in the past few days. And it appeared that meant spending a lot of time in the library. An idea raised its hand. "I'm doing a research paper on...on Michelangelo."

"For what?"

Good question. "For myself."

"For fun?"

Claire shrugged. "I'm odd that way."

Merry shook her head. "Whatever floats your boat. I'll show you what we have on him."

Claire spread books on Michelangelo across a table. She'd gone across the street and purchased a notebook, paper, and pens. Since she'd gotten herself into this thing, she might as well really learn something. She was feeling quite the scholar when Sim appeared at her side.

"What are you doing here? Spying on me?"

"I'm doing a research paper."

"What for?"

"None of your business."

Sim's eyebrow raised. "Getting testy, are we?"

Claire's eyes flitted to the mural that Ivan was desecrating. She *was* feeling testy.

"Hey, I'm all for this 'none of your business' attitude. But just remember what goes for you, goes for me." Sim turned on her heel and left.

Great. Just great.

At the end of the day, the three women left the library and Merry locked the front door. Claire hoped she'd remained less diligent about the door in back. Merry went down the steps toward her car, then stopped. "You two want a lift to the motel?"

Claire covered quickly. "No thanks."

Merry shrugged. "See you tomorrow then."

Sim and Claire walked down the sidewalk, waiting for Merry to get in her car and drive away. They waved as she drove past.

The illusion complete—and now unnecessary—Sim turned on Claire. "What's this about a motel?"

"Merry assumed that's where I was staying. You too, I guess. I don't have a better explanation, so I don't correct her assumption." She sighed. "I hate it."

"But you do it so well."

Claire did a double take. Certainly all this deception was not what God had in mind when He sent her to Steadfast. But what choice did she have? "Maybe we should move into the motel for real. Make it legitimate."

"You do what you want. I'm fine."

Claire thought of Sim sleeping across the chairs. "You *can* sleep in the attic with me, you know."

"I like my space."

"Maybe we should tell Merry the truth about you not being my niece."

Sim stopped walking. "No!" She looked around, lowered her voice, and continued. "Okay, so I was upset at the time. But I think it's a good idea they believe we're related. A lone kid is odd. They'll ask where my parents are, and I won't be able to answer. You pretending to be my aunt makes me look legit."

Sim had a point. "And having a niece makes me look legit."

"You use me and I'll use you."

"That's a callous way to look at it."

Sim shrugged and started to walk—away from the library. "See you later."

"Don't you want to eat dinner? I bought groceries."

"I'll grab something."

So much for family ties.

Claire looked out the attic window. She'd watched Sim leave the square, disappearing into the streets of Steadfast.

If only God didn't give people choices. If only Claire could force Sim to do the right thing from the right place in her heart. If only

Claire knew exactly what *she* was supposed to do.

Claire grabbed a book she'd checked out. She'd wanted free time to read? She had it.

She opened the pages of *Atlas Shrugged*.

Loser town. Nothing to do.

Sim heard the boom of a radio coming from the right. She turned toward it.

She hung back to watch three boys. They looked older. Sixteen, seventeen maybe. One had a belly that couldn't be hidden by a baggy T-shirt. He looked the type who would play football on the defense because he liked to tackle people. The middle-sized boy was growing out his hair and had two earrings. The one who seemed to be the leader was spooky looking, with circles under his eyes, but not too far-out. Sim felt at home. They were better than nothing.

I can take these country hicks any time.

Sim noticed the beer and wanted one. She'd started drinking after she moved in with her aunt and uncle. A strange neighborhood meant finding new friends. What better way to belong than to be a drinking buddy? Instant friendship.

She noticed the earring-guy looking her way. Her legs twitched, wanting to run.

"Hey, girl."

"Yeah?"

"You a watcher or a joiner?"

Good question. She walked toward them.

Jered eyed the girl, trying not to stare. Normally he wouldn't have anything to do with someone who looked younger. But something had nudged him into calling out to her as though his mouth had a mind of its own. So now, even if he had second thoughts, it was too late. The girl was there.

He handed her a beer. She took it, popped the tab, and took a swig like she knew what she was doing.

"I'm Sim."

"Sam?"

"Sim."

Moog burped. "Weird name."

Jered laughed. "You should talk?"

Moog slapped him on the head. "Don't bug me about my name, remember?"

Jered glanced at the girl. He hated when Moog took control. He was always smacking one of them like in those Three Stooges movies, like he had to remind them he was the leader. Not that Jered wanted that position. He was content to let Moog do the planning and scheming. He'd follow. He was good at following.

Moog pointed with his beer. "This is Darrell, that there is Jered, and I'm Moog." The boys nodded at her, then took a sip of beer.

"How old are you anyway?" Moog eyed Sim with an extra gleam in his eyes. Jered had seen that look before. He looked away.

"Eighteen."

"Bull."

Sim lifted her chin, and Jered had to admire her spunk.

"What makes you think I'm not?"

Darrell cocked his head and his eyes made a pass over her chest. "You ain't got the equipment."

Sim blushed but stared Darrell down. "Obviously, neither do you."

Jered crushed a can against his leg, ignoring the pain. "You new in town?"

"Just passing through."

"To where?"

"Don't know yet."

Moog threw a wave at her. "You're too young to be passing through anywhere."

Sim chugged the beer and tossed the empty in the back of the truck. "Got another one?"

Moog laughed and put an arm around her shoulder, his hand draped down her front. "Hey, maybe you're not too young."

Jered knew what came next. He thought about stopping it. She was just a kid. *Let it be. So what if Moog has a little fun?* As if he could stop him.

Moog's hand found what it was looking for.

"Hey!" Sim shoved him away. "Get your hands off me!"

Darrell laughed. "Don't waste your time on her, Moog. She's just a kid."

Sim shuffled her shoulders and opened another can. "I am *not* a kid and I don't need you defending me."

Darrell backed up a step. "Sorry. It won't happen again."

Moog stuffed his hands in his pockets and eyed her, though he kept his distance. "What did you cut your hair with? A dull ax?"

"A sharp one. Care to see it?"

"Sure. Anytime, any—"

Jered jumped out of the truck between them. "Cool it, you two."

Moog flashed him a look. "Watch it, Jer. Don't butt in unless you can handle the consequences."

Jered backed off. What had gotten into him? It was stupid to cross Moog. Everybody knew that. And it was obvious the girl could handle herself.

She leaned against the side of the truck. "This place is boring. In Kansas City we—" She stopped.

Moog grinned. "You're from Kansas City."

She looked at him, then away. She'd said more than she meant to. "What do you do for fun around here?" Sim eyed them, brow arched. "Plow a field? Pluck a chicken?"

Darrell grabbed a hunk of her hair. "I'll plow you, you little—"

Jered was relieved when Moog slapped Darrell's hand away. "Back off."

"But you—"

"Back off!"

Darrell stared at Sim before flipping the girl's chin. "Just trying to teach the girl some manners."

"By showing her some of yours?" Jered stared. Sim didn't sound the least bit frightened. "Brilliant."

Darrell reddened. "Who are you to talk, Miss Etiquette?"

Moog pulled Sim under his arm. "This is our new friend. Our new mascot. Our new—"

"Partner in crime?" Darrell laughed.

The girl looked down at that, and Jered thought she was uncomfortable. He was glad when Moog let her go. Yet she was one of them now. For some reason beyond his understanding, Jered wanted Sim on his team.

It was after midnight when Sim entered the library. Although she'd wanted to leave within fifteen minutes of meeting up with the boys—that Moog gave her the creeps—she'd hung around. One evening couldn't hurt. She had the feeling if she got too chummy with them—especially Moog—they'd want more than she had to give. Darrell was pretty worthless. An overweight bully. She could handle him. And that Jered…he was hard to figure. He seemed tough—had to be tough to hang around with the other two—but there was something softer there. Approachable? Almost pathetic, like a puppy that needed shelter.

Either way, her aunt and uncle would never approve. Yet wasn't that the point? Pushing their buttons was the reason she'd opted for the nose ring, dark-lined eyes, and red hair. Making waves was the only weapon she had.

The boys offered to drop her somewhere, but she begged off, said she would walk, and slipped behind the library. She clicked the door shut as silently as she could. She looked up the attic stairs. All was dark.

Claire's going to be mad.

What did it matter? She didn't have to answer to her, not to anyone. It was great to be independent and in control.

Sim slipped into the library, moved her chairs together, and went to sleep.

Nine

Consider it pure joy, my brothers, whenever
you face trials of many kinds,
because you know that the testing of your faith develops perseverance.
Perseverance must finish its work so that you may be mature
and complete, not lacking anything.

JAMES 1:2–4

"MOM!"

Sim bolted upright and fell onto the floor with an *oomph*. There was light from a window, but the window was in the wrong place. It should have been on her left.

My mom is dead. My dad is dead!

Though sleeping brought forgetting, waking brought fresh remembering—like a twisting knife in the belly.

Sim pulled her sweatshirt off the chair, wadded it into a pillow, and curled on the floor. She squeezed her eyes shut, willing the pain to leave but knowing it wouldn't. Not completely. Not ever. She felt like an amputee who suffered pain in what wasn't even there, who tried to adjust to a missing leg, but with each movement, each task, was reminded of what was lost. Nothing would ever be the same. Life had changed without her permission.

But never again. Never again.

After a few minutes of trying, Sim knew she would not be able to get back to sleep. She checked the time: 6:45. Yesterday Claire had gotten her up at 6:30.

What gives?

She thought back to her midnight return after spending time

with Moog and the boys. She hadn't seen Claire. The attic was dark, and Sim assumed it was because Claire was sleeping.

But what if she was gone?

Sim sprang to her feet. She may not have wanted to accept Claire's mothering, but that didn't mean she wanted her to leave without telling—

She heard a key in the front door.

Merry!

She ducked into the stacks, then remembered her backpack, her sweatshirt, and the three chairs pushed together to form a bed. There would be no way to explain them away. No way.

The lights came on. Sim pulled back even farther. She peeked between the books and saw Merry drop her purse on her desk. She was humming. The humming turned into a song, "I love coffee, I love tea…"

Coffee?

Merry got the pot behind the counter and headed to the rest room for water.

It was Sim's only chance.

She made a dash for the chairs, pulling them apart, only clanking them once. She grabbed her pack and loose sweatshirt and hurled herself toward the storeroom, calming the door's swing behind her. Then she bolted for the stairs and burst into the attic, pasting her body against the closed door.

Too close.

Claire turned around from brushing her hair. "What's—?"

"Shh! Merry is here!" It was hard to breathe even in a whisper.

Claire turned back to the broken mirror, the silk in her red pajama top making a *swish* sound. "Nice to see you, Sim."

There was anger in her whisper.

Sim moved closer. "Didn't you hear what I said? Merry is here. I nearly got caught."

"Is that a concern of mine?"

Sim took a fresh breath. "What's got into you?"

Claire put her brush down. "Not a thing. I'm just surprised you shared that information with me. From what I saw last evening, it was everyone for herself. No accountability. Two separate beings, going their own ways."

Sim leaned closer, keeping her voice down. "You're mad."

Claire's eyes grabbed hers. "Disappointed."

Sim hated that look. "You're not my mom. I don't have to check in with you. I can stay out until two in the morning if I want to."

"Two of your statements are correct. One is not." Claire took a step toward her and Sim resisted the urge to back up. "I am not your mother—thank God. And you *can* stay out until sunrise if you want to. But the statement that is not true is that you don't have to check in with me. Everyone has to check in with someone, Sim. You and I have been placed together. We have a different view of what that placement means and the extent of our ties, but in the end, those details don't matter. It's common courtesy to let anyone who would worry about us know what's going on, know we're okay."

She worried about me? Sim shoved the thought away. There was a principle here, a principle to be fought for. She could not give in to this woman's control. "So now you know. I'm fine. I'll always be fine."

"So you say."

"I don't need this." She grabbed her stuff and left the attic, continuing through the back door. Though she wanted to stomp and slam, she let her anger flow inward.

Where it could do the most damage.

Claire sat on the edge of the bed, the brush in her limp hand. Why had she been so brusque?

She made me worry. She should have let me know where she was.

In principle, Claire was right. In an ideal setting, Sim would have been a good little girl, home by nine, safely tucked in a bed they'd make in the corner of the attic. They would get up in the morning, have some PB&J sandwiches for breakfast, and discuss *Atlas Shrugged*.

Claire glanced at the book, sitting on the chair. She was on chapter 4. Sim was right. It was thought provoking, even if Claire didn't agree with everything it said. She'd wanted to tell Sim she was reading it, hoped it would be a bond between them, an act of goodwill on her part.

But now she wouldn't get the chance. Her pride had been hurt and she'd behaved badly. Maybe it was a good thing God had never blessed her with children. Some mother she'd make.

With a groan, she let herself topple to her side, where she pulled herself into a curl full of regret.

Sim took a bottle of grape juice from the grocery shelf and added it to her basket. If Claire hadn't been so mad, Sim wouldn't be forced to spend her own money on breakfast. Claire had a cooler full of food, and yet so far, Sim hadn't been around to share anything beyond a few donuts.

Speaking of… She headed for the pastries and chose a package of miniature chocolate donuts. The sight of them brought back the memory of yesterday in the park. Claire had brought her donuts, not knowing they were her favorite. Claire had shared with her, cared about her.

And what have you done for her? Left her to eat dinner alone? Stayed out late? Run out at the first disagreement?

She tossed the donuts in the basket, shaking her head. She would *not* let this stranger make her feel guilty. She didn't owe her—didn't owe anyone. She was a free agent.

As she headed to the checkout lane she passed the candy aisle. A bag of black licorice beckoned.

She'd made two enemies since coming to Steadfast: Claire and Harold. True, Harold was a weird old guy, but Sim knew what it was like to be accused of something she didn't do.

She snatched the bag of licorice and went to pay.

When it was time to go in to work she said her hellos to Merry, then took a right and headed to the chair in the corner where Harold spent his days. She placed the bag of licorice on the seat and adjusted it so it was straight and centered on the vinyl. She took a step back to check the effect.

Perfect.

She wasn't such a bad person. She wasn't.

Claire knew it was going to be awkward seeing Sim at the library, but she steeled herself to do it with grace. She would get Sim alone and apologize. Make things right.

But when she got there, Sim was already working with Merry, getting some explanation about logging in new books. They exchanged a glance, but that was all that was possible.

Claire went to work on her study of Michelangelo. The apology would have to wait.

Claire seemed to be drawn to Ivan and the mural like an injured athlete drawn to watching a game she couldn't play in.

Ivan looked up from placing a bunch of brown tiles in the wrong place. "May I help you, Claire?"

"Just checking your progress."

He sat back. "Slow but sure. An artist's job is never done."

It took all her willpower to remain silent. This was *not* her mural—or her business.

"Anything else? I can't create with people watching, you know."

"No, nothing else. I'll leave you be."

As she walked through the reading area on the way to her table, she did a double take at the magazine on one of the chairs. It was the May issue of *Newsweek*, the issue that contained a short article about her commission for the lobby of a Chicago museum. The article had a nice picture of her. She'd framed a copy for her office. If anyone saw it now…

So what if they did? It would feel great to have somebody acknowledge her for who she was. She wasn't some nobody, she was an artist—a real, bona fide artist who could turn the library mural from dilapidated to divine. Did she really have to keep her status a secret?

She glanced around to make sure no one was looking. She heard the sounds of kids in the children's section and Merry's voice at the front counter. But no one was close. She opened to page ninety-six and placed the opened magazine on the chair.

Way too obvious.

She took another magazine and haphazardly placed it overlapping the page facing her article.

Better.

Then she returned to her table, her heart racing. She imagined what would happen when someone found it.

"Claire! Is this you? This is *you! Why, you're famous!"*

Everyone would come running, and they'd fight over the article, oohing and aahing that their Claire was *the* Claire in the magazine.

Pride goes before destruction, a haughty spirit before a fall.

Her lungs deflated as the verse from Proverbs interrupted her fantasy. Why, of the verses she knew by heart, did she happen to think of this one?

You know why.

That was it. She couldn't do it. She *wanted* to, but she couldn't. The accolades of the world were her past. Her future was here.

Such as it was.

Merry's voice grew louder, heading her way. Claire sprang from her seat and bolted toward the seating area. She scooped the magazine from the chair just as Merry turned the corner, a library patron in tow.

Merry eyed Claire, as if she'd just caught the tail end of her movement and found it confusing.

"I was just straightening up," Claire said.

"Glad to hear it."

Once Merry moved on, Claire picked up the other magazine and dropped it into the shelf housing the magazines. She put the *Newsweek* in back.

She hoped God was proud of her sacrifice.

Sim tapped a pencil on the desk and stared at the door. Where was Harold? He'd been in first thing yesterday.

Merry came up beside her. "You waiting for someone?"

Sim went back to checking in books. "I was just looking for Harold. Isn't he usually here?"

Merry checked her watch. "Actually, yes. Why the concern?"

Sim thought fast. "He's just…interesting, that's all. I've never met anyone who quotes Shakespeare all the time. Has he always been like that?"

"Ever since his wife passed away. He used to teach Shakespeare at the high school, but when she died…" Merry looked to the ceiling. "It was eight or nine years ago. I heard he was devastated. It broke him. His wife loved Shakespeare as much as he did—they used to act out scenes in the square on the Fourth of July." Sim shrugged. "She died, and he began to speak Shakespeare exclusively—as a tribute to her, I guess."

"He never says anything normal?"

"People say no. And not that I've heard. I've gotten used to it, and actually, his words usually fit into the conversation so well, that I often forget they're not his."

Sim didn't want to say it but figured now was her chance. "He seems a bit odd."

"A broken heart will do that." She stared into the middle of the room for a moment, then blinked and shook her head. "Harold doesn't care what the world thinks. He lives in his own world."

"That's sad."

"Oh, I don't know. Sometimes I envy him. He's found a way to be content. That's not a bad achievement."

Sim could tell Merry was talking about herself. "You discontent about something?"

Merry pulled the spine of a book between her fingers. Forward, then backward. "I lost my husband and son last year in a plane crash. At the moment, being content is not an option."

Sim took in a breath, ready to commiserate, but stopped herself. She wasn't sure she could share her grief. She was Claire Adams's niece. She was supposedly happy. Telling Merry about her parents would complicate things.

Merry pointed to the door. "There he is."

Harold came in, flicked a quick salute in Merry's direction, then scurried toward his corner. Sim didn't see him as a weirdo anymore. Harold had been a teacher. He'd been a husband. He grieved. They had something in common.

Sim slid behind the book cart. "I'll put these away." She pushed it toward the stacks, turning into the far side of the row nearest Harold's chair. She pretended to rearrange some books. Peering through the stacks she caught a glimpse of the licorice—and Harold standing in front of it.

The man was staring at it. Didn't he like it?

Then a crooked smile lit his face and he reached for the bag. He held it in his hands like a treasure, stroking the cellophane, making it crackle. He pulled the bag to his chest, lifted his chin, and closed his eyes.

He opened his mouth as if to speak, but apparently the words of Shakespeare were unavailable.

Claire read the same paragraph about Michelangelo's feud with Pope Julian II for the fifth time. Although she found the details of the artist's life fascinating, her mind kept wandering, going back to her own art, asking questions—but *not* necessarily getting any answers. Her thoughts focused on the studio and gallery. Had there been any sales since she'd been gone? Had Darla and the others found new jobs?

It's not your business anymore.

Claire arched her back, its ache making her think of other things she'd left behind. If only she could dive into a nice, soothing whirlpool bath, with Vivaldi playing in her ear and a cup of mint-pekoe tea steeping in a Wedgwood cup nearby.

She glanced toward the storeroom door. No whirlpools for her. Just a miniscule shower in a forgotten bathroom. No classical CDs, no radio, no TV, and no mint-pekoe, in a china cup or otherwise.

Stop thinking about what you gave up. Think about what you have.

She expelled a puff of air, rubbing her face. Her skin screamed for special attention. How about the pricey, three-step moisturizing program she'd had in the top dresser drawer back home?

There are no fancy moisturizers, there is no dresser. There is no home.

Tears threatened. This wasn't working out. She'd expected sacrifice to be more fulfilling. Certainly God wouldn't have her give up her entire life for this…this…life of endless days, meaningless study, and dry skin?

"Claire?"

She looked up to see Sim standing before her. "Hi."

"Hi."

Their morning argument stood between them. *Come on, Claire. You're the adult here.*

"I'm—"

"I'm sorry," Claire said.

"—sorry."

They laughed as their words overlapped. Sim pulled something from behind her back: two mini chocolate donuts on a paper towel. "I saved some from breakfast."

Claire's throat tightened. She must be pretty far gone to cry over donuts. "Thank you."

Sim beamed. "I'd better get back to work."

Claire was left staring at the donuts. Sim was a lot more complicated than she thought. There were no easy answers about her either.

Claire ate the donuts. Did they taste extra good because they'd been a gift? That was silly.

She took up her book and got back to work. *Forgive the complaints, Lord. Help me leave the past behind. Help me believe in Your plan—whatever it is.*

What was that saying Pastor Joe used to spout? *"If you have faith, have faith."*

Easier said than done.

Merry looked up from her computer to see Harold standing in front of the counter, grinning.

"What's up, Harold? You look as though you've discovered the cure for the common cold."

He pulled a bag of licorice from behind his back. He held it toward her, allowing her to take her own piece. She slid one out, for once assured it would not be brittle or covered in lint.

"A new bag?" She took a bite. "To what do we owe this treat?"

"Fie, foh, and fum, I smell the blood of a British man." He pointed back to his corner of the library.

Merry tried to interpolate. *A man. A stranger.* "Someone gave you the candy back in your corner?"

"The prince of darkness is a gentleman."

This one was tougher. "Did you see the person who gave it to you?"

Harold shook his head. "Sweets to the sweet! Farewell." He tucked the licorice and his newest book beneath his jacket and left.

Sim came up to the counter. "What was all that about?"

"I'm not sure." Merry chewed her licorice along with her thoughts. "Apparently someone gave Harold a bag a licorice."

"Did he say who?"

"No, not directly. But that would be impossible unless the man's name was Hamlet or Benvolio. Shakespeare didn't use many Toms, Dicks, or Harrys. According to Harold, it was either the Prince of Darkness or a gentleman—who was British." She shook her head, giving up. "Whoever it was, I thank him. I like seeing Harold happy." She gave a little laugh and waggled her hands next to her head. "But then again, maybe it's the library ghost."

"Ghost?"

"It's a tall tale Blanche told me about."

"Tell me."

Merry finished chewing. "Apparently the librarian used to live here during the depression, when money was tight. Up in the attic."

Sim cleared her throat. "Oh, really?"

"She died up there. Blanche said it was really sad. She was an old woman who died alone in a dusty old attic."

"So now her ghost haunts the library?"

Merry laughed. "That's what they say. It adds a little spice to the place, don't you think?"

Sim beamed, as if the story fed some need. "I think it's cool. Very cool."

The three women stood at the door at closing time. Sim tugged Claire's shirtsleeve. "I'll be back—I'll be home—in a little bit."

"I'll wait to eat—"

"No, don't do that." She filled her lungs. "I need to be outside. I'll grab something for dinner." Almost as an afterthought she said, "Is that all right?"

Before Claire could fully nod, Sim waved good-bye and ran across the street. *She always seems to have a place to go to, and yet I stay here. Stuck.* After their reconciliation, she had assumed they'd spend time together.

Merry locked the door to the library and they headed down the stone steps. "She's a good girl."

"Yes, she is." *But what am I supposed to do with her?*

"Since Sim's taken care of for dinner… I'm really hungry. Want to join me for some fine dining at Bon Vivant?" Merry walked to her car. "Don't say no. Get in. I'll drop you off at the motel to get cleaned up."

Claire's heart raced. The thought of a nice dinner was enticing. But the logistics of her secret nagged. "Actually, I've got to get some paper supplies. Why don't I meet you at the restaurant?"

"I'll see if I can get us in about six-thirty."

Claire walked across the street toward the dime store until Merry's car was out of sight. Then she snuck into the library to change. She was sweating—and not from the July heat.

It was only a matter of time before they were found out, and then where would they go? Deception was exhausting.

Sim knew she was strutting but didn't care. *Let the whole world know how good I feel!* She probably looked like John Travolta in the opening scene of *Saturday Night Fever,* strutting down the sidewalk carrying a can of paint like he owned the world.

All because of a bag of licorice and two donuts.

She wanted to celebrate. She'd seen a pizza place a couple of blocks off the square. The thought of a large pepperoni with extra cheese beckoned. Maybe she should bring it back to the library to share. After eating out of a cooler it would taste like a delicacy.

As she turned the corner she heard the pulse of familiar music and saw the boys. She turned back to go around the block the other way. She wasn't in the mood to meet up with—

"Hey, Sim!" It was Moog.

Just keep walking. Pretend you don't hear.

Out of the corner of her eye, Sim saw Jered jump from the bed of the pickup and walk toward her. There was no escape.

"Hey! Girl! Don't ignore us."

Sim stopped walking. "Hi, guys."

"Hi, nothing. Where you been all day?" Darrell asked.

Sim took a step away. "I've been working. At the library."

Jered coughed once. "What?"

"At the library. I'm helping out Merry."

Darrell chucked Jered in the gut. "Hey, isn't that your job?"

By the quick way Jered averted his eyes Sim knew his next words would not be the truth—at least not all of it. "I quit. I didn't want to work in any library. Where's the fun in that?"

"Exactly," Darrell said. "Who wants to be a bookworm like loser-girl here?"

Moog flicked a lock of Sim's hair. "You got a job, you got money. You owe us for the beer you drank."

Sim thought of the money in her pocket. She glanced toward the pizza place.

As if Moog read her thoughts, he pointed down the street. "Go order us one, Simmy girl. We're hungry."

"But I—"

"Or are you a mooch? Sponging beer, not wanting to pay us back?"

She had the urge to toss the money in their faces and call it even. But she knew these guys wanted more than cash. They wanted an act of loyalty. And though she didn't want them as friends, she certainly didn't want them as enemies. She glanced at the library. So much for her idea of sharing pizza with Claire.

But what choice did she have?

Sim stretched out in the back of the pickup. She was glad they'd run out of beer. Her mind was fuzzy, and every time she moved, her eyes dragged her vision a half-beat behind. Besides, if they got any drunker, Jered would sing even louder—and it was loud enough as it was. Actually, his singing was good—but loud. The whole town could hear.

"Hey, Elvis, hold down the 'Jailhouse Rock' or you'll be put in the jailhouse to rot for disturbing the peace."

Sim laughed at her own joke, until Jered grabbed her pant leg and yanked her so hard her head hit the truck bed. "Don't make fun of my singing!"

Sim resumed her position, rubbing her head. "I wasn't. You're good. It's just that your singing is awful—"

"Awful?"

Sim was caught in a whirlpool from which there was no escape. "Not *awful*. Just awful loud." Ever since she'd told them she worked in the library, Jered had been testy.

Moog laughed. "You are that, Jered." He belched. "Loud."

Jered suddenly stood above Sim and pointed down at her. "Nobody, *nobody* makes fun of my singing. I'm going to be famous someday. And I'll do anything to get there."

Darrell snickered, and Jered whipped in his direction. Darrell lifted his hands in surrender. "Hey, Jer, I don't doubt your talent, I just doubt the odds. Besides, we all know what your dad says."

"My dad can go to—"

Sim interrupted. She didn't want Jered to finish the sentence. She'd said such spiteful things about her own parents off and on— and look what happened to them. "What does your dad say?"

Jered sat back and smashed a beer can against his upraised knee. "He wants me to work with him in the restaurant."

"Yeah, a singing waiter."

Jered flashed a look, cutting Darrell's laugh short.

"What do *you* want?"

At Sim's question, Jered looked past them, his eyes seeming to focus on something far beyond the here and now. "I want to sing in front of tons of people. Compose. Have people know my name."

"Hey, rob a bank and they'll know your name," Moog said.

Jered's shoulders heaved. Sim felt sorry for him—and envious. "It must be great knowing what you want to do."

"I know what I want to do." Moog belched louder and winked in Sim's direction. He kissed the air between them.

She ignored him. "I think you should go for it, Jered. If you don't, you'll always wonder."

His eyes lit up and he sat forward. "That's what I keep telling my dad." Then he sat back with a huff. "But he won't listen. He's so proud of that stupid restaurant, as if a town like Steadfast needs such a place. The food at the diner's good enough for me."

"Don't you have any brothers or sisters?"

"It's just me and my dad. My mom left us when I was little. Haven't seen her since."

"Shouldn't you leave Steadfast if you want to get famous?"

"Can't leave without money. And then it takes more money to get a music company to listen to an unknown. Money and connections."

Connections. Sim thought of her uncle and aunt. They lived next to a guy who was in the music business. Jamison Smith. Sim wasn't sure exactly what Jamison did, but she'd heard her uncle talk about the guy dealing with gigs and dates and—

Sim opened her mouth to say something, then closed it. She couldn't hook Jered up with anybody back home. If she did, the neighbor would call her uncle, and they'd find out where she was, and—

Jered kicked Sim's foot. "What? It looks like you got something to say."

Sim let out a breath and shook her head. "No, it's nothing. I wish you luck, that's all. It'll happen. You'll get your chance."

For a moment, Jered's eyes cleared, and Sim saw a spark of innocence and hope she hadn't seen there before. "You think?"

"Yeah, right." Moog waved his hand in the air. "You'll get your chance to clear the tables and wash the dishes. Serve people like some peon."

Jered drilled an empty beer can at him. Then he dove across the truck bed and got in Moog's face. "Shut up! Shut—"

Sim scooted to the tailgate. "I gotta go."

Jered put a foot on her hand. "No, you don't. The fun's just beginning."

Sim looked at the storm in Jered's eyes. The innocence and hope had been replaced by frustration and hate. Sim wanted to look away but couldn't.

Darrell jumped to the ground. "Jered's right. Let's do something. We gotta show our mascot some excitement."

Sim carefully moved Jered's foot aside. "Don't knock yourself out. I really gotta go."

"There!" Moog pointed. "Old Harold. We can have some fun with him."

Harold hurried across the street.

Moog finished the last of his beer and tossed the can onto the ground. "We can't let Harold be a party pooper, can we?"

The boys jumped to the ground. Jered held out a hand for Sim. "Coming?"

"What are you going to do to him?"

"What do you care? He your dad or something?"

"He doesn't hurt anybody." *He knows Shakespeare and likes licorice. He can read an entire book in one night.*

"He hurts my eyes. And that dive he lives in is a disgrace."

The boys took a few steps away from the truck. They stopped and turned to Sim. "Coming, Simmy girl? Or do you just take advantage of our hospitality and then not want to play our games?"

She jumped down from the truck.

The boys turned the corner, following Harold, hiding behind trees and trash cans like they were on enemy reconnaissance. Sim spotted Harold turning onto a street that was full of empty lots with overgrown weeds and junk cars without any tires. He knew they were there. He looked back and scurried faster, hunched over his sack of groceries. Sim tried to stay hidden.

His sack slipped to the ground. He bent to retrieve it. The boys pounced.

Moog grabbed a can of beans. "Ooh, my favorite." He hurled it into the street, denting it.

Sim took two steps back, but Moog grabbed the edge of her

sleeve and pulled her close. "Don't go soft on us, Simmy. You've got a past lurking behind you out there. I may not know the details, but I feel it. You want to belong in Steadfast, then you do things the Steadfast way. Got it?"

The boys rifled through the sack. Darrell ripped open a box of macaroni and cheese, letting the pasta rain over the toppled Harold. Sim picked up a can of corn. Jered pulled the top off a carton of yogurt, grinning at Harold like some kind of gargoyle.

Harold stumbled toward a house with a screen door that was missing the bottom screen.

The boys let out another volley, the yogurt coating the sidewalk. Then apples flew through the air, hitting Harold, the door, and the porch, some splatting open. He fell on the steps and pulled himself into a fetal position, covering his head.

Sim threw the can into the yard where it did no harm. Darrell noticed. He tossed Sim an apple. "Throw it!" He looked to the others and laughed. "Get a bull's-eye and win a prize!"

Moog made clucking noises. "Come on, little girl."

Harold peered out from beneath his arms.

"Throw it!"

Sim tossed it underhand, but it still hit Harold on his back. He winced.

Screaming with laughter, Moog slapped Sim on the shoulder. "Way to go!"

With that, the boys turned and ran away. With a last glance at the cowering man on the steps, Sim followed Moog and his goons, her steps as heavy as her heart.

Sim read Claire's note. She'd gone out to dinner with Merry. Just as well. She didn't want to face her. Face anyone.

Sim didn't line up the chairs to make a bed. She didn't deserve even that comfort. She moved to Harold's chair and sat. When she realized she'd curled into the same position as Harold on his front steps, she began to cry.

Ten

Hope deferred makes the heart sick,
but a longing fulfilled is a tree of life.

Proverbs 13:12

"CLAIRE! HAVE YOU COME BACK to work for me?"

Claire had feared Bailey Manson might give her a hard time when she showed up at his restaurant. "I'm here to dine tonight, Bailey."

"But if we get busy?"

She smiled. "I'm here to *dine* tonight."

"C'est la vie."

Merry came in the door and Bailey's face lit up.

"Hey, Claire," Merry said. "Bailey."

"You two know each other?"

Merry nodded at him. "Claire's been spending a lot of time at the library, doing a paper on Michelangelo."

Bailey's left eyebrow raised. "A waitress who's studying Michelangelo?"

"Give her a break, Bailey. Give both of us a break." Merry glanced into the dining room. "Think you can find us a table?"

He seated them next to a window. "If there's anything I can get you, let me know."

It was an innocuous comment, but when Bailey put his hand on Merry's shoulder and smiled down at her, it took on added meaning.

As soon as he left, Claire studied her companion. "Are you and Bailey dating?"

Merry glanced up from her menu. "Oh, please."

"He's interested. Surely you noticed?"

Merry made a turn-the-key motion in front of her lips. "I refuse to talk about men until *after* the Caesar salad. What happened to small talk? Work talk? Or even a compliment, like, 'That's a nice outfit you're wearing, Merry'?"

Claire glanced at Merry's attire: a nondescript challis skirt and a blouse that was too big for her, as if she'd lost weight and hadn't gotten around to buying new clothes. She was a pretty woman, but her hair had no real style and hung straight from a center part. Her makeup was minimal and could be done more effectively to bring out her beauty. Merry Cavanaugh was a perfect candidate for a makeover.

"Uh-oh." Merry grimaced. "I see judgment in your eyes. I must warn you, I avoid dining with the fashion police."

Claire kept her thoughts to herself and looked at the menu.

Merry sighed. "Okay. Out with it. Tell me my fashion faux pas so I can drown my embarrassment in some decadent dessert."

Claire studied her, trying to choose her words carefully. "Have you lost weight?"

Merry turned up the cuff that hung halfway over her hand. "You sound like Blanche. She's been trying to fatten me up. She brings food over all the time."

"I'll leave the food to her. But I'd love to take you shopping. I'm good at shopping." *Or I used to be good at shopping.*

"Is it that bad?"

Claire shrugged. "Hey, every diet deserves a celebratory shopping spree."

Merry kept her eyes on the menu. "The grief diet. I don't recommend it."

Claire pulled in a breath. *Fool!* "Oh, Merry. I didn't mean to be flip."

"You weren't. It wouldn't be a proper woman-to-woman dinner without talk about our diets."

Claire wanted to change the subject. She remembered Bailey. "And men?"

"You don't give up, do you?"

"So you *are* interested in him?"

She shook her head no. "It's not just him…it's any man."

"But if you found someone who'd slow dance to Johnny Mathis you'd give it a shot?"

Merry laughed. "I've never heard Johnny Mathis cited as criteria for a relationship."

"I adore love songs, and Johnny's written some of the best. Swooners, all of them."

"You swoon often?"

"Not nearly often enough."

Merry looked across the restaurant to where Bailey was chatting with some other diners. "I guess I should be flattered by Bailey's interest, but…" She shrugged.

"It's too soon?"

"It's more complicated than that." She let out a snicker. "Bailey Manson is *not* my husband. He's not Lou."

"Does he have to be? Should he be?"

Merry stared over Claire's shoulder, as if there were a cheat sheet there. She finally looked back. "Lou was down-to-earth. He was flannel shirts and country music, meatloaf and sitting on lawn chairs watching Justin catch fireflies."

"That sounds nice."

"He *was* nice. Too nice."

Claire blinked. "You'll have to explain that one."

Merry closed her menu. "Have you ever had the most scrumptious piece of apple pie sitting right in front of you, where you could smell the cinnamon and see the ice cream melt over the crust?"

"You're making me hungry."

"But have you also eaten that pie so quickly or so distractedly, that you suddenly realize you've just taken the last bite and you don't remember eating it?"

"Too often."

"That's what I feel regarding Lou. He was the most delicious piece of homemade apple pie. I should have savored every bite, but I didn't. I let our life together slip by, and I got so distracted with my own thoughts of dissatisfaction—thinking about eating a slice of cheesecake or a piece of something exotic, like tiramisu, that I didn't notice what I had in front of me until it was gone—*he* was gone. It was too late. Now the taste of our life together is something I can't hold on to, something that with each breath grows a little less distinct, until I find it hard to remember it at all."

Claire put a hand on Merry's. "That was quite poetic."

Merry jerked her hand back, shaking her head. "There's nothing poetic about being unappreciative and selfish."

Claire was at a loss. There wasn't anything in her own life that could compare with Merry's loss.

Merry looked up, her eyes brimming. "Because I didn't appreciate my life God took it away. My family died because of me."

Claire stared at her. "Don't say—"

"Just because it sounds horrid doesn't mean it isn't true."

"God wouldn't take your family away to punish you."

"Then why did He take them?"

Claire closed her mouth.

Merry nodded. "You don't have an answer to that one, do you?"

"I…"

It was Merry's turn to touch Claire's hand. "I don't mean to jump on you like this. Your intentions are good. Everybody's intentions are good. But in seventeen months I've yet to come across someone with a satisfactory answer to my why question." She shrugged and sat back. "That's because there isn't an answer."

There has to be. Doesn't there?

Merry opened her menu again. "The veal is good."

Claire had a question but was afraid to ask it. Merry must have sensed her hesitation because without looking up she said, "Go ahead. Ask."

Claire leaned on her arms. "Maybe Bailey's your next piece of apple pie. Maybe he's your second chance."

Merry glanced in Bailey's direction. "He's a hundred miles from apple pie."

"Then maybe it's time you try some of that tiramisu."

Merry shook her head and returned to the menu. "Bailey has his own appreciation problems. He's too much like me. Too wrapped up in himself."

"What doesn't he appreciate?"

"His son."

"That Jered kid?"

Merry nodded. "Jered's a good boy at heart, but I see him running around town with the wrong crowd. I'm trying to encourage his music dream, but sometimes I think I'm more determined than he is. Right now I see him being in a boat without a paddle."

"Music's a hard dream to have. The odds—"

"Are astronomical. He knows that. And Bailey hounds him about that. Which is why I help."

"Bailey's not supportive?"

Merry laughed and leaned close over the table. "Bailey Manson? Supportive of anyone else's dream? He's too wrapped up in his own dream of being a high-class restaurateur in small-town America."

Claire *had* thought that was kind of strange.

Merry continued. "The point is, he hurts Jered. Repeatedly. Not physically—that I've seen—but mentally. Bailey seems intent on breaking his son's spirit." She sat back, shaking her head. "And when he does, we'd better stand back."

Claire mentally scanned her old acquaintances. "I wish I had some music connection who could help Jered get a shot, but I don't—"

"I don't either. I can only listen when he dreams, which is more than his father does."

Claire found herself without words. The people around her had so many problems, yet she had no clue how to help them.

Merry patted the table. "Let's order."

Claire had never had to worry if she had enough money to pay for her own meal. Until tonight. She'd accepted Merry's offer of dinner without a second thought. She was used to eating out many times a week, and restaurants as fine as Bon Vivant were her normal fare. In fact, she was used to picking up the tab. Budgeting her money was a new experience. She could pay for her meal tonight, but she'd have to eat cold cuts and peanut butter to compensate for the splurge.

Claire turned the bill in her direction, mentally divvying it up. "Mine is twenty-six—"

Merry interrupted. "Uh-uh. I'm picking up the tab tonight."

Claire tried not to show her relief. "You don't have to—"

"Shush. Consider it a welcome-to-Steadfast dinner."

After Merry paid, they moved to the parking lot. Claire immediately realized the situation was awkward. Merry had her car. She had none. Merry thought she was staying at the motel, which was the opposite direction of the library. Claire was tired. It was dark. She wanted to get to bed, yet she had to play out her lie. "Night, Merry. Thanks for the nice—"

Then came the words she'd dreaded. "Claire, let me drop you off at the motel."

"No thanks. I could use the walk after that delicious dinner."

"Nonsense. It's nearly ten. I'm not going to let you walk a mile in the dark alone. Not even in Steadfast." She opened the passenger's door and waited for Claire to get in.

Claire had no choice. They headed toward the motel.

"How do you like the luxuries at the Sleepy Time?"

Claire assumed Merry was being sarcastic. She'd never even seen the place, but she could make an assumption based on the size of Steadfast and the name of the motel that its luxuries did not go beyond a plastic drinking glass and a box of scratchy tissues. "It's nice. Simple, but nice."

"What room are you in?"

"Uh…105." She hoped it was a safe guess. Every motel had to have a first floor, didn't it?

"You mean Five?"

"Yeah. Five." She clenched her teeth.

Merry turned a corner, and the motel came into view. It was typical small-town fare with eight units and an office on one end. There was a car in front of Unit Five. The light was on.

"You sure you're in Five?"

Claire thought fast. "Sim must be up."

"Oh, that's right. Sim. We've been talking about other things this evening. Horrible me, I temporarily forgot about her."

Me too! Claire's gut swelled with panic. Poor Sim was probably frantic with worry back in the attic, wondering why she was so late.

After their argument about the girl staying out late…

As soon as Merry came to a stop, Claire was out the door. She had to restrain herself from running back to the library. She leaned down to peer in the car. "Thanks for the ride, Merry—and the dinner. I'll see you tomorrow."

"Night." Merry put the car in drive, then put it back into park. "I'll wait to see you safely inside."

Claire spotted a pop machine. "Don't bother. I'm going to get Sim a Dr. Pepper—a peace offering for being late."

Merry nodded and finally pulled away. Claire wasted no time. She ran back the way they had come.

That was close. Too close. Her sigh was heavy with relief, yet edged with the weight of her continuing and broadening deceit. It was costing a great deal to weave this intricate web of lies, and she knew the Father's heart must be pained over her deception.

She paused behind a lilac bush, grabbing a breath and a prayer. *Lord, please help me find a way out of the lies. I want to live in truth, yet thinking about my secret coming out also makes me nervous. Handle it, please.*

As she resumed her jog she added, *Because I can't. I can't.*

Merry pulled into the driveway of her home and shut off the car. When she was collecting her purse she noticed Claire's purse on the floor of the passenger side. She could run it back to the motel or bring it to the library in the morning.

I'll call.

She went inside, looked up the phone number for the Sleepy Time, and dialed. She recognized the owner's voice. "Hey, Oscar, Merry Cavanaugh here."

"Long time no see, Merry. How you doin'?"

"Fine, fine. I know it's late, but I needed to speak to one of your guests. Claire Adams? She's in Unit Five."

A moment of silence.

"No Claire Adams here, Merry."

"Maybe I got the room number wrong."

"The number don't matter. I don't have any Claire Adams checked in, period."

Merry's stomach clenched. "Are you sure?"

"I only have eight rooms. I may be getting old, but I can still keep track of eight rooms. Besides, only three are filled."

Merry mumbled a good-bye and hung up. What was going on? Why would Claire lie about where she was staying?

Merry grabbed her keys.

When one *had* to comb the streets, Steadfast was the place to do it.

Merry backtracked to the Sleepy Time, then drove toward Bon Vivant. She tried to think of every place she'd ever seen Claire. The choices were slim: the grocery store, Bailey's restaurant, and the library. With each block traveled, her anger grew. Why would Claire lie to her?

Merry turned onto the square. The grocery was closed. So was the libr—

She stopped the car in the middle of the street. Was that Claire running through the drive-through of the bank? There was nothing in that direction except—

The back of the library.

Although no clear thought formed, a vague suspicion caused Merry to pull over and shut off the car. She got out and walked toward the back of the library. She hesitated at the corner, peeking around. She caught a glimpse of Claire turning into the alcove that held the back door.

What is she doing?

Merry hugged the wall and edged closer. The door was just clicking shut when she reached it. *How did Claire get in? The door should be locked.*

She put her ear to the door. Faint footsteps. She cracked it open. The storeroom was dark. Claire was walking around in the dark?

Merry had had enough. She threw open the door. It banged against some boxes. She flipped on the lights, spotting Claire on the stairway leading to the attic. Claire froze like a deer caught in headlights.

Merry didn't even try to hide her anger. *"What* do you think you're doing?"

Claire had to remind herself to breathe.

"Hi, Merry."

Merry slid inside and let the door close. She crossed her arms. She lifted an eyebrow.

Claire glanced upward to the attic, then to the main library. If Sim was back, she didn't want to give her away. One of them caught was enough. If only she could keep Merry right here in the store-room. "Care to hear an interesting story?"

"Absolutely. Let's go." Merry headed to the main library.

"But—"

Merry was already at the door. *Oh dear. Ready or not, here we come.*

Either Sim was not around, or she was a good hider. They sat in the reading area where Sim usually slept, Claire on one vinyl chair, Merry on another. Claire told Merry how she'd ended up in the library attic, about giving up her fortune. She mentioned that she'd had her own business but left out the details of her profession and her fame.

Merry's laugh was bitter. "You felt strong enough direction to give up the fabric of your entire life on the basis of a few verses and the fact that you liked a painting? On a whim?"

"Not a whim. God told me to do it."

"No, that lady, Michelle Jofsky, told you to do it."

"What about the old man in McDonald's? Or the hymn that said, 'Go, labor on'?"

"So you give up your life because of two strangers and an old hymn?" Merry shook her head. "That's crazy."

"I am *not* crazy!"

Merry raised her hands, fending off the outburst. "You seem like a nice lady, but nobody—*nobody*—does what you did."

"But they should."

Merry laughed. "Oh, that would be productive. What would happen if the entire world roamed around aimlessly, waiting for the skies to open up so God's voice could filter down?"

Claire blinked back tears. She liked Merry. She wanted her to understand and support her. "You're bitter and confused about your family's deaths. I understand that. But God does direct people's lives. I know it."

Merry shrugged. "Oh, I do too. Pawns on a chessboard, that's what we are. Knock us down, move us out without a second thought."

"I am not God's pawn."

Merry raised an eyebrow. "You act like one. This is not the fifteenth century, where people become monks and roam the Italian countryside like St. Francis of Assisi. You don't see people stripping naked in the town square to show they reject the trappings of the world."

"I don't need your approval for what I've done."

"Don't you? Isn't that why you told me your story?"

Merry's question stabbed. Claire moved behind a chair. "I told you because you asked for an explanation as to why I'm living in the library attic."

"Freeloading in the library attic."

"Fine! I'll leave in the morn—"

"Stop it, both of you!"

They turned to see Sim emerge from the stacks.

Merry extended a hand in her direction but talked to Claire. "We haven't even talked about you dragging your niece through all—"

"I'm not her niece."

Merry's eyes widened. Claire moved to Sim's side and touched her shoulder. "Sim, don't—"

Sim shucked off her touch. There was a crease between her eyebrows, and her jaw was set for a fight. She looked to Merry. "Claire and I are not related."

"So who are you?"

"I'm a runaway. I ended up in Steadfast, and Claire was already here. There's no connection. No matter what she tries to tell you, God did not send her here to help me."

Merry snickered and arched a brow at Claire. "You've tried to brainwash the girl into believing your God scenario?"

"It's not a scenario. It's the truth."

"So you're both staying in the attic?"

"Not me." Sim eyed Merry. "You're sitting on my bed. I move three of the chairs together. The attic is Claire's home, not mine."

"The chairs can't be comfortable."

Sim shrugged. "They're better than the floor. At least Claire's got a bed."

"I offered it to—"

"There's a bed in the attic?" Merry's eyes flitted, and she changed her question to a statement. "There's a bed in the attic. I remember seeing it when I first came here. The attic was the librarian's apartment in the thirties. The one who died. The library ghost."

"What?" Claire stared at Merry.

The other woman flipped the question away and turned to Sim. "Why did you run away from home?"

Sim's jaw tightened. "My parents are dead."

Merry's face showed her shock. "Your…?"

Sim pulled the third chair around and straddled it, going eye-to-eye with Merry. "You lost your husband and son in a plane crash. I lost my parents in a car crash, last Christmas."

Merry reached across the space between them and touched her arm. Sim did not pull away. "I'm so sorry. I know exactly what you're going through."

"Yeah, I guess you do."

"I came to Steadfast because Blanche is a good friend of my mom's. She told me about the job opening." Merry shrugged. "I wanted to start fresh."

"That's what I'm trying to do. I was handed off to an aunt and uncle who don't want me. And I don't want them. So I ran away."

"Things must have been bad to make you do that, to prefer staying in a library with a stranger."

"Like I said, I'm not *with* Claire. We're here separately."

Claire felt like a smudge on a clean cloth.

Merry's face lit up. "You can stay with me. At my house."

"I can?"

"Sure. I have an extra room that has an old couch in it. The room's crammed with boxes I haven't unpacked yet, but a couch has got to be better than three chairs pushed together."

Sim backtracked into the stacks, coming back with her pack. "I'm ready."

Claire's thoughts crashed. *What was happening?* "But she has to stay here. With me."

Sim stared her down. "I was never *with* you, Claire. You've got the attic, and that's great. But frankly, I'm tired of sleeping on chairs. I know a good offer when I hear it." She turned to Merry. "Can we go now? I've had a hard night. I'm beat."

Merry stood. "Sure."

Claire knew her mouth was open but she had trouble closing it. "What about me?"

Merry and Sim stopped at the front door. "For the time being you can stay in the attic, Claire. You're not hurting anything. But I wouldn't tell anyone else. They may not approve of a city building being used as a boarding house."

"After all, you can't turn down what God provided, can you?" Sim's smile was nasty.

Merry hesitated. "If there was more room at my place, I'd ask you to stay too."

Sim opened the front door and was gone into the darkness. Merry got her key ready to lock the door behind her. "See you tomorrow. Turn off the lights."

Claire stared at the locked door. What had just happened?

Claire flipped off the lights of the library. She stood in the foyer and looked out over the darkened room. The shadowy recesses mirrored her thoughts. Nothing was clear. Nothing was lit by understanding. All was vague and dark and uncertain.

It wasn't fair. Not fair at all. She'd done everything God had asked of her. She'd been open to His guidance. Then why weren't things working out? Why was her charge this independent, arrogant, unappreciative kid? Why didn't He give her a child who was moldable, teachable, lovable?

With her next breath another thought entered. Was it possible Sim wasn't a part of her journey after all? Had Claire projected an agenda of her own, missing God's entirely?

She noticed the mural on her right. Either way, she was living a joke. Claire Adams, the great mosaic artist brought to a library in need of her services. Yet she couldn't help. Shouldn't help. Like it or not, the mural was being handled by someone else.

The situation was laughable. It was ridiculous. It was stupid. And she wasn't going to be a part of it anymore.

She strode toward the swinging doors leading to the attic. She'd pack up her things and be at the bus stop when the bus arrived at one in the morning. She'd go back to Kansas City, crash at Darla's, and see what could be salvaged of her studio. Her life. She'd plead temporary insanity, take the I-told-you-sos that would surely come, and start over.

She pushed open the door, then let it bounce against her hand.

No. She couldn't give up this soon, this hastily. God had never promised it would be easy.

But there *was* something she could do to feel better…

She looked over her shoulder, her eyes pegging the phone on Merry's desk. *Yes, that I can do.*

She sat in Merry's chair and dialed a number she'd purposely memorized. Darla answered after the second ring, her voice groggy from sleep. "Hello?"

"Did I wake you?"

"Claire?"

"Hi."

"Hi?" She sounded wide-awake now. "Where are you? How are you? Are you okay?"

"I'm fine." She found herself crying. "Really. I'm just a little homesick."

"Then come home."

She doesn't know how close I've come. "I can't. I think I need to stay awhile longer."

"Uh-uh. Forget that. You're needed here. I've been half-crazed trying to figure out how to get ahold of you."

"What's wrong?"

"Nothing's wrong. Everything's right. Too right. Regina from the gallery called and said you've been offered a commission."

Claire rubbed the space above her eyes. "From whom?"

"St. Michael's is building a new church—a campus, really—out south of town, and they want you to create a mosaic mural that would wrap around the entire front of the sanctuary. We're talking twenty-five feet high by a hundred wide."

Claire let her mouth drop open. Most of her murals averaged eight by sixteen or twenty. To have one that was two—no, more than *fifteen* times as large was beyond her ken.

"They saw that one religious piece you did at that Nazarene college and said they could tell your faith is…what words did Regina use? *On track?* Something like that. They said they can tell you're a godly woman. Regina said they'd give you free rein as to content."

The commission of a lifetime.

"Claire? Are you still there?"

Her throat tightened. Oh yeah, she was *there* all right—if *there* meant Steadfast, Kansas.

"Claire!"

"I'm here."

"They said you could practically name your price. They've had a donor stipulate that his or her donation be toward a Claire Adams mural."

"Someone asked for me by name?"

"You bet. Whether you run away to who-knows-where or not, your name is still known. Your art is still in demand. And this would be a way to get you beyond the work you do for the movie-star set, right? It would be doing something big—huge—for the Big Guy in the sky."

"I *am* doing something for God. Here."

"Oh, right. I forgot."

Claire twisted the telephone cord around her finger. A commission for a church. Surely God would approve of that?

"Why don't you give me a phone number, and I'll have the man from the church call—"

"No." She hadn't meant to say it. She hadn't wanted to say it. But she'd said it.

"What do you mean, no?"

Yeah, Claire. What do you mean, no? She examined her motives. "I…I can't do it. I gave all that up."

"Which proved you *could*. You've had a nice sabbatical, but now it's time to go on with your life."

"But I was sent here."

"By the way, where is *here?*"

"I can't tell you."

"Forgive me for saying this—" impatience overflowed Darla's words—"but you're acting foolish. You wanted to follow Jesus, and that's commendable. But now He's placed this commission—for a church—right in your lap. He wants you to take it."

Darla's brazenness made her sit up straighter. "He does, now does He?"

"Well, yeah. He certainly wouldn't want you to give *this* up."

"Are you sure about that?"

"No."

Claire rubbed her eyes. "I didn't call to be confused."

"Sorry. I can't help that. Call the man. What can it hurt?"

"Maybe…"

"You got a pencil?"

She found one and took down the number of Dwight Avery.

"I'd better go, Claire, but I'm glad you call—hey, why *did* you call?"

Her reason had evaporated and she couldn't recapture it. "I just needed to hear a friendly voice."

"Anytime. I mean it. Call Avery, okay?"

"I'll think about it."

Claire hung up, completely drained. Why was God doing this to her? Offering her a big church project—which she'd longed for—for big money, when she wasn't supposed to be doing *any* commission for *any*body or *any* money. Why couldn't anything be simple?

Tears threatened. She needed sleep but feared she'd get little. And yet when she stood, her legs were rubber. Did she even have the energy to make it up the stairs?

No need. There was a place to sleep right here. The chair Sim had straddled was out of place, but Claire turned it around and set the other two chairs in line. Three chairs in a row.

A makeshift bed.

She lay down, using her arm as a pillow. Then she cried herself into a fitful sleep.

Sim pulled the sheet over her shoulder. Merry's couch *was* more comfortable than the chairs in the library.

But not *that* much more comfortable.

On the way to the house she and Merry had really hit it off. And though they'd gone right to bed, she felt a bond with the young woman that she hadn't felt with Claire. Merry was a fellow survivor. She knew grief. She knew pain. She knew anger, and bitterness, and frustration, and hatred.

Merry let Sim be Sim. She didn't try to change her or analyze her. And more than anything, she didn't try to help her. Sure, she'd given her a place to sleep, but there was no intense need to be Sim's savior. Claire expected too much, wanted to give too much. She was too desperate in her need to help.

It was creepy.

Sim turned over, and with the movement her thoughts of Claire changed. She pictured her all alone in the library. Sim hadn't planned to leave her alone. It just happened. Merry offered a place to sleep, and Sim would have been a dope to refuse.

Wouldn't she?

She buried her face in the pillow. She'd still see Claire at the library during the day. Neither of them was really alone. They both had Merry as a friend. And there were Blanche, and Ivan, and Harold.

Harold.

Sim squeezed her eyes shut, trying to block the memory of Harold cowering, his eyes searching hers, asking her, *Why?*

She hadn't wanted to do it. She tried to miss him. It was the boys' fault, not hers.

You. You hurt him. And you hurt Claire.

Suddenly, the need to be near Claire consumed her. Although

she didn't like Claire's God-talk, somehow in the woman's presence, Sim felt safer, as if there were answers floating all around her…if only she could reach out and grab the right one. There were no answers alone in this room.

Sim threw the covers back and sat up. She got her pack and shoes and tiptoed downstairs. In Merry's kitchen she wrote a note, propping it against the coffeemaker.

Sim slipped in the back door of the library and carefully clicked it shut. There was no light in the attic. She wasn't sure whether she should wake Claire or just go to bed and talk to her in the morning.

It was after midnight. She decided on the latter.

Sim went into the library, heading to her bed of chairs. But when she turned the corner, she saw they were already set in a row. And occupied.

Claire must have sensed her presence because she looked up. "Sim."

"Hi."

"You're back."

"I'm back."

Claire got up, stumbling. "I was just trying out the chairs."

"What do you think?"

"They're not bad."

"No, they're not." Sim dropped her pack on the floor. "And if you don't mind, I'm really tired."

Claire backed away. "Sure. Certainly. I'll…I'll see you in the morning?"

"I'll be here."

Claire's smile made everything feel right. Or at least better.

Eleven

Let love and faithfulness never leave you;
bind them around your neck,
write them on the tablet of your heart.
Then you will win favor and a good name
in the sight of God and man.

PROVERBS 3:3–4

CLAIRE WOKE UP AND REMEMBERED.

Sim was back, and with her presence, Claire's confusion eased. A little.

She rolled onto her back. She'd come so close to leaving Steadfast and going back to her old life. What would have happened if Sim had returned only to find Claire gone for good? Sim was independent and tough—and she would have gotten tougher as she endured yet another rejection.

Thank You, Lord, for helping me stay. Forgive me for my weakness and my doubts. I still don't understand how all this is supposed to work, but I guess I have to trust You anyway. You're the boss.

Her prayer was immediately followed by a second memory. She'd been offered a project that was beyond the scope of anything she'd ever done. With a religious theme. For big money. If she accepted the project, was she betraying her initial sacrifice?

Thanks a lot, God. Is this some kind of test?

She got dressed and went downstairs to wake Sim. At least Merry was privy to their presence now, so that pressure was off—though they *would* have to keep up the pretense for everyone else.

She found Sim lying on her back, her arms folded across her chest. Although Claire realized she'd made a lot of mistakes in her handling of the girl—mainly coming on too strong—she must have done something right. Sim was back. That was the important thing.

She nudged her arm. "It's morning."

Sim opened one eye, then closed it. "So it is." She looked at her watch. "It's seven-thirty. It's late."

"Since Merry knows we're here there's no need to rush out."

"True."

"You want the shower first?"

"You go ahead."

Claire headed for the back room. "I feel like celebrating. Let's eat breakfast at the Plentiful. My treat."

And that was that.

Merry was ready to rap on Sim's door, but she found it ajar. The sheets lay rumpled on the couch. Sim's backpack was gone.

Merry headed downstairs. Had Sim gone to the library early to keep up the pretense? There was no need. From now on, she could ride to work with Merry every day.

Suddenly, she stopped on the landing, her imagination demanding her full attention. Something didn't feel right. Sim was a runaway. Was she gone? Really gone?

Merry realized she was holding her breath. She rushed downstairs. She flipped on the kitchen light. A piece of paper leaned against the coffeemaker. She snatched it up. *Thanks for the couch, but I need to go back to the library.*

Merry sighed. Sim was safe.

She should be relieved.

But she wasn't.

Obviously the bond between Sim and Claire was stronger than they let on.

Why did that make her jealous?

Sim was nervous about going to breakfast with Claire. So far her homecoming had been low-key, and Sim liked it that way. She didn't want a lecture or a renewed strategy session about how they should work harder to discover exactly why God had sent them both to this place. Couldn't Claire just let it happen? Did she have to analyze everything to death? Sim was back. Couldn't that be enough?

Apparently so. Claire was a different woman at breakfast. Gone was all lofty talk of finding their purpose. In its place was someone who talked about normal things like movies, and school, and her favorite foods.

Claire was an okay lady. And the biscuits and gravy were awesome.

It was going to be a good day.

Back in the library, Sim and Claire watched Merry's car drive up. Sim's stomach knotted.

"You as nervous as I am?"

Sim looked at Claire. "I didn't mean to hurt her. I didn't mean to hurt anybody."

"It will only be awkward for a moment."

"Promise?"

Claire didn't answer.

As they watched Merry climb the front steps, Sim had a change of plans. "I need to see her alone first. Go get the water for coffee or something, okay?"

Claire picked up the pot. "You sure?"

"I'm sure."

She headed to the rest room, leaving Sim alone.

Merry had her keys out but didn't have to use them. She came inside. "This is strange, coming to work and having the door unlocked."

"Claire's making coffee. But we left the lights off."

Merry switched them on. They could see each other clearly. "You left."

"I came back here."

"Why?"

It was hard to explain. "I couldn't risk not being here."

"I don't understand."

Sim glanced at the restroom. "I couldn't risk not being here if Claire's right about God…about us being brought here for a reason."

Merry nodded and took a long breath. "The couch is there for you, anytime you need it. And I'll be here too."

"Thanks, Merry."

Sim walked toward the stacks where she had work to do. Merry called after her. "But let me know what you find out from God, okay? I'm doing a little searching for purpose myself."

"You'll be the third to know."

There. That wasn't so bad.

It took Sim half the morning to get up enough courage to approach Harold's chair—and even then she had to make two passes at it because each time she came close, Harold showed her his back.

The third time, she didn't back off. She stood next to the chair. Harold looked up and pulled his book closer.

"Mr. Shinness, I have to talk to you."

His eyes flared. "How sharper than a serpent's tooth it is to have a thankless child! Away, away!"

Sim looked around, hoping no one was listening. "I deserve that. That's why I'm here. Throwing your groceries, pelting you with apples…it was wrong. And I want to apologize for all of us."

"A pair of stocks, you rogue!"

Sim extended both arms. "Make haste, and put me in yon stocks."

Harold hesitated, then smiled and shook his head.

Sim smiled with relief. "Sorry. I'm not up on Shakespearese. Do you forgive me?"

Harold looked at her a moment, then unfolded his body and nodded. "Give every man thine ear, but few thy voice; take each man's censure, but reserve thy judgment."

"You got a deal."

❧   ❧   ❧

Ivan lowered his arm from placing a tile and glared at Sim. "Shush, girl."

Huh?

Ivan pointed to Sim's mouth. "That whistling. This is a library, don't you know."

"Oh. Sorry."

Ivan went back to the tiles. "What're you so happy about anyway?"

Sim shrugged. "Stuff."

"Hmm." Ivan's face screwed up, like he hadn't thought about *happy* for a long time.

Sim studied him. "Aren't you happy?"

"Happy is for kids and clowns, not for old cauliflowers like me." He peered at her nose ring. "That thing has *got* to hurt."

Sim ignored his comment. She glanced at Blanche, who was busy at a computer across the room. "Why does she always call you a vegetable name?"

"Because she loves me."

"She does?"

Ivan straightened a tile with his index finger. "She just doesn't know it."

"Do you love her?"

He glanced at her. "Why should I?"

"Because you're her old sugar snap pea."

Ivan smiled. "Good one, girl. You're a regular greengrocer."

"You're not married then?"

"Was. For fifty-two years."

"Wow."

"You bet your sweet whistling, wow." Ivan sighed. "Hardest and best thing I ever did."

"Is Blanche married?"

He shook his head. "Bob died the year before Martha did. We used to play cards every Friday night. Two couples."

"One couple now."

Ivan squirmed on the stool. "Blanche doesn't think of us as a couple."

"*You* said she loves you."

He pointed toward the computers. "That Net-thing is taking her away from me."

Sim thought for a moment. "Fight for her."

"Ain't that simple."

"Does she know how you feel?"

"She should. I'm here every day with her. What more does she want?"

Sim looked from one to the other. "But you're over here and she's over there."

"Close enough."

"Maybe she wants romance? Candles and flowers. Stuff like that."

He shook his head. "Blanche is too old for that schmoozy stuff."

This was ridiculous. "I may not know much about love, but I do know you can't court a lady with you sitting on one side of the room and her on the other."

Ivan picked up a bowl of tiles and shook them. "That's *her* choice, not mine. If she wanted to, she'd take time to know how I feel." He set the bowl down with a clatter. "Now leave me alone, girl. And stop that whistling."

Sim headed back to work, but suddenly detoured down a far book aisle. She had an idea…

Late afternoon, Bailey Manson came into the library. As usual, his clothes were impeccable. Merry wondered how long it took him to get dressed every morning. She should challenge him to a race. She'd probably win—makeup and all.

Bailey strolled to the counter. Merry kept her eyes elsewhere.

"You can't ignore me forever."

She still didn't look up. "I can try."

"One of these days, you'll have to pay attention to me."

"No, I won't."

He flicked the tip of her nose so she looked up. "And today's as good a day as any. How about a date, Merry? Dinner?"

"With you?"

"Well, yes, with me. Who did you think I was asking for, Ivan?"

"Two artichokes in search of a salad."

"What's that supposed to mean?"

She was weary of fending him off. "We've been through this."

"I know, I know. You're a widow. You don't think you're ready."

"That's only one reason."

He raised an eyebrow.

She tapped a stack of note cards into place. "Don't force me to tell you the real reason I keep telling you no."

"You think I can't handle it?"

"Bailey…"

He planted his feet. "Go on. Give it your best shot." Bailey's face revealed he wasn't as sure of himself as he put on.

Merry lowered her voice. Her first thought was to hit him hard by mentioning Jered and what she considered Bailey's lack of parenting skills. But that was something better discussed in private.

"I'm waiting."

Merry had to think of something else. It didn't take long. "I've heard about your exploits, and I do not wish to be another chink in your cog."

"Chink in my…? What *are* you talking about?"

"I'm not an easy woman."

"Don't I know it."

She tried again. "I'm a widow."

He leaned over the counter to whisper. "If you were married, I wouldn't be asking you out."

"That's reassuring. But I don't think… I may be single, but I'm not loose."

He put a hand to his chest. "Am I asking you to be loose?"

"I've heard that's the kind of woman you prefer."

He stepped back, then toward her again to whisper, "Who's saying this drivel?"

People. And from what Merry had seen, Bailey did little to discourage it. His women, his clothes, the fact that he hated living in Steadfast and used his restaurant as a way to lift himself higher than anyone else—it all played into the image. "I can't remember at the moment."

"Then don't give me a hard time. I'm not a Casanova, sweeping women off their feet."

No, but you are *tiramisu, and I don't even know how to spell it.*

"So how 'bout it, Merry? Want to go out with me?"

"Not now, Bailey." She looked to the desk. Maybe it was best to quell all his hope. "And probably not ever."

He shoved his hands in his pockets. "Maybe you should remember that there aren't that many eligible bachelors in Steadfast."

He showed her his back.

Claire looked up and found Bailey standing over her table.

"Hey, Bailey."

"Morning, Claire." He handed her an envelope.

"What's this?"

"Your paycheck. One night's wages."

She stuck it between the pages of a book on the Sistine Chapel.

"Aren't you going to look at it? Don't you want to know how much it is?"

"Unless you're surprising me by giving me a hefty bonus, I have a pretty good idea. Thanks."

"You're welcome." He pinched a piece of lint from the sleeve of his jacket. "The job's still available, you know."

"No thanks. I have research to do."

He offered a smirk. "Why?"

"Why not?" She fumbled through a stack of papers, dropping a book on the floor.

Bailey reached to get it, and they nearly knocked heads. He brushed the book off and put it on the table. "You've got to admit most people don't spend time researching a paper unless they have to."

"Maybe I like knowledge." It sounded lame—and defensive.

He eyed her, tapping his lower lip. "I'm having a hard time

figuring you out, Ms. Claire Adams." He stroked her name as though it were an alias.

She looked away. "Don't waste your time."

"I don't intend to." He took a seat. "Why are you in Steadfast, anyway? You appear to be jobless, so it isn't because of work."

A dozen lies surfaced, vying for attention. She didn't want to get caught in that snare again. It took her a moment to think of a solution. Maybe part of the truth would appease him.

She set her pencil down and leaned on the opened book. "It's an odd reason, Bailey, one that doesn't make any sense to anyone but me."

He leaned close. "Sounds intriguing."

She leaned back. "I saw a painting of Steadfast in a museum and was drawn to the picture, to the place." She thought of something honest she could add that might lend credence to her story. "I've recently gone through a divorce. I'm starting over, and the essence of Steadfast portrayed in that painting appealed to me."

He sat back, making a face. "Sheesh. What is it with you women? Merry comes here to start over. You come here to start over. You're putting a lot of pressure on little ol' Steadfast. I'm not sure it's strong enough to take it."

"But you're here. You must like what it has to offer."

He shoved his chair back and stood. "Yeah, well, I was born here. What can I say? It's as good a place as any."

"Exactly." Her nod was quite triumphant.

He stared at her a moment, then wagged a finger. "I'll buy your story. For now. But I've got a feeling there's more to your presence here than you're telling me."

She turned back to the book. "Don't strain yourself."

When he didn't respond, she looked up. *Go away. Please go away, Bailey.*

He planted his arms on the table, leaning close, his grin smug. "I've got my eye on you, Claire—and it's not because you're pretty. You have a secret, and I intend to find out what it is."

"Good-bye, Bailey."

With a wink, he executed a perfect pivot and left.

It took Claire a good fifteen minutes to calm herself enough to read what was on a page.

Claire's nerves plagued her all day. She couldn't stop worrying about Bailey's curiosity. The world wouldn't end if people knew who she was, but things *would* change. Whether they recognized her name as an artist or not, they would be affected by knowing she was somebody that a lot of people *did* know. When the most famous Steadfast citizen was a ninety-year-old man who had been the campaign manager for Hubert Humphrey's presidential run, any *name* was news. And once the town anointed her a *name*, all hope of discovering a new purpose separate from her past would be impossible.

She had to stay anonymous. But how could she dissuade Bailey's interest? She hadn't done anything suspicious—except be a stranger.

Perhaps that was enough.

Claire heard the jangle of Merry's keys. It was time to close down the research shop. She started to pile her books onto a corner of the table. It was nice to know they'd be left undisturbed until tomorrow.

"You two leaving for dinner, or staying?" Merry called out.

"We're staying."

Claire was surprised at Sim's reply. "We are?"

Sim didn't answer. Merry said her good-byes and locked the door behind her.

They were alone.

Claire looked at Sim. "What's this about dinner? You've made it clear you prefer spending your evenings away from the library."

Sim shrugged. "What's on the menu?"

Claire thought about the meager pickins in the cooler. "Nothing exotic, but I'm sure I can find something."

"Good." Sim headed toward the back room. "Want me to do the fixing?"

"Sure. I'll finish straightening up and be there in a minute." She thought of something. "Actually…Sim?"

The girl stopped at the door. "What?"

"Over dinner…there's a book I'd love to discuss with you."

"Which one?"

"Atlas Shrugged."

Sim's smile made John Galt's ninety-page monologue worth the effort.

Twelve

Direct me in the path of your commands,
for there I find delight.
Turn my heart toward your statutes and
not toward selfish gain.

PSALM 119:35–36

"MERRY! COME SEE THIS."

Merry joined Blanche, who stood beside the computer she always used. Blanche waved a piece of paper. "I found it taped to my computer."

Merry read the paper.

There are lots of things
With which I'm blessed,
Tho' my life's been sunny and blue,
But of all my blessings,
This one's best:
To have a friend like you.

In times of trouble
Friends will say,
"Just ask, I'll help you through it."
But you don't wait
For me to ask,
You just get up and do it!

And I can think
Of nothing in life

That I could more wisely do,
Than know a friend,
And be a friend,
And love a friend like you.

Merry looked up when she saw it was from Ivan. "What do you know?"

"Amazing, isn't it?" Blanche shook her head. "I never knew the old kumquat had it in him."

"Apparently that old kumquat loves you."

"Temporary insanity. He's afraid of rotting on the vine. He just wants to be picked."

"Pick him while he's ripe, Blanche. You have to know he's been upset about you spending so much time with your on-line acquaintances."

Blanche put a finger to her lips. "Speaking of...I wondered if you had a photo of yourself I could send to a man in Cincinnati."

"A photo of me? I'm not *that* desperate."

"You don't understand." Blanche leaned close. "I'd pretend you were me. He wants a photo, but he thinks I'm thirty and—"

"No way."

"But Merry—"

"That's deceitful. And dangerous." She put a hand on Blanche's, remembering her apple-pie conversation with Claire a few days before. "Why are you looking elsewhere when right here, in this town, in this library, you have a man who loves you?"

"A kumquat in the hand?"

"Is worth three on-line veggies in the bush."

Blanche read the verse again. "This *is* nice."

"So, what are you going to do?"

Blanche screwed her mouth to the left, then the right. "Where *is* the old kumquat this morning?"

"He should be here any minute."

She sighed and wiggled her toes. "Then I suppose I'll have to pin him down and tell him thank you."

Merry smiled. "Can I watch?"

She put a hand to her chest. "Why, Merry Cavanaugh! What would your mother say?"

"This *is* a public place, Blanche."

Blanche folded the note in half. "Then I'll make every attempt to contain myself."

Sim pumped a fist in the air. One down, one to go. She glanced toward the mural. She'd taped the note to Ivan's stool. It was ready and waiting for him—if he ever got here.

At that moment she saw him come through the door. Merry greeted him with a mischievous smile. "Morning, Ivan."

He flipped a hand, a gesture that could be taken as a greeting or something worse. He headed for his stool. His eyes locked on the note. His forehead furrowed.

Sim slunk into the stacks to watch.

He opened the note. His left eyebrow raised, then lowered. "Well, I'll be."

"You'll be what?" It was Blanche, standing on the edge of his territory, her note in hand. She moved from side to side, making her skirt sway like a schoolgirl in the midst of a flirt.

"I'll be busy." He folded the note, slid it in his shirt pocket, grabbed a bowl of green tiles, and took his seat. He rifled through the bowl, as if looking for one specific tile, ignoring Blanche's courting dance.

She stared at him a moment, then picked up a bowl of blue tiles, doing her own sifting.

Ivan's right pinky twitched.

Sim couldn't believe it. How could they be so stubborn? She was tempted to—

Suddenly, Blanche put the bowl down with a clatter.

Ivan's hand momentarily stopped, then resumed its digging.

Blanche took a pen out of her shirt pocket and began to click the end of it, down, up, down, up.

His fingers delved deeper into the dish.

She began humming the "1812 Overture," zipping straight to the climax.

"Shush!"

Blanche smiled. Throwing all subtlety aside, she cleared her throat repeatedly, raising the volume as well as the pitch until it was nearly a squeak.

She got him. He spun toward her, losing a dozen tiles over the top of the bowl. "Will you *please* be quiet!"

Blanche put a hand to her chest. "Why, I'm sorry, Ivan. Was I disturbing you?"

He groaned and picked up the fallen tiles. "The gig's up, Blanche. I know your game."

"Game?"

He patted his shirt pocket. "What's this about, woman?"

She shuffled her shoulders. "I hate it when you call me that, you old squash."

"I can't call you *woman,* but you can call me *squash?*"

"An *old* squash." She let her shoulders settle. Her voice softened. "But actually, I love vegetables. It's a sign of affection."

"Maybe calling you *woman* is a sign of affection too."

She crossed her arms and glared at him. "Is it?"

"Could be."

Sim closed her eyes. This was not how she had thought this conversation would play out, which, considering the dialogue participants, was not a total surprise.

Blanche pulled the love note from her pocket and held it out to him.

He took it. "What's this? A recipe for arsenic stew?"

She threw her hands in the air and turned on her heel. "You're impossible."

"I…" He read the note. "Hey! I didn't write this."

Blanche did an about-face and returned, her finger extended ahead of her, ready to impale the note. "Your name's on it."

He drew the other note from his shirt. "And your name's on this."

She moved her lips as she read the words. "It's the same! But I didn't leave this for you."

"Your name's on it."

"Well, I didn't—"

He took the note back and folded it. "I should have known it wasn't real. A token of love from a woman who longs to slice and dice me?"

"And kind words from an old rigatoni? Ridiculous."

"Rigatoni is not a vegetable."

"I've moved on to pasta. I'm tired of dealing with vegetables like you."

When she started to walk away, Sim was on the verge of popping out of the stacks to explain the whole thing. But then she heard something that froze her in her tracks.

Ivan's voice lost its edge. "Blanche, please come back."

She turned slowly. "And why should I, Mr. Manicotti-breath?"

He rose from the stool and took a step toward her. "Because the words in the notes…I like them."

"You do?"

He nodded. "They're better than what I could have put together."

She came closer. "Me too. I never was good at lovey-dovey stuff. But that doesn't mean I don't feel it, want to say it."

"Yeah. Me too."

There was a moment of silence. "So you really think I'm a blessing?"

"Sure I do."

"'Cause I think you're a good friend."

"Good."

Blanche beamed.

"But if we didn't send the notes, who did?"

Blanche looked to the ceiling, then her eyes lit up. "Must be the library ghost."

"Nonsense. Nobody's brought that up in years."

"That doesn't mean it doesn't exist." Blanche swished her skirt again. "Merry told me Harold got some new licorice the other day. No one knows how. And now the notes…"

"I refuse to believe in ghosts." He looked toward the far corner. "Maybe Harold wrote the notes."

Blanche shook her head. "Harold would have quoted Shakespeare."

"Then maybe Merry."

"Merry's methods are more direct."

"Then who?"

They both looked at the notes, then at each other. Sim pulled back, deeper into the stacks.

"That only leaves Claire and that girl."

Blanche considered it. "They don't know us well enough to do this for us. Besides, why would they?"

"Then I guess you're right."

"I am?"

He grinned. "It must be the library ghost."

"Well, I'll be."

"That's *my* line." Ivan put the bowl of tiles down. "You want to go to the Plentiful and have a cinnamon roll?"

"Love to."

Sim did a little jig. The library ghost had struck again.

Merry turned off the television. The sounds of TV people going through the highs and lows of their lives were often distracting, but tonight their inane existence—they dared to be happy—got on her nerves.

She hated them.

The sudden silence reinforced her depression and loneliness. A quiet house in the morning didn't bother her, nor one after work. But once the sun went down, it was disconcerting to have no hope of hearing anyone's voice but her own until morning, when she went back to the library. She had two lives: the one with people at work, and the one without them. Alone. Her public and private faces were not the same. Two masks, veiling the real Merry Cavanaugh.

If only Sim were here.

A quick thought sped in and then out. Had she invited Sim to stay with her for her own benefit more than Sim's? Was she *that* desperate to not be alone?

What bothered her more than aloneness was the fact that she was getting used to it. There was shame in that. Since her family was gone for good, shouldn't she be grieving for good?

Yet acceptance was not assent. Battles were still fought daily. Merry lived in a constant state of frustration at her family's absence. Every time she'd get a notion to share a thought, ponder a decision, or discuss her day, she'd find her sounding board gone. Without Lou's response, the details of her life were not free to return to her nourished and refreshed. Without his input, they fell to the ground half-formed. And because she was getting used to not receiving feedback, she feared she was getting used to not receiving anything from anybody. The wall that separated her from the world was getting higher. And the bricks of grief were very strong, rough, and heavy.

Hadn't God created man and woman to be together? Two by two? Wasn't she obligated to be half of a couple? Wasn't that the right order of things?

Everyone said she should date again. Bailey had certainly made his intentions known. Yet even when her interest flared, she couldn't bring herself to do it. Dating led to commitment, and commitment to grief.

Besides, it wasn't like she needed a man. She'd done all right since Lou's death. She wasn't one of those women who didn't know how to balance a checkbook or unstop a toilet. She'd always prided herself on being able to do whatever needed to be done. She didn't need a man to *do* for her.

But did she need a man to *be* for her?

If she were to date…the main advantage of living in Steadfast was also the main disadvantage. What Bailey said was true: The small population limited her options in the dating game. Sometimes it seemed the only answer was to move back to the city for a few months, tap into the larger population pool, find a companion, and then return to Steadfast. But such schemes weren't feasible. And so she waited.

Would her heart ever be ready to let a second man into her life? Maybe if she started slowly? Lunch? Or even dinner?

Dinner.

Blanche and Ivan were going out to dinner together after accepting each other's love notes. A start. A friendship working toward commitment.

Yesterday, Bailey asked her to dinner. She'd gotten out of every date with him by using a variation of Lou's death as an excuse. It was a bad habit. Whenever she didn't want to deal with something, she fell back on her widowhood. *"I'm not ready."* Would she ever be ready—even if the right man *did* come along?

The right man would have to be full of determination. He'd have to pass her long mental checklist: good-looking, kind, funny, ambitious to the right degree, smart enough to discuss the newest books in the library, and laid-back enough to watch Abbott and Costello movies. Considering the condition of her Victorian house, he would need to be handy at repairs and even-tempered. She'd prefer he had a job that made him happy so he wouldn't be moody and complain all the time, making Merry work to the point of exhaustion to build his ego at the expense of her own.

And he needed a strong faith. Even though her own faith rode the roller coaster, that was one of the things she missed most about Lou. His faith. Whatever had happened in their lives, he had a way of looking to the good of it. So much so that sometimes it drove her crazy. How many times had she heard him say, "God is in control, Mer. He's got it. We don't have to worry; we just have to give it up to Him."

Yeah, right.

Lou had been big on *giving it up to Jesus.* Can't pay the bills? Give it up to Jesus. Lou's boss treating him unfairly? Give it up to Jesus. Justin needs tubes in his ears? Give it up to Jesus.

Yes, in these instances everything *had* turned out for the best, but it galled Merry that Lou could make it so incredibly simple. Such a faith seemed naive and immature. Shouldn't believing in one almighty God, Creator of heaven and earth, be complicated and hard?

Faith *was* hard. There was no way Merry could find any good in her family dying. And if she was a woman of faith, shouldn't she be able to do that? Think a certain thought, pray a certain prayer so it would all make sense? And where, oh *where*, was the promised comfort of Jesus' *everlasting arms?*

It was God's fault. If He loved her so much, He'd *make* her faith strong. He'd grab her from the pit and pull her into His arms like a father pulling a petulant child into his lap, rocking and making soft noises until the child finally relaxed and accepted the love he needed and longed for.

She threw the remote to the floor. She had to quit passing the buck. It wasn't God's fault. It was hers. Everything was her fault. She was a failure on every front. She had been a mediocre wife, a passable mother, a reluctant friend, an average librarian, and a doubting, bitter child of God.

She mentally gathered the smothering feelings, as if they were bed linens she needed to wash clean, and stuffed them into the back of her mind to deal with later. She pushed herself off the couch. There was only one thing that could make her feel better.

It was nearly dark, that gloaming time of day when the eyes had trouble focusing in the half-light. Better true dark or true light than this ambiguous in-between.

Merry stumbled through her garden to the place of her relief. The shrine—her secret shrine. She was glad it was tucked into the far corner of her fenced yard, hidden from view by a row of huge lilac bushes. People would never suspect an abandoned shed contained a place of mourning. They'd never understand her need to remember when they all thought she should forget. Maybe if she hadn't moved to Steadfast, had stayed near the place where Lou and Justin were buried, she wouldn't need a shrine. A place to visit, connect, and grieve.

She shoved open the rickety door, flicked on a flashlight, and found the matches. She lit two candles so she could turn off the artificial light. The wavering flicker reminded her of Christmas Eve church services, when only candles lit the holy place.

The walls of the shed were covered with ancient shelves and hooks for rakes and brooms. Merry wasn't interested in what was above, but what she'd created below the trappings of the shed. She'd carved out a clean corner and placed a rag rug on the clapboard floor. She sat on it now, drew her knees to her chest, and looked upon the two crosses on the wall. She'd created them from fallen branches in the yard. She smiled at the photos of her family. Lou standing in front of his new truck. Justin showing off a fresh haircut. A picture of the two of them displaying their fishing catch.

Merry's eyes did inventory. One picture was gone.

She turned on the flashlight and swiped its beam over every corner. The picture was gone! Someone had taken it.

She shivered. This place was secret! No one knew about it. And even if they did, who would take a picture of herself and her son at a baseball game? Why would they do that? How *dare* they do that!

She rubbed a hand over her face, trying to collect her thoughts. When was the last time she'd been here? A week ago, on the seventeen-month anniversary of the crash. The picture was there then.

A sudden weariness fell onto her shoulders, like a pack too heavy to carry. She flipped off the flashlight and toppled over on her side, curling into a ball. She pulled Justin's stuffed monkey to the place beneath her chin. The flowers from her last visit were wilting, and she chastised herself for not bringing replacements. She didn't have the energy. She plucked one of the daisies and spun it near her nose. Its fragrance was bitter.

As was her heart.

Jered belched loudly as he drove around the square on his way to pick up Darrell and Moog. He took the final swig of a beer and tossed the can behind the seat just as he spotted his father tiptoeing down the steps of the library. How strange.

His father drove away, and Jered pulled into the vacated space out front. He looked at the library. It was completely dark. So why was his father sneaking around its entrance? What was he up to?

Jered put the truck in park but left the engine running. He ran up the library steps and stopped short when he saw a vase of flowers. They looked like the kind they had in their backyard.

He plucked a note out of the stems. *Merry, I won't give up on us. Bailey.*

No way. His dad was two-faced, conniving, selfish, lustful—

His dad didn't deserve Merry. If she ever agreed to go out with his dad… The thought was disgusting. Merry was *his* friend. His dad couldn't have her.

He crumpled his father's note and stuffed it in his pocket.

Thirteen

Friend deceives friend, and no one speaks the truth.
They have taught their tongues to lie;
they weary themselves with sinning.

JEREMIAH 9:5

MERRY AND BLANCHE PULLED INTO the library parking lot at the same time. Merry got out first and opened the door for the older woman.

"Morning, Blanche. I should give you an award for always being my first customer, but aren't you a bit early?"

With a groan, Blanche swung her legs out of the car. "I woke up early, so decided I might as well get a jump-start on my e-mails. And as far as the award, cash is always appreciated."

"Sorry, fresh out." They started up the walk. Merry stopped at the foot of the steps, not quite registering what she was seeing.

A vase of flowers.

"Wow," Blanche said.

"Wow," Merry echoed. But her *wow* came from a different center of response. She stared at the flowers. How could something so beautiful bring back such bad memories?

"Aren't you going to get them?" Blanche started up the steps. "If you don't want them, I'll—"

"No!" Merry reached them first. "I want them."

"I would think so."

Merry ran a finger along the perfect petals.

"Who are they from?"

Merry rotated the arrangement, looking for a card. "There's no note."

"Oooh…a secret admirer—or maybe it's the library ghost."

"Maybe they're not even for me." Merry held the flowers in one hand while negotiating the key to the front door.

Blanche pushed the door open for her. "Ah, you're probably right. There are *so* many people working at the library."

Merry flipped the lights and set the flowers on the front counter. "Maybe Ivan sent them for you."

Blanche turned the vase so the best side faced the room. "If that man ever got the notion to send flowers, he'd send them to my house, not to the library. Face it, Merry, these are for you."

"I wish they had a note."

"Nah. This only makes it more interesting." Blanche put a hand beneath a blossom. "But I'm mad at you."

"Why?"

"You've been holding out on me. I didn't know you had a boyfriend."

"I don't."

"Wanna bet?"

Merry started when Sim and Claire came into the library through the storeroom. They stopped.

Merry's heart skipped a beat. She hurried behind the counter as if nothing were amiss. "Sim, you have got to quit coming in to work early. You make me look bad." She turned to Blanche. "I gave Sim a key since she's such a good worker."

"A workaholic at such a young age. I'm impressed."

Sim helped change the subject by pointing to the flowers. "Where did those come from?"

Blanche answered. "Merry has a secret admirer. There wasn't a card."

"They're beautiful." Claire moved close. "I bet they're from Bailey."

"Not hardly. Not after I rejected him again." Merry pulled the stem of a daisy into a better position. "Besides, I don't think anonymous flowers are his style. If he sent flowers he'd make sure I *knew* he sent them. There'd be a neon sign so he'd be sure to get credit."

Blanche flipped a hand. "Then that settles it. It's the library ghost."

"Merry!"

She looked up from checking out Mrs. Griswold's books on gardening to see Stu Noxley from the *Steadfast Beat* striding toward her. It was obvious by his gait he was not here for books.

"Shhh, Stu. This is a library."

Stu looked left, then right, as if just realizing that fact. "Oops. Sorry." He put a hand on the counter. "I'm here on official business." He pointed to the camera around his neck. "I got a lead on your library ghost, and I've come over to do an article on it, him, her... whatever. Wanted to take a few pictures too."

She did a double take at Mrs. Griswold, whose mouth had formed an *O*. "An article?"

Blanche came running, rubbing her hands together. "Yee-ha! It's about time we got some action in this town."

"The whole town's talking about the ghost," Stu said. "I'm not too late, am I? I mean, the ghost is still doing its stuff, isn't it?"

Blanche pointed to the flowers. "You bet! The ghost left flowers on the front step this morning."

Merry let her frustration out on a huff. "Stu, I don't think this is a good idea. It's not a ghost at all; there's no such thing. It's just someone doing nice things without taking any credit."

"Now that *is* a big deal." Stu readied his pad and pencil. "So what's this about love notes and licorice?" He raised a finger, then jotted down the words. "Oh, I like that. 'Love Notes and Licorice.' Alliteration is great for headlines."

Merry put a hand to her forehead. "Who told you about the—?"

He tapped a pencil on his pad. "I have my sources. Come on, Merry. You know the supersonic speed of the Steadfast grapevine. It's to your advantage to give me the correct information."

"But there's no information to give."

Blanche slipped a hand through Merry's arm. "Merry will be happy to give you an interview. And me too, Stu."

Mrs. Griswold raised a hand. "Me too. I thought I saw the library ghost once back when I was thirteen. I was in the corner back there—" she pointed to the corner near Harold's chair—"reading an Agnes Turnbull novel, when suddenly I saw a smoky apparition float by."

"Now we're getting somewhere!" Stu looked at his watch. "If I make the four o'clock deadline, I can get it in tomorrow's edition. I've got the one-hour photo place primed and waiting."

Merry waved him off. "I think this has gone far enough. Let's stop it right—"

"Getting greedy on me, Merry?"

"What?"

"Trying to keep the library ghost all to yourself?"

"That's ridiculous."

"Then why not cooperate?"

She thought back to the fiasco after the plane crash. "No offense, Stu, but I'm not too keen on the press."

He leaned toward her, and she saw the broken blood vessels in his nose. "Hey, I know you got burned, but I'm not like that. I won't camp outside your house or delve into your love life."

Merry's shoulders straightened. "I was *not* having an affair with George Davanos!"

Stu flipped a hand. "Never said you were. That's old news." He put an arm around Mrs. Griswold's shoulders. "I just want a local story. There's no harm in that."

"Come on, Merry." Blanche nudged her. "It will be fun."

Mrs. Griswold's head bobbed eagerly, like a child trying to cajole her parents to let her go to the circus.

Merry was surrounded. But she hoped Mrs. Griswold wouldn't get her circus.

Sim was in the middle of helping a six-year-old find the *Curious George* books when she noticed Merry talking to some guy with a camera. The man was taking notes *and* pictures. What were they up to?

Since Ivan wasn't a part of the mix, she went over to him. "Ivan?

Sir?"

He grunted.

"Can you tell me who that man is, talking to Merry?"

Ivan looked over his shoulder. "Oh. Him. Stu Noxley. He runs the paper."

"Why is he here?"

"Probably going to make a front-page story about someone who owes a buck on overdue fines. Stu can make mud out of orange juice."

Blanche rushed over, her arms waving. "Come on, you two. Stu's doing an article about the library ghost. He may want to interview you."

Ivan's head moved side to side. "Uh-uh. No way. If you let Stu have that story, the next thing you know we'll have ghostbusters in here, messing with the peace and quiet."

Sim found it hard to swallow. "Why would he want to do an article on the library ghost?"

Blanche was pinching her cheeks like Sim had seen Scarlett O'Hara do in *Gone With the Wind*. "Not much news in Steadfast, Sim, unless you count Mildred Hannigan getting a joke printed in *Reader's Digest*. You take what you can get. And this is big."

"But how did he find out?"

Blanche's shrug was half-hearted. "The main drawback of living in a small town is the speed and degree of its grapevine. News travels fast. If you aren't careful, it'll come back and whip your backside before you finish telling it in the first place." She smoothed her flowered top over her ample hips and looked at Sim and Ivan.

They looked back.

She rolled her eyes and fluffed her hair. "Fine. You two be party poopers. I plan on being famous. Ta-ta."

Sim's heart beat in her throat. If they figured out she'd done the ghost stuff, then there was a chance they'd find out she and Claire lived in the library, and they'd send her back to Kansas City.

"What's wrong, girl? You look like an animal caught in a trap."

Close.

❧   ❧   ❧

Claire sat at her table and watched the pandemonium at the front counter. Everyone who had been in the library when the newspaper man came in was now vying for his attention, all talking at once. Her mind swam with what-ifs. If the reporter wanted the truth, it was up for grabs. The attention and scrutiny were worrisome. How were she and Sim going to slip in and out after hours with a crowd of ghost-watchers on the prowl?

Harold hung back on the edge of the group. His face was contorted. Then he shook his head, hugged a book to his chest like a shield, and scurried out. It wasn't good. Stu was scaring off the regulars.

Sim came beside her, her eyes locked on the crowd. "What are we going to do?"

"What can we do? It's like stopping an avalanche."

"But I didn't send those flowers."

Claire did a double take. "No one said you did. Why—?"

"I was the one who gave Harold the licorice and I wrote the love notes."

"Why did you do that?"

She shrugged. "But now…"

Now the truth didn't matter. Claire watched the crowd. "I'm sure the ghost is getting credit for all sorts of things. The legend has been reawakened, and there's no way the town's going to let it go back to sleep."

"It's crazy."

"Absolutely."

"I want them to leave."

"Dream on, kiddo. The town was dying for some summer excitement, and this is it."

"If only I'd taken credit for the notes and stuff, not done it anonymously."

Claire put a hand on her arm. "Your heart was in the right place. Not many people do good deeds without wanting credit."

"But it may ruin everything."

"Hopefully not."

Bailey came in the door. His eyes scanned the crowd at the front desk as he joined Sim and Claire. "What's going on?"

"Your basic feeding frenzy," Claire said.

"About what?"

"That newspaper guy got wind that the library ghost was doing good deeds and—"

"That old tall tale? That's ridiculous."

"Tell *them* that."

They watched as Stu juggled the attention of the ghost-sighters. Blanche got pushed and nearly knocked the vase of flowers off the counter.

Bailey flinched. "My flowers!"

Claire turned to him. *"Your* flowers?"

"Merry's flowers. The ones I left for her. Maybe I should go rescue—"

Claire laughed. "They're not from you anymore, Bailey. They're from the library ghost."

"What are you talking about?"

"You should have put a note on them. They've been attributed—"

"I *did* put a note on them!"

Claire shook her head. "It must have blown away. No note. No credit."

He took a step toward the counter. "That's absurd. I'm going up there and tell Merry the flowers are from me."

"You do that, Bailey. It's been nice knowing you."

He stepped back.

"Wise choice."

His breathing was labored, and Claire felt sorry for him. He was a little arrogant and snooty, but he *had* brought Merry flowers. That always earned a man extra credit.

He shoved his hands in his pockets. "Forget this. I'm going to work."

"Want me to tell Merry you were here?"

He shook his head. "No thanks. One-upped by a ghost. I can't win."

❧   ❧   ❧

"I have never been so ready to close as I am this evening." Merry got out the key to the library.

Sim peered through the front windows. "Should we make a show of leaving? Or do you think it's safe to stay in here?"

Merry looked over Sim's shoulder. "There's no crowd, but I see people in the square looking this way. There is definitely a buzz in Steadfast."

"And the article's not even out yet."

Merry made a decision. "You two have to stay with me tonight."

Claire turned surprised eyes in her direction. "But you said you didn't have room."

"I don't. Not really. I have the couch Sim almost slept in, and there's a love seat in the living room. If you curl up…"

"We'll take it." Claire glanced out the window again. "I have a bad feeling about staying here."

"I'll get my pack," Sim said.

"I'd better get a few things too."

While they were gone, Merry plucked the fallen petals from the counter. At least the ghost had good taste.

Claire came back with a shoulder tote. "You know those are from Bailey, don't you?"

"How do you—?"

"He came in this afternoon when Stu and the gaggle of ghost-busters were swarming. He told me."

"Why didn't he leave a note?"

"He said he did."

"Why didn't he come over and tell me?"

"You were busy."

The whole day had been a fiasco.

"You have a nice home."

Claire meant what she said. Merry's home *was* nice. Warm. Cozy. Merry made one last stir of the spaghetti sauce and put the spoon on a spoon rack. "It's small but all I can afford. Being the sole bread-winner is new to me."

"Didn't your husband...? I mean, wasn't there insurance money?"

Merry shook her head and tipped the lid on the boiling pasta. "What did two twentysomethings need with life insurance?"

"So you got nothing?" That didn't seem right.

"I got a little from selling our house, but I used that money to buy this one. And someday I may see some cash from the lawsuit."

"Lawsuit?"

Merry handed Sim a loaf of French bread. "Would you slice and butter this, please?"

"Sure."

Merry opened the cupboard and handed three plates to Claire. "There's a class-action suit going on against the airline, but it will take years. And Sun Fun Airlines has declared bankruptcy, so even if we do get a settlement..." She shrugged.

"I didn't get anything from my parents' crash." Sim's words were matter-of-fact. "But it was Dad's fault. He was drunk."

"How awful."

"It's okay. I've got plenty of money. We were rich. Now my aunt and uncle are rich, thanks to my trust fund."

Merry exchanged a glance with Claire. "Since they're using your money, maybe you should go back and—"

Sim spun around, her shaking head spurring the movement. "I don't *care* about the money." Crumbs fell from the knife. "Not really."

"But the money can assure you of a future. College."

Sim turned back to the bread. "I'll get to college on my own. I'm smart. I'll get a scholarship or something."

"But you need a home, Sim. It's summer now, but school will be starting and you need to go back and—"

Sim put the knife down and faced them. "Why can Claire give up her money but I can't give up mine?"

There was a pause, and Claire grappled for an answer. "Because I'm supposed to give up mine." It sounded more like a question.

"Because God asked you to?" There was derision in Sim's voice.

Claire's throat was dry. "Yes."

"Maybe God's asked me to give up mine too. You've said you were brought here for me. Then maybe I was brought here too. Maybe God brought me here. Maybe He wanted me to leave my aunt and uncle and be out on my own."

"You can't be on your own. You're only fourteen."

"But I'm not alone. I'm here with you two."

Claire moved to touch the girl's shoulder. "It's not the same. I haven't called the authorities because I'm trying to figure out what God's up to, but eventually you *will* have to go back."

Sim knocked her hand away. "So this is all a ploy? You've been pretending to be my friend while planning to betray me?"

"Claire's right, Sim. There are rules." Merry sounded as dismayed as Claire felt. "Rules to protect—"

Sim moved so the kitchen table stood between them. "Protect me from who? Bad people? Those *rules* chose bad people as my guardians. They gave me over to an aunt and uncle who made me stay in a basement without any windows, with no bathroom—"

Merry's eyes widened. "They locked you in the basement?"

Sim looked away. "Not locked. But it was dark."

"It didn't have a bathroom?"

"Well...there was a toilet, but the room wasn't finished."

Aha. If Sim exaggerated about one thing, perhaps she'd exaggerated about the rest. Perhaps her aunt and uncle weren't horrible people, stealing her trust fund. Maybe they were nice people who'd used the money to care for her. Maybe Sim's complaints had to do with her parents' wealth compared to the more middle-class position of her relatives? When you're used to bottled water, tap water is a hardship.

I need to contact the aunt and uncle. I'll call—

Claire suddenly realized she didn't even know Sim's last name. All she knew was that the girl was from Kansas City. Before she could formulate a way to ask, she found herself saying aloud, "What's your last name?"

Sim shoved a hand between them as if it could keep the question from finding its mark. "Uh-uh. No way. I see where this is headed. You are *not* calling my uncle. I won't let you."

"But maybe if you talked—"

Sim's face crumpled. "I thought you were my friends!"

"We are—"

"I get led here, just as much as Claire gets led here, but I'm not allowed to have any time to figure out why." She pointed at Claire. "You talk the big talk, but when it comes down to it, you only think the lofty God-stuff belongs to you. You're hoarding Him."

"I am not!"

"You are!" Sim began to pace. "All the stuff about how God sent you here, how He told you to give up everything and follow Him. Well, maybe He told me to give up everything too. Isn't that what I've done?"

"You ran away, Sim."

"And you didn't?"

The words were like a wedge being driven into a log. A fracture split Claire's carefully formed decision. She looked at Merry and Sim. They were waiting for her answer.

"I didn't run away. I was offered the chance to *go* away, voluntarily. As an act of obedience. As a chance to discover my purpose."

"So you can discover your purpose, but I can't discover mine?"

Sim was making things difficult. Claire needed to get things calmed down. She lowered her voice. "Everyone has a unique purpose, Sim. I do. You do. Merry does. The trick is to find out what it is. But in order to do that, you have to be tuned in to God. He's talking, but if we're not listening…"

"I *am* listening."

"Sim…" Claire looked to Merry for support, but Merry's face was drawn tight.

Sim's breathing was heavy. "At least *I'm* doing something to help people since I came here. At least I'm not sitting around waiting for something big to happen. Where's God's purpose in that? At least I'm doing *something*."

"Sim!" Merry's eyes were wide.

"Name one thing you've done since God got you here." Sim's blazing eyes threw a clear challenge at Claire.

She didn't like being on the witness stand. "I've helped you."

Sim's eyebrows raised. "Really? I found the library on my own, and I'm *not* staying in your attic. In fact, I found the shower for *you*. *I* got myself a job at the library, *I've* helped Harold and Blanche and Ivan, and *I've* gone out in the town and met new friends. What have you done but hide out or work on your stupid paper?"

Merry intervened. "Sim! That's enough."

"Yes, it is." She spun on her heel. "I'm going to my room."

She left the two women to suffer the silence. Finally Merry said, "I'm so sorry, Claire. She shouldn't have said that."

Claire sank into a chair. "Even if it's the truth?"

Claire noticed that Merry couldn't think of any words to dispute her. Claire pointed to the stove. "The sauce is bubbling over."

Sim didn't come down to dinner. Merry and Claire shared the meal in silence. When Claire begged off having dessert on the front porch, saying she was tired, Merry helped her make a bed on the love seat and withdrew upstairs to read.

Claire was left alone to ponder the awful truth.

Maybe she should walk away. It wasn't too late to accept the mural commission.

Her brain was mush.

Fourteen

*I fear that there may be quarreling, jealousy, outbursts of anger,
factions, slander, gossip, arrogance and disorder.*

2 CORINTHIANS 12:20

CLAIRE LET OUT A SIGH OF RELIEF when Sim came down for
breakfast. She hated that they lived with the possibility Sim would
bolt. Living one day at a time—in uncertainty—was a new experience.

"Hi."

Sim took a seat on a stool. "Hi."

Merry shook a box of Life cereal. "Gourmet eating at the
Cavanaugh residence."

"Cereal's fine with me." Sim filled a bowl, poured the milk, and
dunked the cereal with the back of her spoon.

Too quiet. Way too quiet. Claire had to take the initiative. "I'm
sorry about last night, Sim. I never want to imply that I understand
what you're going through or that I have all the answers."

The girl glanced up. "You sure have enough opinions."

Claire smiled. "We both seem to have plenty of those."

Sim took a bite. "Touché."

Claire fingered her coffee mug. "And your point about not doing
anything was valid. Guilty as charged."

Sim finished chewing. "Sorry if I hurt you."

Claire shrugged. "Sometimes a little hurt is necessary to get on
the right track."

"So you're on the right track now?"

Claire wished she could answer definitively, but truth made her
say, "I haven't a clue."

Sim laughed. Merry joined in, then Claire. It was nice how laughter made everything seem a little more doable.

Sim ran ahead and grabbed the newspaper off the library stoop. Merry and Claire hurried up the steps after her.

"What's it say?" Claire asked.

Sim positioned the front page so they all could read the headline: "Love Notes and Licorice: The Saga of the Library Ghost."

"Stu followed through with his alliteration," Merry said.

"Read on."

It did not get better. Stu had turned what should have been a story about anonymous good deeds into a sensationalized account of the supernatural and how the ghost was giving people presents, acting like a paranormal Santa Claus. A quote from Merry was taken out of context, and Blanche was misquoted to have said she'd seen the ghost.

Sensationalist journalism at its worst.

Claire stepped back. She'd read enough. "I was up half the night worried that people would connect me and Sim being new in town and the sudden activities of the long-dormant ghost legend. But good old Stu didn't take that tangent. He presents the ghost as a *ghost*. I'm not sure whether we should be relieved or annoyed."

"It's all my fault." The edges of Sim's mouth sagged.

"Why is it your fault?"

She looked at Merry. "Because I'm the ghost." Sim told her about her part in the ghost-activities.

Merry unlocked the door. "Stu's to blame, not you. But I do wish you would have told me sooner."

They went inside and were greeted by a ringing phone. Merry answered it, listened a moment, then said, "You're welcome to visit the library anytime, ma'am, but honestly, there's no ghost to see. None." Merry jerked the receiver away from her ear. "She hung up." She put a hand to her forehead. "This is not a good sign."

Blanche and Ivan burst through the front door, Blanche waving the newspaper in the air. "Did you see?" She slapped the paper on the counter.

Merry shoved it away. "We've seen it, Blanche."

Ivan pointed at Merry's face. "You look way too serious for a person who's just been quoted in the paper."

Merry took a seat behind the counter. "We were all *mis*quoted, and I plan to express my displeasure to Stu. I've already had one phone call from someone wanting to know when the ghost was scheduled to show itself. They're taking the ghost tag literally."

Blanche smoothed the paper on the counter. "Why shouldn't they? We don't know for sure that it isn't a real ghost."

Ivan poked her arm. "But that didn't give you the right to say you'd seen it."

Blanche shuffled her shoulders. "I didn't lie, I merely implied—"

Ivan crooked a thumb in her direction. "She said it plain as day. I heard her."

"Blanche, how could you?" Merry shook her head. "Here I've been blaming Stu for false reporting, when you were the one who led him astray. On purpose."

Blanche stuck out her lower lip. "I was just trying to make things interesting. This is the most exciting thing that has happened in Steadfast since old man Briscoll claimed to see an outline of Frank Sinatra on the side of his barn."

Ivan squinted his eyes. "It did look pretty real if you squinted and the sun was hitting it—"

Merry stopped his words with a hand. "This is hardly the same. There is no ghost. For anyone to tell people otherwise is a downright lie."

"Well!" Blanche crossed her arms. "I won't tolerate being called a liar."

"Now, now, Blanche." Ivan patted her hand. "You *are* a liar."

"I *embellished*. For the sake of the library."

They all looked up when the first of a crowd of two dozen swarmed in the front door. Merry leveled Blanche with a look. "I'm not sure the library can take any more of your help."

Blanche raised her chin, did an about-face, and headed out to greet the crowd.

❧   ❧   ❧

The ghost enthusiasts poured into the library like water flowing through a break in a dam. Merry hoped they wouldn't be as destructive.

"Forget the licorice," one woman said. "I want a new washer and dryer."

"Or a big-screen TV."

"You can't have that."

"Why not?"

"Ghosts don't have charge cards."

Merry moved into the center of the crowd and raised her hands. "Come on, folks. There is no ghost."

Jered Manson sidled forward, settling in beside her. "But you were quoted in the paper, Merry. You're the one who called it the library ghost."

She noticed Jered's friends standing nearby and bemoaned the fact that the first time she'd seen them in the building had nothing to do with reading.

"I meant it figuratively. I mentioned the old legend, but I guarantee you, there is no apparition, spirit, or poltergeist."

"But the paper—"

"Was misinformed." When Merry glanced in Blanche's direction, she saw her entertaining some stragglers, most likely with tales of love notes and ghostly sightings.

The crowd mumbled. Then a woman asked, "Hey, I have something practical to ask the ghost." She grinned and poked a friend in the ribs with an elbow. "I need a babysitter Friday night, and if the ghost isn't busy…"

The woman beside her laughed. "You'd need more than a ghost to take care of your kids, Sue."

Then a man asked, "Are you sure we can't leave a wish list for the ghost? Just in case?"

"I'm very sure." Merry moved to shoo them out. "Go home, people. This *is* a library. You're much too noisy. Besides, being greedy never got anybody anything."

"Wanna bet?" The man headed to the chairs in the reading area. "I'm staying. I'm not going to miss the appearance of any ghost."

"Joe's right. This only happens once in a lifetime. I'm staying too."

A swarm of people headed toward the middle of the library. Merry moved between them, trying to stop the flow, getting a hint of what it must feel like to be in the middle of a stampede. "Please. Go home. There's nothing here."

Oscar from the motel put a finger in her face. "You just want the pickings for yourself, Merry. That's it, isn't it?"

"There's no pickings to be had. It was just a bag of licorice, some love notes, and a vase of flowers. Nothing big. Nothing at all like what you're asking for."

Lyn from the grocery store stepped forward. "The point is, the gifts from the library ghost were just what people wanted. The ghost *knew*, it *knew* what they needed and gave it to them."

"Exactly. Like I said, I know what I want. I want a big-screen TV."

More laughter. A planter tipped over and dirt spilled on the carpet. A question came from a man who'd sat at one of the computers. "You got any video games on these things?"

Ivan edged through the crowd, waving. "Merry! Get these squatters out of here. Oscar's sitting on my stool!"

Oscar crossed his arms. "This is a public library, Ivan. You can't claim a spot."

"I can too. I'm an artist. I'm recreating the mural."

Oscar took a look. "What's this red stuff in the middle of the blue?"

"Oscar! Out! You have no right to criticize my work, nor do you have the right to be in this library at all. You have to be able to read more than the Sunday funnies to come in here."

Oscar got in Ivan's face. "Don't make me punch you, old man."

"You're calling *me* old? You graduated three years ahead of me."

Blanche yelled from the sidelines. "Go, Ivan!"

The crowd roared.

Merry had had enough. But she was no match for a teeming

mob. Her stomach threatened to do something nasty. Her face burned. Maybe if she splashed some cool water on it…she glanced toward the rest rooms. Jered and his friends were congregated around the storeroom door.

Oh, no! Not in there, boys. She hurried toward them. "Jered, what are you doing?"

Their three heads moved apart. "If there's a ghost, we need to search the place, find where it's hiding."

"Don't be ridiculous. Your dad didn't raise you to believe in ghosts."

The bigger kid laughed. "But he *is* kinda spooky."

Jered glared at him. "If there's a ghost, we're going to find it."

The toughest kid raised an eyebrow. "You hiding something, lady?"

She shooed them away from the storeroom, having to physically push them toward the main part of the room. When they blended into the crowd, she allowed herself to breathe.

The arguments continued as if she'd never left. "It's not fair of you to make us go, Merry. This is public property."

"It's public *quiet* property. People come here to study and read, not to be harassed by ghostbusters."

"We should have a sit-in." Oscar dropped to the carpet. "Come on! Sit!" Others followed, many claiming the floor. Merry couldn't believe her eyes. These were grown people. Normally sane people. Steadfast was not known for its rebels.

She began to protest but suddenly noticed Jered and his friends were gone. She looked toward the storeroom. The door was finishing the last of its swing. *No. They wouldn't. They didn't.*

"Got any coffee, Merry? That's what this library needs. A coffee bar."

"And frozen yogurt. I love frozen yogurt."

"Fruit smoothies, that's the ticket."

As the crowd got sidetracked discussing food she raced to the storeroom. As she pulled the door open, it was pushed toward her. Jered burst into the main room, throwing her off balance. "Hey, people! Someone's living in the attic!"

The crowd changed their point of attention. It took a moment for Jered's words to register. "What attic?"

Jered held open the door. "In here. There's an attic. It's got a bed in it. And clothes. Someone's been living up there. It belongs to the library ghost!"

The crowd swarmed toward the storeroom. Merry extended her arms, but they pushed her out of the way. She heard feet stomping on the attic stairs. Loud voices echoed.

Blanche pulled Ivan by the arm. "Come on you old turnip, let's go see."

"No, Blanche." Merry wanted to weep. "Stay here. Please."

"But we want to see where the library ghost lives. Maybe he's still up there."

Merry shook her head, her eyes seeking out Claire and Sim. She found them huddled together by the mural, their faces frozen in shock.

With each loud footfall overhead, with each shout of discovery, Claire's body tightened. The gig was up. Her hiding place was found.

Sim looked up at her. "They're going through your stuff."

"I know."

"What are we going to do?"

"I'm open to suggestions."

Two women burst through the storeroom doors with a stream of people close behind. One was holding Claire's denim dress against her body, discussing how it looked. The other woman held her Bible.

Enough.

Claire strode across the room and grabbed the dress and Bible. "If you'll excuse me, those are mine!"

"No, they're not. I got them up—"

One. Two. Three. Finally, they got the connection.

Just do it. Get it over with. Claire wrapped the dress around her Bible and hugged it. "There's no ghost in the attic. There's just me. I'm living—"

Blanche spun around. "Where's the ghost?"

Sim took a step forward. "Here. *I'm* the library ghost."

Ivan slapped his hands together. "I *knew* she was a strange kid."

As the crowd gathered for the next portion of the library ghost show, Claire tucked Sim close. "She is not strange. She's a good kid who has done some nice things for people. *You're* the ones who've gone overboard, making it into something it isn't."

"The kid's been living in the attic?"

"I live in the attic."

Sim spoke up. "I live down here."

The two women who'd taken Claire's things looked at each other. "They can't live in the library."

Blanche took the floor. "Claire's her aunt."

"No, she's not," Sim said. "We're not related."

A moment of silence.

Oscar pointed a finger at Claire. "I betcha she's some sexual pervert. She's kidnapped a young girl and has kept her prisoner in the attic. It's just like in the movies."

Claire pulled Sim closer. "I am *not* a pervert. And I did not kidnap Sim."

"Then why is she here? With you?"

Claire didn't know what to say. Sim made up her mind for her.

"I'm a runaway."

There was a gasp from the crowd, as if she had said she was a serial murderer. They were getting out of control. Merry stepped forward. "Listen, people. Sim is an orphan. She was living with some relatives who weren't treating her well. She came to Steadfast looking for a safe haven."

"And found it with *her?*"

"Claire is a good woman. In fact, she is so good that she gave up all her possession, her home, her money, and her job—gave up everything, became poor—in order to come here. Those few things in the attic are all she has in the world."

Merry's words were true but they sounded completely lame. How had Claire ever expected people to understand when it sounded crazy even to her?

"So she's a *loony* pervert." Oscar turned to Claire. "What were you doing in the attic in the first place?"

Claire fingered her cross necklace. "I had no home. Like Merry said, I gave everything away. I was led to Steadfast to—"

"Led here?"

"Who led you here?"

Claire hesitated and looked to Merry, then to Sim. There was no way out. Did God want her to chicken out or speak the truth? "Actually, God led me here. I gave it all up for Him."

The laughter started out nervously, then gained strength. "Next time, ask Him to lead you to Hawaii."

"Or at least Eldora. I bet *they* have a fancy library with all the modern conveniences. I bet there's wall-to-wall carpet in their attic."

An older woman grinned. "Haven't you been listening? She doesn't want any conveniences. She gave up everything to be poor."

"She *wants* to be poor?"

"That's what Merry said."

"No way. Nobody wants to be poor."

"I do." Claire lifted her chin in an attempt at dignity. But from their laughter she knew it was too late. People had made up their minds. She'd been deemed a wacko extremist. There would be no understanding now. Yet, maybe if they knew… "I'm Claire Adams."

They stared at her. Finally one man said, "This is supposed to mean something?"

Claire's ego deflated and blew away. *Forget it. Forget the whole thing.*

"Has anybody called the sheriff yet? She's a squatter, and the kid's a runaway."

Merry shook her head. "There's no need for that. I knew they were staying in here. I agreed to the arrangement."

"Then you're as crazy as they are."

"It was just temporary until they—"

"But they're not even related to each other. They need to go back where they came from before she draws the girl into some weirdo cult where she wants to be worshiped or something."

Sim made fists. "Claire's been good to me."

"Oh, I bet she's been good, sissy. *Real* good."

Sim pulled away from Claire's protective arm. Her face was red. "You're mean. And unfair. We came here to start over. We haven't done anything wrong." She took a step toward the door. "But you want me gone? I'm gone."

She ran out the door.

After a moment's hesitation, Claire ran after her.

Merry wanted to run after them both, but the crowd wouldn't let her. It gathered close, demanding answers she did not have.

Where was Sim going? Would Claire find her?

Would they ever be back?

"Sim!"

Thankfully, Sim stopped on the far side of the town square. Claire ran to catch up, out of breath. "Don't run. Please don't run."

"Why not? It's falling apart."

Claire shook her head. "Maybe it's falling into place."

Sim stomped a foot. "Stop it, will you? Stop all that unique-purpose God-talk. Nothing is working out how either one of us planned."

No words of wisdom came to mind. "You're right."

Sim raised an eyebrow. "You're admitting it?"

"It's the truth."

"So what do we do now?"

"Assume God knows what He's doing—even if we don't have a clue."

"There you go again."

Claire decided to take a different tack. "You need to stop being afraid, Sim."

"I'm not—"

"What's the worst that can happen?"

Sim looked at her, mouth gaping. "The worst has *already* happened. They found us. They found out *about* us. And they don't understand any of it."

"No one's hurt you."

"But they will. They'll hurt me by sending me back to my aunt and uncle, where I'll be in the way while they have their own passel of babies. I won't go where I'm not wanted. Talk about having no purpose."

"Maybe your relatives have realized how wrong they've been. Maybe your running away snapped them out of their selfishness."

"*If* they've noticed I'm gone."

"Aw, come on, Sim..."

She showed Claire her back. "Can't everybody leave me alone? I'm not hurting anybody."

"No, you're not. But being alone is no way to live. It's not enough. As I've been telling you, God has a—"

"Plan. I know. And you'd think that would make me feel better about things, but it doesn't. So far I'm not too keen on God's plans." She began walking but ended up circling back, her fists framing her head. "I haven't felt this messed up since I was at the hospital the night Mom and Dad were killed. I hate when things change without my permission."

Now *that* Claire could relate to. "Everyone does."

Sim's fists lowered and she wrapped her arms around herself. Then she shook her head. "I need to be alone. I need time to think." She looked down the street. "I gotta go."

"Go where?"

"Anywhere." She ran down the sidewalk, calling over her shoulder, "Hooking up with you was a mistake, Claire."

The words slapped Claire into immobility. Such awful words, such rude words.

But were they true?

People came out of the library and Claire tensed. She didn't want to face them, endure their insults, or endure their ignorance of who she was. But where should she go?

"Psst!"

Harold stood in the alley. He motioned her to come with him.

What choice did she have?

⁓   ⁓   ⁓

Sim turned onto a side street, wishing once again that Steadfast were a big city with tons of people. It was hard to blend in when the streets were empty except for a few kids riding bikes or a grandma tending a garden.

She ran through a neighborhood, needing a place to hide out. Finally, the residential street ended and Sim spotted a dilapidated barn on a corner lot. It appeared to be unused, probably abandoned after Steadfast got too close.

She looked around and waited until a car passed. She hurried toward the barn and opened the door, cringing when its hinges whined. When the door closed she gave herself a moment to let her eyes adjust. The barn was full of leftover hay and garbage—beer cans, chip bags. If Jered and his friends didn't use this place, other kids did. There was a ladder leading to a loft. She climbed it and claimed a spot by a small window.

Home sweet home. Such as it was.

Fifteen

HAROLD'S HOME WAS A SURPRISE. Claire expected it to be as rumpled as his personal appearance. And it was—from the outside. The rose-bushes were overgrown, and the grass—where it was growing—needed cutting. One of the shutters was off-kilter, and the screen door was missing a section.

Yet inside… Harold's home turned into a cozy showplace.

The furniture was antique and the aroma that assailed Claire was one of lemon oil and wood. The knickknacks on the mantle and buffet were sparkling and the doilies beneath them were crisp and white. She'd had pretty things once.

When Claire picked up—and set back down—a figurine of an eighteenth-century woman in full court dress, Harold rushed to the table and adjusted its position a half inch to the right.

"Were these your wife's things?"

Harold nodded, stroking the edge of a crystal decanter as if it were the curve of his wife's neck.

"She'd be very pleased to see how nicely you've kept everything."

He beamed, and Claire knew her assessment of his tidiness was on target. His wife had cared for the inside of the house and probably hadn't touched the exterior. And so he had taken up the chores that were important to her—that reminded him of her.

There was a photo of a woman on an end table, a fresh rose placed in front of it. "Is this your wife?"

Harold's face changed from its usual look of perplexity to one flushed with love, wistful with longing. "Harriet."

"She's lovely."

"She was my life."

Claire was shocked—not by his emotion, but by the fact that his words were not from Shakespeare. Yet she didn't want to bring it to his attention lest he revert to the difficult verse.

He smiled and shrugged. "At home I can be me. In the world I honor her with the Shakespeare she loved."

"Does anyone else know this?"

He stroked the picture frame. "It's our secret." He looked at Claire. "And yours now. Will you keep it?"

"Of course. If you'll keep my location a secret. I need some time."

"Don't we all?"

She fell into a wing chair by the fireplace. The ashes had been cleaned out for the hot weather, but the brass andirons still stood guard. "I'm beat."

"There's a room above the garage. It's not much, but you could stay there if you'd like."

"I'd like. Thank you." She remembered that her clothes were divided between the attic and Merry's. Oh well, it couldn't be helped.

"Would you also like some iced tea?"

Claire smiled. "That would be wonderful." What would Ivan and Blanche think if they saw Harold being the host?

He returned with two glasses and a plate of cookies.

"You bake too?"

He smiled. "Nabisco bakes. I buy."

Claire took one. "We have a lot in common, Harold."

He sat across from her and slipped his hands under his thighs. "Indeed. We've both lost what's important in our lives."

He'd taken the trivial and turned it profound. "I haven't lost anything. I gave it up willingly."

"Did you?"

What kind of question is that? "Of course. No one forced me to do it."

"You forced yourself."

Claire stopped with the cookie halfway to her mouth. "Sure it was hard, but I was willing to do it. I *wanted* to do it."

"Why?"

"Because God wanted me to. It was a way I could obey Him."

Harold tucked his feet into his chair, like he did in the library. "You thought it would be impressive, didn't you?"

She took a bite of cookie and chewed. "I'm not out to impress anyone."

"Aren't you?"

She swallowed. "Harold! Maybe you should go back to Shakespeare. You're not being very nice."

He smiled. "I'm being honest—and trying to get you to be the same."

"So I've been dishonest?"

"You're Claire Adams, the famous artist."

"How—?"

"I saw the article in *Newsweek.*"

Somehow, having one person know the complete truth felt wonderful. "So you understand I had a lot to give up."

He shrugged. "Why did you do it?"

"I told you. For God."

"Then what does it matter what people say?" He tossed a hand toward the west, toward the library.

"It doesn't. Not really. But they think I'm crazy."

"So?"

"I'm not crazy."

"Neither am I."

Suddenly, Claire got the connection. "Doesn't it bother you that people think you're odd?"

"I *am* odd." He held up a finger to make a point. "But I'm not crazy."

"They don't understand that."

"I don't need them to understand. I have no desire to be the world's version of normal. Acting as I do makes them leave me alone. And who's happier? Them or me?" He put his feet on the floor. "When Harriet died, I wanted to die too. But I knew God wouldn't want that. I had to go on living. I had to find a *way* to go on living without her. You married?"

"Divorced."

He shrugged. "So you've lost too. And Sim…I understand why she ran away. Grief makes you want to hide. Who knows if her aunt and uncle are good or bad? Right now it doesn't matter. She's trying to find her way through the grief. Just as I found my way."

"And your way involves quoting Shakespeare?"

"What do I have to say to the world that he hasn't already said?"

"But you're talking normal to me. Now."

"Only because you're here. In my house. In my world. You and I each have our own world. We're both outcasts. The difference between us is I'm happy in my world, whereas you're fighting yours. You want people to know how your world came about. You want them to pat you on the back and say you made a good decision. You want their praise and applause, like an actor on a stage."

"No, I—" She couldn't finish the sentence.

He softened his voice. "If you truly gave up everything for God and God alone, you wouldn't care if people knew of your sacrifice or who you were before. You wouldn't care if they approved or even understood. As long as *He* understood and approved. I think you need to face the fact that you liked the idea of what He asked you to do, and you've used it."

Her throat was dry. Parched by the truth. "Used it to what?"

"To hide out from life."

"I'm not hiding from anyone. I want to help people. I'm here to help Sim."

Harold considered this a minute. "Maybe Sim is here to help you."

She choked on a cookie crumb. Or his words. She wasn't sure which. "But now we're apart. How can either of us help the other if we're apart?"

"I guess you'll have to wait it out."

Great. Waiting. Her favorite pastime.

❧   ❧   ❧

Merry was just getting ready to lock up when Officer Ken Kendell came in the library. Although she'd expected him all day, when closing time approached without a visit from him, she'd let herself relax.

Too late to escape now. At least everyone was gone. At this point she'd count her blessings.

He strode toward the counter, one hand resting on his never-used firearm. "Hey, Merry."

"I guess you heard about the library-ghost ruckus."

"It's not the ghost I'm concerned about."

"Oh?"

He looked around the library. "Care to tell me why you let two strangers live in a public building?"

"It was temporary, Ken. And they weren't hurting anything."

"Then maybe we should open up the town hall for tenants too?"

He had a point.

He leaned against the counter. His class ring could have fit on her thumb. "I did a computer check on your Claire Adams."

Merry laughed nervously. "And she's a felon on the run, right? She's an infamous serial killer who stalks people who don't have the same reading taste as she does."

"She's not infamous, but she is famous."

She blinked. Twice. "What are you talking—?"

He pulled a folded page of a printout from his back pocket and opened it. He talked as Merry read. "She's a world-renowned mosaic artist. She has her own gallery, she's had showings in London and Lucerne. People—movie-star types—pay tens of thousands of dollars for her work."

Merry tried to stop her head from shaking, but she couldn't. "She never said a thing. She was doing research on Michelangelo—for fun."

Ken laughed. "According to her press, she could have given Michelangelo lessons." They both looked toward the mosaic Ivan was massacring. "It makes you think, doesn't it? All that talk about her giving up everything." He turned back to Merry. "Quite a sacrifice."

Merry couldn't fathom it.

"Makes you wonder why she came here."

"She said God led her here."

"I heard that."

"And?"

He stood and arched his back. "No way to prove it one way or the other, is there?"

"So what happens now?"

"You tell her she can't stay here."

"She's left. I don't know where she is."

"Just as well then."

Not really. Now that Merry knew the whole truth she wanted to talk to Claire. Right now.

"Then there's the girl," Ken said. "She's a runaway."

"And she's run away again. I haven't seen her since this morning."

"We need to get her back to her relatives."

"Even if they don't treat her well?"

"According to whom?"

"According to her."

"Hmm."

"She could be telling the truth."

"Or not. The point is, it's not up to you and me to decide, Merry." He took out a notepad and pencil. "I need her full name so I can put it in the computer and search the missing children database."

"I...I don't know her last name. She'd said she was Claire's niece, so I assumed it was Adams. And when Claire asked her, she never did tell us. I'm not even sure where she's from."

"You're not much help."

"Sorry." Actually, Merry was relieved she *didn't* know Sim's last name. She didn't want to be put in the position of withholding it from Ken.

He headed for the door. "If she comes back, you call me."

When Merry didn't answer, Ken turned to look at her. "You'll call me. Right?"

She drew a cleansing breath. "Can't we just let things be a little while longer? Give the girl the benefit of the doubt? Wait until we know the whole truth?"

He put his hands on his hips, looking at the floor. Finally he looked up. "I shouldn't. I'm not promising anything. And I guarantee if I find out you're hiding her, I'll come take her. You keep me informed. Let's be on the up-and-up, all right? Work together on this?"

"I suppose."

"That's not a strong enough answer, Merry."

"Yes, yes. If she comes back I'll let you know."

Sim opened her eyes to a single thought: *Claire!*

It was dusk. She'd fallen asleep in the barn loft. The good thing was that no one had found her. She was safe.

But what about Claire? Had she gone back to the library? Was she at Merry's? Or was she gone, completely gone from Steadfast? She had every right to leave. Especially after what Sim had said: *It was a mistake hooking up with you, Claire.*

Why had she said such a thing? It wasn't true. She wasn't keen on all of Claire's ways, but she was glad she'd met her. Knew her. And she didn't want her to be gone.

Sim needed to check the library before it got dark. If Claire wasn't there, maybe she'd left a note. Knowing something was better than nothing.

The back door to the library was still unlocked. And why shouldn't it be?

The ghost fiasco had swept into Steadfast like a summer storm, only to dissipate, leaving behind only the mud, puddles, and humidity of the excitement.

Sim went inside, bounding up the stairs. "Claire? Where are you?"

No answer.

She scanned the attic. Maybe Claire was out looking for her. She'd been gone for hours. Maybe—?

Sim did a sudden three-sixty. All of Claire's belongings had been tossed by the ghost-seeking crowd. Obviously Claire hadn't been back since the attic was discovered.

Then where was she?

Sim went downstairs. It was quiet.

As quiet as a library.

A horrible sound.

Merry parked in front of the building. Since she'd spent so much of her day dealing with the issues of the ghost and Claire and Sim, she hadn't gotten her work done, so she'd come back after dinner.

When she unlocked the front door and went inside, she was shocked to see Sim come out of the fiction stacks.

Merry flipped on the lights. "Sim?"

"Claire's not here."

"I know. She never came back from running after you. And where have *you* been?"

"Places."

"Don't. I'm not in the mood."

The girl turned toward the storeroom. "I'm going to wait for her in the attic."

"No, you're not."

Her eyes blazed. "Oh yes I am! This place is my home."

"Not anymore, it isn't." *Not when the police are looking for you.* "You're coming home with me."

"I've got to wait here."

Merry closed her eyes. "Look, Sim, we both have to face facts. Claire hasn't been back and she may not be coming back."

"Thanks to this stupid town."

Merry put a hand on her shoulder. "Home is where you place your head. And tonight, your home is my home. Okay?"

Sim bit her lower lip. "There's one condition."

"What's that?"

"I want you to promise you won't call my aunt and uncle, and you won't call the sheriff on me."

"Sim, you can't continue to live in limbo like this."

"Wanna bet?"

Merry sighed. "Fine. I won't call anyone, at least for now. Just come home."

Merry pulled in the driveway and shut off the car. Sim didn't move, so she walked around and opened the door for her. "Last stop. Everybody out."

Sim complied, but without enthusiasm. Merry led her inside and tossed the keys on the entry table. She turned on some lights. "You hungry?"

Sim shook her head. Merry looked at the clock. Thank heaven—it was nine. A respectable time to turn in, if you were desperate. "I bet you're tired."

The girl headed upstairs, accompanied by the creaking of each step. Merry followed after her, opening the windows, letting in the summer breezes.

Come on, Sim. Say something. They both stopped at the door to the extra bedroom. "Well then...good night."

Sim went into the room and began to close the door.

"I'm glad you're here, Sim. I'll help you through this. You're not alone. Not with me around."

Sim continued the door's gentle swing, closing it in Merry's face.

Claire hid behind the bushes at Merry's house and watched Sim go inside. She clutched a hand to her chest and realized her ache was caused by regret. Sim wasn't her charge anymore. Not that she ever truly had been.

Merry could probably take better care of the girl than she could. A real house. A real room. Food prepared in a kitchen, not eaten out of a box or can. But the question remained: Why had God arranged for Claire and Sim to meet up and stay in the library if it was only for a few days? How could she help the girl when she couldn't even spend time with her?

She couldn't risk seeing her. Not after the townspeople called her a pervert. Yet even that she could handle. That was so far beyond the truth, she could defend herself with ease. But the rest…

They'd laughed at her sacrifice. They hadn't understood at all. Called her loony. Crazy. *"Nobody wants to be poor."*

Were they right? Was she crazy? Had it all been for nothing?

For that's what she had now. Nothing. Truly nothing. No calling, no goal.

And no Sim.

Harold's house was quiet. Claire slipped the kitchen phone off the hook, muffling the dial tone. She punched the numbers. When she heard the first ring, she moved to the far side of the refrigerator to mute her words.

"Hello?"

"Darla?"

"Claire! I've been waiting to hear from you. The church has been calling the gallery, and the gallery's been calling me. They want your decision about the commission. What am I supposed to tell them?"

She'd actually forgotten all about the commission. She'd called Darla for some commiseration, a connection, a comforting word. Not pressure.

"Claire, answer me."

"You sound upset."

"I am. I mean, it's awkward. I don't like being in this position."

Claire pinched the bridge of her nose. Poor Darla. Left to take the heat. "I'm sorry. I never meant for you—for anyone—to have to handle such things."

"Yeah? Then give me something to tell them. What's your decision?"

"I…I don't know."

"Well, when *will* you know? They're not going to be kept hanging forever. In fact, they're asking Dermont Davis to submit a proposal."

"No!" She'd spoken too loudly. She lowered her voice. "They can't use Dermont. The most original idea he's ever had was when he decided to start copying *my* style."

"I know, I know. He's a Claire Adams wanna-be. But he's here, and you're not. To a church that's raring to go, that's a plus."

"Did he approach them? I bet you a million dollars he approached them."

"You don't have a million dollars, Claire. You don't even have a thousand dollars. Not anymore."

"That's beside the point. Dermont has no right taking advantage of my absence—"

"Absence? You make it sound like a temporary condition. Does that mean you're coming back?"

Claire let the refrigerator guide her to the floor. Tears caught her by surprise. She flicked them away.

"Are you crying?"

"Yes, I'm crying."

"Hey, don't do that. I'll put the church off. Don't let Dermont's presence push you into anything. We both know he could never handle such a big commission."

"But the church doesn't know that. They'll give it to him because he's there and raring to jump on it, and then he'll get into it and mess it up and the church will hate me for not taking the commission in the first place."

"My, my, a regular mosaic soap opera."

Claire sniffed and groaned. "Why does everything have to be so complicated?"

"I take it the complications extend beyond Dermont Davis?"

She told Darla about the library ghost fiasco and the town's reaction to her sacrifice. "They think I'm bonkers."

"You are bonkers. But don't let some town stop you from doing what you need to do. Just wait it out."

"But the commission. Dermont..."

"Is God telling you to get all blubbery and give up what you're doing there?"

"I...I don't know. I haven't consulted Him."

"Don't you think you should?"

Claire began to laugh. "What would I do without you, Darla?"

❧   ❧   ❧

As Claire slipped outside to go to the room above Harold's garage, a window on the second floor opened and Harold peered out. "You feel better now?"

Claire looked back toward the kitchen. "Sorry. I didn't mean to disturb you."

"You didn't. But living alone I notice small sounds. Did your friend help?"

Claire shrugged. "She gave me the same advice you did: to pray and wait." She sighed. "I fear there's a conspiracy to curtail my impatient nature and I'm not sure I like it."

"Advice can be hard to take."

"And harder to apply. But I promised Darla I'd give it a shot."

"Can't ask for more than that. You're a good woman, Claire Adams. Let me know if you need anything." He disappeared inside.

She went up the steps to the room, but sleep would have to wait. Being a good woman could only start in one place.

She fell to her knees.

Sixteen

Anyone, then, who knows the good he ought to do
and doesn't do it, sins.

JAMES 4:17

IT WAS FIVE O'CLOCK in the morning. Merry Cavanaugh couldn't sleep. Was it because there was another person in her house?

How ironic. Her lonely house often kept her awake, and yet now, when she had someone with her, she couldn't sleep.

She turned over and had to adjust the twisted shirt she slept in. Lou's shirt. Although she'd long ago gone through his things, she'd kept a few odd items intact. Like this shirt she slept in, his Bible on the bedside table, his toothbrush in the drawer, and the bookmark in the book he'd been reading. Slices of him. Things that brought to mind daily scenes she never imagined she'd forget. And yet, even with these small life-markers, she found the memories fading, like a veil being drawn across them, softening their edges, making her strain to see them clearly. Maybe someday, she'd get the book out and start up where Lou left off. Finish it. Read it blind.

That's what her life felt like, as if she were starting up where Lou's life had left off. Trying to finish it. Trying to read it blind.

No…not blind. Unlike an unknown book, they had shared a life and a history. In truth, she'd known him better than he knew her. Where Lou was an open book, Merry was a locked diary with secrets and private thoughts that had nothing to do with loving her family or being a good wife and mother. She was never unfaithful or anything so blatant, but in her heart she experienced plenty of mental infidelities and embraced far too many thoughts about being alone, being *away*, being a different Merry in a different life.

She hugged her pillow, squeezing her eyes shut. How much had Lou known? It was a question that could never be completely answered. And when she'd been in the throes of one of her dissatisfied moods, she walked the tightrope between never wanting him to see the black side of her heart and wanting to confront him with every petty complaint, real and imagined.

He'd known some of it. And it cost him his life. He knew she was flying to Phoenix because of her dissatisfaction, to have fun with a girlfriend. That's why he surprised her by bringing Justin on the plane. To be with her. To try to save her from herself. And to try to save their marriage.

She remembered his words on the plane: *"I know you're not happy, Mer."*

Not happy? The level of the unhappiness she'd felt then compared with the unhappiness she felt now was laughable. A cut finger compared with an amputation. If only she'd been content with what she had—counted her blessings instead of weighing her happiness. If only she'd been nicer. Such a simple thing, being nice, and yet she'd failed horribly at it.

Be nice now. *You're not alone* now.

Sim needed her. A child alone who could use some kindness.

Merry got out of bed and tiptoed into the hallway. The door to the guest room was closed. She tried to remember if there was a lock on that door. She hoped not. If Sim locked herself in, then it meant she was afraid, or angry, or upset, or…

How would I feel if I were an orphaned runaway and I'd been brought to a strange house after my newest friend had disappeared?

An answer came in a flood of emotions that spurred Merry to open the door. She needed to know how Sim was doing. Even at five in the morning.

She flexed her fingers like a safecracker and forced herself to use deliberate movements. It wouldn't do to barge in and scare the poor girl. She took a deep breath and wiped her hands on Lou's shirt. Then she turned the knob. Unlocked. She inched the door open. The lamp beside the couch was on.

The couch was empty.

She's left! She ran away!

Merry opened the door wide. Then she saw her.

Sim was sitting on the window seat, her knees drawn to her chest. Her head lay on her arms, her face turned toward the window. She sniffed.

Merry's heart, which she thought was broken beyond more hurting, ached for a heart more hurt than her own. She went to the window seat and sat. Sim looked up. Their eyes met, and with that one glimpse into a pain beyond her own, Merry discovered a hidden place in her soul.

And she began to heal.

Sim was glad Merry came into her room. She'd felt so incredibly alone. Maybe the fact that she'd been alone, then not alone, and now alone again, made it hurt more.

Alone and guilty. Claire was gone, rejected by everyone. But who had rejected her first? Sim. Every time Claire tried to be nice, tried to get to know her, Sim pushed her away.

I'm so sorry.

Sim and Merry looked out the window, seated at opposite ends of the window seat. "Do you mind living alone?"

Merry hesitated. "Widows don't have a choice. But you do. You can stay here—for a while."

Sim nodded at the implications of "a while." "I wish I were older. Then there wouldn't be laws against me. They'd leave me alone."

"The laws protect you."

"I can do that myself. And what I can't do, between you and Claire—"

"Claire's gone."

"But she'll be back. People scared her away, that's all. She must have things to do."

"Like what?"

"I don't know…stuff for God. She wouldn't leave me now."

"She *did* leave."

Sim dug her chin into her knees. When Merry touched her

head, she didn't pull away, but a part of her wanted to. She didn't want pity.

Well, maybe a little wouldn't hurt.

"How about some breakfast?"

Sim let her attention move to her stomach. She *was* hungry. Odd how life went on, even in the midst of a crisis.

Sim juggled three eggs.

Merry pointed a whisk at her, admiring her talent while fearing for her floor. "Don't get cocky on me. Not unless you want to settle for a bowl of cereal again."

Sim caught the last one behind her back, then presented them to Merry.

"You're very talented with your hands."

"My dad used to say the talent is *all* in the hands. He hated when people said he got where he was because of luck."

"Meaning, you make your own luck?"

"Luck is bogus. Using your talents and making the right decisions at the right time have nothing to do with luck."

"Maybe."

"You've got a talent for cooking." Sim sat on a stool at the cooking island. "I used to watch Cook like this. But I've never had a breakfast casserole. Not many casseroles period. Dad said they were poor-food. Besides, he didn't like different foods touching. He'd never go for them being mixed together on purpose."

"He sounds a bit compulsive."

"Cook called him—them—obsessed."

"About what?"

"Being rich. Playing the part."

"Wearing the right clothes, driving the right car?"

Sim nodded. "And not eating poor-food like casseroles."

Merry looked at Sim's clothes. A plain red T-shirt and gray gym shorts. She was barefoot. "Do you feel like they feel—felt?"

She shrugged and traced a crack on the countertop. "I'm not them." Sim looked as if she wanted to say more.

"And?"

"They didn't like so many things."

"Such as?"

Sim thought a moment, then counted on her fingers. "They didn't like two-door cars, instant coffee, showing photo ID at airports—" she looked to the ceiling—"margarine, coffee mugs, sheets that were less than four-hundred-count percale, terry kitchen towels, drive-throughs, regular mustard."

"Goodness."

Sim wasn't through. "Drinks served in a can or bottle, tap water, handicapped parking spaces, Monday holidays…and Rico."

Merry looked up from measuring flour. "What's a Rico?"

"Rico's a who. Rico Garcia. He's a kid I met at summer camp. He was there on scholarship; some church paid his way. We were best friends. He could hold his breath for two minutes, nine seconds."

"That's quite a feat. Your parents didn't like him?"

"We didn't travel in the same circles. That's what they said after I got home and wanted to hang out with him. He lived in another part of town. I snuck out to see him once, but I got caught, so after that, we just talked on the phone. At camp he taught me how to swim."

"What did you teach him?"

"Me?"

"Rico taught you how to swim; what did you teach him?"

Sim's eyebrows dipped. She reached for one of the eggs. "Let me separate one. Cook showed me how."

Merry pulled the egg out of her reach. "Answer me, kiddo."

Sim looked down. "Don't call me that."

"What?"

"Claire called me—calls me kiddo."

After a moment's hesitation, Merry handed her the egg and the bowl.

Sim expertly separated the egg. "Claire's weird."

"How so?"

"The God-talk."

"That hardly makes her weird. Maybe a bit unique."

"Same difference."

"Not really." Merry threw away the eggshells. "Weird is when something *isn't* like it should be. Unique is when it's *exactly* as it should be."

Sim tilted her head. "Hmm. I like that."

"So is Claire weird or unique?"

Sim's smile revealed her certainty. "Oh, Claire is definitely unique. She is exactly as she should be. I've never known anybody who was so driven to do the right thing."

A new wave of uncertainty rushed over Merry. Claire was gone. Officer Kendell wanted Merry to help find out where Sim belonged. She poured the egg whites into the mixer and turned it on high. The noise covered the arguing of her inner voices.

Merry was already at the car when she noticed Sim's absence. She was at the front door, but she wasn't coming or going.

"Come on, Sim, we're running late."

Sim held the doorjamb on each side, stuck her head out, and looked both ways.

"Sim!"

She stepped back into the foyer. "You go on ahead. I think I'll stick around here today."

Merry did her own scan of the street. No one was outside. She backtracked to the porch, speaking softly. "You're acting as if people are stalking you, getting ready to nab you. They're not."

"Can you guarantee that?"

Actually, she couldn't. Though Ken Kendell had given her a reprieve from turning Sim in—mostly because no one knew her last name—that didn't mean there weren't any other well-meaning citizens of Steadfast who would call other authorities.

"There's not much to do here." Merry glanced around. "I don't have cable or a single video game."

Sim grinned. "You have books, don't you?"

"A few."

Sim spread her hands.

Merry retrieved a piece of paper and a pen from her purse. "Here's the number at the library. Call if you need anything."

"I'll be fine. Really."

As soon as Sim closed the door, Merry called after her. "Lock the door!"

The bolt clanged into place. The girl was safe.

Wasn't she?

When the phone rang at the library, Merry's first response was dread, fearing more fallout from the Claire-Sim-ghost incident. But as soon as she answered it, she was faced with another, more tangible kind of anxiety.

It was her mother. She needed emergency surgery. Tomorrow, first thing. "Come home, Merry. I need you."

Blanche was close by when she hung up. "Great bananas, Merry. You look whiter than any ghost I've never seen."

Sudden fear clamped Merry's heart. She'd lost so much. Certainly God wouldn't take her mother too.

"My mom needs me. Surgery. Tomorrow."

"What's wrong?"

"She had a suspicious mammogram. She was so scared that she pressured the doctor to do a biopsy tomorrow."

"Then go. Right now. She needs you. We'll take care of things here."

Merry shook her head, her mind juggling the logistics. Blanche and Ivan probably *could* take care of the library. But then there was Sim. Claire was gone. Sim needed Merry's protection.

Blanche was talking. "...anything else I can do, you let me know."

There was only one solution. "Is Ivan here yet?"

"As always."

"Go get him, please."

Blanche looked skeptical but went after Ivan. They returned immediately. Ivan took Merry's hand and patted it. "Sorry to hear about your mother. Whatever you need, just ask."

"Thank—"

When Merry spotted Bailey coming in, she cringed. She wasn't up to his dating game today.

He came toward the counter. "My, my, such attention. Three sets of eyes stuck on me. What did I do?"

Merry turned to Ivan and Blanche. "We'll discuss this in a few—"

"Discuss what?" Bailey asked.

"Merry's mom needs an operation," Ivan said. "Merry has to leave ASAP."

Blanche nodded. "She needs our help."

Bailey bowed. "At your service." He actually sounded sincere.

Merry rubbed her head. She had no choice. Best get on with it. "I need help with Sim. Since it's obvious she can't stay in the library anymore, she stayed with me last night."

"Ask Claire to help."

"Claire never came back. She's disappeared."

"You'd better call the authorities on that girl."

Merry shook her head at Ivan. "I've talked to Ken. He's given me some time before we go that next step. So for now, we're it. She needs us."

"Us?"

"Someone."

Bailey placed his hands across his middle. "You're asking *us* to take care of her?"

"For just a few days, until I get back."

Blanche raised an arm. "Merry's friends to the rescue!"

Ivan rubbed his chin. "It will never work. I don't care what Ken said. Time's up. We need to turn her in to the authorities. We have no right to—"

Blanche swatted his arm. "To be nice to her? To give her some attention and a place to sleep?" She pulled her blouse over her hips. "Actually, I've been going through grandkid withdrawal. It's been six weeks since I've had a little one around."

"Sim's hardly little." Ivan directed a pointed look at Blanche. "And your place is so cramped none of your grandkids stay over. They just come for the day."

"She could sleep in my recliner."

Ivan shook his head. "And no way can she stay at my place. It's smaller than Blanche's. And what if Claire comes back? Are we supposed to give the kid up to her?"

"No way." Blanche shuddered. "I liked her at first, but now…she's too strange for my medicine."

Everyone started talking at once, and Merry glanced at her watch. Decisions had to be made. Now. She raised a hand to quiet them. "Discuss Claire later. I need a real volunteer."

A hand shot up, but not the one she expected.

"I'll take her," Bailey said.

Merry had never considered Bailey a contender in the guardian race. "You're…single."

He glared at her. "What does that have to do with anything? Claire's single. Truth be, we all are." He raised a hand, as though taking an oath. "I promise I won't let her stay up too late, let her watch any nasty things on television, lose her, or teach her any cuss words she's never heard before—though I can't vouch for Jered's vocabulary." He looked at his audience. They seemed unconvinced. "Come on, people. I was the oldest of six brothers and I didn't kill, wound, or maim any of them. I know how to deal with an extra kid for a few days. Give me a chance."

"What about Jered?"

"He'll be fine. Maybe they'll become friends."

Merry wasn't sure she liked the sound of that.

Ivan slapped his hands on the counter. "Let's get this wrapped up. I've got a mural to do."

Bailey traced a figure eight near her eyes. "Don't look at me like I'm some alien who's threatened to eat your baby. Sim will be fine in my care."

She couldn't say what she wanted to say.

"What? You think I'm a bad parent?"

Jered's no gem.

"Goodness, Merry—" Blanche planted her hands on her hips— "give the man a break. He's trying to help."

Bailey took the in Blanche gave him. "Then it's settled. Sim will stay with me."

What choice did she have?

❧   ❧   ❧

"Bailey's taking her in?"

Claire yanked a weed from the ground and tossed it in the garbage can that was already full. Cleaning up Harold's overgrown backyard was the least she could do to repay his hospitality. She wore an old straw hat as a disguise just in case anyone could see through the jungle.

"He volunteered."

She pushed herself to standing. "Bailey only volunteered to get on Merry's good side. And from what I hear he has a problem teen of his own. This is no good at all. I can take care of Sim better than any of them."

"But where?"

Claire hesitated. "I could move back to the attic. Or even the motel. I have *some* money. Anything would be better than strangers passing Sim around like a used book. She needs me."

Harold rocked on his heels. "Maybe the town needs her more."

"The town?"

Harold pushed the weeds deeper in the garbage can. "Maybe Sim's situation will force people to think past themselves, past their own lives. Caring for someone else can be a blessing."

"But I miss her. And I feel responsible for her."

"I know."

"So what am I supposed to do while Sim goes from house to house?"

"It's just Bailey's."

"For now. But later? Who knows where this will lead? I repeat, what am I supposed to do?"

"You have to wait some more."

"Or?"

"Move on."

Claire used the gardening claw to tear through a wad of weeds. *Move on.* Maybe that's what she should do. Go home, accept the church commission, take up where she'd left off. And keep the likes of Dermont Davis from giving art a bad name. "I'm not needed here. I was never needed here."

"You know that's not true."

She tossed the gardening tool aside. "Then tell me what good I've done. I've been instrumental in creating a ruckus that caused an orphan girl to be tossed around like a beanbag."

"You're overreacting."

She stood, needing to pace. "I got Merry in trouble for letting us stay at the library, I wasted days and days researching a paper I could care less about, I befriended nice people then left them in the dust." She stopped in front of him. "I'm completely confused."

Harold smiled. "How 'bout some carrot cake? Genuine Betty Crocker."

"Is carrot cake an antidote to confusion?"

"It can't hurt."

"Go on—" Merry nudged Sim—"Bailey's waiting for you."

Sim held her position at the front door. Merry stood behind her, blocking her retreat.

She felt Merry's hand on her shoulder. "It will be all right. Bailey's a nice guy. He'll take good care—"

"I don't need taken care of. I want to stay in the library and wait for Claire. Or let me stay in your house while you're gone. I promise I won't mess anything up."

Merry looked down but shook her head.

Sim's muscles tensed when Bailey opened his car door to come get her. *No! I won't be a baby who has to be helped to the car.* She cast a backward glance at Merry. "Fine. Be that way. Have a good trip. Hope your mom is okay."

Merry reached out to hug her, but she slipped away and pushed through the door.

"Great." Bailey got back in the car. "Glad you're ready. Time's a'tocking."

"You make that saying up all by yourself?" Sim got in the car, noting it was an older model Mercedes. Not bad for a small-town hick.

"You get that snotty attitude all by yourself?"

Touché.

They pulled away from the curb. "Seat belt."

Sim didn't move. "I don't believe in them. They didn't save my parents, so why bother?"

"Because it's my car and my rules. Put it on."

With a sigh, Sim fastened the belt and looked at this man who had volunteered to take her in. The big question was why? Bailey certainly hadn't done it out of pity. "Why aren't you being all gushy to me?"

"Gushy?"

"Feeling sorry for the poor orphan girl. Being sickly sweet."

"You like sickly sweet?"

"Not especially."

"Then stop complaining. Bad things happen. That's life. We have to live with it."

Sim ran a hand across the dash. "Nice car. But you should have picked a better color. This one's too blah."

"Silver is classic."

"Boring."

"Elegant."

"Stodgy."

Bailey glared at Sim. "I am *not* stodgy. If people only knew the amount of time I spend on *not* being stodgy."

"Maybe you try too hard."

"You should talk."

"Huh?"

Bailey glanced at her, motioning to her face. "What's with the eye makeup and that nose thing? And the red hair. No way is *that* natural. You trying to look like a hooker?"

"It's the style."

"Whose style?"

"Girls'."

He shook his head. "Not the girls I see."

"Kansas City is miles ahead of Steadfast in the style department." Sim realized what she'd said. "I mean…"

"Too late. You blew it, girl." He sang a blues song, "'I'm going to Kansas City, Kansas City here I come.' Claire's from there too."

"Along with a million and a half other people. Maybe you should mind your own business." Sim crossed her arms. She felt a pout start but held it back. No way was she giving this pompous man the satisfaction.

Bailey snickered. "Don't worry. I won't tell."

"Whatever."

"But since I know your roots, care to tell me more? All I know is that your parents were killed, and you ran away from your aunt and uncle, and—"

"I don't like the idea of everyone knowing about me. It isn't fair. I don't butt into your business."

"Go ahead. What do you want to know?"

Now that she had the chance, Sim wasn't sure what to ask. "How come you have such a fancy restaurant in such a little town like Steadfast?"

"Why not?"

"And your clothes. People are pretty casual here. You dress up."

"All to complete the image, my dear."

"Image of what?"

"Success. You have to dress the part."

"Even if it makes you stick out?"

"Especially if it makes you stick out. You should talk."

She couldn't argue with him. She liked looking different.

"Actually, different is fun. And Bon Vivant meets a need in Steadfast."

"The need to be snobby?"

Bailey pinned her with a look. "The need to be discriminating."

"You discriminate?"

"No, no. Discrim*inating*. Refined, tasteful. A chance to treat oneself to something special and out of the ordinary. To feel pampered."

"You probably charge way too much."

Bailey shrugged. "You charge five bucks and serve a meal on a paper place mat, and people gobble down the food and go home to watch TV. You charge twenty and serve it on starched linen, and they take their time and relish it. The five-buck meal may be just as good, but the presentation—the ambience—affects the attitude as well as the stomach."

"You trick them."

"I don't trick anybody. People want what I'm selling. It's as if we have a contract. When you go for fast food the contract is for food that is quick and cheap—and you get it. When you come to Bon Vivant the contract is for a relaxed, elegant dinner—and you get it. Everybody's happy."

"Especially you, raking in the dough."

Bailey shrugged again. "I like nice things, so I created a job that provides them for Jered and me. Is that a—?"

"Jered?"

"My son."

Sim's mind swam. Jered had talked about his father owning a restaurant, and she'd known that Bailey owned a restaurant, but why hadn't she put the two together? Probably because the two didn't fit. Oil and water. Beaches and snow. Reggae and opera.

She grabbed the car handle. "I can't stay with you."

"Why not?"

"Just 'cuz."

He studied her a couple seconds before looking back to the road. "Jered won't bother you. You'll be in the guest room. It has a lock, if it makes you feel better. Besides, half the time Jered isn't home. I don't know what he does with his time."

I do.

Bailey pulled into a driveway. "Here it is. Home sweet home."

That was yet to be determined.

Bailey started by showing Sim around the house. It wasn't much to look at from the outside—just one among many houses in a row. It looked similar to Merry's in age but didn't have the curlicue wood-work on the porch. It was simple and homey. But inside it changed and turned sophisticated. There was a leather couch, oak antiques, and framed black-and-white photographs of mountains and canyons.

Sim had to admit it was nice, but she could have done without the play-by-play. She wasn't in the mood.

"And this piece I got at an estate auction." Bailey pointed out a carved bookshelf. "I was willing to pay $400 for it, but no one else knew its worth so I got it for $110. It certainly pays to do your home-work. And this painting over here is a genuine—"

Sim rolled her eyes. "Who am I? Someone to brag to?"

"What?"

"Is that why you volunteered to take me in? So you'd have some-one to show off to?"

"No, of course not."

"I want to be someone people brag *about,* not *to.*" She tapped her teeth shut, wishing she could lock her lips once and for all. *Why did I just say that? He's going to think I'm all weak and needy.*

She was surprised to see Bailey falter and his cheeks redden. He lowered his arm. "Me too, Sim. Me too."

This had gotten *way* too serious. Sim plopped down on the couch, liking the *scrunch* of the leather. "Don't you have to go to the restaurant or something?"

"Not tonight. I commandeered one of the waiters to fill in as host. I'll stop in later to check on things. But other than that, the evening is free."

Goody. "So what's there to do around here?"

Bailey looked around as if he'd never considered having to *do* anything. "I don't know…" His face lit up. "You like Monopoly?"

Sim tilted her head. *Why not?* "Only if I get to be banker."

Bailey clapped his hands. "Ha! Boardwalk! With a hotel, that will be—"

"This is not fair." Sim counted out the rent money.

"This is the epitome of fair. Can I help it if you land on Boardwalk or Park Place every time you come around the board?"

Sim looked under the kitchen table. "Do you have this thing rigged?"

"It's only rigged by my dynamic presence and business acumen. Quit complaining. I've landed on your Marvin Gardens enough."

"Not enough." Sim straightened her meager piles of money.

"Care to sell something?" Bailey stacked his five-hundred-dollar bills. "I feel generous."

"I wouldn't give you the satisfaction."

The phone rang. Bailey looked from it to the clock, then his face flushed. "Oh no…" He answered it. "Stanley, I'm so sorry. I meant to stop by, but we got sidetracked playing…we got sidetracked. How did everything go?"

They talked a bit more. Sim felt kind of good—but guilty—that Bailey had been having so much fun with her that he'd neglected his duties. To be truthful, she'd been having fun too.

"I'll be right there." Bailey hung up and turned to Sim. "I've got to run to the restaurant to pick up the night's proceeds. Want to come with me?"

"Nah. I've had enough of money tonight. I think I'll turn in."

Bailey grabbed his keys. "Be back soon."

Sim slipped under the covers and turned on her side. The moonlight fell across the floor, spotlighting her dirty clothes. Another day, another place to lay her head. But no place hers. No place home.

She closed her eyes and was surprised to find herself thinking about God. Really thinking about Him. Was He actually out there somewhere, looking down at her? Claire believed in Him. So did Merry. Should she?

She thought of all the times Claire mentioned God. And yet Sim had managed to let all reference to Him skim off as though Claire were mentioning someone as unimportant to the moment as George Washington or Santa Claus. But now, tonight, to think of Him as soon as she closed her eyes…it was as if *He* had come to *her*, as if He had set Himself before her in such a way that He couldn't be ignored.

She opened her eyes to see if the feeling of His presence faded. It did not. And somehow she knew He wasn't going anywhere.

Might as well acknowledge Him then—though she had no idea what to say.

Uh…hi, God.

She felt a sudden swell, as if she'd inhaled a breeze. It filled her body with a freshness that tingled her cells while wrapping her in a warm embrace she never wanted to leave.

Wow.

The warmth seemed to appreciate her reaction and hugged her closer than ever. She closed her eyes and let it—Him—take over. Then she realized she didn't need any more words. Somehow He *was* the Word and could handle both sides of the conversation.

Cool. Very, very cool.

When Jered came in, he found his dad putting the zipper bag of receipts on the desk in the kitchen.

"Where have you been?"

Hi. Nice to see you too. "What's it to you?"

"Behave yourself. We have a guest."

Jered looked around, his eyes resting on the Monopoly board. "Who?"

"Sim."

Jered let out a puff of air. "You're kidding."

"No, I'm not."

His jaw tightened. "Why her?"

"You know her?"

"Probably more than you."

His dad's eyebrow raised, but as usual, he didn't ask for details. "Ever since the fiasco at the library, the girl has had no place to stay. And her aunt—who wasn't her aunt…Claire's gone."

"Good riddance."

"Jered!"

He shrugged. He didn't want to hear about Sim's problems. He had enough of his own. He picked up the dice. "Why don't you ever play this with me?"

His dad blinked. "I didn't think you'd want to play anymore."

Maybe not, but I'd like to be asked. Jered tossed the dice—and his moment of weakness—on the board. He headed for the stairs. "I'm going to bed."

"Fine, but be quiet. Sim's in the guest room."

"Give it a rest, Dad." He went upstairs, making his shoes pound on the wood.

Great. Just great. Competition.

Seventeen

If anyone thinks he is something when he is nothing,
he deceives himself.

GALATIANS 6:3

"COME ON, LET'S GO!"

Sim heard Bailey's call from the kitchen but didn't answer because she was right outside Jered's bedroom door. She quickly slipped downstairs, hoping to be gone before Jered woke up.

Bailey held the door open. "Ready to see the sights of Bon Vivant?"

Sim stopped with one foot on the threshold. "I can't go with you, Bailey. I have to work at the library." It was a lie—Merry had told her she didn't have to work—but spending the day with this man was not what she had in mind.

"Au contraire, mademoiselle." Bailey shooed her out. "It's Sunday morning. The library doesn't open until one. Besides, Merry gave me free rein to do with you as I will. And today you are mine."

"A scary thought."

Bailey rushed by her and opened the car door with flourish. "You have no idea."

After he got in the car, she eyed him. "You like Merry, don't you?"

The ignition ground against itself; the engine already engaged. He blushed. "A lot of good it's done me." He turned in his seat to back out of the driveway, flashing her a look. "Now be quiet. Aren't children supposed to be seen and not heard?"

Bailey pulled into the parking lot behind Bon Vivant. He got out of the car. Sim did too, reluctantly. "Why are you going into work in the morning? Nobody comes to eat until lunch."

"To make a meal look effortless, you must expend effort."

"I don't like the sound of this."

"What?"

"You must expend effort, or *I* must expend effort?"

Bailey paused before going inside. "Are you a lazy bum?"

"Not usually."

"Then you should have nothing to worry about."

Sim put a hand on Bailey's arm. "Just remember the child labor laws, all right?"

"I'll keep them in mind."

They entered a huge kitchen. Stainless steel was the norm. A Hispanic man wearing a white cook's uniform stirred a pan on the industrial-size stove.

"Morning, Sanchez."

The man's eyes touched on Bailey, then landed on Sim. "Got yourself a new partner, Bailey?"

With a hand on Sim's back, Bailey urged her forward. Sim moved away from his touch and held out a hand. "Hi, I'm Sim. Bailey's slave."

"Welcome to the club." When Sanchez grinned, the corners of his eyes crinkled.

"Hey, you two. Quit acting like I'm Simon Legree."

Sanchez leaned toward Sim. "He keeps his whip in the pantry."

"I'll remember that."

Sanchez resumed stirring. "Why are you in here so early, Bailey?"

When Sim saw Bailey blush, she knew their early-morning outing had been another ploy to show off. But feeling she had an ally in Sanchez, she didn't rub it in.

"There's a good chance we've got a food reviewer coming tonight. Everything has to be perfect."

"A food critic?" Sim looked at him. "My uncle—"

Bailey raised an eyebrow. "Your uncle what?"

Sim shrugged. Her uncle wrote about food for a magazine, but she sure wasn't going to tell him that. "Nothing. I always thought reviewers came on the sly."

"They do. Usually. But I have connections and found out they were coming tonight. I don't know what they look like, but I'm going to be prepared."

"That's why I'm here too," Sanchez said. "I wanted to perfect the sauce for the Chocolat Bordeaux."

Sim peeked into the pan of melted chocolate. "It smells great."

"Only because it is." The chef's eyes lit up. "It starts with a macaroon and caramelized sugar crust with layers of strawberries soaked in Bordeaux wine alternating with a thin white cake that has been baked with chunks of chocolate. On top is the sauce." He lifted the spoon and the smooth chocolate flowed from it into the pan. "This recipe came about because my grandma broke her hip. I was only twelve, and my mom was baking—"

Bailey waved his hands, stopping the story. "I don't care how you came up with it, only that you *did*—and that it's perfect."

Sanchez made a mock bow. "Anything you say, oh mighty master."

Bailey looked toward the other room. "Help Sanchez a few minutes, will you, Sim? I have things to do in the dining room. I'll come get you when I need you."

Sim made her own bow. "Anything you say, oh mighty master." She was glad to be rid of the man.

Sanchez laughed. "I promise I won't bake, broil, or fry her."

"If you do, don't make a mess." Bailey left the kitchen.

Sim sighed. "Is he always so hyper?"

"Oh, Bailey's a good guy. He just likes things the way he likes them. His whole life is this place. He wants it to succeed."

"Is it?"

"Succeeding? As far as I can see. He had the bucks to hire me, didn't he?"

"You're not a cook, you're a real chef."

Sanchez bowed. "Chef Sanchez Sanders, at your service."

"You went to school for this?"

"Good food is more than measuring cups and turning on the oven." He scraped the sides of the pan. "Bailey has his dream and I have mine."

"What's yours?"

"To create one perfect recipe that is mine alone."

"The chocolate stuff?"

Sanchez laughed. "*Stuff* is not exactly the word I was going for."

"You were telling me how you came up with the recipe."

Sanchez dipped a spoon in the chocolate and held it to Sim's lips. Sim blew on it and then tasted. "Wow. I'd eat this plain."

"And only get half the experience." Sanchez turned off the burner and moved to a white cake on the counter. He took a long serrated knife and began to slice it into thin horizontal layers.

"The story?"

"Ah yes. I was twelve and my mother was mixing the batter for a white cake—just one of those cheap mixes—when the phone rang. It was news that my grandmother had fallen and broken her hip, so Mom had to leave. The last thing she told me was, 'Finish up, Sanny, and don't make a mess.'"

"I bet you made a mess."

"An act of God would have left less debris. Of course, turning the mixer on high didn't help. Batter was everywhere."

Sim pulled a stool near the counter. "How did you go from a cheap white cake to Chocolat Bordeaux?"

Sanchez put a finger to his lips. "My mother left behind her glass of red wine and—"

"You got drunk and created the recipe while in a stupor?"

"Whose story *is* this, anyway?"

"Sorry."

"Anyway, it was spring and we'd just picked some fresh strawberries from our garden, and I dunked one of them in the wine and tasted it. It was good, even to my twelve-year-old taste buds. In the pantry I found chocolate chips and poured a bunch in the batter. I topped the cake with some chocolate frosting from a tub. When Mom got home from the hospital, I cut her a piece of cake, sliced through the middle so I could slip in a layer of the wine-soaked berries, and put a berry on top."

"Did she like it?"

"She thought it was wonderful, but she forbade me from ever making it again—the mess, you know. But when Bailey wanted me to create a new chocolate dessert that could be exclusive to Bon Vivant, I remembered the experience. I've been working on it for a month now."

"I'd like to eat the rejects. I bet they're good too."

Sanchez patted his belly. "I do my own testing, thank you." He started to layer the strawberries and cake on the bed of crumbled macaroons. "So that's my story. What's yours, little lady? Why are you hanging out with the likes of Bailey?"

"I'm a runaway orphan living in the library."

He stared at her. "That's you?"

"That's me."

"The waiters were talking about you."

"I hope my fifteen minutes of fame is up."

"You might have a few seconds left."

"Lucky me."

"So Bailey took you in? Sorry, but that doesn't sound like—"

"He's trying to earn brownie points with Merry Cavanaugh. After the library, I was staying with her, but she left because her mom's having an operation." She twisted the stool back and forth.

"Wasn't Claire involved in all that?"

"You know Claire?"

"Sure. She worked here one night as a server."

"She told me that." Sim squinted at the chef. "What did you think of her?"

"Unflappable. Nothing fazed her. On a busy night, it's like recess at a grade school in here, everyone running around, yelling for something and wanting it now. She'd stand still with this little grin on her face as if she alone recognized the absurdity of the situation. Dave— he's the salad man—said he was so impressed with her calm that he'd make *her* salads first. As a reward, I guess. There was something about the lady that made all of us want to please her."

Then why didn't I try to please her?

"Where is she? We sure could use her."

"She had to go away for a while. But she'll be back, I know she will."

Sanchez stopped his work and Sim saw the pity in his eyes. And kindness. It was the same look Cook used to give her when her parents did something hurtful.

Maybe a heart for cooking and a heart for compassion went together.

Sim was tired. She'd spent two hours helping Bailey clean the dining room even though it looked clean enough. Working at the library was one thing, but this scrubbing, vacuuming, and dusting was another. No fun at all.

Bailey's attitude didn't help. Sim had been kidding about being his slave, yet Bailey barked commands like a vindictive overseer. An *obsessive* vindictive overseer. He had made Sim rewipe all the salt and pepper shakers because she missed a speck of food on one. Ridiculous.

Once the Sunday lunch crowd started, she bussed tables.

When she noticed Bailey alone in the waiting area, she took her tub of dishes with her and dropped it on a chair with a clatter.

"Hey! Be careful."

Sim leaned back in a chair and crossed her arms. "Can slaves resign?"

Bailey straightened the menus. "Don't exaggerate. I haven't worked you that hard."

"Without looking at your watch, what time is it?"

Bailey put a hand over his watch as if the mere order not to look at it would prove too tempting. "I don't know...one-thirty?"

"Almost three."

Bailey removed his hand and stared at his watch. "No, it couldn't—"

"It is." Sim gathered the cleaning supplies. "I said I'd help bus tables tonight, but if I'm going to do that, I'd really like some time off in-between. I want to go to the library and see if Claire's come back."

"Sure, sure." Bailey rubbed his head. "I had no idea...the time...hey, sorry, Sim. You've been a big help, and I know I haven't been easy to work for today. I'm just nervous about this reviewer coming. A lot rides on these things."

Sim put a hand on Bailey's shoulder. "It'll be fine. The place is glowing and Sanchez's dessert…you tasted it at lunch. It's great."

Bailey glanced at her. "You're a good girl, Sim. Jered could learn from you."

Speaking of… "I thought Jered worked for you."

Bailey's laugh was bitter. "Jered and work go together like jalapeños and chocolate."

"Maybe the restaurant business isn't his thing."

"If it's his *thing* he's after, he'd have to find a job drinking beer and sleeping late."

"Why don't you want him to be a musician?"

"He told you about that?"

"If it's his dream, why don't you let him go for it?"

Bailey straightened the already-straightened menus. "So now you're a parenting expert?"

"No, but—"

"If my son *ever* showed me he could stick to something for more than two days, I'd consider it. Going after your dream is hard work." Bailey put a fist to his heart. "You've got to live it in your soul. You've got to *have* to do it or die."

Sim had never seen someone with so much passion. She couldn't imagine feeling that way about a restaurant, but Bailey's fire cast him in a better light. "I wish I felt that driven about something."

Bailey let his fist relax and looked at it as if he hadn't realized he made the gesture. He took a breath. "Go on now. If you're back at six, that's soon enough."

Sim stopped at the door. "Everything will be fine tonight, Bailey. I know it will."

Since Merry was gone, and Blanche and Ivan were filling in, Sim didn't want to go in the front door of the library and risk running into anyone who'd been present when the library ghost fiasco came down. Not yet. Plus she didn't want to answer any questions about how things were going with Bailey. All she wanted to do was check the attic for signs of Claire.

She slipped in the back door and took the stairs. Even before she opened the attic door, she sensed Claire wasn't there. She slumped onto Claire's bed.

Where are you?

Sim opened her eyes. She looked at her watch. Five o'clock. She hadn't planned to spend her free time sleeping. She stretched and looked out the attic window. Kids rollerbladed through the square by City Hall and two more rode their bikes as if nothing was wrong in the world. A surge of envy hit her. Would she ever be a normal kid again? Had she ever been a normal kid?

She slipped down the stairs and out, heading back to Bon Vivant. She heard a vehicle driving slowly behind her. Her arms prickled.

"Hey, little orphan Simmy."

Jered. Maybe if I don't turn around...

"Talk to me, ghost." It was Moog. "Or do you think you're too good for us, making a fool of the town by doing that library ghost junk?"

Sim took a strengthening breath and turned. "I didn't make a fool of anybody. I was only trying to—"

"Trying to butt in where you had no business butting."

"Yeah." Darrell sat in the middle of the other two. "You tricked us."

"I didn't *trick* anybody."

Moog pointed a finger across Darrell. "We took you in as a friend. And this is how you repay us? By lying to us?"

"And taking over my father?"

They all looked at Jered.

"Well, she did."

Sim's gut wrenched. "Your dad's just being nice, letting me stay with you guys while Merry is—"

"You're staying with *him*, not me." Jered glanced at Moog and Darrell, making sure he had their attention. "Did you have fun playing Monopoly with Daddy, Simmy?" His voice hardened. "How old are you, anyway? Ten?"

Sim felt herself redden. "I like Monopoly. I will always like Monopoly."

"Ooooh, such a woman. Taking a stand for Boardwalk. What are you going to do tonight? Play Candy Land?"

"Actually, I'm going to work my tail off at your dad's restaurant. He's expecting a restaurant reviewer this evening, and I spent most of the day helping him get everything perfect."

Moog squealed and offered a limp wrist. "That bernuz sauce is simply too-too mahvelous fer words."

"*Béarnaise* sauce." Sim looked at Jered. "Why aren't you helping him?"

"I don't have to work in my father's busin—"

Moog laughed. "Unless he makes you."

Jered leveled him with a look. "It's his business. Not mine."

"And your business is?"

Darrell laughed. "Getting into trouble."

"Want to go for a ride with some real men?" Jered revved the truck's motor.

Sim rolled her eyes. Bailey was right. Jered would never achieve his dream. Not when all he cared about was messing around. "No thanks. I have a really important game of Chutes and Ladders to get back to." She walked away. The sounds of the boys' laughter faded with the roar of the engine.

Morons.

Jered headed out of town.

"I thought we were going to rent some movies and have pizza at my house," Darrell said.

"Yeah," Moog said. "I want to see that new slasher movie. We should have gotten Sim to watch it with us because she'd get all scared and want to cuddle, and I could—"

"Twenty-two people get killed in that movie." Darrell grinned. "I think it's so cool when the victims walk through their house in the dark and then this knife comes out and..."

Jered tuned them out. He liked horror flicks as much as the next guy, but at the moment they seemed inconsequential—like discussing which shoes to wear to Judgment Day. Ever since seeing Sim, his insides had begun a frenzied dance, wanting to leap through his skin. It was like he had something to do but he didn't know what it was.

"Enough cruising. Jered, turn back to town. We don't want—"

Jered swerved the truck onto the shoulder and jerked to a stop, sending his friends forward into the dash.

"Hey!"

"Out!" Jered ordered.

They stared at him. "What?"

"Get out. I've got something to do."

"Like what?"

Not knowing the answer to that question only fueled his anger. Jered shoved the truck in park and opened his door, not quite believing what he was about to do. "Do I have to drag you guys out or—?"

Moog opened the passenger door and got out. "You'd better watch it." He pointed a finger. "I don't know what your problem is, but I don't like it."

"You can't just leave us here." Darrell was almost whining.

"Sure I can." Jered shut his own door, then reached across the seat and pulled theirs shut. He forced his eyes to focus on his friends standing on the edge of the highway. *What am I doing?* He called to them through the window, forcing his voice to be friendly. "Got things to do. Sorry about this. I'll make it up to you."

As he drove away, Moog's yell followed him: "You'd better believe it!"

Jered's head hurt. He gripped the steering wheel so as not to veer off the road with the pain.

First Sim takes my job at the library, then she stays with Merry, then she gets my *dad to take her in. Then she works for him in* my *place.*

He continued away from Steadfast, the urge to drive straight and fast accelerating with his anger.

As soon as he surrendered to the impulse, his headache lessened.

And with the absence of pain, he began to enjoy himself. He noticed the speedometer inching upward into the eighties. He was invincible. No one could stop him.

He spotted an oncoming car on the horizon and fixed on it. As it got closer, he leaned over the steering wheel, the car an objective.

He found the thought odd but didn't have time to analyze it. He flexed his fingers and positioned them on the wheel, ready for action. When the car was seconds away from passing alongside him, Jered jerked the wheel toward the center line.

The other driver reacted, turning away from danger. Too much. His right tires found the soft shoulder.

Jered looked back and saw brake lights. Another glance let him see the car fishtail as it tried to get back on the road. And yet another let him witness the car's descent into the ditch.

He looked in his rearview mirror in time to see the dust settle around the accident. His stomach lurched.

What have I done?

He pulled to the side of the road, flung open the door, and hurled himself onto the shoulder. Then he threw up.

Sim watched Bailey wipe his palms on his pants. The man was oozing politeness, pasting on his best host-smile. "Good evening…lovely weather…you look beautiful this evening…"

A lone man entered the restaurant. When Bailey did a double take and straightened his shoulders, Sim realized he'd deemed this man the reviewer. *Watch out, buddy. You're in for some heavy schmoozing.*

Bailey stood his full height and straightened his tie. He cleared his throat and smiled. "Good evening, sir, may I help you?"

"Morrison. Table for one. Nonsmoking."

"Right this way, Mr. Morrison." Bailey led the man to one of Stanley's tables. He told him the specials. As he passed Stanley, he crooked a finger at him—and Sim—leading them back into the kitchen.

"The man dining alone. Mr. Morrison. That's the reviewer."

Stanley peeked out the window in the door.

"Don't look at him!" Bailey yanked him back. "We aren't supposed to know it's him."

"Then how *do* we know it's him?"

"We just know." Bailey glanced through the window himself. "You'd better get out there. Make me proud, everyone."

"So it's show time?" Sanchez asked from the stove.

Bailey held up two sets of crossed fingers.

It was pitiful. The man was obsessed.

Sim was glad Mr. Morrison ordered Chocolat Bordeaux for dessert. From a discreet distance, she watched as he took a bite. As the food hit his palate, his chewing slowed, as though he was savoring the taste. His head cocked and he nodded.

He likes it! Sanchez would be so happy.

But just as she was going to go give the chef the news, Bailey approached the table.

"How is your dessert, Mr. Morrison?"

The man brushed his napkin against his lips. "Truly delectable. Such an unusual combination of tastes."

"It's an exclusive creation of Bon Vivant."

Mr. Morrison nodded. "I'm a bit of a rookie chef myself. I'm always curious how such recipes come about."

Sim's stomach engaged. Bailey hadn't listened to Sanchez's story. What would he do? What could he do?

In a flash, she knew.

He'd lie.

Even as she heard Bailey's words, Sim had trouble believing what she was hearing.

"Actually, my grandmother came up with the idea of the basic cake," Bailey said. "I merely added the sauce."

"Then I compliment the chef—your grandmother."

Bailey glanced in Sim's direction. His eyes widened. He looked back at Mr. Morrison.

Sim couldn't stand the sight of him. She retreated into the kitchen.

Sanchez looked up from his stirring. "What's wrong, Sim?"

Her thoughts played darts, none of them hitting the bull's-eye. "Nothing."

Plenty.

Sim couldn't stand it any longer. She sought Bailey out in the waiting area. "Why'd you do it?"

He looked up from the reservation book, giving Sim an employer-to-employee look. "Excuse me?"

"Why'd you take credit for Sanchez's dessert? It's his creation, not yours."

Bailey glanced toward the dining room and pasted on an amiable face in case any diners looked his way. "Don't lecture me, kid."

"It was wrong."

"It was necessary. I didn't know the real story, and the reviewer wanted an explanation as to how the dessert came about. What was I supposed to do? Say 'I don't know'?"

" 'I don't know' is better than a lie."

Bailey stacked the menus. "I won't take this from you."

"You could have gotten Sanchez, brought him out, and introduced him. Couldn't you have done that?"

Bailey's silence was proof that he'd never thought of it.

"My dad used to pull stuff like this. I'd hear him on the phone, arguing with someone after he'd taken credit for their ideas."

"I'm not your dad."

Sim raised her chin and looked Bailey straight in the eye. "No, you're not." She turned toward the dining room. "I've got work to do. Honest work."

As she returned to the kitchen, Sim thought about the words she'd just said to Bailey: *honest work*. The reality of what she'd witnessed was the epitome of *dis*honesty, and it was a blow to the concept of rewards coming to those who did the work. Sanchez had worked hard to create that recipe. He deserved the appreciation that went with it.

Like he deserved to know what had just gone on.

Sim went over to the stove. Sanchez was pouring a sauce over a cut of veal. He gave her a glance. "What's up, little lady? And don't say *nothing*."

Sim checked the location of the waiters and other kitchen help. They were all scrambling with their orders, not paying attention to her, though she could tell by the occasional glance that their curiosity had been piqued.

"Can I talk to you a minute? Alone?"

Sanchez chuckled. "There's no such thing as alone in the kitchen of a restaurant, Sim. Not during eating hours."

"Oh."

Sanchez studied her face for a moment, then scanned the kitchen. The curiosity of the others had turned to a deeper interest.

"Don't you people have anything to do? Shoo!"

The bustle resumed full force. He turned to Sim. "How 'bout you whisper it in my ear while I cook up this salmon?"

It would have to do. Sanchez leaned down, and Sim leaned close. She put her lips to his ear. "Bailey took credit for your dessert with the restaurant critic. He said it was his creation."

Sanchez jerked back. "He *what?*"

Sim nodded, not wanting to say it again.

Sanchez shook his head. "So if the man likes it and gives it a good review, Bailey will get the credit."

Sim shrugged.

Sanchez noticed the salmon smoking and turned it over. "Well, that's that, then."

"That's what?"

"I quit."

"You—?"

He turned the knobs on the stove to *off* with a flourish. "I'm gone. I can't stay in a place where the owner steals my dream out from under me."

Stanley appeared with a tray. "What's wrong?"

Sanchez told him. And then he told the others. The kitchen activity halted as all listened to his story and his harsh words.

Sim slunk away. *What have I done?*
I have to get out of here. Now!

Sim went into the dining room, nearly bumping into Bailey as he headed into the kitchen. She took his arm, stopping him.

"What?" He lowered his voice. "Not now. I'm busy and I intend to find out why I'm the only one who is. Where is everybody?"

She held on to his sleeve. "I don't feel very good, Bailey. Can I go home early?"

Home. What a joke. She had no intention of going back to *his* house. Another bridge burned. Another haven deserted.

"No, you cannot. I need you here. Can't you hold on another hour?"

"I—"

Loud voices came from the kitchen. "What is going on in there?" With a backward glance to the customers, he took Sim's arm and pulled her into the kitchen with him.

As he entered, the staff slid out of the line of fire. Sanchez was packing his personal utensils in a tomato paste box.

Sim felt Bailey's fingers tighten around her arm.

"What are you doing?"

Sanchez didn't even look at Bailey as he answered. "Leaving."

"You can't leave."

Sanchez pointed a whisk at Bailey. "Why did you take credit for my recipe?"

Sim pulled away and tried to sneak behind the ovens.

"Sim! Get over here!" Sim showed herself but kept her distance. "Feeling sick, my foot. This is your fault, isn't it?"

Sanchez tossed the whisk into the box. "This is *your* fault, Bailey. You knew how important it was for me to create one great recipe. You knew how hard I've worked on it. Yet you took the credit." He waved his hands to encompass the restaurant. "Isn't this enough for you? Do you have to grab my dream too?"

"I didn't grab—"

"You did." Sanchez dipped his head. His voice softened. "You can't have it all, Bailey. You need to leave some pride for the rest of us."

"I didn't give you credit because I didn't know your story. The reviewer put me in a bind—"

"You didn't know my story because you've never taken the time to listen to it." He waved a hand at Sim. "This little lady took the time. She knows more than you do. Admit it, Bailey. You said it was yours because it made you feel important. You stole the glory for yourself. You smuggled my accomplishments as if they were your own."

Bailey's features paled. "Look, I'm sorry. I was wrong. I won't do it again. Just don't leave. We can work something out. I'll hunt the guy down, I'll tell him the whole truth."

Sanchez shook his head. "It's like my grandma used to say, 'Consequences are inevitable.' I can forgive you, Bailey. But the forgetting part...I don't know. We'll see."

Bailey grabbed on to this bit of hope. "Then you'll stay?"

"Stay? No. I quit. I won't be at work tomorrow. As for the next day...?"

Sim glanced up at Bailey. He looked as if he was going to be sick. "But if you leave, how will we finish out the night? How will we open tomorrow? You're the only one who knows how—"

Sanchez lifted the box and headed for the back door. "Consequences, Bailey. Without truth, there are consequences. Deal with it."

Sim hugged the passenger door of Bailey's car. The silence was stifling. If only Bailey would yell. She was used to yelling. She could hold her own against yelling. But silence? She could barely breathe under the weight of it.

She'd tried to skip out of Bon Vivant, but every time she headed for the exit, Bailey was there, pulling her back. Being in his presence was the ultimate torture.

When they got to his house, Bailey didn't wait for her to get out of the car, or even to come up the walk. He let the kitchen door slam, and Sim heard his keys tossed on the counter.

Her legs tensed. Now was her chance. He was out of sight. She could run away.

And yet, suddenly she didn't want to run. She was tired of running. Would running make the past go away? As Sanchez had said, "Consequences are inevitable."

She surprised herself by slipping inside and closing the door. She leaned against it to wait for the storm that would surely come.

Bailey busied himself with a pile of notes on the kitchen desk. He did not look up. "You've been trying to escape all night, so what I am about to say should please you. You can stay here tonight, but in the morning, you're gone. I'll call Blanche tomorrow and see if she'll take you in, recliner or no recliner. The great philanthropic experiment is over."

Tears were imminent, but Sim would not let them come. "I'm really sorry—"

Bailey's nostrils flared. He kept his distance but pointed an accusing finger. "You had *no* right to tell Sanchez what I said to the reviewer. You're a kid and I'm an adult. You have no idea what grief your interference has caused me. I spent months trying to find a chef as good as Sanchez. Do you know how hard it is to get a decent chef to move to a small town like Steadfast? I'm paying him a big-city salary to live in a small town. It's killing me. But I figured it would be worth it because he's good. Very good."

"Then why didn't you give him credit for the dessert?"

Bailey's jaw tightened. "I'm not going to go over this again. It would have worked out. I'd have made sure Sanchez got his due. I had to make an instantaneous decision. And I made it. You can't just butt into people's lives."

Sim's voice was small. "You're butting into mine."

"I'm trying to help you!"

"And I was trying to help you!"

Bailey shook his head, his breathing labored. "Get out of my sight."

Sim's feet were lead. Each step dipped into her reservoir of energy. As she reached the landing, Bailey added, "Are you sure your aunt and uncle didn't kick you out?"

She wanted to die. Even climbing onto the bed was too much work. She sank to the floor like a discarded sack of potatoes. She wiped her nose on her sleeve and pushed the tears into her hair. How could everything go so wrong? Just a few hours earlier, she'd been defending Bailey's business to Jered and defending Jered's dream to his father. She'd even secretly enjoyed bussing tables, helping Bailey out. Why had she told Sanchez what she'd overheard? If only she hadn't heard it in the first place. If only she'd given Bailey her loyalty instead of betraying him. If only she'd kept her mouth shut.

I've blown it.

With those three words, she knew what she had to do.

As soon as he heard his father's angry voice, Jered turned down the volume on his computer video game. *Finally, someone else is in trouble.* He stopped playing until Sim's bedroom door clicked shut and, soon after, his father's slammed. *Ha! One orphan girl bites the dust.*

He was just about to turn the volume back up when he heard soft footsteps in the hall. He recognized the sound of sneaking when he heard it. He cracked his door in time to see Sim turn the corner on the landing. She was carrying her backpack. He waited for the victory sound of the front door closing.

Click.

He smiled. Things were looking up.

Sim climbed into the loft of the barn and settled by the window. She picked up a piece of straw and broke it in pieces.

She wasn't sure why she'd returned here. All logic said she should have kept going, out of Steadfast, on to another town where they didn't know her. Judge her. Hate her.

See what happens when you try to belong? Maybe it was time to face the fact she never would. Not in Steadfast, not with her aunt and uncle, not anywhere.

She fell onto her side, cushioning her head with an arm. She closed her eyes. A tear snuck through and skimmed her cheek. If only Claire were there to say just the right thing.

But what would Claire say?

You're not alone, Sim.

She knew it was true. Deep down, she knew it. She felt it.

Please, God. I'm so sorry. I can't handle things anymore.

She and God had been in opposite corners. But after last night's time with Him, and with her simple prayer just said, it was as if a bell sounded and God crossed the space between them—not with fists raised, but with arms outstretched. Sim rose to meet Him, then hesitated.

With all she'd done, could she really move forward...toward Him? It wasn't just the Sanchez incident that weighed on her heart. It was every questionable thing she'd done since her parents died— since *before* her parents died. Her clothes, her hair, her pierced nose, her drinking, her I-can-do-it attitude. Her rudeness toward Claire. Throwing apples at Harold. Her sins—her motives—it all sat on her like a huge boulder. The only way to breathe, to move, was to surrender, right there, in front of God.

She moaned. *I can't believe I'm doing this...but I...I need You, God.*

As soon as the words took flight, Sim was free. She took a step forward. God made up the distance and pulled her into His everlasting arms.

She'd never be lonely again.

Eighteen

*Consider it pure joy, my brothers, whenever
you face trials of many kinds,
because you know that the testing of your faith
develops perseverance.*

JAMES 1:2–3

JERED WOKE UP TO THE BLARE of one of his dad's oppressive
Wagnerian symphonies. He snuck to the top of the stairs and peeked
down. His dad sat in the living room, his hands clasped in his lap, his
eyes straight ahead. He looked at his watch.

Was he waiting for Sim?

It would be a long wait. Suddenly his dad looked toward the
stairs. "Sim?" He had to raise his voice to be heard above the music.

Jered came down. "No, father dearest, it's not your precious Sim.
It's just me, your detested son."

His dad turned back around, crossing his arms. "Don't get cocky.
I'm not in the mood."

"By the way, if you're waiting for Sim, she's gone."

In a single movement, his father pushed himself out of the chair
and shut the music off. The amputated notes dissipated in the silence.
"What did you say?"

Jered scratched his chest and headed for the kitchen. "She's gone.
It's just you and—"

His father grabbed his arm. "Why didn't you stop her?"

Jered shook the touch away. "I say good riddance."

His dad took a step back. "Don't be petulant."

"Since when did we start taking in strays?"

"It's too early in the morning for sarcasm, Jered. Get to the point."

"It's never too early for sarcasm, and who's being sarcastic?" He moved into the kitchen, yanked open the refrigerator door, and took a swig of milk from the carton. "You're getting bent out of shape over a stupid girl."

"I was responsible for that stupid girl. Merry was depending—"

Aha. "So that's it. You aren't worried about Sim as much as impressing a woman who doesn't even know you exist." He grabbed an apple and polished it against his shirt. "Merry doesn't like you, you know."

"Hold it right there. You have no right—"

"Everyone can see it except you. She thinks you're sickening."

His father perched his fingers on his forehead and took a breath. "I don't need this. When did Sim leave?"

"Middle of the night."

His dad's eyes widened. "Where did she go? She's just a kid."

"So am I."

His dad's eyebrows touched as if Jered had spoken the words in Russian. "You're nearly grown. Sim's just starting out."

Jered withdrew the unbitten apple from his mouth. "And she's full of potential, right? She's not a lost cause like I am. You *bet* it's different. You *care* about her."

His dad took a step forward. "I didn't mean—"

Jered raised a hand, fending him off. *If he were a good father, he'd still come hug me. He'd force me to hug him.* "Of course you meant it."

"Jered—"

"I know I'm a disappointment. The dream of a music career isn't on the same level as the dream of running a restaurant, right? What I want isn't important."

"You're being childish again."

Jered inhaled a huge gulp of air and, with one swift movement, heaved the apple against the kitchen wall. It splattered like shrapnel, the pulp slipping to the floor with sickening whispers of *shlup.*

Jered's chest heaved, his face hot. "My dreams are childish?"

His dad looked toward the door. "I didn't—"

"You *did!*" Jered took a step forward, and his dad raised a hand to fend off a blow. Jered stepped back, going cold. *He thought I was going to hit him!*

His dad's hand dropped and his face mirrored his own realization of the awful truth.

So this is how it is…

Jered swept the Monopoly game to the floor.

They stood in silence a moment, studying the mess.

"That was totally unnecessary, Jered."

"Actually, it was extremely necessary if it got your attention. And it's symbolic. Trouble-child Jered is being replaced, swiped off the family roles, just like the game."

"Don't be ridiculous." His dad blinked and seemed to change gears as he shifted from one foot to the other. "You stay out too late, you sleep too late, you—"

"Maybe everything's too late."

His father stood behind a chair. "Listen, Jered, I'd love to have you—"

"Disappear off the face of the earth."

"What?"

Jered paced in front of the counter. The feeling consuming him was like the disturbing exhilaration he'd experienced when he'd driven the car off the road. A frightening mix of anticipation and dread, power and weakness, confidence and doubt. "You'd be thrilled if I was gone instead of Sim. Maybe she's the brave one here. Leaving this loser house. Finding a better life anywhere else." He stopped and faced his father. "Admit it. You'd like me out of here so the path would be clear to train some other, more *worthy* successor."

"Jered—"

"You've hated me ever since I got old enough to use my own brain."

"When was that?"

Jered felt the slap of the words.

"Hey, I'm sorry. I didn't mean…it just slipped—"

Jered raised his chin, forcing it not to quiver. "The truth slipped out, didn't it, Dad? You think more of a stranger than you do about me."

"That's not true."

"You hate me."

"That's not true either. I hate your attitude. Your choices."

"You've forced me into those choices."

"That's a lie." His dad's hands began to shake. He clasped them together. "I've done nothing—"

Jered gave a harsh laugh. "Exactly. You've done nothing to make me think I was worth anything. For years you've been telling me what I don't do right. Ignoring what I want. Making fun of my dream."

His father laughed this time. "You bet I make fun of it. You say you want to be a famous singer, yet I never hear you sing."

"I don't sing in front of *you* because you don't want to hear me sing."

He hesitated. "If I felt you really had *any* chance, I'd be right behind—"

The fight spilled out of Jered and pain rushed in to replace it. "You don't think I have a chance? At all?"

His dad rubbed a hand across his shirt. "Jered, face it. The odds are against you. I don't want you to get hurt."

"But I *am* hurt! I'm hurting *now.*"

His dad winced. "If I let you try the singing thing—"

"*Let* me?" Jered resumed his pacing. "So I don't know where to start with this music business. So what? I deserve a chance. Everyone deserves a chance."

"Then look into it. Do some research. Show some…gumption."

Jered stopped pacing. "You're always throwing my faults in my face."

"You're the one who flaunts your faults. You seem proud of your disrespect, your lack of responsibility, your loser friends, your drinking. And lately—"

"Did you ever consider I drink because I don't get any respect and because you don't trust me to assume any real responsibility for my life?"

His father hesitated. "You haven't shown much interest in the restaurant."

"That's because I don't *care* about the restaurant!"

"You don't care—?"

"You are deaf, dumb, and blind! You don't know a thing about me. You think because I'm your son I want to do what you do, be what you are."

"But you just complained I was showing Sim—"

Jered flicked a tear from his cheek as if it were acid. "I complained because you show more interest in Sim than you do in your own son."

"Jered—"

"No!" He turned toward the kitchen door, grabbing the knob like a falling man needing a handhold. He flexed his fingers but held on. When he spoke again, he found his voice surprisingly soft. "I want you to love me."

"I do—"

Jered whipped around. "Don't lie to me!"

His dad sucked in a breath and put a hand to his chest. His eyes widened in shock. In a single moment of clarity Jered knew what was happening, but all he had time to say was "No!"

His father collapsed to the floor.

Sim shot to a sitting position.

Go to Bailey's!

She held her breath. She looked out the window of the loft to see who spoke to her. She was alone. It was morning. A few cars drove by on their way to work. Sim shook her head, discounting—

Go. To. Bailey's.

She didn't take more time to think. She ignored the ladder and jumped down from the loft, running as fast as she could.

Sim pounded on Bailey's front door.

No answer.

She cupped her hand to the window. Bailey wasn't in the living room or the dining room. She looked beyond to the kitch—

Is that a pair of legs?

She tried the door. It was locked. She ran around back. The kitchen door was open. Bailey was in a heap on the floor, Monopoly pieces scattered around him.

Sim grabbed the phone and called 911.

Jered hid behind the neighbor's garage and watched as the ambulance took his father away, Sim riding in the back. *Like the daughter.*

Yet if it weren't for Sim…

His father was alive but the heart attack was Jered's fault. *If* his father woke up, he would remember their argument and any love he had for his son would die.

In spite of everything, Jered cared about his dad. He even loved him. *I'm so sorry, Dad, so sor—*

An arrow flew through his organs. He clutched his middle and moaned.

He forgot about love—and the pain went away.

Nineteen

"Therefore my people will know my name;
therefore in that day they will know that it is I who foretold it.
Yes, it is I."

ISAIAH 52:6

MERRY WAS EAGER TO GET HOME. In so many ways it had been a wasted trip. Not that her mother hadn't had an operation, but the needle biopsy had been far less involved than she'd described. Outpatient. Thirty minutes, tops.

In fact, within three hours of the procedure, Merry's mom suggested they order takeout. They'd actually stayed up until eleven watching an old Jimmy Stewart movie.

Not that she begrudged her mother some attention, but the timing was awful. Leaving Sim just after Claire left her? And leaving her in Bailey's charge? What had she been thinking?

She tested the speed limit.

Sim tore the paper cup into pieces. She stared at the floor of the hospital waiting room. They'd been doing tests on Bailey all day. They were shooting dye into the arteries to see where the blockage was. After the test they'd know what to do next. Balloon-something-or-other, or even bypass surgery. Procedures that meant nothing before now took on vivid meaning with huge consequences.

I hate hospitals. Bailey could die. Wasn't that what happened in hospitals?

"You're making quite a mess."

Merry stood in the doorway of the waiting room. Sim jumped up and gratefully accepted a hug. "When did you get back?"

"Just now."

"How's your mom?"

"She's fine. But Bailey…?"

"How did you find out?"

"I stopped at the library. Blanche said you've been here since early morning?"

Sim sank into a chair and resumed her shredding. "Bailey's having tests right now."

"It's good you were staying with him."

But I ran away.

Merry looked around the waiting room and shivered.

"What's wrong?"

She took a deep breath. "I hate hospitals, and two hospitals in two days is testing my tolerance."

Sim nodded. "People die in hospitals."

Merry lifted the girl's chin. "But not today, Sim. Not today." She took another look around the waiting room. "Where's Jered?"

"I don't think he even knows what happened."

"That kid. We need to find—"

The doctor came in. He winked at Sim but went to Merry. "Merry. Glad you're here to help our heroine out."

She turned to Sim. "Heroine?"

Sim shook her head. She didn't want this kind of attention.

"Bailey needs an angioplasty—a balloon to open up the blocked artery."

"But he's so young."

The doctor shrugged. "It happens. Rich foods, little exercise, stress."

Sim sank into a chair. *It's all my fault.*

"When is he scheduled?"

"As soon as possible."

"What are the risks?"

"Angioplasty is routine. Although there is always risk, with the proper diet, exercise, and treatment, he should be fine." The doctor squeezed Merry's hand and put his other hand on Sim's shoulder. "We'll let you know when it's scheduled. Sim, if you'd like to go see him now, you can. He asked for you."

"Can I go too?"

The doctor nodded at Merry. "If you keep it short."

Jered stood across the street from the hospital. He'd tried to go closer a dozen times, only to retreat to this spot.

STAY AWAY! THEY DON'T WANT YOU THERE.

But he's my dad!

HE'S REJECTED YOU AND FOUND ANOTHER.

But he needs me!

HE NEEDS THE ONE WHO SAVED HIM, NOT THE ONE WHO HURT HIM.

Jered ran out of arguments.

Merry stuck her head in the door to Bailey's room. "Up to a couple of visitors, Bailey?"

There was a smile in his weak voice. "Merry, you're back."

"Just in time, I see. Slacking off again."

Sim followed her in. She wasn't sure what reception she'd get. Would Bailey still be mad about Sanchez and her running away, or would he remember that she'd helped him?

Merry came to his bedside, but Sim stayed near the door. Bailey swallowed with difficulty and Merry handed him a glass of water.

"Where's Jered?"

"We haven't seen him, but as soon as we do…" With her next breath, she changed the subject. "You scared about the surgery?"

"More scared *not* to have it."

There was a moment of awkward silence. Merry squeezed his hand. "We'd better let you rest. Take care and—"

He raised a hand in Sim's direction. "Sim."

She took a step closer, expecting a full frontal assault.

"I'm sorry, Sim. About being mad."

Merry looked puzzled, but Sim nodded. "It's okay."

"Are *you* okay?"

"Sure. Just get better."

"I want to thank you. Thank you for saving me."

Sim nodded, then hurried away. How come some compliments were as hard to take as complaints?

In the hallway, Merry pulled Sim aside. "What was Bailey mad about?"

Sim punched the button for the elevator. "Nothing."

"It didn't sound like nothing."

She punched it again. "It is."

Merry looked to the numbers lit above the door. "Have you heard from Claire?" Sim shook her head. Merry didn't know what to say. "Want to come to work?"

"Sure."

Merry was underwhelmed by her enthusiasm.

Claire swept Harold's porch. The yard was looking good. She'd gotten it cleaned up and had even repaired a sagging shutter. It was a good way to spend an afternoon. They'd had some hamburgers and a half hour ago she'd sent Harold to the hardware store to buy some wire mesh so she could fix his screen door.

In spite of being out of the loop, in spite of being away from Sim, she marveled in the simple high of her domestic achievements. Yet her motives were twofold. She was helping Harold to repay him for his hospitality, but it was also to prevent herself from going bonkers while waiting to hear news about Sim *and* from having to make a decision about taking the mosaic commission.

The other perk about doing manual labor was that it gave her a chance to pray. The pull of her muscles fueled the pull of her mind as she searched for direction from the Lord. Since being Sim-less, she had gone through the entire gamut of techniques to hear God's promptings. She'd prayed harder, faster, longer; she'd tried to empty her mind of all thought, hoping God would fill it with inspiration; and she'd taken short naps, praying that divine dreams would show her the way.

But all she'd gotten was silence. A peaceful silence, as if the silence itself was God's answer. A heavenly "not yet."

She finished the sweeping and paused to look at her handiwork.

"You're spoiling me." Harold came up the walk, carrying a roll of wire mesh.

Claire set aside the broom. "What's the newest news of Steadfast? Is there a search party combing the streets for the crazy lady from the attic who gave away her fortune to rake leaves and live undercover? Should I be wearing a full disguise when I work on your yard? Your neighbor looked at me funny."

"There *is* news."

When he didn't smile, her heart skipped. "Is Sim all right?"

"Sim's a heroine. She found Bailey collapsed from a heart attack."

"Is he okay?"

Harold shrugged. "He's having angioplasty surgery tomorrow morning."

A question surfaced. Claire hated that her mind had so quickly set aside Bailey's pain for her own, but she voiced her thought. "Where is Sim staying?"

Harold took a breath, as if bracing himself. "Merry is back."

Claire's hope deflated. "Oh." She took a breath that started at her toes, but the fresh air did not make the ache go away. And she wanted it away. Desperately. More than anything she wanted to feel normal again. She made a decision and headed for the garage. "I'm going home."

"Home?"

She stopped and faced him. "Back to Kansas City. Nothing's working out the way I planned."

"The way *you* planned?"

All she could do was stare at him.

Harold swallowed. "He who learns the most has faced struggles."

She wiped a hand across her forehead. "Shakespeare?"

"Harold Shinness." He carried the wire mesh to the porch, set it by the door, sat on the top step, and waited for her to join him.

She resisted. She didn't want to be talked out of it. "I'm not doing anybody any good here, Harold."

"You're doing me good."

"Sure. The yard work. But—"

"I know yard work isn't a big thing. It's not fulfilling some lofty purpose."

She let a breath in, then out. "I gave up *everything.*"

"And helping me with chores isn't proper compensation."

A fire sparked. Her arms flailed. "Hey, I'm helping you without *any* compensation. I was trying to take care of Sim without a single moment of encouragement. I'm doing all of this out of the goodness of my—" His look stopped her final word.

"It doesn't have to be big, Claire."

"What doesn't have to—?"

"Your purpose." He squirmed on the porch, getting comfortable. "People are always looking for the big thing, the big sacrifice with the big reward. They want something showy, something worthy of their trouble."

"Are you saying God *didn't* ask me to give up everything?"

He shrugged. "I'm saying maybe you made it bigger than it needed to be. Maybe all He really wanted from you was a *yes.* A blanket surrender to go in whatever direction He chose, addressing whatever aspect of your life He wanted to bring to your attention. You took it to mean giving up your possessions, your art, but maybe that wasn't at the core of His charge."

"You're saying I gave up everything for nothing?"

"Not for nothing. And your motives were honorable. You knew your *everything* involved possessions and position. So you gave them up as a gesture—"

Her laugh was bitter. "Let me tell you, it was more than a gesture."

"Wrong word. And I know it was hard. It should be hard. And I wouldn't be so presumptuous as to tell you it was wrong."

"Isn't that exactly what you're doing?"

"No, no." He ran a hand over his face. "I don't mean to muddle your mind; I want to clarify it."

"You're not doing a very good job."

He made a tent with his fingers and was quiet a moment. "We have a tendency to complicate things, to make them more involved and intricate than they actually are."

"If I hadn't given up everything, I never would have come to Steadfast."

Harold's face showed new wrinkles as he tried to find the words. When he did, they came out in a rush. "The big question relates to the main call, the all-encompassing call."

"What *are* you talking about?"

His face cleared and he sat up straighter, as if he'd found the right direction of his thoughts. "People are detail oriented. We want direct answers to specific, detailed questions."

"You bet we do."

"We want to know the when, what, who, where, why of everything."

"Absolutely."

"If I came to you and said, 'Claire, I want you to say yes to me,' what would you say?"

"I'd say, 'That depends. Yes about what?' "

"Exactly. We treat God the same way. He gets our attention—which is no small feat in itself—and then He says, 'I want you to say yes to Me.' At that point we hedge and say—"

The idea fell into its proper slot. "'That depends. Yes about what?'"

Harold touched the tip of his nose. "But God doesn't want a conditional yes. Where's the faith in that? He wants us to just say yes, without knowing *any* details, without knowing what aspect of our lives the yes pertains to, without knowing anything."

"He wants us to say yes blindly?"

Harold popped to his feet. "But we're *not* blind. We know who *He* is. If we didn't, He wouldn't be asking. The yes question is not one that's asked until we're ready, Claire. We have to know Him, know how He works, know about Jesus, the Holy Spirit, the whole shebang. We're not blind when He asks the big question. He's given us the basics, tested us, taught us, carried us along a road that's been fraught with chuckholes, detours, and accidents. And He's asked many other yes-or-no questions along the way."

"Like what?"

He looked at the sky, then counted on his fingers. " 'Do you trust me?' 'Do you believe I can do this for you?' 'Do you believe I am who I say I am?' Those kinds of questions."

Claire's mind was on fire. "And if we say yes to all those specific questions, then we're ready for Him to ask the big question?"

Harold came down the steps and put his hands on her shoulders. His eyes locked on to hers. "Yes, Claire. Yes."

Tears burned. "I want to say yes, Harold. But what's the big question?"

He took hold of her shoulders, led her to the steps, and pushed her to sitting. Then he went in the house. He came back with a Bible and pressed it into her hands. "Isaiah 6:8."

He went inside.

Claire watched a bird land on a telephone wire. It fluttered its wings and looked down at her. Waiting. She took hold of the cross around her neck.

I want to say yes to the big question, Lord. Help me do it.

She opened the Bible, finding the verse: "Then I heard the voice of the Lord saying, 'Whom shall I send? And who will go for us?' And I said, 'Here am I. Send me!'"

Chills rippled up and down her spine. Michelle had quoted this very verse in her parting note. Claire put a hand to her mouth and felt God's question deep inside, melding her physical, mental, emotional, intellectual, and spiritual beings.

Will you go for me? Whoever, whatever, whenever, wherever, why ever, however?

Claire bowed her head in her hands and said the words God had been waiting to hear.

"Yes, Lord. Yes."

Twenty

But Jonah ran away from the LORD.

JONAH 1:3

JERED SNUCK INTO HIS OWN HOUSE. It was a weird concept, but that was how it felt. He didn't belong there anymore.

He went into the kitchen and stepped over the Monopoly pieces lying all over the floor. Then suddenly he couldn't stand the sight of them. They were evidence of his anger and his father's pain. He picked them up in a rush and stuffed the game onto the highest shelf in the entry closet. *There. Nothing happened here. Nothing at all.*

But something had happened. Certainly by now his father had told everyone Jered caused his heart attack. It was only a matter of time before someone came to the door and dragged him away to face the consequences of being a terrible son.

Sim saved him.

Sim would live here now. Permanently. Sim was everything Jered was not. He was expendable. She would make the perfect child.

And she might be home soon. Which meant he had to be gone.

Jered ran upstairs and stuffed a backpack with clothes and scraps of paper containing the songs he'd written. Looking around his room, he was surprised at how few things really meant anything to him. He noticed a picture stuck in the edge of the dresser mirror. It was of his dad and him, taken years ago at the opening of Bon Vivant. They were both smiling. Another time. Another world.

He shoved it in the pack.

❧   ❧   ❧

Jered was headed out of town when he found himself turning down a side street. Only after the turn did he realize his intent.

He parked a few houses away from Merry's and walked down the sidewalk, hands in his pockets. He started whistling but stopped. He didn't want to draw attention. Luckily, it was hot and the neighbors were inside.

At Merry's he bypassed the front door and slid into the fenced yard. He made a beeline for the shed in the back. It looked like any other shed. But Jered knew different. One day when he'd been walking past, he'd seen her slip inside. Nothing odd there. But then she'd closed the door and hadn't come out. For a long time.

After dark he'd come back with a flashlight and found her stupid shrine. He felt bad that she lost her family, but didn't she see how weird it was to keep a shrine like that? Jered didn't keep a shrine of his mom.

Which had made him realize how little he knew about his mother—the woman who'd left when he was tiny. He didn't have a picture of her displayed in his room. He barely thought of her. *I think of her just as much as she probably thinks of me. Wherever she is...*

That's when he took the picture of Merry and her son. A poor substitute, but better than nothing. There was probably something weird in that, but he didn't let himself dwell on it.

Jered stood before the shed-shrine. His gut clenched. He hated all it represented. Love, family, longing, loyalty. Where were those things in his life?

He shoved open the door until the sunlight bathed the rug, the photos, the flowers, the crosses. He went inside and nudged the stuffed monkey with his foot.

An idea formed.

Merry left work early, spurred by Blanche and Sim's assurance that they could handle the library the rest of the day. She was mentally weary, what with her mother's health, Bailey's attack, and life in general.

When she pulled into her driveway, she noticed someone moving around her backyard. She turned off the car and ran toward the fence. "Hey! What are you—?"

It was Jered. He froze. He was next to the shed holding a cross made of small branches, one hand on each section. His aborted movement continued its work and the cross tore in two.

She ran toward him, her eyes grabbing onto the desecration: the ripped photos, the shredded rug. "What have you done? Why have you—?"

Jered tossed the branches aside. He pointed to the shed. "That's sick."

"*That's* none of your business!" She spotted Justin's stuffed monkey sticking out of a mound of impatiens, and she retrieved it. She petted the brown fur, checking for damage, then hugged it to her chest.

Jered headed for the gate.

She ran after him, grabbing his arm. "You stay here and fix this!"

He pulled away from her, his chest heaving. His mouth contorted as if words were wanting out, yet being held prisoner within. There was something wild in his eyes, and Merry felt a tingling of fear. She lowered her voice. "I don't know why you did this, Jered, but I want you to put it back together."

He set his jaw. Then he fled.

She yelled after him, "I'm calling the police!"

Merry heard footsteps on the porch and drew her knees tighter to her chest. The doorbell rang.

She didn't answer it.

"Merry? It's me, Officer Kendell."

She uncurled herself and answered the door.

Ken studied her. "You okay?"

She nodded.

"Did he hurt you?"

She shook her head.

"Can I come in?"

She let him in, yet found herself backing away from him.

He seemed to sense her unease and stood his ground. "Tell me what happened."

She told him the story and led him into the backyard. He took notes.

"You say that was a shrine?"

She cringed. She'd never intended for the entire world to know. "You ever lost someone close to you, Ken?"

"My grandfather died last year."

"That's not the same."

"I suppose not." He dropped it. "We've got a call out for Jered's truck, and I've sent someone to his house. When we find him, we'll bring him in and—"

"I don't want him arrested."

"But he destroyed…" He nodded toward the backyard.

Merry was torn. This new fear of Jered was real, and yet he was still Bailey's son. He was misguided, needy, almost pathetic. She came to a compromise. "If you find him, bring him in and let me talk to him—with you there. I'll decide the rest later."

"We can do that." He put his notepad away. "And Merry? About that other thing…the girl?"

"Oh."

"I've been more than fair, giving you way too much time."

"I know, Ken. And I appreciate it."

"I have to do my job."

"I know."

"So what's her last name?"

"I still don't know. And you can be sure she won't tell."

"Then I'll have to proceed with what I have. Contact Kansas City. Give them a description of her."

The weariness Merry felt before the Jered incident overtook her. "Do what you need to do, Ken. I'm tired of fighting it."

Merry took the elements of the shrine into the house. She looked out the kitchen window at the backyard. There was no way a stranger would know anything of importance had ever existed out there amid the rakes and old flowerpots.

Perhaps nothing of *importance* had.

Merry looked at the pitiful collection of memorabilia on the counter. A few torn pictures, Justin's monkey, a couple of candles. Lou's pocket Bible. Were these things she should bow down to? Worship? Jered had called it sick.

She'd argued with him, but was he right? Were these things unhealthy, keeping her anchored in the past, in her grief? If only there were rules about grief, giving hallmarks of emotions the bereaved should feel at one month, three, six. As it was, grief was way too volatile and hard to handle, like pinning down a breeze, a wind, or a tornado.

She sank onto a kitchen chair and pulled the monkey into the crook of her arm. She fingered the pages of the Bible, finding an odd comfort in the *swish-swish* of page against page. At least she'd stopped Jered before he'd ripped it apart. She noticed a red ribbon, cutting through the pages. Why had she never looked at the page before?

She turned to it now. It was in the book of Revelation. One verse was marked, 21:4: "He will wipe every tear from their eyes. There will be no more death or mourning or crying or pain, for the old order of things has passed away."

No more death or mourning or crying or pain.

I wish.

But even as she closed the pages, she let another thought nudge the doubt toward trust.

Maybe…

Jered drove too fast.

But not fast enough.

Each memory fueled the accelerator, the could-have-saids and should-have-saids assaulting him like pointing, jabbing fingers.

He'd blown it. His little side trip to Merry's as he was heading out of town had blown everything. He had no choice. He *had* to leave.

And stay away.

For how long?

It would depend on whether his father died.

He's my dad. He can't die!

The tears made him mad, and the anger made him drive faster.

Twenty-one

"I am the true vine, and my Father is the gardener.
He cuts off every branch in me that bears no fruit,
while every branch that does bear fruit he prunes
so that it will be even more fruitful."

JOHN 15:1–2

THE MORNING AFTER THE JERED INCIDENT, Merry called the
Manson house searching for him. So far, none of the Steadfast police
officers had seen him or his truck. He'd vanished. Unlike Sim, who'd
had to resort to buses, Jered had his own wheels—wheels that could
take him a long, long way from home.

He was such a confused and confusing kid. His destruction of
her shrine unnerved her, and she'd racked her brain trying to figure
out why he would do such a thing. She came up empty. She'd been a
friend, listening to his dreams, helping him as much as she could.
Something his own mother would do if she were here.

If she were here.

She shivered, and as the phone at the Manson house rang for the
twentieth time, she hung up, feeling more relief than regret.

"Merry?" Sim stood in the kitchen doorway. "Ready to go see
Bailey?"

Not really. What could she tell him about Jered? What *should* she
tell him?

Claire opened her eyes and saw a spider climbing the wall. *I need to
call the exterminator.*

A few more seconds of wakefulness reminded her she wasn't in

271

her townhouse. She was staying in a room above Harold's garage, where spiders were welcome. She looked at her watch, then looked again. Eight forty-six in the morning?

Yet instead of feeling panic at the late hour, she grinned and stretched, wallowing in the first truly good night's sleep she'd gotten since coming to Steadfast. She stopped in midstretch as she remembered the reason for her contentment.

She'd said yes to God.

It wasn't that she hadn't agreed with Him at other moments in her life, but this time was different. This time it was all-encompassing, like writing a blanket disclaimer for her life: *I, Claire Adams, do hereby relinquish all rights to myself.*

And so, in the quiet of the room, she said the word again, making the *s* linger, not wanting it to end: *"Yes-s-s-s!"*

She whipped the covers off. Today was *not* like any other day. Today was heady with a new air of possibility. Anything could happen. Anything. All because she'd given God a free hand to do whatever *He* thought best. All because she'd quit living for man—or herself—and was living for an audience of One.

Audience of One? What an odd phrase, and yet so perfect.

As Claire put on her one pair of pants, three words popped into her head: *Biscuits and gravy.*

Her mouth watered.

She knocked on the back door and found Harold reading the paper in the kitchen. "Care to join me for biscuits and gravy at the Plentiful, Harold? My treat."

"You're going *out?*"

"I think it's time."

"You're not…nervous about it?"

She realized his question mirrored his own fears. She took a seat across from him. "Maybe it's time both of us quit hiding out."

"I don't hide."

"Not physically like me, but what about the Shakespeare? What about the scurrying, odd man who isn't the real you?"

He got up to refill his coffee cup. "I like maintaining a distance."

"You like hiding."

He stopped with the pot midway to the cup. "Yes. It's safer."

"It's cowardly."

He poured his coffee and returned to his seat, looking into the swirling darkness. "O thou monster ignorance, how deformed dost thou look!"

She put a hand on his. "Ignorance, indeed. You're depriving people of knowing a wonderful man."

He shrugged. "Maybe someday." He turned her hand and squeezed it, then gave it back to her. "But you go. Today is your day to reenter the world."

So it was.

Walking to the diner, Claire was a little disappointed that cars didn't scream to a halt at the sight of her, nor did ladies scamper toward each other, whispering behind their hands. The extent of the town's reaction—if there was any reaction at all—was a double take and a slightly delayed, "Good morning."

Ah, the delusions of the self-absorbed.

Claire chose a table in the corner.

Annie approached with a coffeepot. "You want cream, right?"

"You remembered. I'm impressed."

Annie shrugged. "You going for the biscuits and gravy again?"

"Absolutely."

Annie nodded but didn't leave. "People been asking about you."

"What do they want to know?"

"Where you been, for one."

She thought about saying, "With Harold," but realized she had no right to blow his cover. "I've been around. Waiting for the whole library ghost thing to blow over."

Annie nodded. "It doesn't take long. Give us five minutes and we'll find a new fish to fry."

"Double-dipped?"

It took Annie a moment to get it. Then she laughed. "We like our scandals extra crispy." She changed the coffeepot to the other hand. "Breakfast will be up in a jiff."

Claire settled in. She looked out the window just as Merry's car pulled into the library lot. Merry got out—and then Sim. They exchanged words at the car, then Sim took the front stairs two at a time, juggling the keys in her hand. Claire checked her watch. It was 9:20. Why were they opening so late? And why wasn't Merry going up the steps?

When Merry turned toward the Plentiful, Claire's heart did a somersault. Although she'd wanted to end her confinement, she wasn't sure she was ready to meet up with her friend—the friend who had taken over her spot in Sim's life.

Too bad she didn't have a choice.

Merry nearly missed the curb when she spotted Claire through the window at the Plentiful. Their eyes met, and a rush of conflicting emotions bombarded her. Relief and anger. Joy and anxiety.

She attempted to calm herself as she went through the door. She tried on a smile and hoped it looked better than it felt. Claire lifted a hand in a half-wave. Merry moved to greet her.

"You're back."

"I'm back."

"Where were you?"

"Around."

Merry nodded, buying time. She didn't know what to say next.

"Care to join me?" Claire nodded at the opposite seat.

Merry glanced at the library. "I've promised Sim a cinnamon roll."

"You're opening late."

"We've been to visit Bailey. He had his angioplasty. He's doing fine."

"Glad to hear it."

Silence.

Claire patted the place setting across from her. "Please sit. For just a minute?"

How could she refuse? Annie appeared, and Merry ordered two cinnamon rolls to go and let Annie pour her a cup of coffee. The rising steam made her already warm face too hot.

"This is awkward, isn't it?"

Merry shifted in her seat. "A little."

"I'm sorry I ran away like that, leaving you to take care of Sim. I'm glad she's not staying at the library anymore."

"How do you know that?"

Claire seemed startled, as if she realized she'd said too much. "Is she okay?"

"She's fine. She's a joy. She's the one who saved Bailey."

"How?"

Merry explained about the visit to her mother's and then Bailey's heart attack. "Have *you* seen Jered around?"

"Bailey's boy? No."

Merry warmed her suddenly cold hands on the coffee mug. "He's run away."

"Why?"

She decided to give the condensed version. "He did some vandalism at my house. I called the police on him."

"Oh, Merry."

"I don't know what to tell Bailey. I'd planned to tell him this morning, but I chickened out."

"Is there anything I can do?"

For some reason, these innocuous, much-heard words shocked her. It took her a moment to figure out why. "So you're planning to stick around?"

In turn, this question seemed to shock Claire. "I…I don't know. I'm kind of waiting."

"Waiting for what?"

The biscuits and gravy came, and Claire took up her fork, though she didn't take a bite. "During my absence, I've had what you might call a God-moment." She suddenly reddened and gave a little laugh. "Funny, when I try to explain it to someone else, it seems less momentous. And yet when it happened, it was as if the earth moved."

"You've certainly captured my interest."

Claire took a bite of biscuit and chewed slowly, as if chewing through her words. "I've come to realize that the verse that brought me here, 'sell everything and follow me,' was only part of something bigger."

"Actually, you can't get much bigger than that."

"Actually, you can."

Merry listened as Claire told her about the "big question"—and the big answer: yes. As she heard the details of Claire's progression from giving up everything in the way of possessions to truly giving up *everything* by saying yes to *anything* God wanted, Merry's insides came to attention, as though readying themselves for inspection.

Claire finally took another bite of her food. "It's so hard to explain the feeling of elation when I woke up this morning and said yes again. I mean, what a way to start a morning, as if anything could happen. And what a feeling of freedom to know God's got it—He's got everything. 'If God is for us, who can be against us?'"

Merry laughed. "Loads of people."

"But He'll take care of it." She sat back. "I'm not naive enough to think that just because I said yes to God I'll never have any struggles. But I *do* know I'll be able to handle whatever—and I mean whatever—comes because He's in charge." Claire looked sheepish. "I know it sounds trite and simplistic, but it's because He loves me."

It *did* sound trite and simplistic—but it also sounded wonderful. What might happen if she—?

"You look like you want to say something, Merry."

Did she? After a moment she realized she did. Maybe if she voiced it to someone else everything would be made clear. Clearer. "I think Jered's vandalism was a good thing."

"Talk about positive thinking."

"Let me finish. What I didn't explain was the thing Jered vandalized was a shrine I'd erected in the backyard, to my family." She waited for a reaction.

"Continue."

Claire's calm acceptance fueled her. "You thought the everything you needed to give up to follow God was your possessions. I'm thinking my everything is my past. My guilt. My grief. As long as I had the shrine, I was holding on to it. But now that it's gone…"

"You're free to say yes to the big question?"

"I'm free to think about saying yes."

"That—" Claire cut off a big piece of gravy-dripping biscuit and put it in her mouth with flourish—"is a start. A very good start."

Claire paid the bill for breakfast, including the rolls for Sim and Merry. She walked Merry out.

"You coming to the library to see Sim?"

It was tempting. "Not yet. I'm still not sure what my next move is supposed to be, and until I do, I don't want to insert myself into Sim's life. Stir things up."

Merry nodded. "You've changed a lot from the woman who grabbed Sim by the scruff of her life and declared, 'We *are* going to find our purpose. Now! Whether we want to or not.' "

"My intentions were good. And I still want us to find our purpose. The thing I didn't realize was that hers may not be intertwined with mine."

Merry touched her shoulder. "I know what a big concession that is."

"Yeah, well…"

They parted, each woman going her separate way.

For now.

Claire stood in Harold's kitchen and washed the bowl she'd used to stir up a batch of brownies. When was the last time she'd baked? Suzy Homemaker in the making.

As she rinsed the dishes, she found herself glancing at the telephone. She repeated the glance three times before she stopped to figure out what her subconscious was trying to get her to do.

Call Darla.

She looked to the phone a fourth time. If she called, Darla would want a decision about the commission. Had she made one?

Did recovering alcoholics feel like this? Did they ever feel strong enough to resist the temptation to indulge in their old ways? She imagined temptation would always be there on the outskirts of her reach; but as each day passed, would she become stronger and be able to resist with less effort?

Acknowledge and resist. And find strength in the big *yes*.

She wiped her hands on a towel and picked up the phone.

She dialed Darla's number.

"Hey-ya, Darla."

"We meet again."

"I'd give you a hug, but my arms won't reach."

"How convenient."

She had to sit down. "Where's this antagonism coming from?"

Darla took a breath. "You're off *finding your purpose* in who-knows-where, while I'm left here to take the heat for your abandonment."

"I didn't abandon—"

"Yes, you did. You spent your life getting people to notice and appreciate your talent, then you ran off. It's like holding a piece of your cheesecake under someone's nose, letting their taste buds kick into gear, letting them want it, need it, only to pull it away. You teased the world with your talent. And no one likes to be teased."

Was her speechlessness a by-product of hearing the truth?

Darla took advantage of her silence. "Few people can do what you do, Claire. It's a God-given gift. You've said as much." She took a breath. "Remember when you gave me that hand-knit sweater for my birthday?"

"The one you put in your closet, never took out of the box, and never wore?"

"That's the one."

"You made me mad, Darla. That's was an expensive, beautiful sweater."

"I know. It was rude. I'll wear it the next cold day. But to the point…how do you think God feels when you take the gift *He* gave you and put it in the closet?"

"I took it out of the box. I *did* use it."

"For a while."

Claire stood to pace. "But I thought the temptation of the commission was just that—a temptation to return to my old life. A test to see if I still cared about money and fame."

"I think you already proved you don't care about those things."

"But going back and taking it—"

"Would prove you *do* care about appreciating and using the gift of your talent. Hey, Claire, do it for free, or take the money they pay you and give it to some mission in India. Sign someone else's name. I don't care. But come back and do the work. Your work."

Claire couldn't believe the surge of excitement that overwhelmed her. *Could* she go back? *Could* she return to her art?

Then practical matters raised their hands. "Where would I stay, Darla? I sold—"

"Oh, please. You can stay with me."

Her mind swam. She hesitated long enough to send up a prayer. *Yes, Lord? Is this what You want me to do?*

Before she could formulate a cognitive answer, she heard herself telling Darla yes.

Again, what a glorious, glorious word.

"Say a prayer for me, Darla."

"What do you think I've *been* doing?"

Claire found Harold reading in the living room. He looked up from his book. "You're glowing like a hundred-watt bulb."

She moved to stand beside his well-stocked bookshelves. "I'm happy."

"I can see that."

"I've made a decision."

"Glad to hear it."

"I talked to someone back in Kansas City. She approves."

"Is that important?"

Claire fingered the top of a book. "I didn't think it was, but it is. Darla's not just my colleague; she's my friend."

"Then count yourself as having at least two of the latter."

She nodded her thanks. "I'm leaving Steadfast."

He put the book down, and she told him about her decision to accept the commission.

"I do think it's time you leave here."

Although she wanted his approval, his words seemed rude.

He must have seen the shock in her face. "I don't mean to be brusque, but when you talk about your art, your entire face lights up. That glow is from God and cannot—and should not—be denied. I haven't seen that glow in you until now. Not while working in the library, nor even when you've been with Sim."

It was a blow. She moved to a shelf and let her fingers skip over the bindings of the books as her memory skipped over the events of her time in Steadfast. Staying in the attic, meeting Sim, meeting Merry, Bailey, Blanche, Ivan, Harold… And just as her fingers only skimmed the covers of the books without delving into their rich content, so her memories proved she had only skimmed over the people of Steadfast, without delving into the rich content of their lives. If she removed her hand from the books, they lost nothing. If she removed herself from the people of Steadfast, they lost…

Pride invaded the room. "It's been a waste. I haven't done anything here."

"Nonsense." Harold put his book down and pointed out the window to the backyard. "It's like all the pruning you've been doing for me. Maybe God had to do a little pruning on you. Cut you back so you could grow stronger, with even more blooms and branches. Although it's a hard process—and even seems negative at the time of the pruning—in the long run, it's for the best." He took a deep breath, then faced her. "Consider it a compliment. Like a gardener, God cuts off the dead branches, but He takes the time to prune the good ones, to make them better. Stronger."

"I like the sound of that. And I hope you're right."

"Your life and art weren't wrong or dead. They were good, but they could be made better. Giving up everything and coming here got you to the point of saying yes to the big question, right?"

"Yes."

"It got you to quit playing your life to other people and start playing it to an audience of One."

Claire gasped. "That's the phrase I thought of this morning!"

Harold smiled. "I wish we could claim it, but the Danish theologian Søren Kierkegaard came up with it first. He says we're all players to an audience of One."

Claire shivered. "Oh my. That's so perfect."

Harold closed the book. "The point is, would you have said yes if you hadn't been pruned?"

"Maybe."

He dropped his chin.

"All right. No. Probably not. At least not for a while."

"Exactly. God knows what it takes to move us toward the center. *His* center. And sometimes He has to stir things up to get us to quit dancing around the edges and take a strong step toward Him."

Claire smiled. "You do have a way with words, Mr. Shinness."

"Glad to be of service."

She sat across from him. "Before I go, I do want to say good-bye to Sim and Merry."

"As you should."

"But I'm nervous."

"Why?"

"After all my big talk to Sim about my being brought here for her, her being brought here for me—I'll sound like a fool."

"But, O, how oddly will it sound that I must ask my child forgiveness!"

"Shinness?"

"*The Tempest,* act 5, scene 1. The audience of One, Claire. *He* won't think you're foolish. He'll be proud."

Ultimately, what else mattered?

Jered couldn't stand not knowing. He stopped at a gas station, dialed the operator, and got the number for the hospital.

"Bailey Manson's room?"

"Please hold."

"Hello?"

At the sound of his father's voice, Jered didn't know what to say. His dad sounded okay. A little tired, but considering...

"Who's there?"

Jered wanted to answer but couldn't.

"Jered? Is that you?"

He broke the connection.

Sim had trouble concentrating. She couldn't get Jered out of her head.

Something was wrong. No one had seen him in two days, and she had a terrible feeling. She'd even run over to Jered's house and banged on the door, but no one answered.

Sim was no angel, but she recognized that Jered was on a path to bad things, shady people, and dangerous places. Although Moog and Darrell were currently content with drinking a few beers and tossing a few apples, she knew that wouldn't satisfy them forever. They would seek the bigger thrill, the larger crime. Were the three of them together, planning something even now?

What Jered should be planning was his music career.

How terrible to have a dream that no one else believed in. Sim didn't have a dream yet, but she knew what it was like to have people push. Her dad wanted her to be a businesswoman, but Sim wasn't interested in deals and numbers. She liked people. She wanted to do something with—

Do something.

Sim stopped with a book halfway to a shelf. She let the thought repeat itself. *Do something.*

She put a hand to her chest. *Help Jered achieve his dream.*

Sim put the book away and stood in the stacks a moment. She didn't know for sure if her nudging was from God or herself.

If it wasn't from God, it should have been.

Sim approached Merry. "Can I make a long-distance phone call?"

Merry raised an eyebrow, looking way too hopeful. "Are you call-ing home?"

Sim shook her head adamantly. "No, no, I still don't want…" Maybe this wasn't such a good idea. If she made the call, her aunt and uncle might find out where she was.

"Sim? Who are you wanting to call?"

"It's a secret. A good secret." She raised her right hand. "I promise."

Merry eyed her suspiciously but handed over the receiver. "Have at it." She walked away, giving Sim a backward glance.

Sim took a deep breath and dialed information for Kansas City.

Jamison Smith rocked in his executive chair and nodded at the phone. "Yes, Sim, I promise not to tell your aunt and uncle you called as long as you follow through with your promise to call *them* as soon as we hang up." He snickered to himself. Little did the girl know he had caller ID. He glanced down at the number and reached for a pen to jot it down. *Where was that pen?*

"If you ask me, your uncle's an arrogant tripe who acts way big-ger than his britches, and I don't owe him any favors. If we weren't neighbors, I'd have nothing to do with him. I don't approve of you running away, but as long as you're staying with other relatives… I don't involve myself with domestic squabbles."

"Thanks, Mr. Smith. I'll have my friend, Jered, get ahold of you and set up a meeting. I really appreciate it."

He finally found a pen and positioned it to write down the phone number. "I'm not making any promis—"

The caller ID was blank. Jamison tapped on the display. It remained blank.

"Mr. Smith?"

"I'll be waiting for his call, kid." Jamison hung up. He turned his chair so he could see the skyline of Kansas City. *Should I call Forbes and tell him the girl called?* He looked back to the malfunctioning phone. If only he'd gotten a number.

He shrugged. Without the number, what good would it do to call? Besides, Forbes was an annoying creep. He didn't deserve more than a neighborly nod, driveway to driveway.

Jamison went back to work. It was good to keep a promise—even to a kid.

Sim felt great, as if she'd just earned some brownie points. The only question was, who was keeping track? Did God care about such small acts of kindness?

She hoped so.

Twenty-two

*For he has rescued us from the dominion of darkness
and brought us into the kingdom of the Son he loves,
in whom we have redemption, the forgiveness of sins.*

COLOSSIANS 1:13–14

A NEW MORNING CAME, and Claire knew it was time. Time for things to draw to a close, time for lives to move on. Hers, and everyone else's. She'd imposed long enough.

She was pouring her second cup of coffee when Harold came into the kitchen. He did a double take.

"What?"

"You look more…confident this morning. More determined. Flushed with excitement."

Claire put a hand to her cheeks. They *did* feel a bit warm. "I must be a good actress, because my insides are tied in knots."

"Confident, determined nervous knots?"

She took a sip of coffee, enjoying its bitter bite. "I'm going to the library first thing, to say good-bye."

Harold nodded once. "You want some company?"

Claire laughed at her relief. "I feel like a little girl getting her dad to come with her on the first day of school."

He put a hand on her shoulder. "Then I'll say what every dad has said at every such moment: Everything will be all right."

"And I'll take up the kid's part: Promise?"

"Promise."

❧   ❧   ❧

As Merry was doing the breakfast dishes, she suddenly thought of Bailey and realized she *hadn't* thought of him for a full twenty-four hours. Was he home or was he still in the hospital? The fact that she didn't know was disconcerting. She found the hospital's phone number and called.

"Is Bailey Manson still a patient?"

"Yes, ma'am."

She hung up and grabbed her keys.

A nurse came in for Bailey's breakfast tray. "You ready to go home?"

"I was ready yesterday."

"Patience, patient." She pointed to the half-eaten food on the tray. "I thought you'd be finished."

He shoved it an inch. "I am."

She smiled. "Don't you like our oatmeal?"

"No comment."

She took the tray. "You can get dressed now. We're just finishing up the paperwork." She took a few steps toward the door, then turned. "Who's picking you up?"

His reaction was the same as if she had asked him to name the capital of Kazakstan. "Uh, I'm not sure."

"You do have someone coming, don't you?"

"Of course I do."

She lowered her chin, then left him ready, but unable, to go. His car was at home. His son hadn't visited, called, or answered the phone. Steadfast didn't have a taxi service. How *was* he going to get home?

He pulled the phone into his lap, but his mind was a blank. "This is ridiculous."

Yes, it was. Bailey Manson, local restaurateur, was stuck in the hospital with no way home and no one to call to take him home. No buddy, no relative.

No nothing.

He shook his head. It couldn't be true. He wasn't this pitiful.
Was he?

His hand gripped the phone as he realized his life was full of
acquaintances: people he talked *at* but never *to,* people he swept by
but never touched. He'd set himself above and apart, and now, when
he needed contact, he found the cupboard bare.

His chest tightened and he grabbed at his hospital gown. Yet he
knew the pain didn't stem from any physical defect, but from a
deeper disease. One that was far more deadly.

"You arrogant fool."

It was odd, hearing his own whispered voice condemn himself.
But the title was true, and it had dire consequences. He'd ostracized
himself from his son. He'd lost the best chef in the region. And he'd
repeatedly ruined any chance of having a relationship with Merry. All
for the same reason.

Because he was an arrogant fool.

One, two, three strikes you're out.

He covered his eyes, shocked by his own tears. He was out, all
right. Nearly all the way out. Dead out.

I'm so sorry. I've been so wrong.

"Bailey?"

At the sound of Merry's voice, he looked up.

She came toward him. "What's wrong?"

He swiped away his tears. "What are you doing here?"

"I came to see you." She pointed toward the hall. "A nurse said
you're going home?"

He started to yank the covers back so he could swing his legs over
the side of the bed, then realized he was only wearing a hospital gown.
He smoothed the covers. "I was just going to get dressed."

She angled toward the door. "Oh, I'll leave then."

"No!"

Her eyebrows raised.

"I mean…" He smoothed the top of the sheet a second time.
"Oh, great Gatsby."

She returned to the side of the bed. "I've never heard that one
before."

"That's because I've never felt this way before."

"What way?"

He could only risk a glance. "Vulnerable."

"Well, I'll be."

He looked up. She'd crossed her arms.

"Stop gloating."

She laughed. "I will not. I've earned this gloat and intend to make good use of it."

"I wasn't *that* bad."

She put a hand on his forearm. "Oh, Bailey, I don't want to be too hard on you—you just having had surgery and all—"

"Oh, why not? What's another slice or prick or stab?"

She gave him one of her looks. "You do have a tendency to come off as the Prince of Steadfast."

"I was going for King."

"But we don't need a king or a prince—nor want one."

"What do you want?"

"A friend."

His throat tightened, making him unable to speak.

She squeezed his arm. "I'll leave you now so you can get home."

He grabbed her hand. "I don't have a way home."

He accepted her shocked look.

"Could you be my friend and take me?"

"I'd be happy to, Bailey. As a friend."

In the car on the way to Bailey's, the subject Merry dreaded came up.

"I can't believe I haven't even heard from Jered."

How much should she say? Could she say? "Actually, no one's seen him, Bailey. Ken and the other officers have even been looking and—"

"The police?"

"It's nothing serious."

Bailey ran a hand along the dash. "He shouldn't have run. He shouldn't feel responsible."

"But he was responsible. I saw him do it."

Bailey's head jerked. "You saw us arguing?"

"When did you argue?"

"The night I had the attack. We were arguing when I had the attack." When she didn't answer, he added, "We aren't talking about the same thing, are we?"

She shook her head.

"What did you see him do?"

It was easier to tell the whole rather than pick and choose particular points. She told him about Jered destroying the shrine.

"I didn't realize you knew each other more than 'hi' and 'bye.'"

"We don't, other than the few times I helped him look up information about the music business at the library."

"Ah. The kind, attentive adult, encouraging his dream."

She hated the edge in his voice. "There's nothing wrong with having dreams, Bailey. We'd all shrivel up and die if we didn't. Jered has his music, you have the restaurant, and I—"

"You?"

Compared to starting a restaurant or becoming a singer, Merry's dream seemed inconsequential, like comparing a diamond to cut glass.

"Tell me."

How did we get on this subject? She drove faster. "My dream is to go through a day and not think about surviving."

A pause. "The plane crash."

She held in a *duh!* "Surviving then, and surviving now, is like a wool blanket on a hot day. I'm suffocating and want to throw it off, but it's too heavy. In fact, surviving the crash was the easy part. My instincts took over. My body did what needed to be done. But now..." She put one hand to her collar. "Now I have to think about breathing in and out. I have to make an effort to move, to sleep, to eat, to think, to feel." She looked at him. "To *be.*"

"I'm so sorry." Bailey actually sounded as though he meant it. "Do you really think about such things all the time?"

"There are times when I forget, when life grabs hold and takes me along for a ride." Her hand stroked the steering wheel. "Remember what it was like to be on a trip with your parents and fall asleep in the backseat? You'd stop hearing their voices, the sound of tires against pavement, or even the *schwoosh-schwoosh* as other cars passed. Until the car slowed down. The change in momentum was like a clanging bell, waking you out of your sleep. That's the way it is when life takes me for a ride. I'm fine until it slows. Then I remember and I have to make myself take a breath. And let it out. And take another one in."

They turned onto his street and she recognized the moment for what it was: Bailey, coming home from the hospital to an empty house, his son gone who-knows-where; and her, pouring out her woes, adding to his stress.

"Don't worry about Jered." Merry patted his arm. "He'll get through his crisis, just like we all do."

Bailey took a deep breath. "The thing is, I love him. I never told him that. I want him to come home so I *can* tell him that."

What could she say? She, more than anyone, knew about regrets.

Claire watched Sim emptying the book-return box. The girl looked up and smiled. "Claire!"

Sim ran to her and surprised Claire with a hug. Claire exchanged a look with Harold. The act of affection suddenly made everything harder. Why didn't Sim show she cared before? Why now?

Sim pulled back. "Are you crying?"

Claire was surprised to find she was. "I always cry at reunions." She wrapped an arm around the girl's shoulders. "I missed you."

"I missed you too."

Really?

Sim drew Claire to the front desk like she was the owner of a prized possession. "Look, Merry. Look, Blanche."

Blanche shook her head. "We saw, we saw. Well, I'll be…"

Merry nodded a greeting. "Hi."

"Hi."

Sim's eyebrows dipped. "That's it? Claire is gone for days and that's all you can say?"

Obviously Merry hadn't mentioned sharing a cup of coffee at the

Plentiful. She tapped a stack of papers against the desk. "Glad to see you, Claire."

"Long time no see."

Sim rolled her eyes. "You guys are ridiculous. There are questions to be asked, things to find out." She turned to Claire. "Why did you leave? Where have you been?"

Claire hesitated.

"Maybe she doesn't want to tell," Merry said.

"Sure she does." Blanche nodded. "Because if she doesn't, I'll sic Ivan on her—as soon as he gets back from the hardware store."

Claire glanced at Harold. How much should she say? When he scurried off to his corner, she knew she had to keep his secret. "Let's just say I've been around."

"But why did you go?" Sim put her hands on her hips. "We didn't get in any real trouble for staying in the library."

That was such a small portion of the bigger situation. "It went way beyond having our hiding place discovered." Claire looked at the others. Having a public forum for her faults was not pleasant, but it was necessary. "The truth is, I left because I was a coward. I didn't like what people said about me when my story came out." *I didn't like that they didn't recognize my name.* She took a deep breath. "I wanted them to ooh and aah over the great sacrifice of giving away my fortune. My motives were pitiful. I ran away because of my pride."

"To my house." They all turned around to see Harold standing nearby. He stood tall.

Sim looked at Merry. Merry looked at Blanche. Merry spoke first. "What did you say, Harold?"

"I said, *to my house.*" He grinned and looked ten years younger.

Blanche waved a finger at his mouth. "What happened to Shakespeare?"

Harold shrugged. "'Part, fools! Put up your swords! You know not what you do!' How's that?"

Claire giggled and drew him into the group.

Merry shook her head. "What's going on?"

He glanced up, then down, a part of the old Harold coming through. "Quoting Shakespeare was *my* way of running away." He looked wistfully at Claire. "It happens to the best of us."

Blanche took his hand and patted it. "Glad to have you back with the rest of us, Harold. Deciphering your Shakespeare was exhausting. I'll be glad to revert to 'Hi, how are you?' instead of 'What light through yonder window breaks, you cowardly knave.'"

"That's pretty good, Blanche."

She curtsied.

Claire moved to the counter and traced its edge between her thumb and finger. Should she tell them she was leaving *now?*

She didn't have a chance. Sim bounced twice on the balls of her feet and grinned. "I'll be right back." She headed to the storeroom.

"Where are you going?" Claire called after her.

"You'll see."

Blanche crossed her arms. "So. You're not the loony pervert we thought you were, huh?"

"Blanche!"

The older woman pulled a face at Merry's reprimand. "I didn't say anything she hasn't already heard."

Claire slipped her arm around Blanche's shoulders. "Have you ever been friends with a loony pervert?"

Blanche looked toward the ceiling. "A few."

They laughed. All seemed right with the world.

Merry only partly heard the chitchat between Claire, Blanche, and Harold. Harold speaking sans Shakespeare was surprisingly easy to accept. It was Claire's presence that unleashed the butterflies in her stomach. Just yesterday, Claire had told Merry she didn't want to insert herself into Sim's life until she knew what to do next. Did her presence here mean she'd made a decision? What was it? Unfortunately, with Blanche babbling on, there was no way for Merry to take Claire aside to find out.

All conversation stopped when Sim popped back through the storeroom door with a bang. "I'm ready."

She was carrying an armload of Claire's stuff from the attic. She dropped the things on the counter. A shoe slipped to the floor. "Can someone else get the cooler? My hands were full."

Merry was glad when Claire spoke first. "Sim, what are you doing?"

"Getting your stuff. The rest of it is already at Merry's. I was thinking…you can have the couch in the bedroom and I'll sleep on the love seat."

Merry felt a twinge of jealousy and didn't like it one bit. It was repulsive. She looked to Claire, who had a pained look on her face.

Sim kept glancing between them. "Hey, that's the only solution. I don't want you staying at Harold's anymore. No offense, Harold, but…"

Claire spoke up. "Harold's house is lovely—on the inside."

"And the outside too—" Harold smiled—"since Claire's been working on it."

Merry found that hard to believe. She'd seen it. The outside, anyway. It was a disgrace. And it wasn't that she minded Claire staying with them; it was Sim's exuberance at the idea that bothered her.

Sim refolded Claire's black pants. "Do you have a sack or something, Merry?"

Before Merry could answer, Claire stilled Sim's hands. The girl looked up. "What?"

"I'm going home, Sim."

A crease formed between the girl's eyes.

"Home, Sim. My home. Kansas City."

Merry froze, then suddenly shook her head. She knew she should say something, but what?

"Had enough of us, eh?"

Claire ignored Blanche and took Sim's hand. "This isn't where I'm supposed to be. It's where I was supposed to *come*, but it isn't where I'm supposed to stay."

Sim jerked her hand away. "But you said—"

"I know. And everything I said I believed 100 percent. But a lot's happened."

"Nobody's making fun of you anymore. No one's said a thing about you or the library ghost for days."

"It's not that. Truly, it's not."

"Then what?"

Claire glanced at Blanche, and Merry knew she wanted some privacy. But Merry wanted to hear what she had to say too. Luckily, Harold came to the rescue. He sidled up to Blanche and took her arm. "Come show me how to work a computer, Blanche. I hear you're a real expert."

Blanche looked over her shoulder as she was led away. "But…"

There was an awkward moment of silence. Merry broke it. "Is it all right if I hear this too?"

"Certainly." Claire smiled at her. "You deserve that. And so much more."

Sim shoved Claire's possessions aside, making half of them fall to the floor. "You can't go! There's nothing for you back home. You gave it all up to come—"

Claire took a deep breath. "I've been offered a huge mosaic commission from a large church. I accepted."

Sim shook her head and said what Merry was thinking. "You're selling out."

"I'm buying in. Buying in to what I think is God's plan for my life."

"But He sent you here! *That* was His plan. You said so."

"Yes." She took their hands. "Because of coming here, I met both of you. And I've realized that giving up my talent—temporarily—was God's plan. He had to do a bit of work on me through my obedience, but now that He has…He's giving it back. I have a responsibility to use the gift He gave me. Use my art."

With an intake of breath, Sim ran out of the library.

Claire took a step toward the door. The thought of Claire going after Sim made Merry's stomach roil. Hadn't the woman teased their affections enough? She grabbed Claire's arm. "Let her go. She needs time for it to sink in."

"I feel awful."

"You should." Claire opened her mouth to speak, then closed it. Merry was glad. The woman had said enough. "When did you decide all this about accepting a commission and going home? Yesterday, you were all gung ho about saying yes to God. You even got me thinking about it."

"Leaving is a part of saying yes to Him. I think it's the right thing to do."

Merry flipped a hand. "Whatever, Claire. Come, go…it's hard to keep up with you." Claire's face fell. And even as Merry said the words, she questioned what she was doing. She was acting as if she wanted Claire to stay. But did she? Hadn't she liked this time alone with Sim?

"Don't be that way, Merry. This is hard enough."

The painful sincerity in Claire's voice made Merry's questions dissipate. Wasn't Claire the one in tune with God? If she felt God was leading her to leave, what could Merry offer to counter it?

Claire looked to the door Sim had used only moments before. "I'm worried about her."

"You should be. Her time's running out."

Claire did a double take. "What do you mean?"

"Officer Kendell held off as long as he could, but he's had to contact the authorities in Kansas City to see if he can find her aunt and uncle."

"Has he found them?"

"I haven't heard anything. But it's inevitable he will. The hard aspect about missing-children cases is not finding the relatives, but finding the child. We have the child."

"Does she know what he's doing?"

"No. I was afraid if she did, she'd run."

"She would. She just did."

A solution raised its hand, and Merry found herself verbalizing it at the same moment it entered her mind. "Everything else aside, maybe you should hang around a little while longer to see Sim through the hard time ahead." She shook her head. "Truthfully, I could use the help."

With a breath out, then in, Claire nodded. "Yes. Absolutely."

They both looked toward the door. One of them had to go talk to Sim. Would it be Surrogate Mother 1 or Surrogate Mother 2?

Claire headed for the door. "I'd better find her."

Merry was left to clean off the counter. There was no joy in being number two.

Sim looked up from her position on the bench in the town square to see Claire come out of the library. Her legs twitched, wanting to run again, but her torso seemed to lodge itself heavier on the bench. She was tired of running away. She was tired of people leaving her.

She was tired. Period.

Claire approached as if Sim were a squirrel that would bolt at any quick movement. Finally, she stood in front of her.

"I wish I had a chocolate donut to offer you as a peace offering."

Sim wouldn't let herself smile. "It's not that easy. *I'm* not that easy."

Claire nodded and scuffed a toe on the edge of the grass. "May I sit down?"

"Must you?"

Her toe stopped its movement and planted itself. She did not sit. "I know you don't understand."

"My, you're smart." *What am I saying? Why am I being so rude?*

"There's nothing further for me to do here."

"I agree." *God, make her stay!*

Claire blinked. "You agree?"

Sim drew her knees to her chest, balancing her heels on the edge of the bench. Unable to get comfortable, she dropped her feet to the ground and pretended to chip away at a fingernail.

"I'm sorry I pulled you into all this, Sim."

Sim abandoned her nails, hating the tears that threatened. "Hey, *you* didn't pull me into anything. I came here on my own, I dealt with things here on my own, and I will leave here on my own." *I'm so alone!*

"You're leaving?"

Sim risked a glance. *I don't want to. I really don't want to.* "What's it to you?"

Claire looked toward the library. "Actually, I told Merry I'd stay a few more days."

Sim eyed her. That made no sense, but she was glad anyway.

Claire held out a hand. "Let's go back to the library. Merry needs you."

Sim ignored Claire's hand, stood, and brushed past her. "At least *somebody* does."

Three females staying in the same house after a tension-filled day. Not exactly a formula for a pleasant evening.

Gone was the usual banter. In its place was a dinner of chopped salad combined with chopped sentences. Pass this, pass that. Thank you very much.

Going to bed was a relief.

Yet kindness *was* present. Merry was proud of Sim when she gave up the couch in the guest room for Claire and slept sprawled on the love seat in the living room. That simple act said a lot about the girl's character. She deserved a better hand than the one life had dealt her.

Didn't they all?

Merry flipped sides for the tenth time. She couldn't sleep. Memories of Lou played on the screen of her mind, like a family newsreel.

But it wasn't enough. She found herself needing actual pictures. She tiptoed downstairs to find the photo albums in the living room, careful not to wake Sim. She took the photos into the kitchen and spread them on the table. She ran a hand over the top of the newest album, thinking of all the times she'd seen Lou working on them. Taking snapshots had been his thing. He would pester her mercilessly to "Hold that pose. I need a picture of this." Hence, the albums were full of pictures of Merry hammering, Merry and Justin cooking, Merry dancing with Justin to the old Neil Diamond song "Porcupine Pie."

Lou took such pride in arranging the photos in an artistic manner, adding funny captions and even poems or clippings to the pages to create a unique presentation of their life together. But since he took most of the pictures, there were few with him in them, which was one reason Merry had not opened the albums since his death. But even a few pictures were better than nothing.

She opened the newest album for the first time ever. It contained photos of Christmas. No one could have known that just one month later...

She paused at the picture she'd taken of Lou holding Justin in his lap, his strong arms wrapped around the boy like a seat belt.

The plane had had seat belts. Little good they had done.

Merry's eyes were drawn to a poem Lou had added to the page:

The Creator descends on family moments
with a warm hug and a soft word.
Man shakes his head in awe, "Surely, this is perfection."
The Lord, our Christ, descends on mankind
with a warm hug and a soft word.
God nods his head,
"Surely, He is perfection. My perfect Son."

It was signed by Lou.

She stroked the words with her fingers as if they had physical as well as spiritual depth. Lou had had such a strong faith; he had been an unmovable rock compared to her pebble that could be kicked aside on a whim. How many times had he tried to get her to truly commit to Jesus? And how many times had she only pretended to believe, to shut him up so she could think about "more important things"?

Merry let the tears come. She wanted to believe. It was lonely keeping God on the outskirts of her life and rude living a faith of convenience, only going to Him when she needed something. God was so giving and forgiving...

What would happen if *she* gave a little?

She closed the album, her thoughts skimming over the events of the past few days. The destruction of her shrine and the subsequent surrender of that icon. Her discussion with Claire about saying yes. And Claire's strong, sure decision to go back. Did that strong, sure decision come directly from her saying yes to God?

She wanted to feel strong about something. She wanted to be sure.

Then say yes.

As she thought, *Why not?* she realized her motives were far from pure. At the moment, saying yes to Jesus was a means to gain something precious: peace. Once more she was using God to get what she wanted. And yet she had the feeling Jesus would forgive her flawed motivation. He—all man and yet all God—would understand and be so pleased at finally having Merry Cavanaugh's full attention and dedication that He would overlook its imperfection and zone in on the least bit of purity it possessed.

She folded her hands beneath her chin and bowed her head. "Dear Jesus, I'm so weary. I'm tired of just surviving. I want more. I want strength and certainty and determination…and joy. I want joy."

She decided a confession was in order. "You know my motives. It's true I'm hoping that saying yes will bring about good changes in my life." She laughed softly. "I'm certainly not considering it because I want things to get worse. But know that I also am doing this because it's the right thing to do. I know it will please You—and somehow please Lou. He tried so hard and for so long to get me to this point."

She put a hand on the album, connecting to her husband. "So here I am. Saying yes to you without even knowing the question." She drew a breath from her toes. "Yes, I say yes. I give you my everything. Take me, I'm yours."

She lowered her head to her arms, blanketing the pictures of her family. And then she cried every kind of tear left inside. Sorrow, guilt, relief, joy…

And she was cleansed.

Twenty-three

Therefore judge nothing before the appointed time;
wait till the Lord comes.
He will bring to light what is hidden in darkness and
will expose the motives of men's hearts.
At that time each will receive his praise from God.

1 CORINTHIANS 4:5

CLAIRE STOPPED OUTSIDE THE KITCHEN to listen to Merry's song. She wasn't good, but she was loud.

When Merry ended with an exuberant "Hal-le-lu-ya-a-a-h" Claire made her presence known by walking in with applause.

Merry blushed but recovered nicely with a deep curtsy.

"What's got into you this morning?"

Merry pulled out a stool for her. "You're not the only one who has God moments. I had one last night."

Claire suffered a twinge of jealousy. "Where was I?"

"Sleeping."

"What happened?"

Merry brandished a spatula to make her point. "I said yes, Claire. Just like you did. I said yes to God."

Without me? "What brought that on?"

Merry shrugged. "A lot of things. I'm tired of treating the Lord like a four-letter word, I'm tired of holding on to the past and my guilt as if it will change something. I'm tired of making it so hard by thinking I have to attain a certain state of perfection before I can commit to Him. Truth is, God will take me as I am."

Claire thought of a well-known song—"Just As I Am, Without One Plea."

"I'm tired of handling things by myself," Merry said. "I figure He can do a better job of it."

Claire knew she should be happy for Merry—and for God. This was a victory for the Lord. This was proof He was working in Merry's life. This was—

"Aren't you going to say anything?"

"That's great." Her voice had the dull resonance of a spoon against a tin cup.

Merry flicked the spatula at her. "Aw, come on, Claire. Don't be so...*contained*. Today is a day for joy." She flipped a pancake with a flourish. "It feels so *good* to move on with my life."

"Haven't you been moving on?"

She shook her head. "I've been a sleepwalker. If something threatened to wake me, I'd run away until I could slip back to sleep."

Sim came in the kitchen, her eyes half-closed. "What's going on in here?"

Merry ruffled the girl's hair in a gesture full of joyful abandon. "I was just telling Claire that you two had a big part in waking me up."

Sim stumbled onto a stool. "Who's awake?"

Merry was on a roll. "Actually, Claire started it. Her appearance in Steadfast made me think about someone other than myself and my predicament."

"Oh," Claire said flatly. "I'm...glad."

Merry stopped, an eyebrow dipping. "What's *with* you anyway?"

"I don't know what you're talking—"

"Don't give me that. It's pretty noticeable when the head cheer-leader has lost her pom-poms." Merry waggled a single finger next to her own head and deadpanned, "Yay, team."

Claire had to smile. "It's not that bad."

"Yes, it is." Merry eyed her. "I thought you, of all people, would be jumping up and down, doing a funky end-zone dance."

Why *was* she being so lukewarm, acting like a little girl who'd been served lima beans instead of chocolate?

"You having second thoughts about staying on for a while?"

That woke Sim up. "Are you?"

Claire looked past them into nothing. She let the notion settle and found it false. "No. I'm okay with staying—and then going back."

"Then what is it?" Merry asked.

Explaining it was like grasping fog. "Change makes me…wistful." Claire traced the edge of the counter. "I'm aware of a change about to take place. I want it to happen yet don't want it to happen."

Merry piped up immediately. "You mean you're human."

Claire laughed. And the wistfulness was appeased.

Merry served the pancakes. "Eat up. Eat up now, but save room for a big dinner. I want to take you both to Bon Vivant this evening to celebrate—celebrate everything. Celebrate life."

How could Claire argue with that?

The restaurant critic sipped coffee from his travel mug. He glanced at the woman in the passenger seat. "You feeling any better?"

The woman did not open her eyes. "I'll be all right. Get me a good meal, and I'll be fine."

"We didn't have to come. The magazine said they'd assign the review to someone else. They understand we're going through a hard time. And I've already tried to do this once. Stupid, crazy driver, running me off the road…"

The woman moaned. "If only I'd remembered to bring along my motion-sickness medicine." She shook her head. "I thought I was over such things. I haven't gotten sick like this in years."

"We can stop and get some."

"No. It's okay." She sank deeper in the seat, holding the litter bag close, just in case. "Actually, I'm glad we can spend some time together. We've both been so stressed."

"I know. This is nice."

She opened one eye. "Just don't go driving into any ditches this time, okay?"

"It's a deal."

Sim stared into the mirror of the library's rest room. It was so wonderful to have Claire back at the library with all the regulars, and have
life feel normal.

Normal.

Suddenly she noticed her makeup as if seeing herself for the first
time. The darkly-lined eyes. The glossed lips. The patch of red hair
amid the gelled shocks. And the nose ring. She'd gotten it pierced on
a whim.

A stupid whim.

She rubbed a finger across her lips, spreading the goo around.
Then she smiled. She had an idea. All she needed was a little time.
Maybe Merry would let her off early.

Merry and Claire were ready and waiting. They'd come back to
Merry's to meet up with Sim and change for the celebratory dinner
at Bon Vivant. They hadn't seen the girl since she left the library at
four, and ever since they'd gotten home Sim had been ensconced in
the first-floor bathroom.

Claire looked at her watch and rapped on the bathroom door.
"Sim? Come on. The reservations are for six-thirty."

Merry sat on the love seat and buckled her sandals. "She's taking
an awfully long time. Something's up."

The bathroom door opened, drawing their eyes. A creature
appeared—a creature that resembled Sim but far surpassed her in
beauty.

"Whoa, baby!"

Claire echoed Merry's outburst as the girl paraded in front of
them like a runway model. Her lilac flowered skirt swirled as she
made a pirouette. Her chopped-off hair was layered, curled, and dyed
a soft chestnut brown. Was that a headband? And her face… "What
happened to you?"

Sim placed herself front and center. "You like it?"

"You are an angel."

Sim laughed. "I wouldn't go that far, Merry."

Claire nodded her agreement. "You certainly look like one. My, my, you clean up good, kiddo."

Sim fanned her skirt and curtsied. "All in honor of the celebration."

Claire's throat tightened. "Absolutely. Now come over here and give me a hug."

The wistfulness returned.

The waiting room of Bon Vivant was empty when the women arrived. Bailey was busy talking to Stanley in the dining room.

"I didn't think Bailey would be at work," Claire said.

"It's probably less stressful to be here than worrying about the place from home." Merry sat in the waiting room, right below Claire's mosaic.

Claire looked at the mosaic, then her friend, then her mosaic again. Her two lives merged. She was tempted to take credit but decided against it. She'd come this far…

Sim glanced toward the kitchen. "I'd like to go see everyone, see if Sanchez is back. Is that okay?"

Merry smiled. "You just want to show off the new you."

Sim's blush was lovely.

"I'd like to go along." Claire rose. "I know the gang too."

Merry waved them on. "Go on. I'm fine here."

Sim rushed toward the kitchen, Claire close behind, but Claire got sidetracked when Stanley waved her over. Bailey was off attending to some customers.

Claire got an update about Sanchez from Stanley, telling how Bailey had apologized big-time and lured the chef back. Then Stanley did a double take when he looked over at Bailey. "I don't believe it."

"What?"

Stanley put a finger to his lips and nodded toward Bailey, who was talking with a couple. The man had his hands resting on his ample stomach in a gesture of satisfaction. The woman fingered her wine glass. They were listening to Bailey with intent interest.

"Actually, our chef, Sanchez, came up with that Chocolat Bordeaux. It all started when he was twelve…" Bailey glanced toward the kitchen, hesitating just a second as he noticed Claire and Stanley listening. "If you're really interested, I could have Sanchez come out and tell you the story."

The couple looked at each other and beamed. "That would be wonderful."

Bailey went to the kitchen, returning with Sanchez in tow. He let the chef get his accolades solo as Bailey came over to Claire.

"Evening, Claire. Your table's ready. I saw Sim—a new and improved Sim, I must say—but where's Merry?"

At that moment, Merry peered around the corner of the waiting room. Bailey gestured her toward an empty table. He held their chairs.

"Sim must still be in the kitchen. I'll get—"

Sanchez came over. He was practically glowing.

"Does your hat still fit?" Bailey grinned.

"I think so." He nodded to the couple. "They want to see you."

"Me?" Bailey glanced at them.

"They have a surprise for you."

"A surprise?"

Sanchez gave Bailey a gentle push. "Go on. It's *your* turn."

"But what—?"

Sanchez turned serious. "It's your turn, Bailey. Go on. And thanks. You made my day. You made me glad to be back."

With a shrug to the ladies, Bailey headed for the couple.

"What's going on?"

Claire gave Merry a shrug. "I don't know, shh. Let's listen."

"You wanted to see me?"

The man grinned at Bailey like he was about to present a winning lottery ticket. "I am a restaurant critic from Kansas City, and I—"

"You're—"

"Yes, I am. And I just wanted you to know that I plan on giving Bon Vivant five stars in all categories. Your restaurant is charming, well staffed, and serves food that makes the trip well worth it. Bravo."

Diners at nearby tables applauded. Bailey beamed.

Claire noticed Sim come out of the kitchen with the other staffers, no doubt drawn by the applause. But suddenly Sim's curious smile changed to a look of horror. She took a step back into a waiter, sending his tray and all its contents crashing to the floor.

Sim didn't seem to notice. She just stared at the restaurant critic, stricken.

Eyes followed eyes until all in the restaurant were looking her way.

The critic rose from his chair. "Sim?" He frowned, as though trying to decide if the girl standing there really was who he thought she was. "Sim! What are you doing here?"

The woman stood, her chair nearly toppling. "Sim!"

Merry looked between them. "You know her?"

"You bet we do. She's our niece."

Sim ran. She heard footsteps running after her.

They'll catch me and take me back—

"Sim! Stop!"

She risked a glance behind. Claire huffed, trying to catch up. Sim turned the corner, putting the restaurant out of sight, and waited.

Claire staggered the last few steps. She gasped. "I'm...not used...to running."

"Well, I am." Sim crossed her arms. "And I'll keep running as long as I have to."

Claire held up a hand, grabbing a breath. "You don't have to. Merry and I are not going to let anything bad happen to you. I promise."

"But Bailey asked my uncle and aunt to his restaurant. He had them there, waiting for me."

"He didn't know they were your relatives. The man said he was a restaurant critic. He came to critique Bon Vivant. You saw his face; he didn't know you were going to be there."

What Claire said made sense.

"Talk to them, Sim."

She pulled the headband off and flung it in the street. "What good does it do to change when everything will go back to the way it was? You're already on their side. You don't even know them and you're on their side."

"I'm on *your* side. But running away again is not the answer."

"What choice do I have?" Sim looked toward the restaurant, ready to flee. "Now that they've found me, they'll want me back." She looked at Claire. "They'll want me back!"

Sim couldn't hold the tears any longer. She fell into Claire's arms and wished she never had to let go.

Claire and Sim walked back to the restaurant with Claire's arm strung protectively across Sim's shoulders. There was no way Claire would let them take the girl. Not yet.

An audience waited for them in the parking lot. Claire could feel Sim tense. She whispered out of the side of her mouth, "It will be okay. Stay calm."

Sim's aunt ran to meet them. She held out her hands to touch her niece but withdrew them when Sim stiffened. "You look…so different! Absolutely lovely."

The girl didn't say a word.

Her aunt tried again. "We were so worried. Why did you leave?"

"You know why I left."

The aunt and uncle exchanged a puzzled look. The uncle spoke up. "We have no idea, young lady. We know you've gone through tough times these past months, but we've tried our hardest, taken you in, provided—"

"You provided nothing. It's my *parents'* money that provided for me—and for *you.* In grand style. You don't care about me. All you care about is the money that comes with me."

"That's not true." Sim's aunt sounded shocked. Claire wondered if it was because of regret at being misunderstood or anger that Sim had given them away.

Sim's uncle took the girl's arm. "There's our car, right over there. You get inside right now, and we'll take you home and—"

"No!" Sim shook his arm away and hid behind Claire.

He tried to grab her, but Claire dodged out of his way. She raised her hands. "Let's calm down. There's obviously a lot to be worked out, and that can't be done when everyone's upset."

"We have a right to be upset," Sim's uncle said. "The girl ran away, and then we find her in a strange town, brainwashed against us."

Merry raised a hand. "We have *not* brainwashed Sim, we've *cared* for her. We care about her. We only want what's best for her."

"Is that why you've broken the law, hiding her from her legal guardians?"

Claire stepped forward. "This may be a legal matter, but it's also a moral one."

The man flashed an incredulous look. "Who are *you* people to talk of morals? What's moral about keeping a girl from her family?"

"We've been her family." Claire felt her own anger building.

The uncle laughed. "You've got to be kidding."

Sim pushed her way between Merry and Claire. "They're not kidding. I choose them. They're my family now. I want to stay here. I don't want to go back with you."

Sim's aunt put a hand to her mouth. Claire saw the woman's tears and felt a wave of sympathy. This was a complicated matter that couldn't, wouldn't, and shouldn't be decided in a parking lot. "There's a motel on the edge of town. Why don't you check in, and we'll work through this in the morning."

Sim's uncle gave a curt nod. "Fine. Sim, come with us."

The girl hung back, shaking her head. Merry spoke for her. "She's been staying with me and will continue to do so until a decision is made." She got out a paper and pen. "Merry Cavanaugh. Here's my number." She handed the paper over. "If that's agreeable with everyone, I think we'll call it a night."

"That is *not* agreeable!" Sim's uncle crumpled the paper in his palm. But his wife put a hand on his arm and took the note. They got in their car and drove away.

As the three women walked to Merry's car, Sim looked as if she were taking her final steps.

⨎   ⨎   ⨎

No one talked as they drove back to Merry's. A single thought bored its way into Claire's mind: *It's over.* Sim's aunt and uncle had found her. Sim would return to them and that would be the end of everything.

It didn't seem right. If God wanted Sim to remain in her old life, then why had she and Claire been brought together in the first place? Why had Merry been brought into the mix to care for the girl? It didn't seem logical. The aunt and uncle couldn't have her. *She's mine.*

She's not yours, she's Mine.

That was the bottom line. Either Claire believed God was in control or she didn't. Either she trusted Him or she didn't.

Either their yeses meant something…

Claire said a quick prayer but received no immediate insight. All they could do was wait for Him to show them the right way. His way.

Someone knocked on the door. Merry's stomached clenched.

Sim ducked behind the love seat. "Don't open it!"

"Don't be silly." Claire motioned for Sim to come out of her hiding place. She patted the love seat beside her. Sim fell onto the cushions like a rag doll.

"There's nothing to be afraid of." But Merry looked through the peephole just the same. It was Bailey. She opened the door.

He came inside. "Is the girl okay?"

Sim tucked her feet beneath her. "I'm fine. For now."

Merry touched Bailey's arm. "How about you? With all the excitement…your surgery. Shouldn't you be at home?"

"I'm going. I just wanted to check on you." He looked to Sim. "Your uncle's not the kind to try to nab you, is he?"

"I don't think so."

"I could stay here. Sleep on the couch. Protect you."

Merry smiled. "Where's your shining armor?"

"It's at the cleaners." He took a deep breath. He was way too pale. "Sorry your dinner was scrapped."

"We'll do it another time," Claire said.

Bailey pointed a finger at Sim. "Be brave, kid. Everything will turn out fine. I promise."

Ten minutes later, Merry hung up the phone. This was not going to be easy.

Sim must have noticed the crease between her eyebrows. "Who was that?"

"Ken."

"Who's Ken?"

Merry hesitated. "He's a police officer."

"A cop?"

"Your uncle called him. Ken wants to hear our side."

"Yeah, right."

"He's a good guy, Sim. He's been concerned about you and has been very nice about letting you stay here *without* contacting anyone."

Sim stomped away. "It's a conspiracy."

"It's reality, Sim."

"Then I'll take fantasy."

Merry sighed and flipped through the pages of the phone book, finding a number. She drilled it with a finger. "I'm calling your aunt and uncle at the motel."

"No way."

Merry put the receiver to her ear. "This isn't a question of *want*, Sim. This is a question of *right*. Ken wants to meet tomorrow and agreed to do it over here instead of at the station. Your aunt and uncle need to be here. They have a right to be here."

"To decide *my* fate?"

Merry dialed the number.

A noise woke her. Merry opened her eyes and waited to hear it again to prove to herself that it was real and not a part of a dream.

A soft shuffle. A muted bump. *Someone is in the house!*
Sim's uncle!

She threw off the covers and ran downstairs. The love seat in the living room was empty.

Claire appeared on the landing behind her. "Where is—?"

"Sim! Sim?"

A glass broke in the kitchen. They found Sim standing above the mess, fully dressed, her backpack over one shoulder.

Merry put her hands on her hips. "What are you doing?"

"Getting a drink of water."

Neither woman responded.

Sim let the backpack slip to the floor. "I was leaving."

Claire pointed to a kitchen chair. "Sit."

Sim walked around the broken glass, her shoes crunching small shards. She sat.

"You can't run away again. Ever. You have to face this."

The girl's head shook back and forth. "I know how these things work, Claire. Relatives always get custody of the kids. Plus I'll get in trouble for running way. Because of that, the authorities won't listen to me. They'll think I'm a delinquent. I've watched the news. These things never work out."

"It sounds like your aunt and uncle want you back because they care about you," Merry said.

Sim kept shaking her head. "Don't I have a say in this?" Her voice was choked with tears. She put her head in her hands.

Merry witnessed a tear fall onto Sim's knee and chastised herself for being surprised to see it. Why did Sim always seem older than her fourteen years? Merry wrapped her arms around the girl. Within a moment, she felt Claire's hands on her back.

"Dear God—" Claire's calm voice filled the kitchen—"take care of this child. You were the One who brought us together. And now…we want what's best for her. Please control this situation and help us do the right thing. We're saying yes to you. Whatever you want." Claire's voice changed. "Aren't we saying yes?"

Merry sighed deeply. "Yes, I'm saying yes."

"Sim?"

The girl hesitated. Then she nodded. Three for three.

A cord of three strands is not quickly broken…

Twenty-four

I will be glad and rejoice in your love,
for you saw my affliction and knew the anguish of my soul.

PSALM 31:7

BY EIGHT-FIFTEEN THE NEXT MORNING, they were ready for the meeting at Merry's.

At least, Claire *hoped* they were ready.

Officer Kendell stood at the bottom of the stairs, his elbow resting on the baluster. The smell of cinnamon coffee cake filled the room. Claire set two chairs near the love seat.

Merry came in from the kitchen and handed Ken a cup of coffee. "I sent Sim to get ice. Quick. Let's devise a plan. We've got to have a plan." She looked to Ken. "Don't we?"

"You can plan all you want, but..." He shrugged.

That said it all. This meeting was an act of futility.

Claire put a calming hand on Merry's arm. "I think it's imperative we react logically yet show compassion. No angry voices. No threats. We don't want the aunt and uncle to think we're the enemy. It's important we handle this situation with dignity."

"I vote for dignity." Merry glanced at Ken. "We'll never convince them that Sim belongs in Steadfast unless we can show them we are good people who'll care for her and bring her up right."

There was a moment of silence.

"Whoa!" Ken made a *T* with his hands. "Time out. Bring her up? Since when are you talking about a permanent situation?"

Yeah, since when, Merry?

"I don't know. I just—"

"Temporarily taking care of a runaway is one thing, finding out

312

the truth about her situation is a second thing, but having her stay…"
He shook his head. "There are courts to think about. Lawyers. Laws."

Merry and Claire exchanged a glance. What *was* Merry talking
about?

Merry's hands flew up and down, back and forth. "But we can't
let Sim live in limbo any longer. If it turns out she shouldn't be with
her relatives, then *someone* has to take her. We need to make a commitment." She turned to Claire. "Right?"

Claire swallowed hard.

Ken looked at Merry, then Claire. "You talking foster care here
or adoption?"

"Hey, don't look at me." Claire held her hands up. "This is
Merry's ball game."

Merry's face sagged. *"Claire!* Don't you want to take her? Keep
her here?"

Claire moved to Merry's side, lowering her voice. *"Here* is the key
word. *I'm* not going to be here, Merry. I'm going home."

"But…" Merry looked as if she'd been hit in the stomach.

Ken moved between them. "I know your heart is in the right
place, Merry. But you're thinking short-term, while the girl needs a
long-term answer. I advise you not to get her hopes up by letting her
think she's going to stay. I truly doubt the aunt and uncle will go
down easy."

Claire pressed a hand against her forehead to fend off a headache.

Merry adjusted the doily on the back of a wing chair. "I was hoping…maybe they want to give her up."

"They were pretty adamant last night."

Merry turned to Claire. "And rude. I don't like the uncle at all."

"He was just surprised," Claire said. "It was a shock seeing his
niece at the restaurant."

Ken sipped his coffee. "So what exactly are you offering, Merry?"

Claire joined Ken in waiting for an answer.

"I'm…I'm offering her a home." Merry suddenly sounded certain. "A loving home. That seems to be more than she has—"

They heard the kitchen door slam. Sim rushed in, carrying a bag
of ice. "They're here! They're just driving up." She dropped the ice on

the floor and took a position behind a wing chair, as far away from the front door as possible. "I don't want to do this. Let's call it off."

Claire patted her hand. "Calm down, kiddo. Nothing's going to happen to you."

They heard car doors slam. Then footsteps on the front walk and the hollow sound of shoes against the wood porch. A knock. Merry tensed. It did not add to Claire's confidence. "Dignity, people."

Merry answered the door.

Claire thought Sim's aunt looked like she was going to be sick. She kept her arm linked through her husband's, as if it was his strength that was holding her up. His jaw muscles twitched.

"Welcome." Claire was relieved that Merry sounded sincere. "Come in."

The aunt sought out Sim and offered a smile, but Sim raised her chin.

Merry introduced Officer Kendell.

"And your names are?" Ken asked.

The aunt opened her mouth to answer Ken, but the uncle answered for both of them. "She's Susan. And I'm Forbes. Forbes Kellogg."

Merry nodded once. "Won't you have a seat?"

"We're not staying long." They sat on the love seat. Merry sat on an added chair, while Claire took the wing chair with Sim at her back. Ken moved into the room but remained standing.

"Coffee, anyone?" Merry looked around the room. "And I have coffee cake."

"I *said* we're not staying long."

So much for dignity.

Claire drew in a breath. Nerves ricocheted. Perhaps it was up to her to start? "When Sim appeared—"

Forbes laughed. "Appeared? You make it sound like she popped out of thin air."

"Nearly so." Claire actually managed a smile. "She came to town in the middle of the night and…" How should she word this? "And we found each other. It was not a coincidence."

"God brought me here."

The air quivered at Sim's bold statement. Finally Forbes pointed at his niece. "Like I said last night, you've brainwashed her. She didn't used to be a fanatic."

"I'm not a fanatic now," Sim said. "But Claire helped me see that God was in on this and—"

"Oh, please." Forbes rolled his eyes. "Let's not go overboard with the God business."

Although this was *not* the direction Claire wanted to take, she couldn't stop it now. "Why can't Sim's presence here be an example of God at work? Why are you so quick to dismiss it?"

"It was *Sim's* decision to come here, not God's."

"How do you know?"

Forbes laughed. "So you think God *made* Sim run away to Steadfast?"

"Not at all. But I do think He offered her choices that fit into a larger plan, even if she didn't realize it."

He waved off Claire's words. "You people are over the edge. A bunch of religious weirdos. A cult."

Ken took a step forward. "Hold the insults, Mr. Kellogg. We're here to discuss the matter, not make false accusations."

"But they—"

"*They* are not in a cult. And I, most certainly, am not in a cult." He leveled Forbes with a look. "Is that understood? Can we move on?"

Forbes shrugged.

Merry sat forward. "Sim's being here saved a life. If she hadn't been in Steadfast, Bailey Manson—the owner of Bon Vivant—might have died of a heart attack. She found him. She saved him."

Forbes snickered. "Coincidence."

"It wasn't any such thing!" Sim's voice cracked, and she cleared her throat. "I woke up in the barn and just knew I had to go to Bailey's. I found—"

"You were sleeping in a barn?"

Sim bit her lower lip. "They weren't making me stay in a barn. I ran away and found one on the edge of town and—"

"You ran away?" Forbes cast a glare from Merry to Claire.

Ken's eyebrows raised.

Sim's gaze flitted across the room, looking for help, but there was no way to save her. "It wasn't anything bad. I'd just run away from Bailey's because he was mad I tattled on him, and Sanchez quit and…it was my choice. Bailey didn't send me away."

Forbes folded his arms across his chest. "Seems running away is getting to be a habit with you."

Sim looked away, then gripped the back of Claire's chair.

Forbes slapped his thighs. "Well, that certainly clinches it. You're all irresponsible zealots who forced my niece to take refuge in a barn. And she proved she's mentally disturbed by running away—again. She needs stability, that's what she needs." He turned to Ken. "Officer, certainly you see what a bunch of crazies these people are. There is no way any responsible person could consider letting Sim stay with any of them. They are decidedly unfit."

Ken spoke up. "They are not—"

"They are not unfit." Everyone looked at Susan, who up until now had not spoken.

Forbes stared at his wife as if he'd forgotten she was there. "Excuse me?"

Susan fingered the strap of her purse. "What they say…it makes sense."

"It does not."

"It does." She looked around the room. "I'm not saying I approve of all that's gone on, but I do want to make it clear that I…I believe what you believe. That God can guide us." She looked at her lap and began creasing her skirt between thumb and forefinger. "I've let myself forget that. For too long."

Forbes shook his head, clearly disgusted. "I am dumbfounded at how God got into this discussion. We're talking about very practical matters here, not some spiritual double-talk."

"I happen to think God is extremely practical," Claire said.

Merry nodded. "Don't be so close-minded, Mr. Kellogg."

"I'm not."

"I believe you are."

He opened his mouth to speak but ended up snapping it shut. He looked at his watch.

"You have someplace to go?" Ken asked.

"As a matter of fact, yes. I only came to Steadfast to critique Bon Vivant, not to stay for days on end."

"It's only been one night, Mr. Kellogg. If getting Sim back is an inconvenience, these ladies would be happy to take her off your—"

"Cute."

Susan put a hand to her stomach and closed her eyes. She groaned.

Merry leaned forward. "Are you all right?"

"She's fine." Forbes ground out the words.

"Oh…I'm not." Susan opened her eyes, and Claire saw that she was even paler than before. "Where's the bathroom, please?"

Merry helped her out of the room.

"Now—" Forbes turned to Ken—"let's get down to business. We all know there is no way Sim is going to stay—"

"I'm afraid you're taking a lot for granted, Mr. Kellogg."

Before Forbes could respond to Ken, Claire shook her head. "Aren't you concerned about your wife?"

Forbes hesitated. "She'll be fine. It's just the remnants from her motion sickness yesterday. It has nothing to do with—"

"But I think it does." Claire shifted on the chair. "How you treat your wife is indicative of how you treat your niece."

He glared at her. "She's got an upset stomach. Keep it in perspective, lady."

"Do you see what I mean?" Sim waved a hand at him. "He doesn't care about anyone else. He only cares about himself—and *my* money."

Forbes pointed a finger at her. "That money has been entrusted to us until you turn eighteen."

"At the rate you're spending it, there won't be any *left* when I'm eighteen."

"The things I purchased were for you too Sim. There was the big-screen TV so you would feel comfortable bringing your friends over—"

"Friends who won't come over because you always yell at us. What about the car? Is that for me too?"

"Sure it is."

"And the fertility treatments? How is *that* for me?"

The argument waged on, but to Claire the point was made. Although she'd believed the essence of Sim's story about her aunt and uncle's greed, she'd thought the girl's complaints were exaggerated.

Now she knew better.

Merry tapped on the door to the bathroom. "Mrs. Kellogg? Are you all right?" The door opened and Susan emerged, dabbing a tissue to her mouth. "You don't look so good."

"I don't feel so good."

"Come sit down."

Susan shook her head. "I have to get back to Forbes. He needs—" She was interrupted by the sound of his loud voice berating Sim.

Merry shook her head. "You certainly *don't* need that. And frankly, I don't either." She helped Susan into a seat at the kitchen table, then went to get her a glass of water.

"Thank you."

"You're welcome."

She took a sip. Merry didn't know what to say except, "I want you to know that Claire and I care about Sim very much. Very much."

"Sim's only been here a short time. How can you care for her so deeply?"

Merry looked to the ceiling. "What can I say? It's got to be a God-thing. What else can explain our affection for the girl, and her affection for us?" She arranged the salt and pepper shakers. "I guess I have an open place in my heart for a child." She withdrew her hands. "I had a child once."

"Once?"

Merry chose her words carefully. She didn't want to get into the plane crash. This wasn't about her. "I lost him in an accident. My husband too."

"Oh my. I'm so sorry."

Merry nodded. "So there is a chance my feelings for Sim are selfish. She fills a need in me. A need to mother."

Susan's face crumpled, but she got it under control. "I understand that need completely. We desperately want a child."

"A baby. Sim told us."

Susan drew in a breath, opened her mouth to speak, then covered her forehead with a hand. "We haven't handled things well. I'll admit that." She crossed her hands over her chest. "I have never, ever been as obsessed with anything as I have been with wanting a child." She glanced at Merry. "A child of my own. A baby." She lowered her arms. "Sometimes my arms ache for the weight of one, my nose tingles for the smell of one, my cheek longs for the feel of a tiny cheek against…" Her arms returned to her chest, an invisible baby within her embrace. "I've had two fertility treatments—that haven't taken."

"I'm so sorry."

Susan nodded. "When Sim came into our lives we—I—was still recovering from the last disappointment. I wasn't prepared to take care of her, comfort her, when I was still grieving myself."

Ah. It made sense now. The Kelloggs' treatment of Sim wasn't justified, but was understandable. At least on Susan's part.

"What about your husband?"

Susan glanced toward the living room and cringed. "We handle things differently."

"He seems…stern."

She smiled weakly. "That's one word for it."

Merry leaned forward. "Does he really want Sim?"

Susan shredded the tissue. "I don't know the answer to that."

If Susan didn't know…

"I want Sim." Merry's eyes met Susan's. "I really do."

Susan didn't respond. She pushed her chair back. "I need to get back to my husband."

❧   ❧   ❧

Everyone was quiet while Susan took her seat. Uncle Forbes gave Aunt Susan a quick glance, then continued speaking. "Like I said, no court is going to give any stranger in a strange town custody."

Sim's insides hurt. They just kept going round and round. There was no hope.

Until…

Merry stood up. "I want to pursue custody."

Uncle Forbes snorted at her. "You're single."

"So?"

Ken raised a hand. "This is going to get complicated, Merry."

Forbes laughed. "No court is going to give a single woman custody when there's a couple available—a couple *related* to the child."

Sim stepped out from behind Claire's chair. "They will if I tell them to." She wasn't sure if it *was* true, but it *should* be.

Her aunt stood. Sim hated to see the hurt on Aunt Susan's face. "I know things haven't been great with us, Sim, but we'll be better. I promise. I've let things… I've gotten my priorities messed up. But I'm determined to make things right, make things the way they should be." She took a breath. "We love you."

Sim bit her lip. She wasn't at all sure about the *we* part in her aunt's statement, but she accepted her aunt's love as genuine. "And I love you too, Aunt Susan. I really do. But you aren't being entirely truthful. I know you don't want me around. You want a baby. All you think about is having a baby."

Susan shook her head. "It's more complicated than that."

"But it's not. I'm a kid. I want to be a part of a family who wants me around."

"Oh, Sim. I'm so sorry. We've been so wrong. We've—"

Her uncle waved his hands. "*We* nothing. And enough of this 'rally round the flag' bit. Enough of kids who don't appreciate what they've got. Enough of meddling strangers who want to run our lives." He took his wife's hand and pulled her toward the door. She nearly tripped.

The policeman put a hand on his shoulder. "Ease up on her, Kellogg."

Uncle Forbes made a big deal of raising her hand and then dropping it. "Better?"

Office Kendall nodded. "Much."

He glared at Aunt Susan and pointed to the door. "We're going. Now."

She looked back at the group, and Sim hated the sadness in her eyes. "Excuse us. We need some time alone. I'll phone later."

Uncle Forbes was already on the front step. "Come *on!*"

No one spoke until the sound of the Kelloggs' car faded.

Claire took a long, slow breath. "What do we do now?"

Merry moved to the dining room. "We wait, we pray—and we eat coffee cake."

Forbes stuffed his hands in his pockets. "I don't know why we have to take a walk."

Susan slipped her hand through his arm and pulled him close. "Because I'll go crazy sitting in that motel room a moment longer."

"The Ritz it ain't."

"Our motel is everything it should be for a town this size: clean, comfortable, and homey."

"Are you sure you don't mean *homely?*"

She inhaled deeply and looked up at the pin oaks lining the street. She smelled honeysuckle as they passed a row planted between two houses. She heard the squeal of kids playing in a backyard. "This is a wonderful town, Forbes. I can see why Sim wants to stay here."

"Kansas City is a wonderful town."

She shrugged. "Both have their advantages and disadvantages."

"You bet they do."

"Then maybe it's not the town we need to consider." *Maybe we're the problem, dear husband. Maybe we've let ourselves stray from what's right, what's important. And it's more than just Sim. I know I've let God slide into the backgr—*

Forbes shook his head. "I don't want to talk about any of this. I'm weary of the whole thing."

She hated his penchant for shoving difficult decisions to the back of his mind like they were leftovers being shoved to the back of a refrigerator. And just like leftovers, many of those decisions never saw the light of day until it was too late. "The situation is not going away."

He huffed. "We had the perfect setup."

She pulled him to a stop. "I cringe at the implications of the term *setup*. And perfect? Were we living in the same house?"

He started walking again. "Okay, okay. So it wasn't perfect. But we gave Sim a nice home, her own room—I know it's not the palace she's used to, but the little snot can make do like the rest of us."

Susan stopped again. "Did you hear what you just called your niece?"

Forbes shrugged.

She pulled her arm away from him, feeling sick again. But this time it had nothing to do with motion sickness. "Do you love her at all?"

"Sure I do."

She stared at him. "I'm sure you don't. You never say anything nice about her. You act like she's an imposition." The next bit of truth hit Susan so hard she almost reeled from it. "Sim's right. All you care about is her money."

Forbes began to walk. "It never hurts to sweeten the pot." He stopped when he noticed she wasn't following him. "What now?"

She shook her head as her own complicity surfaced. "Everyone's right."

"About what?"

"We don't care about Sim. You want things, and I want a baby. She was in the way of both."

He pegged a finger into his scalp. "Now they've brainwashed *you*. Expose you to a small-town house with cross-stitched samplers on the wall and coffee cake on the table and you turn to mush."

"But we've ignored her and used her—"

"I refuse to feel guilty because I've spent a fraction of Sim's money bettering our life."

"But *is* it better?"

"Are you saying we're not happy?"

Susan's heart skipped a beat. "Are we?"

He threw his hands in the air. "Fine. I'll take everything back. You can have your old car that died every five miles, and I can watch baseball on an eighteen-inch screen."

Susan had no answer for him. Their crisis of dealing with a runaway Sim had grown multiple arms, multiple facets, multiple implications. She noticed they were approaching a drugstore. "Can we stop in here?"

"Can't it wait until we get back to Kansas City?"

"Humor me." She pointed to a bench out front. "You wait here. I'll only be a minute."

As Susan went inside, a bell on the door announced her arrival. A clerk smiled from behind the counter. "Morning. Can I help you find anything?"

"Just looking." It was a lie. She knew exactly what she wanted, and she headed for a section near the pharmacy. There it was. She picked up a box and headed back to the counter to pay. At the last minute, she grabbed a Snickers candy bar for Forbes. Surely chocolate would soothe the savage beast in him.

The clerk took her money. "Good luck." She pointed to the pregnancy test.

Susan's heart beat double time. "Thanks. I need it."

Twenty-five

"Watch—and be utterly amazed.
For I am going to do something in your days
that you would not believe, even if you were told."

HABAKKUK 1:5

SUSAN SAT ON THE TOILET LID and stared at the test.

I'm pregnant!

There was a knock on the bathroom door. "Come on, Susan. What're you doing in there? I gotta go!"

Curious to see if she looked different, she stood before the mirror. She smiled at her reflection. She *was* different. *I'm a mother!* What miraculous words!

She opened the door but stood in Forbes's way.

"Move it! Move—" He looked at what she was displaying in her hand. "What's that?"

"A pregnancy test."

"Why do you have a—" He looked at her eyes. "You're not...? You can't be."

She nodded, knowing her face was beaming. "I am. I'm pregnant."

Forbes staggered back into the room, feeling for the bed. He bumped into it, caught himself, and sat down.

"But we can't...we've tried for years." He put a hand to his mouth. "The treatments worked?" He ran both hands over his head, a gesture she recognized from back when his hair was plentiful. "I don't believe this is happening."

A new thought eased into Susan's mind, and she placed a hand on the door, steadying herself. *Oh, dear Lord Jesus. You did this! You!*

Please forgive me for ignoring You so long. I don't deserve this. And yet You give it to me anyway. She covered her face with a hand, humbled by the contrast between her disgrace and His grace.

"Susan?"

She gathered her feelings and found her voice. "Claire talked about things not being a coincidence. This is not a coincidence."

"You bet it's not. It's twenty thousand dollars' worth of fertility treat—"

"No." She stepped forward and took his hand. "It's God."

He pulled away and escaped to the other side of the bed. "You *have* been brainwashed."

"Why can't you admit this pregnancy is a miracle from God?"

"It's medical science at its best—and most expensive. You got what you wanted."

"What *I* wanted? You wanted it too."

He shrugged. *The shrug that spoke a thousand words.*

This was all wrong. After trying for years, they were finally pregnant. Had there been a hug? A kiss? Nope. Only a shrug. It was not a good sign.

"I'm not sure I have enough patience for a teenager *and* a baby."

She had to blink twice to grab the train of Forbes's thoughts. He was discarding Sim like an out-of-date computer being replaced by the newest model. "Who said you had any patience at all?"

"That was rude."

She shook her head, her mouth slack. "This isn't how I dreamed this moment would be."

He came to her, and she didn't have the strength to push him away. "Now, now, Susan. You have to be practical. Two kids…"

A rush of adrenaline gave her the energy to sidle away from his touch. "You *don't* love Sim, do you?"

"Huh?"

She put two fists against her forehead and forced herself to calm down. Stress could not be good for the baby.

The baby. *Her* baby. A life that was joined with her own, now until forever. With each second that passed, she was amazed at how this new love grew upon itself, so that the love that had started as a glimmer when she'd first seen the positive test was now infinitely larger. Her entire life had changed.

Thank God.

Susan lowered her fists and found her thoughts clear and distinct.

"Hey, Susan, I—"

She put a finger to her lips, and he was quiet. She didn't want his excuses to taint the perfection of the moment. Her resolve was complete and undeniable. She took a deep breath. "This baby is a gift from God. I accept the gift, even though I know I don't deserve it. And Sim is a gift from God too, though we didn't take the time to realize it."

"You're going overboard. You're—"

She raised a finger, not wanting to hear any more. "So much has been revealed to me in the past few minutes. I have seen my future as a mother presented to me on a platter covered with gold. And I have seen our marriage as a cracked and broken plate in dire need of mending."

His mouth dropped open, closed, then opened again. He huffed. "Just because I didn't jump up and down...that's not fair."

Susan hesitated. "Perhaps not. But it is the truth." She walked past him to the door of their room. She opened it and stood in the sunlight. "I will be a mother to our baby—the best mother I know how to be, because *I* want this baby. And I want Sim."

He shrugged. "Fine. I suppose—"

"No, you don't understand. *I* want Sim. And I will take care of Sim. Alone."

He stared at her. "What are you saying?"

She felt utter calm as she took a step outside the door. "I'll be taking a bus home, Forbes. If it's good enough for Sim, it's good enough for me."

She shut the door, blocking her view of his face.

Since her purse and car keys were in the room, Susan begged a ride to Merry's house from the wife of the motel owner. She rang Merry's doorbell. Sim answered the door.

"Aunt Susan."

"Hi." Silence. "Can I come in?"

Merry appeared from the back of the house. Claire was behind her. "Susan, come in. Sim, let her in."

Sim held the door open but stepped back as if she didn't want to risk physical contact.

Merry gestured toward the love seat. "Have a seat."

Susan sat at one end while Merry sat at the other. Sim took refuge in the doorway leading to the kitchen, Claire's arm around her shoulders. Her hands were in the pockets of her shorts. Her face was wary.

Don't worry, Sim, I've come to make everything better.

"Can I offer you some coffee? A glass of iced tea?"

"Nothing, thanks." A moment of awkward silence passed, and Susan found herself praying for strength. She hoped the God she'd ignored for so long would take pity and listen to her prayers. "I've come to tell you about a decision I've made."

"*You've* made?" Claire studied her. "What about your husband?"

"I'm afraid I've given him no choice."

Sim straightened. Susan had planned to tell them about the pregnancy first but decided not to torture the girl any longer. "I am not willing to give up custody of Sim—"

"But you have to! I don't want to go back with you and Uncle Forbes."

"You won't be going back with your uncle and me."

"Huh?"

"You'll be staying with me. Me alone."

Claire stepped to the love seat. "You're leaving him?"

"For now." She caught Sim's gaze and held it. "Things haven't been good for a long, long time, and it's not fair to either of us—any of us—to live in a bitter, angry world."

"What does Uncle Forbes think of all this?"

Susan tried not to think of the sight of him in the motel room, arguing, not even pretending to be happy about the pregnancy. "If he wants to work on things, I'm willing, but until then, I have to think of you." She smiled. It was the moment she'd been waiting for her entire life. "I have to think of you—and the baby."

It took a moment for their faces to register her news. "You're pregnant?" Sim sounded as incredulous as if her aunt had just told her that she had become a brain surgeon.

Merry leaned over and grasped Susan's hand. "But this morning…"

"This morning I didn't know. I suspected, hoped, and prayed, but I didn't know. I just took a test."

"Congratulations." Claire sounded sincere.

Sim began to pace, her face showing a bevy of conflicting emotions. "I'm going to be a…have a…?"

Susan finished the sentence properly. "A brother or sister."

Sim stopped moving. "But I'm…it's my cousin, isn't it?"

"Technically, cousin. But you'll be a big sister, won't you? I'll need your help like a big sister."

Sim shuffled her shoulders. "I'm going to be a big sister."

Merry's voice cracked. "You'll be a good one."

Susan turned to her. "I appreciate—*we* appreciate—your offer to take care of Sim. I know she would have been fine here in Steadfast. It's a lovely town and—"

"Oh!" With an excited flip of her hands, Sim took a seat on the edge of the coffee table facing them. "Let's *move* here!"

Susan paused. "Move to Steadfast?"

"Sure. If Uncle Forbes isn't going to live with us, then we can move anywhere, can't we?"

"I…" Susan looked to Merry and Claire, searching for the correct answer.

"You *could* move here," Claire said.

"You and the baby would have all sorts of support." Merry laced her fingers together. "And babysitters."

They were jumping *way* ahead. "I'm not ready to give up on my marriage. That wouldn't be fair to Forbes. Or to me. So I can't move—"

"But you *could* stay for a while," Claire said. "Wouldn't some distance be…helpful?"

Susan knew it would. She had a lot of thinking to do. And praying. She would talk with Forbes, tell him she needed some time to sort things through. As did he. "But what about my job?"

Claire pondered that. "What do you do?"

"I'm a nurse."

Merry clapped her hands once. "We have a hospital. I'm sure they could find a position for you."

Susan put a hand to her forehead, trying to take it all in. "But where would we live?"

Merry patted the love seat. "You could live here. For now. Until you get your own place. Until you decide what you want to do with—"

Susan stopped her. "What God wants me to do with my marriage."

Merry shrugged, then nodded.

Sim leaned forward, resting her arms on her thighs. She took Susan's hands in hers and looked her straight in the eyes. "Let's do it, Aunt Susan. It feels right. I know it's right."

After a moment's hesitation, she nodded. Sim sat back. They shared an awkward silence. Susan's emotions collided; she felt relief, but also great sorrow. If she'd thought life was complicated before…

And yet one thing was clear: Sim's coming to Steadfast was not a coincidence.

Nothing was.

Epilogue

Let us hold unswervingly to the hope we profess,
for he who promised is faithful.

HEBREWS 10:23

"YOU LOOK GREAT." Claire stood back to get a better look.

"Very pretty," Aunt Susan said.

"Not bad for a cool chick," Merry said.

Sim shook her head. "I always feel like a freak on the first day of school. Especially this year." She shook her head and smoothed the fabric of her skirt. "Who would have thought I'd ever wear a *skirt* to school?"

"I called the ten o'clock news." Claire winked. "They're doing a special feature."

Sim rolled her eyes, then checked them in the hall mirror. Her eye shadow was a nice, neutral shade, her lids unlined. She liked the look. She noticed the three women watching her. "What?"

"I'm feeling very blessed." Aunt Susan put her hand on her belly.

"Yeah, yeah, praise the Lord, I'm a gem."

"Don't be impudent, Sim." Claire nudged her. "I didn't come visit to hear such piffle."

"Piffle?"

"It's a new word."

Sim ran a finger over her lip gloss. "Actually, you didn't come down here to see me off on my first day of school at all. You came to find a place for your new studio."

"And to see you. And to see you."

Sim gave an exaggerated sigh. "Ah, yes. The pain of second billing."

Claire flicked the tip of her nose. "Oh, you." Then she put her hands behind her neck and unclasped her cross necklace. "Turn around, kiddo."

Sim couldn't believe it. She shook her head. "Claire, you don't have to—"

"I want to. It was my grandmother's. Since you're the closest thing I've got to a daughter, it's yours."

Sim's throat tightened. She turned around and let Claire fasten the clasp. "Thank you."

Claire kissed the top of Sim's head. "You're welcome."

Sim took one final look in the mirror. She liked the feel of the cross against her skin. She touched it and suddenly understood Claire's familiar gesture. There was comfort in the cross's presence. She'd never take it off.

She thought of another thank-you that was due. "And Merry, thank you for the new outfit. I love it. But you shouldn't have spent so much on me."

"Face it, she's a pushover," Aunt Susan said.

They all were. Sim had never been so content. Just two weeks previous she and Susan had gotten their own place—a permanent place, since Uncle Forbes had decided he didn't want to work on the marriage after all. He didn't want to be a husband anymore, or a dad at all. Apparently without the free use of Sim's trust fund, the advantages of having a family had paled. He'd shocked everyone when *he'd* been the one to ask Aunt Susan for a divorce.

Whatever. His loss was Sim's gain.

Her aunt was having a hard time letting him go, feeling guilty and dwelling on if-onlys. But every day she was getting stronger. And Sim's unborn brother or sister was getting bigger. Yes indeed, life was good.

Sim hooked her backpack over her shoulder and pivoted toward the door. "Ta-ta, ladies." She stopped with one hand on the knob. "You're not going to be waiting for me after school with milk and cookies, are you?"

Aunt Susan put her hand on her chin, her eyes wide, considering. "It's a thought…"

"Then make them chocolate chip."

"You got it."

Sim grinned. "And you call Merry a pushover?"

She left them to argue the point without her.

Bailey was just leaving for work when the phone rang.

"I'm calling for Jered Manson."

"He's not here."

"Where can I get ahold of him?"

Good question. "Who is this?"

"My name's Jamison Smith. I'm an executive with Hiptone Music."

Bailey changed the phone to the other ear. "What do you want with my son?"

"A while back I got a call from Sim Kellogg about him. She said he was interested in having some of his songs heard."

Jered really had songs? He'd actually composed something?

"Sir? You there?"

"Yes, yes, I'm here. But I'm afraid I don't know where Jered is."

"Why not?"

"He's…he's taken a sabbatical."

Jamison laughed. "Yeah, right. Whatever. Well, if you see him, let him know I called."

"But what do you have to offer him?"

"Nothing unless I hear from him. Hey, I'm just doing Sim a favor—better late than never. I don't know if your son has talent or not. And even if I heard his stuff, who knows if I could do anything with it. But I certainly can't do something with nothing. Here's my number. Tell him to call."

Bailey jotted down the number, then hung up. He stared at the slip of paper, unseeing. Jered really was a musician. His dream was viable. He had a chance.

But he was gone. And Bailey had driven him away.

❧   ❧   ❧

Jered had chosen the park in Kansas City because he needed a place to sleep. The alley he'd parked in had been the scene of a mugging the night before, so he decided it was time for yet another change of residence.

He pulled his truck into the far end of a parking lot, under the shade of a tree, and curled up on the seat. The lowered window let in some much-needed air, and the sounds of kids playing and a ball game going on nearby helped lull him to sleep. It was a quiet place. A safer place.

Laughter woke him. Hard laughter. Bitter laughter. He sat up and found it was dark. The dome of the nearest streetlight just missed his truck. In fact, no vehicles were parked within the brightness of the lights, as if the other, laughing tenants had purposely chosen the shadows to conduct their business.

And there *was* business going on.

Though Jered had never gotten into drugs, he'd seen enough during the past month to know what a drug deal looked like. And the shadowed meeting that was happening across the lot fit the image.

He scooted down in the seat, hoping not to be seen. He wanted to drive away but knew that the sound of the truck's engine would draw attention, and they would immediately brand him a witness—to whatever was going on.

The bass beat of a stereo preceded the sound of another car coming into the lot. It pulled near the others, and the bass beat died. Shouts. Laughter. Bottles breaking.

Jered's back hurt from the odd position. He needed to move. If only he could turn on his side and slide—

Bam! The truck shuddered with the slam of a hand. "Hey! What choo doin' in der?"

Jered tried to see the face belonging to the voice but only saw two silhouettes standing outside the cab of the truck, one on each side. Suddenly the truck rocked and two more figures jumped into the truck bed.

I'm dead. Literally dead.

A hand reached through the open window and unlocked the driver's door. It was yanked open and a face appeared inside. A sneering face. A mocking face. A challenging face. "You like watchin' what we're doing, don'cha, man?"

Jered swallowed, his mind searching for something—anything—that would make foe into friend. "I like *doing* better. Got any beer?"

The face laughed and withdrew, pulling Jered with him. "Sure. Come on, kid. You want some beer? I'm sure we can find something you'd like."

The face put his arm around Jered and led him away.

⸙

> *Where can I go from your Spirit?*
> *Where can I flee from your presence?*
> *If I go up to the heavens, you are there;*
> *if I make my bed in the depths, you are there.*
> *If I rise on the wings of the dawn,*
> *if I settle on the far side of the sea,*
> *even there your hand will guide me,*
> *your right hand will hold me fast.*
> PSALM 139:7–10

The publisher and author would love to hear your comments about this book. *Please contact us at:* www.multnomah.net/nancymoser

VERSES FOR A STEADFAST SURRENDER

PROLOGUE
Hiding/Job 34:21–22

CHAPTER 1
Riches/James 1:11
Thirst/Psalm 63:1
Opportunity/Colossians 4:2–6

CHAPTER 2
Seek/Matthew 7:7
Sacrifice/Mark 10:17–23

CHAPTER 3
Sacrifice/2 Samuel 24:24
Giving/Luke 12:48
Hope/1 Peter 3:15
Blessings/James 1:17
Widow's mite (paraphrased)/
    Mark 12:41–44
Giving/2 Corinthians 9:7
Calling/John 10:3
Wounds/Isaiah 53:5

CHAPTER 4
Sacrifice/Luke 9:61–62
Blessings/James 1:17
Calling/Isaiah 6:8

CHAPTER 5
Jesus/Philippians 3:8
Light/2 Samuel 22:29

CHAPTER 6
Work/2 Chronicles 15:7

CHAPTER 7
Trust/Proverbs 3:5–6
Waiting/Psalm 37:7
Charge!/Jeremiah 46:9
Waiting/Zephaniah 3:8
Waiting/Psalm 27:14
Waiting/Isaiah 30:18

CHAPTER 8
Pursuits/2 Timothy 2:22

CHAPTER 9
Perseverance/James 1:2–4
Pride/Proverbs 16:18

CHAPTER 10
Fulfillment/Proverbs 13:12

CHAPTER 11
Love/Proverbs 3:3–4

CHAPTER 12
Direction/Psalm 119:35–36

CHAPTER 13
Sin/Jeremiah 9:5

CHAPTER 14
Dissension/2 Corinthians 12:20

CHAPTER 15
Protection/Psalm 91:14

CHAPTER 16
Sin/James 4:17

Dear Readers:

Every novel evolves during the writing process, but some stories go through a drastic metamorphosis. That is the case with *A Steadfast Surrender*. The idea started with a newspaper article four years ago about a transient who was found living in the attic of an old library. *Interesting*. The first character I put up in my attic was an angel named Gilroy who only spoke in Bible verses. Gilroy teamed up with an orphan boy named Sim in a story called *The Secret Son* that focused on the boy—and the town keeping his secret. Whatever. Yawn.

Wisely I let Gilroy dissipate into character heaven and replaced him with a woman named Claire... I have always been fascinated with the story of the rich man who asks Jesus how he can get to heaven. Mark 10:21 says: "Jesus looked at him and loved him. 'One thing you lack,' he said. 'Go, sell everything you have and give to the poor, and you will have treasure in heaven. Then come, follow me.' " Not liking the answer, the man walked away—"because he had great wealth." What if someone felt compelled to give up everything? It's just not done. The world would think they were crazy. I called the hugely revised manuscript *The Outcast*.

Then in 2002 my own faith was challenged. I found myself consumed with a new issue: total surrender to God. Up until then I thought I had surrendered to Him, but little by little, God showed me I was still holding back. It was during this time that I realized my story—about a woman who gives up all her material *things*—was not a complete representation of the biblical story. We each have a different "everything" that's important in our lives, that stands between us and total surrender to the Father. To my character it was her possessions and fame; to someone else it might be pride, or hobbies, or stubbornness, or... At this point, the manuscript went through another transformation that made the story richer, deeper, more applicable to our lives. At this point I sold it to Multnomah Publishers.

But that pesky title, *The Outcast*... I have *never* had trouble titling a book. But this time, I must have made a list of a hundred possibilities, none quite right. And time was running out. The story was in place, but the title was not. Then one day I heard Sara Groves sing "This Journey Is My Own." The lyrics matched the essence of my book exactly. (It could have been written as my book's theme song!) Especially when I heard the line, "Now I live and breathe for an audience of One." Later that day I realized I'd been given that phrase the month before as I listened to Lee Strobel quote Søren Kirkegaard: "We are all players for an audience of One." This could not be a coincidence.

Okay. Go ahead. Point out that the name of this book is *A Steadfast Surrender,* not *An Audience of One.* That's another evolution. But the point is that the phrase "an audience of One" became vital to the book and helped further form the plot into a story about not caring about the accolades of man and saying yes to God (before we even know the question). This phrase is even quoted in the book, affecting the faith and lives of the characters as it has affected me.

As I hope it affects you. So go on. Live your life for an audience of One, in total, steadfast surrender. You'll never regret it.

And may all your metamorphoses be as satisfying as mine has been. The joy is in the journey.

Nancy Moser

Discussion Questions

1. What was your initial reaction when Claire gave up her fame and possessions to follow Jesus?

2. What would people's reactions be if *you* did such a thing? *Would* you do such a thing?

3. If your "everything" is not possessions or status, what stands between you and total surrender to God? Can you surrender that now? Why or why not?

4. Do you think Claire should have gone back to her art? Why or why not?

5. What nudges have you experienced from God and what have they led you to do? Or did you say no?

6. If you have ever lost someone close to you, have you ever created a kind of shrine to their memory? Did it help? Did it hinder healing? Do you still have it?

7. What would you like to see happen in order for Aunt Susan and Uncle Forbes to reconcile?

8. Who have you known like Bailey—consumed with his or her own dreams at the expense of others?

9. What do you think will happen to Jered?

IS THERE A HERO IN YOU?

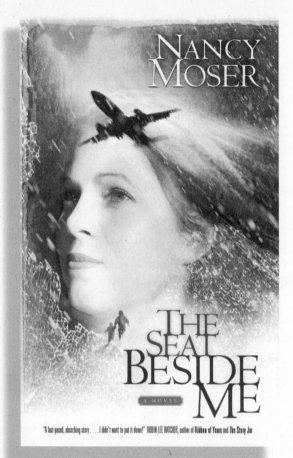

NANCY MOSER

THE SEAT BESIDE ME

A NOVEL

"A fast-paced, absorbing story . . . . I didn't want to put it down!" ROBIN LEE HATCHER, author of Ribbon of Years and The Story Jar

That strange, snoring, legroom-invading person next to you on the airplane—have you ever imagined owing your life to him? Nancy Moser tells the gripping story of five passengers and their seatmates who get casually acquainted—then plunge headlong into an icy river in a sudden plane crash. The moments that follow are more intense than any they have ever lived, changing the way the passengers see God and the meaning of life itself. This book reveals the eternal impact a brief interaction can have and the drastic measures it takes for some to reexamine their souls.

ISBN 1-57673-884-1

"If you have faith as small as a mustard seed, you can say to this mountain, 'Move from here to there,' and it will move."

THE MUSTARD SEED

THEY WERE FOUR ORDINARY PEOPLE,
MYSTERIOUSLY SUMMONED TO A SMALL TOWN
WHERE EXTRAORDINARY THINGS ARE ABOUT TO HAPPEN...

THE INVITATION
NANCY MOSER

Julia, Walter, Kathy, and Natalie: four ordinary people with little in common, until each of them receives a small white invitation from an anonymous sender. It reads: "If you have faith as small as a mustard seed... nothing will be impossible for you. Please come to Haven, Nebraska." At first, they all resist. But amazing circumstances convince them that they should heed the call and go to Haven. In this rerelease of *The Invitation*, Nancy Moser crafts a captivating story of everyday people who come to realize that even a small faith, combined with a heart led by God, can change the world.

ISBN 1-57673-352-1

They never imagined doing God's will would make them targets for evil...

"Nancy weaves a fascinating story showing how God uses ordinary people in extraordinary ways. Get ready for a page-turner!"

—**Karen Kingsbury**
author of *Where Yesterday Lives* and *Waiting for Morning*

Book two in Nancy Moser's Mustard Seed series is the continuing story of four ordinary people whose lives are forever changed after they are invited to the very supernatural town of Haven, Nebraska. The paths of Natalie, Walter, Kathy, Del, and Julia are once again joined in a quest of faith—and a battle against the forces determined to stop them—as they implement the decisions and direction they received in *The Invitation* and discover the meaning of Matthew 7:7: "Ask and it will be given to you; seek and you will find; knock and the door will be opened to you." When the heat's turned up and the enemy unleashes his greatest opposition, the Havenites learn that it's not enough to know what's right— one must, with God's help, do what's right. No matter what the cost.

ISBN 1-57673-410-2

Complacency is Deadly.
The enemy lurks close by.

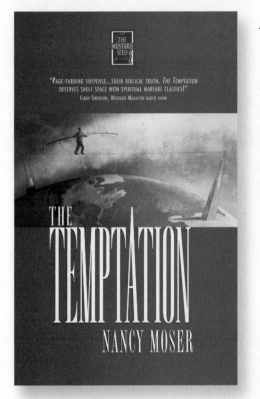

"High drama
and characters
pulsating with
human emotion...
a tremendous
addition to
The Mustard
Seed series."

—**James Scott Bell,**
author of *Final
Witness* and
Blind Justice

The Temptation continues the sagas of Haven, Nebraska, visitors Julia, Kathy, Del, and Walter as they live out the commitments they made in *The Quest.* Now successful in their separate pursuits, the Havenites think all is going well—and therein lies great danger. As complacency attacks the characters' focus on God, they start believing their achievements have risen from their own savvy and power. When Del decides to organize a reunion, the characters face Satan's chaotic interference and learn the true nature of temptation: inevitable, subtle, biting, and potentially disastrous. They must recover their courage to live out their plea to the Lord: "Lead us not into temptation, but deliver us from evil..."

ISBN 1-57673-734-9

A FREE
"BEHIND THE SCENES"
LOOK AT YOUR
FAVORITE
FICTION AUTHORS!

www.letstalkfiction.com

Let's Talk Fiction is a free, four-color minimagazine created to give readers a "behind the scenes" look at Multnomah Publishers' favorite fiction authors. **Let's Talk Fiction** allows our authors to share a bit about themselves, giving readers an inside peek into their latest releases. Published in the fall, spring, and summer seasons, **Let's Talk Fiction** is filled with interactive contests, author contact information, and fun! To receive your free copy of **Let's Talk Fiction,** get on-line at www.letstalkfiction.com. We'd love to hear from you!